... the epic sequel to *Cavalcade*, we ... *n they arrive in Oregon and take* ... *ith their family where they have been granted six hundred and forty acres of land under the Organic Laws of Oregon. They must build their home, farm the land, and eke out a living on this piece of raw land. Wolves, bears, and wildcats are the least of their worries in this new land. Hard work and trusting that each will do their very best are the keys to conquering the wilderness as they pioneer their lives on the high plains of Oregon!*

Come along as the Herriot family lives a life few have attempted in this wilderness near the Blue Mountains of Oregon. You won't want to miss Pioneering, *the final half of the fantastic pair of prequels to* Vetted *and* Vetted Further!

Herriot Family Tree

A K'Anne Meinel novel

In E-Book Format:
Short Stories

Fantasy
Wet & Wet Again
Family Night
Quickie ~ Against the Car
Quickie ~ Against the Wall
Quickie ~ Over the Couch
Mile High Club
Quickie ~ Under the Pier
Heel or Heal
Kiss
Family Night 2
Beach Dreams
Internet Dreamers

Snoggered
The Rockhound
Stolen
Agitated
Love of my LIFE
Quickie in an Elevator,
GOING DOWN?
Into the Garden
The Book Case
The Other Women
Menage a WHAT?

E-Book Novellas

Children of Another Mother
Bikini's are Dangerous
Kept
Ghostly Love
Bikini's are Dangerous 2
On the Parkway
Stable Affair
Sapphic Surfer
Bikini's are Dangerous 3
Bikini's are Dangerous 4
Bikini's are Dangerous 5
Mysterious Malice (Book 1)
Meticulous Malice (Book 2)
Mistaken Malice (Book 3)
Malicious Malice (Book 4)
Masterful Malice (Book 5)
Matrimonial Malice (Book 6)
Mourning Malice (Book 7)
Murderous Malice (Book 8)
Sapphic Cowgirl

Sapphic Cowboi
Mental Malice (Book 9)
Menacing Malice (Book 10)
Charming Thief
~Snake Island~
Charming Thief
~Diamonds are a Girls Best Friend~
Minor Malice (Book 11)
Morally Malice (Book 12)
Morose Malice (Book 13)
Melancholy Malice (Book 14)
Mad Malice (Book 15)
Macabre Malice (Book 16)
Marinating Malice (Book 17)
Macerating Malice (Book 18)
Minacious Malice (Book 19)
Sayyida
Meddlesome Malice (Book 20)
Meandering Malice (Book 21)
Maniacal Malice (Book 22)

E-Book Novels

SHIPS *CompanionSHIP, FriendSHIP,*
RelationSHIP
Erotica Volume 1
Long Distance Romance
Bikini's Are Dangerous
The Complete Series
Malice Masterpieces
The First Five Books
To Love a Shooting Star
Germanic
The Claim
Represented
Timed Romance

Blown Away
Blown Away *The Alternate Cover*
Malice Masterpieces 2
Books Six through Ten
The Journey Home
Out at the Inn
Anthology Volume 1
Lawyered
Malice Masterpieces 3
Books Eleven through Fifteen
Small Town Angel
Pirated Love
Doctored

Dedicated to anyone who thinks I'm writing about them. I am.

K'A. M.

K'ANNE MEINEL

PIONEERING

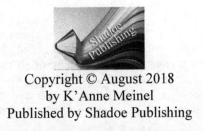

ISBN-13: 978-1721944866
ISBN-10: 1721944869

Copyright © August 2018 by K'Anne Meinel

K'Anne Meinel is available for comments at KAnneMeinel@aim.com as well as on Facebook @ http://www.facebook.com/K.Anne.Meinel.Fan.Page, Google + @ https://plus.google.com/u/2/+KAnneMeinel, LinkedIn @ https://www.linkedin.com/in/k-anne-meinel-a026385a, or her blog @ http://kannemeinel.wordpress.com/ or on Twitter @ https://twitter.com/KAnneMeinel, or on her website @ www.kannemeinel.com if you would like to follow her to find out about stories and book's releases.

www.shadoepublishing.com

ShadoePublishing@gmail.com

Shadoe Publishing, LLC is a United States of America company

Cover by: K'Anne Meinel @ Shadoe Publishing
Edited by: Deb Amia, Grammar Queen grammarqueen.com

PIONEERING

PUBLISHER'S NOTE

This is a work of fiction. Names, characters, places, and incidents are the product of the author's imagination or are used fictitiously, and any resemblance to actual persons, living or dead, business establishments, events, or locales is entirely coincidental.

The publisher does not have any control over and does not assume any responsibility for author or third-party Web sites or their content.

CHAPTER ONE

"Six hundred acres! Can you *farm* six hundred acres?" Molly marveled when Erin explained.

Erin chuckled and shook her head. She too was amazed at the present they had been given for traveling to Oregon. "Well, maybe not *this* year," she answered modestly, sharing a huge smile with her wife. She waited a moment and said with a note of wonderment in her voice, "Six hundred and forty acres. Who'd a thought?" Why, the farm back in Ohio had been only forty acres and they had fought for it with trees and Indians and rocks. She looked at the land they were heading for, thrilled to realize that all they had to do was work it and improve it to claim it. "We can also raise cattle, horses, and sheep," she reminded her, their seed stock having made the trip with them.

"You already filed?" she asked, sounding slightly hurt.

"I did. I didn't know what I'd find here, and I wanted to claim it for our family before someone else filed on it."

"Is the area settling up?"

"I haven't the faintest idea. We didn't see anyone for days, and it will take us a couple days to get there. But it's ours, Molly, all ours!" she said, putting her arms around the smaller woman and swinging her around and around as she shouted.

"What? What's ours? What's going on?" the children came running. Queenie started barking at the noise.

"Your pa has found our homestead and filed on it," Molly announced, pleased to be the one to tell them.

The children cheered and clapped, happy to hear this news and asking questions a mile a minute.

"Wait, wait, wait. We have to head down to our land tomorrow, and it's going to take at least a couple days to get there."

"Can't we go now?" someone asked.

"Well, we could get in a couple miles," she looked around at Molly, wondering if they should. It was late in the afternoon and she was as anxious as any of them to head down to what was now *their* land.

"No, it's too late in the day, and I don't want to camp by lantern light in a strange area. We will start out tomorrow," Molly vetoed, getting up to put together a dinner for them all.

"Let's move those sheep, so they continue to crop the grass until sunset," Erin encouraged the children, signaling the dogs to move them. She didn't need the children, but unless Molly called one or two to help with dinner, it would keep them out of her hair. Erin scooped up Timmy, lifting him high in the air and hearing his giggles. She was happy, and she wanted to share it with her family.

"What's it like?" Molly asked her as they lay side by side later in the tent, the lantern turned low, so they could see each other as they talked.

"There's trees, excellent farmland, and many acres of grazing land," she answered, sitting up to talk, too excited to sleep yet.

"We'll have to plant first thing," Molly marveled aloud, her arms folded under her head.

"We'll have to build a cabin first thing," Erin corrected, already planning it out in her head.

"Shouldn't we–" began Molly, but Erin, in her excitement, interrupted.

"We probably should do everything, but we have to get these children under a roof and then, the stock."

Molly nodded, agreeing but a little aggrieved that she had been interrupted. She let Erin talk on.

"There is a stream nearby that runs through the valley, so we should be able to dig a well for our farm," she continued. "Some of the upper hills are a little parched and won't be good for anything but grazing, but those fields should give us good crops in the coming years…" she would have gone on and on but noticed Molly's silence. Turning, she

tried to peer though the dark at her. "Is something wrong? Don't you want the farm anymore?"

"I would say you are making all the decisions these days."

"You did promise to obey me..." she started to tease, referencing their marriage vows.

Molly sat up slightly, indignant. "I won't obey against my better judgement..." she began angrily and then, realizing the tone in Erin's voice, lay back down with a harrumph.

"Molly, I just couldn't take a chance to let someone else file on it. I rode all over that place, and I think it just might be perfect. I was on pins and needles as the clerk went through the section and checked the filings. I don't think I've ever wanted anything so badly before in my life."

"Anything?" Molly asked in a voice that had Erin turning towards her quickly.

Taking Molly in her arms, Erin answered huskily, "Well, not just anything." She began to turn her excitement over the land into excitement over making love to her wife, kissing her ardently.

Molly immediately returned her adoration, kissing her back, hard.

Erin realized it had been too long since they'd been alone, neither had their periods, and Molly hadn't been ill. She responded immediately, pulling at Molly's clothes to feel her naked skin against her wife's, pressing close, hearing the catch in her voice at the contact.

Molly had worried at the length of time Erin was gone in search of their homestead and being relieved at her return, as well as overjoyed at her find, she expressed herself physically, wrapping her naked body around her wife, rubbing, and murmuring in enjoyment.

Erin kissed her way across her wife's jaw and down her neck, then paid homage to the breasts standing up and peaking in their excitement. First one, and then the other, received devotion as she licked, sucked, and gently used her teeth. The catch in Molly's breath told her how much her wife was enjoying the attention. Her hands weren't idle as she caressed her wife's luscious curves, remembering how she had looked and felt when they had been able to make love without children nearby.

Molly was enjoying her wife's dedication to giving her enjoyment. She was equally determined to love Erin in return and kissed, suckled, and caressed all the bare skin she could reach.

Erin could scent Molly's arousal and that made her want to taste. She slowly made her way between her wife's legs, pleasantly surprised to find that she had bathed recently, and she was fresh and clean and tasted heavenly. Her first lick had Molly arching into her mouth in supplication.

"More," she gasped, reaching for Erin's head to hold her in place.

Erin smiled against Molly's clit, enjoying herself as she licked away the juices from the appendage that stood at attention waiting for her. Suckling slightly, her fingers slipped inside and made a come-hither motion, bringing Molly up off their blankets only to fall back helplessly as she touched the tender tissue within.

"Oh," she moaned and then stifled it by putting her fist into her own mouth, knowing the children were simply yards away. Her body wasn't under her control as Erin played with it.

Erin began an in and out motion with her fingers, and on every third thrust she 'accidentally' curled them to hit the spot that Molly so enjoyed, causing her to gasp at the sensations that were building. Her mouth gently suckled on Molly's clit as her tongue swirled around it. She could tell from Molly's breathing that her crisis was nearing. She held on as her wife's body convulsed in her arms, smiling as she came not once but twice in succession.

Molly couldn't believe how incredibly her wife aroused her. She hadn't known these feelings were inside herself until Erin taught her so long ago. She'd never thought of touching herself, knowing she was meant to save herself for her someday husband's pleasure. She didn't know the woman could receive pleasure too. Learning that another woman could and would give her pleasure had been a revelation and she reveled in learning her body and its responses. Realizing that Erin was learning as well had been such a delight. They learned together, exploring each other to discover whatever means they could to obtain this pleasure. Finding that she could orgasm, that it wasn't an experience solely for men, had been a revelation. She forced herself to come down from her high quickly, entirely satisfied by what Erin had done to her body as she rolled their heated and sweaty bodies over and began to lave attention on Erin, doing many of the same things to her tall, lanky body in return.

Erin loved this moment when Molly turned the tides of their lovemaking. She was hoping that someday they could come at the same time; she was certain it was possible. She didn't analyze it too strongly as she was enjoying herself far too much to think coherently. Molly had been a willing student, and when she realized Erin was learning too, she became less defensive. As each found what pleased the other, they discovered a part of their love they hadn't known was missing. Now, they had it down pat and could instantly push the

other's buttons to quickly arouse them and make them replete. Erin was already aroused from making love to her wife, and it didn't take long for her to come against her wife as she thrust her fingers inside. Seeing her licking them afterwards aroused Erin again, and she took advantage that, rubbing against Molly's leg as she ground herself into completion once more. Molly's answering smile told her it had been deliberate. She turned off the barely lit lantern, so they could go to sleep.

"Maybe I should build a bathhouse first," Erin murmured sleepily afterwards.

"First? Why?"

"So, we can take a hot bath together without the children barging in and seeing us," she answered, tweaking Molly's still hard nipple through the nightclothes she had put back on. She clearly recalled the view of Molly in their house in Ohio, the thin towel barely covering her lush body, her long, dark hair loose about her shoulders. She had modestly tried to cover herself, but the view was forever burned in Erin's mind.

"That sounds wonderful," Molly said as she stretched, not quite as sated from their lovemaking as she had thought. The tweak had caused a corresponding twinge in her crotch, and she really wanted to continue, but they both heard the growls of the dogs.

Erin quickly got dressed and went out, carrying her pistol in her waistband and slinging her rifle over her shoulder as she peered through the darkness to see what the dogs were upset about. It was difficult to see as the moon was behind some clouds, but she could hear the dogs on the far side of the herd. She could see the silhouettes of the cattle all looking off to the west. Billy snorted a challenge of sorts, letting whoever or whatever know he was ready for them and willing to fight. Walking slowly, so she wouldn't spook the animals, she found both dogs alert and posing, looking off into the night. They had stopped growling. Erin quietly petted both dogs, praising them for she knew not what. Still, whatever had upset them might be gone. When she could see the cattle cropping grass again and the hackles on the dogs had gone down, she started to make her way back to their camp.

"What was it?" Molly asked, having pulled on more clothing just in case she was needed. Her shotgun was nearby and ready.

"I don't know, but whatever it was wasn't willing to take on the dogs and Billy."

Molly didn't blame whoever or whatever it was. She wouldn't like her odds either if those three came at her. "Do you think someone was trying to see if they could get our cattle?"

"I don't know," she admitted. She was tired now, and all thoughts of further lovemaking were gone from her mind as she worried about taking her family to the remote area of Oregon she had filed on. They would have to get supplies soon but only after she had built them a strong cabin against the winter snows. She had heard it didn't snow in certain parts of Oregon but having seen some of the mountains they came through, she was pretty sure it would snow where they were. She would soon need the money she had forwarded to Oregon and wondered how long it would take to arrive after the letter she had sent. She heard Molly snoring slightly and decided she would join her after she mentally thought through the building of their cabin. It took a while to walk herself through that. She had never built a cabin but had listened avidly as the settlers and mountain men in their wagon train had spoken of it in detail. She knew the cabin couldn't be very big. She wasn't certain she could do it, but she had to try; she had promised them all a home.

They packed up the next morning. It was odd how alone and different camping felt since the wagon train had moved on. Putting the cages of poultry up on the sides of the wagon, she was disappointed to find one of the chickens dead. Still, they had suffered relatively few losses, and not counting those marked for eating, they had a lot of stock left to rebuild their flocks. They put the chicken in a bag to be plucked and baked later for their dinner.

Erin walked a wide arc with the dogs, who snuffled avidly, but she saw no signs of man or beast that might have caused the animals to become upset the previous night. Returning to the fire, she shrugged at Molly's look.

The children asked a million and one questions until Erin shushed them. She was concentrating on keeping the cattle at a walk on the odd trail she had taken in the previous days. There wasn't an obvious wagon trail south from where they were heading, and she worried if they would be able to get through in a couple places or if they could become lost. Still, their teams and both sets of yoked oxen were strong and pulling the Conestoga wagon effortlessly across the land didn't seem to faze them. She watched as the pigs kept up easily under the back of the wagon in their accustomed place.

There was plenty to graze when they stopped that first night, and the animals fell to cropping it as quickly as they could. The children were disappointed that they weren't on 'their' land that first night, but Erin explained that a horse and rider could travel much faster alone than their large wagon and all these animals.

On the second day, Erin had to ride ahead a bit to make sure they were on the right path. She hoped her memory of the previous trip was accurate. Some of the trail wasn't good for the wagon, and they had to be creative in how they got through, around, and over some of the obstacles.

"Come on, you can do it," she encouraged the teams as they pulled up a rather steep grade. She saw Theo, who was walking, had stopped the flock of sheep behind them, waiting to follow the large wagon. She looked farther behind him and Tabitha was sitting on the mare and signaling to King to slow the cattle, who took advantage of the moment to crop at the grass.

It started raining as they drove along that afternoon, and they had to make camp in the rain that night. It wasn't a gentle rain. They had been warned that some of the rains were coming in off the ocean and would hit the mountains west of them, including Mount Hood, which was now north and west of them. Erin thought about that far-off mountain they said had been a volcano once. She wondered what would happen if it went off. She'd heard stories of volcanoes but had never seen one. It sounded like they must be like the fires of hell.

Coping in the rain, nothing new after their long trip out here, they made a small fire and used lard to cook the chicken, so they could all have a hot meal. Erin had rigged the awning off the wagon, so they could have the fire and keep a relatively rain-free space. The smoke went out both sides of the awning as it flapped in the wind. As she ate, she watched the ducks and geese stretching their necks out beyond the cages trying to catch some water and pecking at the grasses they were placed in to find things only they could see. She was looking forward to getting them out of the cages but wondered at how vulnerable they would be out on the farm, especially in an area that had never seen domesticated animals and birds before.

"It isn't going to be a farm with that many acres," Molly teased her as they wearily got ready for bed. The children had been tucked into both the wagon and the other tent that night. The cats weren't liking having to share 'their' beds in the wagon again.

"Oh, what is it then?" Erin asked, pulling at her boot and pleased when Molly brushed aside her hand to pull on it for her. Her shapely derriere was a fine sight in the low light of the lantern. Erin helped push on the boot with her other booted foot and pointed the toe on the foot between Molly's legs. The boot came off easily with their combined efforts, and Molly took one unbalanced step before turning for the other boot. Both boots were soon off.

"With that many acres, it's a ranch," she contended.

"I think it's a farm or a ranch, whatever we *want* to call it." She pulled off her pants and changed her shirt for a men's nightshirt, doing it quickly, so her bindings wouldn't be exposed too long. That was something she had done many times on the trail until it became automatic.

They chuckled at their teasing, eager to get to their new home, but a wagon was slow traveling, and it took days.

CHAPTER TWO

Molly stared in awe as they came up over the last rise. Erin had ridden up ahead of them to stop their forward march and point it out.

"All this? All this is ours?" she asked, incredulous at the scene before her. She could see gently rolling hills, pastures for their stock, and places they could plow for grain. It was beautiful! She saw the trees up on some of the hills and even on a bluff. They could cut down these trees for their cabin and barn. At Erin's concerned nod, she smiled and said, "You chose well." She could see a slight blush and then, a beautiful smile took over Erin's face. At that moment, you could tell she was a woman if you were looking for it. Otherwise, she looked to be the tall, lanky man she pretended to be.

"This is it? We're home, Pa?" Theo asked as he came up from walking behind the flock of sheep next to the wagon.

"Yep, this is home," she confirmed, looking around once more. "Let's get settled."

They rolled down that last hill and into the little valley where Erin had determined they would build their home. In no time, she had the cattle on one hill and the flock of sheep on the other, each guarded by a dog. The children gathered fresh water from their own stream, bringing filled buckets to Molly, who poured them into the large barrels. Erin had emptied one of them to clean out the silt and put it on the ground where one corner of their tent would go. She was emptying the wagon…this time, completely.

Slowly, piece by piece, bag by bag, box by box, and trunk by trunk, they unloaded the wagon onto the ground. Erin and Molly pulled the canvas of the wagon cover over all their possessions to protect them from the elements and to make a large tent. The cats were confused and intrigued, and went off to hunt in this new area, expecting everything to be put back into their wagon by the time they returned. *Their* wagon, their home for many, many months, was being pulled apart. By the time they had everything out of the wagon, the horses hobbled, and the oxen out on the hillside, it was time to make camp for the night. The pigs had discovered the creek and were playing in the cool mud beside it. The children gladly gathered firewood for dinner as Molly and Erin put together a nice meal.

"Can we let the birds out of their cages, Pa?" Tabitha asked.

"I don't know if we should yet," she admitted. Glancing at Molly, she added, "I think we should build a coop or something to keep out the wildlife."

"What do you think is in these hills?" she asked, looking around at what would be their home. Far off in the distance she could see the mountains that felt like a remote wall of protection, but having come through some of those, she knew they could be dangerous.

"Anything we found along the way and more," she admitted, knowing the animals would have no fear of them and they would have to keep an eye out. It would take time, and there would always be some animals that would hunt their domesticated stock.

"We're low on things," Molly whispered to her later.

"Can you hold out a week or so?" she whispered back, worried about providing them with a home first and wondering if the money they were expecting would have arrived by then.

"I can," she replied, wondering what Erin had planned.

The first thing Erin did the next day was pace off where she wanted the cabin and the barn. She even marked where they would put the pump they had taken from that burned-out church so long ago.

"Can we really build all that?" Molly asked after seeing the dimensions Erin had in mind.

"We can try, Molly my dear. We can try," she said in a happy voice. They were on their own land and they could do whatever they wanted with it. She'd spent the evening sharpening her axe blade and preparing one for Molly as well. Between them, they would try to build a home for their family.

The next day, they were shocked to find that their sow had finally given birth to a litter of squealing piglets. She'd chosen a stand of hay near the stream and Erin had gone looking for them. The older piglets, the ones they hadn't sold, stood by, almost as watch dogs. King had alerted them to the pigs' location, the grass being too long to see them clearly. For now, Erin would leave them, but she needed a pig shed to contain them soon. She didn't want them going wild, which could prove dangerous at some point.

Taking the wagon, they only hitched up one of the teams of horses and brought the oxen. They began by having the children fill the wagon bed with all the firewood they could find. It kept them busy, and it would help them build their winter supplies.

"Don't you go poking and prodding into things, and if you hear the sound of a rattle, freeze and back away slowly. I don't want you getting involved with snakes," she glanced at Theo who rubbed his buttocks unconsciously, remembering the belt punishment he received for bringing a snake into their campsite on the trip out.

"You really think there are rattlesnakes up here?" Molly asked, concerned.

"They can be anywhere, and I don't want to take chances; I want the children to be safe." She watched, nearly laughing as three-year-old Timmy dragged dead wood to the wagon. He couldn't lift it into the high box but he could drag it down the hill for someone else to put in.

Molly and Erin, both wearing gloves, were chopping down trees. When they got to the point the tree could go down at any moment, they did a head count on the children and ordered them far away from the falling tree.

"I don't want you anywhere near this when it goes," Erin had explained, and she repeated herself for emphasis. The children were wanting to explore, not only in their search for downed wood but just out of natural curiosity.

"I don't want any of you becoming lost either," Molly added, worried about them. They were, after all, in unfamiliar territory. "You stay within shouting distance."

They took the full wagon back to the campsite daily and unloaded it into neat piles that Erin insisted on. The longer trees were put aside to be sawn or chopped into firewood. They were building up their supplies for winter. They removed the branches and limbs from the trees they chopped down and put them in a pile to dry. Then, they hooked up one or two trees to the oxen and dragged the long logs back.

"Those piles will attract varmints, so we can hunt and get food," Erin pointed out. That was one of the ways they had gotten rabbits from the brush piles. She'd already seen there was an abundance of rabbits out here on their chosen land and intended to do a lot of hunting, trapping, and even fishing when she had time.

"Pa, couldn't I use an axe and help remove the limbs?" Tabitha asked.

"Me too, Pa?" Theo asked. After all, they had used them occasionally on the trip out here.

Looking at eleven-year-old Tabitha and nine-year-old Theodore, she made an instant decision. "You are absolutely right. You are both old enough not to chop off your legs or feet. Just be careful," she warned as she searched in their supplies and found hand axes for both. They were both ready for use as she sharpened the blades on all the axes each night by the fire.

"How are we ever gonna keep track of the other three?" Molly asked, exasperated at having to stop chopping to look for them constantly.

"They have to grow up fast and be responsible out here," Erin replied, but she too had stopped to check up on now seven-year-old Tommy, five-year-old Theresa, and three-year-old Timmy. All of them had grown older on the long trip out here. All they could do was cope with things as they came up and keep on going as best they could, but they did have a moment of worry when Timmy went missing and they all dropped their work to search him out. It was King that found the boy, curled up and sleeping in some tall grass. It was a worry for them all.

"I can't keep up with all this," Erin admitted as they hauled more wood to the campsite and she had to check on the cattle and sheep. Both herds seemed to be faring well, fattening up for winter, but Erin knew she should be putting in some hay for winter too.

"It's too much," Molly admitted, realizing that they had taken on too much singlehandedly. She wondered if they had been foolish to take on this new land and all these children. She worried about the money and the supplies they needed to buy too.

Still, a week had gone by and the wood was piling up. Erin began sawing the long trees into measured lengths for the cabin, using a string to determine how long each side of the cabin would be. Erin used a saw to cut them to length, and sometimes, Molly would help with the cross-cut saw. When she had a dozen ready, she began to put them in place. Molly helped her cut troughs about a foot from the end, again

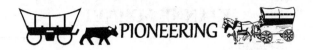

measuring the distance with a string, so they could put the logs on top of each other and build the walls of their cabin.

"We have enough to last a little longer. I don't think we should stop," Molly fretted, looking at the clouds and worrying not only about the rains that had come and gone, but possibly snow. She thought this area would get snow, but they had no neighbors to ask.

"If we have food and supplies, I say we keep going on the cabin as long as we can," Erin agreed. She'd convinced Tabitha and Theodore to duplicate their efforts with the log cabin to build a chicken pen. They'd let the birds out in a limited capacity during the day and put them in the cages every night, so they could keep an eye on them. It was a hassle to capture them each time, but there were varmints around that were determined to eat this easy prey. King and Queenie were on full alert to this, and Erin had set several snares. They'd caught one racoon, but several traps had been sprung and caught nothing. She'd had to hit the raccoon over the head with a shovel to kill it as it growled and spit at the dogs when they confronted it.

"As long as we don't have to delve into our seed, I say we keep going and finish," Molly decided.

Slowly, log by log, the walls rose. The walls were getting too high to simply lift the logs in place, and they had to use skids and the horses to lift the heavy logs up higher. Erin was determined to get the walls at least six feet high, more if possible. Then, she had to figure out how to strongly attach the supports and the cross beams, so everything wouldn't all come crashing down on them. They covered the top with closely-knit wood, but that wouldn't be enough to shed rain and they placed sod on top of it for that. Erin was doubtful this would keep out the rain completely, but she hadn't had a chance to make shingles. Shingles would be one of her winter projects, and she'd already put aside several logs for that purpose. For now, those logs were great for sitting around the fire.

Building their cabin took weeks, and Erin was grateful Molly was there beside her the entire time and not holding her to the promise she had made to get supplies in a week.

The children helped chink the logs, enjoying preparing the mud, straw, and clay combination they mixed up to place between the logs and getting filthy in the process. Erin and Molly made it fun and didn't mind how dirty the children got since they had the nice, clean stream to wash up in.

"I've got this in," Erin told Molly as she applied some of their preparation where the two logs came together, using a stick to push it in and showing the children what she wanted done. Molly pushed and prodded the mixture between the logs using her own stick. Erin knew all the children wanted to be on the outside playing with the mud, but they needed someone inside to keep it from falling through and to keep it neat. There was only bare ground inside the cabin now, but someday, they would have a floor.

When they were done, the cabin had one long room with a fireplace in the middle. The children had enjoyed searching along the stream for the rocks and clay they needed to put the fireplace together. Erin had built it slowly, using fire to harden the mixture. The clay took on a darker patina, but she didn't have time to let it dry in the winds that came through. There had been too much rain, and she worried about running out of time to build them a snug home before those rains turned to snow. Slowly, she built it up, using the planks to keep it straight, waiting until it hardened enough to pull them out and fire the area, hardening it permanently as she built it up higher and higher. Finally, it was a full three feet above the cabin and she felt it was done. She built a little roof from slabs of rock she found, slanting it to keep out the rain and leaving it open on either side, so the smoke could escape.

Erin also built a loft across the inside of the cabin, leaving it open on either side of the fireplace. She built a ladder to get up into the loft, and the children were like monkeys as they climbed up and she handed them things to store there and make it comfortable. She shaped some wood to make bedsteads, using rope to stretch across the box square and make beds. Using the mattresses they had kept in the wagon as they traveled, they now had three beds. Tabitha, as the oldest, had her own bed, but Theo and Tommy shared one, and Theresa and Timmy shared the other.

"I don't want you jumping on these beds," Molly warned them. "Your pa put a lot of effort into making them." She'd heard Erin curse the idea of having sideboards and headboards for them, much less stringing the ropes.

"Your ma made those straw ticks, so don't you be ruining her hard work," Erin warned as well. She'd gone out in one of the fields and used her scythe to cut down a lot of the hay that they'd stuffed the bed with. Once a blanket was placed on top of the straw tick and another on top of that, the beds were cozy warm. They'd spread sheets on top of the straw tick's blanket to also prevent them from getting poked, and Molly was making pillows from all the feathers she had collected.

"Here…is…one…more," Erin said as she shoved another trunk up the ladder with her shoulder. Molly pulled it back from the edge.

They'd emptied the trunks, so they knew what they had left. They would refill them later, but meantime, the children hadn't seen many of the things they'd stored in these trunks and were curious.

"Oh, look, clothes!" Tabitha exclaimed gleefully.

"Those were mine when I was younger," Molly told her, cutting off Erin and sending her a warning look when she had almost blurted out the same comment.

Erin, caught unawares, was grateful for the interruption. Fortunately, they had her brothers' clothing from right up until they had died, and both Theo and Tommy had plenty to grow into. Even Erin couldn't wear some of it because her brothers had been bigger men than she. Poor Timmy, by the time the clothes would get to him, they'd have nothing left or would have had to make them over many times. Both Theo and Tommy were hard on their clothes, and Molly was already doing repairs all the time.

"It's too bad we don't have time to plant these," Molly sighed wistfully as they went through the seeds they had brought.

"I don't know if all of these will grow here," Erin answered, handing her some more to pack away in the cool, dark trunk once again.

"We'd better get the orchard planted. I'm sorry so many trees died on the way out here."

"I planned for that, but yes, we lost a lot," Erin admitted. Many were still being watered, their roots alive and well. She was anxious to get planting. There were a million things she wanted to do but they simply didn't have the time.

"We'd better plan that trip to town. What was it you called it? Sweetwater?"

"Yep, make out your lists, and after we get all this put away, we'll go into town." She was secretly hoping that the mail she had arranged for from the town they stopped in, which would someday be called Pendletown, would make it to Sweetwater along with their money.

"Me too? Me too?" the children all asked.

"Everyone is going to town," Erin agreed as she handed Molly some more seeds to put away. She glanced at the dogs, who were looking up at her through the doorway she had cut in the cabin wall. "Well, maybe not everyone," she admitted, and the two Belgian Tervurens looked crestfallen. They understood as much as Tommy, maybe even as much as nine-year-old Theo. But they were needed here on the farm. They had to guard the land and the animals while the family was away. Although both Tabitha and Theo were old enough to watch their younger siblings, Erin and Molly didn't want to leave them in this new, remote place without adult supervision too long.

While they got the last of their things out of the tent and into the cabin, Erin took some of the boards she had brought from the farm back in Ohio and made a doorway and a door. She used nails to put the planks around the ends of the logs to square it off, measuring once, then measuring again. "Measure twice and cut once," she explained to the children, who helped whenever they could. She'd given them all saws to cut the wood they gathered into manageable pieces, and the woodpiles were growing nicely. She complimented them all on their work. They would work with enthusiasm for a while, and then, she'd let them go play. She didn't want them to resent the work, but there was a lot for them to help with.

Using leather for hinges, Erin was pleased when the door fit snuggly, replacing the quilt they had used in the interim. The cabin was a lot darker with the door closed, so she cut a window in what would be the living space. For now, a set of shutters would have to do for their one window. She wanted another across the way, but they were dangerously low on supplies and Molly wanted to go to town. She used two planks to make them a table to sit at and eat dinner. Logs were used to make seats for them to sit on.

One last thing she did was make a bed for herself and Molly on the other side of the fireplace from the big room. It was below where they had put their supplies. They had done this deliberately, not wanting the children above them in the loft. They had proper mattresses, but Molly also put a straw tick and feather pillows on it after Erin strung the ropes across. It was springy, super soft, and warm when she put their favorite blankets on it.

"That looks nice...like home," Molly said when she saw the overall effect. Their clothes chest was at the foot of the bed and there was a small table next to the bed. The floor was bare ground for now, but they'd cut extra trees and in time, they would have a clean, solid floor. "Let's go to town."

CHAPTER THREE

While hitching up the horses to the wagon, they noticed having just one set looked odd. Since they didn't know how heavy all the supplies they needed would be, they hitched up both teams. They left the oxen with the cattle, and King and Queenie were left to guard the homestead. Looking back over the wagon, the children found the box looked bare without all their worldly goods. The farm was taking on a lived-in look with the little cabin standing to one side and the grasses all worn down around it. The cabin was well above the flood line of the creek but near enough they could get the free-flowing, clean water.

"I want to dig a well and use that pump," Erin murmured, annoyed that she hadn't done more in the weeks it had taken them to build the cabin. The chicken coop looked good. The children had worked hard, but they hadn't seen her out there fixing their errors every night by lantern light.

The ducks and geese walked freely around the farmyard now, protected by the two fierce-looking Tervurens that guarded their yard. The chickens were behind their walls in the chicken coop, and Erin had ideas on how to expand that, so they could peck and bathe in the dirt. The cattle and extra horses could be seen on the hillside beyond where Erin wanted to build a barn. The horses were hobbled to keep them from running off. The sheep were on a hill across the stream, eating to their hearts' content. Erin wanted to plow up this area for her first field but was letting them crop the long grasses. They wouldn't be able to eat it all because there weren't enough of them, but she had let the ram in among them, and he'd covered their small flock. She knew she'd have early lambs but wasn't worried about that right now.

"We'll get there," Molly assured her, taking her hand and giving it a squeeze of support. Erin smiled at her and leaned in for a quick kiss.

"Oooh," cooed Theresa and Tommy, proving they had been watching. That brought their parents to the attention of the others.

"Do you have to do that?" Tabitha asked, sounding indignant.

Molly turned back, laughing. "Someday, you will understand that when you love someone like I love your pa, you want to do things to show your affection for them." She tried to use everyday situations as a learning opportunity with the children. As they had all the way across the country, every mistake, every chance they got, they taught the children.

Sweetwater was smaller than any town they had ever come across. Erin was able to get credit for the bear teeth, claws, and pelt. She had no need of those things, nor did she want the reminder of her encounter with the bear, but anything that helped to pay for the supplies was welcome.

"You say you're a smithy too?" the storekeeper asked when she inquired about mail that hadn't come. Molly had also mentioned they needed some iron to finish the stove that Erin was planning on putting together. They'd brought most of the iron plates but used some on the way and now needed more.

"Aye, a little. I make what I need," Erin admitted. She hadn't had time to set things up the way she wanted; there just hadn't been time to do everything that needed doing.

"I'd be willing to do a little trade with you on some of your supplies. All my horses need shoeing, and there's no one about who is a smith. We get by, but it isn't the same," he admitted.

Erin and he discussed what he needed and how much the work was worth. In the end, they had the supplies they needed, some that would last for many months, and they were towing four of the man's eight horses back to the farm for Erin to work on. She'd get them shod, trim their hooves, and return them. Then, she would take the other four horses and do the same. She'd bring the wagon on that trip and get some more supplies to last them the winter.

"Don't forget the new McGuffy Reader," Erin reminded Molly as she counted her supplies and checked her lists again.

"Oh, Pa, do we have to?" Theo complained upon hearing that directive.

"You don't want to grow up to be an ignoramus, do ya?" Erin asked in return.

"What's an ignor…amus?" the boy asked, frowning.

"See, if you kept up with your lessons, you'd know that," she finished, turning away before she laughed. Even she hadn't learned that word until she was an adult. She saw the pleased look on Molly's face as she added the reader to their order along with a second slate. The first one had been broken on the trip out and they'd been making do.

"We don't need chalk. There's a deposit out by the woods," Erin whispered when Molly went to add that to their order.

They filled the box of the wagon with their initial supplies, the man's sons bringing out the heavy sacks of flour, sugar, and other supplies, some they had long ago run out of. They didn't need salt, still using the supply they had laid in when they came upon a salt outcropping on their journey.

"I'll have these back to you in a few days," Erin promised as she tied the four horses to the back of her wagon.

"I'll see you then," Mr. Laydin, the storekeeper, agreed. He had liked the Herriots, a nice, fine family. When he had mentioned credit, Mrs. Herriot had refused immediately.

"We have no crops yet, and I don't want to be beholden to anyone," she told her husband firmly.

The children had been respectful, not asking for anything but wide-eyed as they surveyed the limited selection in the little store.

"Trees, eh? I bet I can order some more from Oregon City, but they wouldn't be here until spring," Laydin told Herriot as he told of the saplings he had brought out from Ohio.

"I'll get back to you on that. I want to see how the surviving trees fare over the winter."

Although she was taking home a fully loaded wagon, Erin still worried. She worried over the prices they had paid and how long their money would last until she got in a crop. They had to feed this brood over the winter and make it all last. As she glanced back at the children, each eating a piece of store-bought candy that Molly had allowed them, she vowed to work harder and do more for all of them. Glancing at Molly, who had looked back too, Erin could tell she felt the same way.

"It feels weird to be in our own room in our own cabin," Molly commented that night as she lay there. She had made several similar comments as they adjusted to living indoors again.

"I'll get the window up as soon as I can," Erin promised.

"What window?" Molly asked, confused. They hadn't bought glass in town. It was then, she remembered that last trunk they hadn't gone through yet. That was where the glass from that church was stored. "The colored glass?"

Erin nodded, laughing at Molly for having forgotten. She stopped laughing as she heard a noise and lifted her head to listen.

"It's probably one of the cats."

"I'd rather the children didn't bring them into the cabin," Erin told her.

"How do we stop them? They are used to having them around all the time."

"Those are barn cats, and the sooner they understand that, the better."

"We'd better build that barn," Molly stated, still amused.

Erin chuckled. That was another thing they needed to do, but first, she had to shoe those horses.

She set up her small anvil on one of the stumps, lifting it with the help of a horse and a set of pullies on logs. It was simply too heavy for her to lift by herself, which was why it had only been taken out of the wagon once on the entire trip from Ohio. She'd made shoes that time too. Now, she worked with the strange horses, earning their trust and only having to tie one, so it would be off balance if it tried to kick her. The other horses were more sedate, and she managed to not only tighten the shoes they were wearing, but also remade a couple of them and trimmed their overgrown hooves. "Hooves are like fingernails, and they keep growing," she explained to the children, who were avidly watching. She'd built a forge with the extra stones they gathered for the fireplace. The hot fire was made even hotter by the pipe she used to fan it. She'd made the clay pipe by slathering a straight branch with a thick layer of clay and burning it in the fire. The resulting pipe was very useful, and she was going to try that on several things, including the pump they had dismantled back in Ohio. Right now, she had to finish shoeing the storekeeper's horses and get them back to him.

Erin drove the wagon alone. Molly and the children stayed home while she went to town to return the first horses and bring back the others. Showing the shopkeeper her work, she was pleased with how grateful he was for the fine job. Erin was even more pleased to find

that her check had arrived. She arranged for the storekeeper to cash it and credit their account for supplies they would be needing. She also pocketed some ready cash.

"If you need the work, I can send others your way," he promised.

"I can use the work, and I'm willing to trade if they don't have ready cash."

Erin would soon regret that offer as it took away from all the work she had waiting to get the farm ready for winter. Still, it provided them with more supplies and stock, and they got to know some of their neighbors. Although she only had a small forge, she worked harder and faster to get the work done, so she could get back to her own chores. She and Molly were cutting more trees to build their barn but traded some work with another farmer, who couldn't afford to shoe his horses. She reshaped his worn-down shoes and used some of her own iron to make more. In exchange, he helped her cut down the trees, talking disparagingly of 'women' doing 'men's' work. Erin wanted to toss him off the farm but knew she couldn't. Instead, she got the better of him in the bargain, and he helped her start building the barn for her stock.

By the time the snow flew, she had a barn, a small shed for her sheep, a shed around her forge and anvil to keep out the worst winds, and a split-rail pigpen, which their pigs were not fond of after having enjoyed their previous freedom. Next, she turned her eye to digging that well and pumping the water *inside* the cabin. The table and stumps were pulled away from where she was digging.

"Stay away from the hole your pa is digging," Molly warned Timmy, who was fascinated by the process. The others were interested too, but Molly kept them busy hauling the dirt away in buckets she filled according to their sizes.

"Damn rocks," Erin swore when the children weren't around and she was cleaning up a bucket they had filled and hauled from the creek. "Making it harder to dig down," she explained.

"Maybe I should…" Molly offered, knowing she hadn't done much.

"I got it," Erin dismissed. She felt the need to do this alone for some reason, and she'd already dug down nearly twelve feet in the dirt on one side of the cabin.

"What makes you think you'll find water?" Molly asked, practical as ever.

"That would really be a lot of work for nothing, wouldn't it?" Erin asked in return. "If we don't, I guess we'll just expand it and have a cellar," she promised with a smile. She wasn't going to let the fact that she hadn't seen clay or any sign of water dissuade her...not yet. She'd built the cabin above the flood plain of the creek, on the highest level she could see it reached. She knew nothing about digging a well, except to just keep digging. She hoped she'd see some sign of water soon. The rocks and sand gave her hope.

It was at the eighteen-foot level that things began to get damp. The moisture lined the walls and made the weight of the buckets coming up heavier. Molly was having a harder time working the windlass they had installed to pull the buckets up, causing more to spill out when pulling the buckets over the edge. It also allowed the often-exhausted Erin to come up in some level of comfort since she could no longer climb up the rope on her own at the end of a digging shift.

"You're going to kill yourself digging that well," Molly told her. "We should have dug closer to the stream."

"I don't want our water tainted by the animals, and by having the pump inside our cabin, no one else can get at it," she answered, not mentioning that the thought of Indians had crossed her mind. The Indians out west weren't as 'tame' as those back east, and even those eastern Indians had caused troubles in her parents' and grandparents' time.

Molly was pulling up the latest bucket of muck when she heard a distinct thump from the bottom of the well. Looking down, she saw Erin slumped against the side of the well. Dumping the bucket on the floor to divide between the children's buckets, she called, "Are you okay down there?"

Erin didn't answer.

"Erin? Erin? ERIN!" she called, getting progressively louder as the children gathered around. Looking frantically around, she spied the two oldest children. "Do you think you can work the windlass?" she asked, concerned.

Both nodded but looked scared. With that, Molly set the block, so it wouldn't turn, and she put her foot in the bucket. "Okay, lower me down." Her heart was beating a mile a minute.

Slowly, the two worked together to lower the bucket. Molly and Erin had built it, so it wasn't as much muscle work to pull up a bucket, but the weight of the bucket included Molly now, and the going was slow as the two children cranked it. Molly stepped off when she was right next to Erin. Turning her wife over, she couldn't see any reason why she hadn't answered. She was still breathing but it was shallow and a little labored. It was just then, she felt a light-headedness coming over her. Gas! There must be gas in the hole. Erin had mentioned that

once. She took a breath and held it, trying to get the bucket off the end of the rope. The tie had become very tight and she was forced to exhale. Taking another breath, she knew she had to hurry. Spying the ever-present sheath on Erin's belt, she grabbed the knife it contained and quickly cut the rope, dropping the knife in the bucket. "Give me a little more," she called to the anxious children's faces peering from above her. The rope pooled around her at the bottom of the gunky hole. She tied it around Erin's torso, knotting it firmly. Then she looked up, wondering how she was going to get them both out of the muddy hole. She couldn't have the children pull Erin up alone; they'd never get her to the side. She could feel herself becoming sleepy and knew she didn't have time to waste. Looking again at the thickness of the rope, she wondered if she could still climb a rope as well as she had as a child. She was one of the few girls back then who had the upper body strength to pull herself up. Could she do it now? It had been many years since she tried, and she was a full-grown adult now. She looked up at the anxious faces again. If both adults died down here in this hole what would happen to their children? Adopted or not, they loved these children as their own. Taking another polluted breath, she took hold of the rope to try and pull herself out of the hole. Her first attempt had her mentally swearing as the rope burned her hands and she couldn't pull herself up very far. Remembering the mountain men's stories from around the campfires about how they pulled themselves up rock faces, she tried walking up the sides of the well, but the slickness prevented that. She nearly sobbed in frustration.

"Keep trying, Ma," Tabitha called, the only one to realize what was going on.

Knowing her children were up there alone, Molly tried again. This time, she wrapped her feet around the rope too and her legs helped boost her. Although it was only a few inches, she was able to grab higher up on the rope and pull, at the same time bringing her legs up higher. Using this inchworm technique, she slowly raised herself up the rope. She sensed better air midway up and gasped to fill her lungs as she continued to pull her way up. As she came to the top, her head popped up and out of the hole, and she pulled herself to the side, rolling in the dirt to get away from the hole. "Can you pull her...him up?" she shook her head as though to clear it as she corrected herself. She watched as Tabitha began to turn the windlass, Theo also putting his nine-year-old strength into it. It was a pitifully slow process. Molly, worried that her own time in the well had taken precious time away from Erin, slowly got up to help them. Their combined strength turned the windlass, raising Erin's unconscious, heavy body attached at the end. It seemed painfully slow to Molly as she counted the precious seconds Erin continued to breathe those gasses.

Finally, Erin's limp body was high enough that Molly could swing it to the side. Setting the lock on the windlass, she shoved her husband onto the dirt along the side and rolled her over. Untying the rope, which had tightened painfully around her torso, she ended up cutting this too. Erin wasn't breathing well, and Molly began to pinch her nose and push air into her mouth, giving her a kiss to fill her lungs with necessary oxygen. It took several tries before she saw Erin begin to breathe on her own. She sat back, exhausted at the ordeal.

"Is Pa going to be all right?" Theo asked, and for the first time in a while, Molly was aware of the children staring at her in concerned alarm.

"I think so. We shall see. Help me get him to bed and remove these filthy clothes," she told them. Both Theo and Tabitha rushed to help her. "Stay away from that hole," she told the other three when they would have taken advantage of the moment to look down into its fascinating depths. "In fact, go out and play," she ordered them, and they reluctantly obeyed.

Molly removed Erin's boots and pants but ordered the children away while she removed her shirt and dressed her in her nightshirt. With trembling hands, she lovingly washed away the dirt on Erin's face and neck. Tucking her into bed, she didn't know what more she could do for her. Taking the dirty clothes, she put them outside, so she could wash them later. She saw the younger children looking at the mud on the clothes in fascination.

Not knowing what else to do, Molly cleaned up the extra mud on their dirt floor and placed the wooden cover Erin had made over the large hole of the well. Next, she made dinner in the fireplace for the children and fed them.

"What will we do if Pa doesn't wake up?" Theo asked. Tabitha struck him, causing an uproar as he struck her back.

"Theo! Tabitha! You stop that! You stop that right now, you hear?" Molly ordered them. She couldn't fault Theo—she'd had the same thought—but she was angry. "We don't hit in this family," she told the two of them once they stopped. The other three were staring, wide-eyed.

"Pa hit me with the belt," Theo reminded her, unconsciously rubbing his buttocks as he remembered the sensation.

"And I'll leather your backside myself if you don't mind your manners, young man," Molly told him, pointing the butter knife at him. "Your pa breathed in a lot of that gas, and he'll wake up when he's ready," she answered his earlier question, hoping to convince herself.

"What's gas?" Tommy asked as he bit into the bread Molly had buttered for him.

"Gas is like air, only you can't breathe it cause it's bad for you," Molly told him, trying to explain something she didn't really understand herself. "It's heavier than air, and sometimes it sits at the bottom of wells and other holes. You can't see it, but it's there." She was repeating almost verbatim something Erin had explained to her once. "Your pa breathed in more than his fair share, and the gas put him to sleep."

Erin took the entire night to come out of the gas-induced coma. Molly had an awful night sleeping beside her, wondering if she would ever wake up. The coughing they heard in the morning told them Erin was waking up.

"What happened?" she asked with her raspy, sore throat. Between the repeated coughing, gagging, and the gas she had inhaled, she wasn't faring well.

Molly explained about the bad air in the bottom of the well and with tear-filled eyes explained how they had gotten her out.

"And the three of you pulled me out?" she asked, tenderly holding Molly's face in her hand. She could see how upset Molly was.

Molly nodded, tears spilling from her eyes. She was so relieved to see Erin awake.

"Well, I'll…" she began as she started to get out of bed, but Molly pushed her back. Strangely, she was too weak to resist. "Guess I'll wait until I'm stronger," she finished.

"You will stay in that bed the whole day," Molly ordered her.

"But I have so much work to do," she pointed out.

"And it will still be there when you die, but you aren't dying today, and you aren't working either. You stay in that bed! You hear me?"

Erin knew Molly was upset and this was how she showed concern. She was going to listen to her; she was too tired to fight her.

"Pa's awake?" Tabitha asked at breakfast, having heard her ma talking to him.

"He's sleeping now, but yes, he woke this morning. You children aren't to pester him. He needs to recover from that bad air," she told them, fixing them with stern looks. "You do your chores, and I don't want any arguments."

Molly had done the milking. The cows weren't as fresh as they had been earlier in the year, so they weren't giving off as much milk. Erin had taken each of the milk cows to Billy as they came into season and he had serviced them. They weren't sure yet if all four were with calf, but they were hopeful. Erin wanted to obtain a milk bull someday but would have to use Billy for the time being.

"Your husband the smith?" asked the rider who came when Molly responded to his hail. He wasn't getting off his horse though, the two dogs assured her of that.

"Yes, but he's ill today," she told him, shading her eyes from the sun. "Can you come back tomorrow?" she asked, not wishing to lose the money or trade they might need.

"Iyup, I can do that," he told her, eyeing the dogs some more, wondering if they would lunge up and if he'd be able to get his gun into play in time. They looked at him...strangely intent. "I'll come back tomorrow." Turning his horse, he rode away, looking back once to be sure the dogs hadn't followed him.

"That's a good dog," Molly told them, praising them and petting them when they wagged their tails. She looked at the hugely pregnant Queenie and worried when her pups would come, but she needn't have worried. This time, Queenie birthed them effortlessly with no help from Molly, who had midwifed for the dog the first time. They found the pups in a pile of hay in the barn when Molly and the now recovered Erin came out to do the milking.

"Well, will you lookie that," Erin said, pleased to see the litter of five pups. "We're going to have to keep some this time."

"Why is that?"

"Well, we can't breed her this often and not expect to lose some. We should keep one or two to breed later."

"You'd breed siblings? From the same litter?"

"Well, I hear you can breed the dog with his daughter, but I wouldn't do that; the faults would show up. I also wouldn't breed that stallion unless it was totally unrelated to the horses. He's keen though, and he's been sniffing around the farm horses. I wonder what kind of foals I'll get out of them."

Totally distracted by this conversation, Molly asked, "Why? What would be wrong with the foals?"

"Well, the farm horses are so big, and the stallion is more of a riding horse. I wonder how big their foals would be?"

They discussed it as they milked the cows, no young ears listening to their adult conversation. After, they released the cows into the near pasture, so they could eat the hay growing in the field. They wanted to enclose the pasture but hadn't gotten to it yet. They looked in on the new pups and mother, and Queenie wagged her tail good-naturedly. King looked from Queenie to his humans and back again, almost as though to say, "Do you see this? Do you see this?"

"Good job, Queenie. Good boy, King," Erin told them. She glanced up in time to see one of the cats looking down from the small loft in the barn, watching the new family, fascinated. She'd been one of those who had kittens on the trip, and Erin wondered if she was pregnant again. The tom who had ridden with them had disappeared soon after arriving on the farm, and she didn't know if something had gotten him or he got lost while hunting.

The children were thrilled to see Erin up and about and even more thrilled at the puppies. Erin let them each hold a puppy as Queenie looked on anxiously. "Come on, let's let them sleep. We got work to do," she told them, and when they would have argued, she fixed them with a stern look and said, "We have to get the bad air out of the well."

"How are we going to do that, Pa?" two of them asked at the same time and she laughed.

"Yes, how are you going to do that?" Molly asked, concerned. She didn't want a repeat of the previous worry.

"We are going to blow it up with a little gunpowder," she informed them and then proceeded to show them how. She pulled the cover back from the well and looked down at the little pool of water at the bottom. Putting the gunpowder in a little pouch, she then rolled a string in the powder, attached it to the powder bag, and lit it. Once it was burning well, she waited until it was nearly at the bag, then threw it in the hole. They all looked over in time to hear the loud bang and pulled back in alarm at the rush of air that rose from the well.

"What will that do? How will that get rid of the bad air? What are you doing?" the questions had gone on and on as she prepared the little bomb and lit it, and the questions were repeated once the bomb had gone off.

Erin pulled the rope out of the well, warning the children away.

"What are you going to do, Erin?" Molly asked, concerned.

"No worries," she assured her wife with a smile.

She tied a new bucket to the rope, since the other bucket was still down in the hole after Molly had cut it from the rope. She put a lit candle in the middle of the bucket. Slowly, they lowered it to the bottom of the well. Its flame didn't diminish, didn't even flicker, and it illuminated the wet sides of the well's hole. In fact, the explosion had done more than merely clear the gas from the bottom of the well. Erin and the others could see there was water coming in now, rather fast. Erin quickly pulled the bucket up from the bottom of the well and blew out the light.

"Can you pull me up on this again?" she asked, smacking the windlass.

"What are you going to do?" Molly asked, alarmed now. There was no longer any gas at the bottom of the hole but she had seen the water rushing in.

"I'm going to retrieve that other bucket and my knife."

"You certainly are not," she argued, imagining trying to pull up Erin's dead weight again.

"Then I'll climb..." she began, and Molly prepared to argue with her again.

"I'll go," Tabitha put in, and a second later, Theo said the same thing.

Both parents looked at the children in surprise, then back at each other.

"If we are going to do this, we better do something quick. Otherwise, that bucket and my knife will stay buried in the well, and the steel will begin to contaminate the water at some point," Erin pointed out to Molly, who she could see wanted to say no immediately.

Sighing loudly, she listened to the water sloshing in the bottom of the well and finally agreed. Shrugging, she left the decision to Erin.

Erin, although she was female, was more willing to allow Theo to go before Tabitha, but to be fair, she was going to let the older, more mature, and heavier girl go down into the well.

"You won't be frightened?" she asked the girl, tying another rope around her in case she couldn't hang on to the first one.

She gingerly stepped into the bucket. "I got it, Pa," she assured her. She looked pleased to have been chosen. She knew Theo had been favored by the men on the wagon train simply because he was a boy, but her parents tried to be fair and let them both do things. She watched as Erin slowly cranked the windlass to lower her into the hole.

"Are you sure, Erin?" Molly asked, worried as her oldest daughter clung to the rope and was lowered into the deep hole.

"She's got it," Erin assured her.

Tabitha did have it. She was frightened by the dark, deep hole and what had happened to her pa, but she was also excited to be doing something that her pa needed done. Looking down, she saw the water pouring in from both sides of the hole. She also saw the bucket filled with water and slightly below the waterline. Because of the mud she couldn't see the knife inside the bucket, but her ma had assured them it was there. She reached down as soon as she was able, nearly losing her balance in her own little bucket. Pulling up the full bucket, she found it filled with water and mud as well. She poured the water and mud away, nearly losing the knife in the process. Carefully, she held onto her rope and emptied the bucket while holding onto the knife. "Pull me up," she called, her voice echoing oddly in the passage. She felt the strain immediately as the windlass reversed direction and she began rising. As she came over the edge, Molly reached out, grabbing her bucket and handing it to Theo before reaching for Tabitha again and helping her over the edge.

"My, that water is coming in fast," she commented as Molly helped untie the second rope from her middle.

Erin grinned at that. She hadn't imagined that possibility when she thought of the explosion the gunpowder would cause. Putting the planks back over the hole, she saw that Molly had cleared away all the excess dirt. She began to pull apart the windlass to take it outside.

"Are you done with that?" Molly asked, surprised, as she gathered the second rope together.

"Yes, we won't need it anymore," Erin assured her.

Molly handed Theo the rope and he handed Erin her knife, which she returned to her empty sheath after carefully wiping it off. After taking the extra bucket and rope to the barn, the boy skipped off to play. Molly helped Erin carry the windlass out and place it next to the barn. They didn't know what else they would use it for, but it would be a shame to waste it after all the trouble they went to building it. "What's next?" Molly asked as Erin went to grab an axe.

"Well, unless someone comes along to have me smithy for them, I'm going to cut us a floor," she announced.

Taking the axe and some wedges, she began to split some of the logs they had saved. She'd already measured them, and they were a little long, so she cut them and left the halved ends lying about. She continued to split logs with the help of the mallet, sledgehammer, and steel wedges until she had enough logs to use. She began dragging the split logs into the cabin one by one and digging down a little into the dirt to make them fit. She covered the well completely after eyeing and marking one of the logs. Molly and the children helped her with the heavier, longer logs that reached into the bedroom.

"We're going to have to move the table and chairs as well as our bed to get these in here," Erin told her, and they did it together.

Erin found an outcropping of sandstone and made a game of having the children and Molly sand their new floor with it until the wood floor was smooth enough for bare feet. They sang funny and outlandish songs to make the hard work go by quickly. When it was smooth and they had swept it several times, Erin put a finish on it to keep it smooth and easy to clean.

"My, doesn't that look nice," Molly said when they finished. They now had a slight step down to exit the cabin but at least they had a nice floor that wasn't made of dirt.

CHAPTER FOUR

Their next task was to gather as much hay as they could before the snow came. It had rained so much and the fall rains were so cold she worried about the hay drying thoroughly. Erin cut as much as she could, not allowing the children anywhere near her swinging scythe as Molly cut her own swath. Together, they managed to clear the field she intended to plow up next year using the sod-busting plow she would reassemble from their wagon. For now, it lay waiting in sacks in the barn.

If the rains didn't come again, the dried grasses would be raked into long windrows and the windrows raked into stacks. The stacks would be thrown into the back of the wagon and the children would be encouraged to stomp it down, so they could get even more in the box. Molly worried as the children rose higher and higher in the tall wagon on the hay they were stomping down. Taking the wagon to the barn, they filled the loft and the extra stalls with hay, well away from the bitch and her pups. Erin made a haystack beside the barn, fencing it off from the milk cows that she herded in daily. The cats loved the new hay. It provided a new place to hunt as the mice came to feast, attracted by the seeds in the hay. The cats were growing fat with all the abundance and two of them were also pregnant.

"Why can't these animals have their litters in the spring like everyone else?" Erin complained good-naturedly.

Slowly, they gathered what they could. Erin even found the time to put together her plow and plow up two long strips on the far side of the stream just above the flood line where they would plant their saplings. She was sorry there wasn't more shade nearby, but she planted their raspberry bushes out by the woods in an area that looked promising. It reminded her of Picket Road where she had dug up these bushes. She hoped they would take out here. The country felt so different from Ohio, and yet, she felt she had chosen good crop and grazing land. Molly found a semi-shady area in the creek where she planted the watercress, in a spot where the creek was kind of sluggish and the grasses high enough to provide shade. She wasn't positive it would grow, but she was optimistic.

One day, Erin took her rifle and rode the mare out to the lake. It was a bit of a distance and she felt very alone out there. She wished she could have taken King too, but without Queenie to guard the cabin and stock, she felt he was needed for those duties. She was pleased to see a lot of game, some of it coming down from the mountains to graze in the foothills before winter shut them in or hid the rich grasses. She saw the prong-horned antelope, very much like the antelope she had seen on the prairies while heading to the mountains. She wondered if she would see big-horned sheep if she went into the mountains or just those Rocky Mountain goats? She saw signs of deer and elk and was pleased about that. It meant more meat for their table if she could get one. The mare shied at one point as they went by an outcropping, and she was alarmed to see signs of a big cat. She figured it must be one of those cougars she had heard people talking about. She recalled her father telling about the cats in the woods of Ohio when they had settled there. Her grandfather and others had hunted them. They hadn't seen one in this area fortunately, but she worried a cat might come for their sheep or cattle. As she traveled even farther into the mountains, she saw signs of a bear but nothing as big as the grizzly they had tangled with.

Heading back home, she was pleased to spot a small herd of elk. They were downwind, so she tied off the mare and crept up on them. She walked as close as she dared, and when one of them raised its head testing the wind, she froze, not moving a muscle as it looked around. She knew only movement would give her away. When it fell back to eating and she knew she was in range, she brought her rifle up. Another of the herd looked up and she shot, hitting it right in the chest.

Without looking to see if it went down, she quickly reloaded her gun. It would be foolish to be out here without a loaded gun. Then, she looked up and saw that her shot had brought one down because she had hit it in a vulnerable spot and it had bled to death before it could run far. The rest of the herd had been frightened by the gunshot and fled. She quickly ran to the now dead elk and used her knife to open it, getting the gasses out before it could bloat and taint the meat.

Running back to the mare, who shied away at the smell of blood, she led her to a couple deadfalls, pulling out her axe and chopping the trees until she had two poles. Laying branches across the poles, she quickly devised a travois to pull behind the mare. It wasn't a perfect travois, but it would do to get the meat home. As she came back to the carcass, she saw several birds fly off. The crows had already stolen some of the meat, the eyeballs had been pecked, and flies were crawling in the blood. Shuddering her revulsion over that, she tried to pull the elk onto her travois, the horse sidestepping because of the smell of blood, the dead animal, and the biting flies. She got a better idea. Putting the travois flat on the ground, she used a rope around the carcass to pull the dead weight of the elk onto the travois. Backing the horse up, she reattached the now heavy travois to the horse and began to pull it. Seeing that it would work, she quickly mounted her horse and headed for home. She only had to stop a couple times to adjust the travois when it got stuck on rocks and picked up other debris.

"You got one!" Molly said, pleased. When Erin had proposed that she go off and try to hunt a deer or an elk, Molly suspected Erin was really going off on a pleasure ride. She was delighted to see the rather large, dead elk on the travois.

"We have to prepare the meat right away. I wish I had thought to look for a hollow log," she answered.

"Why right away?"

"Well, the flies for one," she said, waving from side to side to swish them away as they congregated.

"Is there a two or a three?" Molly asked, teasingly, seeing that Erin was covered in blood.

"Actually, I saw cat spoor, and it wasn't one of ours," she said in a warning voice, but not willing to elaborate since the children were listening. She didn't want them to be scared. She saw that Molly understood her.

Using a pulley system, they were able to lift the elk up by its back legs and begin to cut the meat. Molly put up a low, long fire to keep the flies away and to dry the meat and smoke it. Having the younger children watching and swishing away the flies who braved the smoky fire, she kept them out of her hair as she, Erin, Tabitha, and Theodore cut the meat into small slices and hung it on strings across the smoky fire.

"Easy there," Erin warned as Timmy got too close to the fire in his exuberance to be helpful. She didn't want him falling into the hot coals.

There was a lot of meat on an elk, and Erin wanted to preserve the head, or at the very least, the antlers because she thought she could trade those. She was pulling the pelt back, intending to scrape off the fat, when someone walked their horse into the yard and the dogs barked to alert them.

"Can I help you?" she asked, wiping her hands on the apron Molly had insisted each of them wear over their clothes.

"I'm looking for the smith," the man said, looking around at them all working so hard to preserve the meat.

"You were here before," Molly greeted him, rubbing her nose with the back of her hand.

"Yep, you said your husband was ill?" He looked curiously around again and then directly at Erin.

"That I was. Got a bit too much bad air from the well," she admitted. "You need smithy work done?"

"Yeah, my horse needs new shoes, and I'll be traveling soon, so I need to have them now."

"Well, I'll have to fire up my forge, but with extra coals here," she indicated the long trench fire they had going to dry the meat, "that shouldn't be a problem." She pointed towards the small shed where her anvil was sitting. "My smithy is over there," she said.

The man got off his horse and nodded, walking his horse towards the shed. Erin quickly put some dry wood into her forge and used a shovel to retrieve some coals from the fire. She swiftly had a fire roaring in her forge and heated it up using the makeshift bellows. Tying off the horse, she inspected each of the shoes for wear and pried out the nails holding them to the hooves. Measuring them, she determined she would have to put four new shoes on them and couldn't even reuse the old ones, which she threw into a pile of iron. She had some she had made previously and measured each of the hooves to determine a fit, reusing the nails they had come with, tapping them in their hooves after she filed away the excess. She had to bend two shoes a bit to get them to fit, but the hot coals helped loosen the iron, so she could hammer away until they fit the horse's hoof.

"You got a nice place here," the man made conversation as she worked.

"Yep, we just moved in and filed our claim this year but it has possibilities. Yep, it shore does."

"You come out from the east?"

"Well, not the full-on east. We were in Ohio near the Pennsylvania border," she answered, trying to be friendly. "I'm Erin Herriot. That's my wife, Molly and our *brood*," she chuckled at the word.

"I'm Daniel Baxter. Say, you wouldn't want to sell or trade your wagon, would you? Do you need a Conestoga out here?"

"I'd be interested in a trade or selling it. I need a good farm wagon."

"I may know of someone who could use it. I will be traveling with a small train of people taking goods to the coast and coming back with others. We need wagons that can hold a lot as well as stand up to the rigors of the trail."

"Well, that wagon," she pointed with her hammer, a nail in her teeth as she spoke, "got us here from Ohio, and she hasn't given us a bit of trouble. She's a good Conestoga wagon." It was hard to talk around the nail.

"I'll let some people know you got one for sale but would be willing to trade."

"Well, a Conestoga wagon and a farm wagon ain't the same," she pointed out warningly as she tapped the nail in firmly. The horse didn't like it and tried to pull its foot back down, but it was the last nail and Erin wanted to make sure it was flush with the shoe and hadn't come out the side before she let the horse pull its foot free of her grasp.

"No, they ain't," Baxter agreed, appreciative of how gentle the smith was with his horse. "I'll point that out when I tell them you have one for sale. Now, how much do I owe you?"

They worked out the price of the work Erin had done, and the man paid her in cash. Putting the money deep in her pocket, she pulled coals out of the forge with a shovel and carried them back to the trough, which took several trips. She looked at the pile of iron she had accumulated in old shoes, deciding one day soon, she'd heat up the forge to the point where she could turn those old shoes into something useful.

The head of the elk was left out back on a post high enough to keep varmints from chewing on it, but airy enough that the flies, birds, and wind could clean it out. Erin forgot about it in the rush of work.

CHAPTER FIVE

The elk meat helped to supplement their supplies, but Erin was ready to butcher a pig. They would need the ham and bacon, and they couldn't feed all these pigs and their piglets over winter. What an awful time to have young, and they also had the puppies and kittens to add to their menagerie.

"Naamah's Ark keeps on giving?" Molly teased, referencing the name they had given the Conestoga wagon and all the animals they had brought west with them. Already, one of the geese had been a victim of their new land. Something, they weren't sure what, had gotten to it.

Not having heard the name for a while, Erin laughed at their long-forgotten joke. She was feeling the strain of making sure they were ready for winter.

Erin had drilled through their nice, new floor in the spot she had previously marked. She was just barely able to see the mark since she and the others had walked over the well and sanded the wood. Into this hole, she slowly inserted a pipe, waiting to hear it hit the water and then, going down a bit farther. She wouldn't go right to the bottom of the well, but she had made a good, long pipe. To the pipe that stuck up out of the floor, she attached the pump she had disassembled and bagged so long ago. She made sure each piece was greased and put back into place and then, she attached it to the pipe. Once she got the fit, she unattached it and built a cabinet using slices of a big tree they had cut down for the boards. Using the sandstone, she smoothed the pieces and then stained them. Carefully, she drilled through a broken washtub to make a basin and put a large piece of wood on top of the cabinet. Onto that piece of wood, she placed a large piece of sandstone. She carefully drilled through both these pieces and pulled the pipe up through the holes to attach the pump. She primed it and then tested it. It took three or four tries, but then it pumped right into the basin.

"What are we going to do when it fills up?" Molly asked, pleased at how clever Erin had been. The water from the pump was cool, clean, and delicious. She understood how important it had been to her husband to provide them with this indoor necessity.

"I'm not done," Erin told her and proceeded to punch through the hole that had formed in this washtub, making a bigger hole and causing the water to drain out onto the floor. Erin looked apologetically at Molly before cleaning it up. Drilling through both the tub, the sandstone, and the wood again, she formed a drain in her cabinet that led outside and through the chinks in the logs. "We'll have to figure out a bit of screening, so nothing can come up that drain," she pointed out. Imagining mice and other things crawling up the drain and no cats allowed in the cabin to stop them, Molly shuddered.

Before the ground froze, Erin quickly dug a privy. She placed it well away from the cabin but close enough they could all use it. They'd been using a bucket, something Erin had started on the wagon train, so they wouldn't have to go off into the woods or onto the prairie and get lost, at least that's what she told the children or anyone else who asked. But it had also been to hide her own private time, so no one would see her or her privates when she had to go. She'd only gone out on the prairie or in the woods a few times with Molly guarding her. There had been a couple of near misses, but no one had suspected she was really a woman until she was injured and someone noticed the wrappings that covered her breasts. She had originally used the wrappings to hide her breasts but continued using them because they kept her from bouncing as she worked. She took them off most nights now that they were in their own cabin. She found so much pleasure when Molly played with them as they made love. They weren't big, but they were very sensitive.

"I can't believe we are finally here," Erin said as she pitched hay into the loft, making room for some more they had gathered against the coming winter. The high bed of the wagon made it easier.

"Somedays, I feel like it's temporary, but I'm so glad we are here and the children are healthy."

"We have so much work to do," she commented, taking a momentary break as she leaned on her pitchfork, the same one she had used back in Ohio and had brought with them so far across the country.

"Yep, and there's no use complainin' about it," Molly answered, easily slipping back into the way they used to talk.

Erin smiled at her wife, pleased to be building this home with her. She glanced across the farmyard at the cabin they had built. It wasn't fancy and it wasn't big, but it was theirs. She returned to pitching hay into the loft of the barn.

There were large fields they could eventually plow that had rich stands of grass that had never known a scythe. Erin thought perhaps fire had come through here a time or two. They had found the charred remains of wood at one end of a long field, but she'd also heard from the old mountain men how the Indians sometimes burned off grass, so their ponies could run through the prairies easier. But what about when they didn't have ponies? Horses had been brought from Spain and let loose to breed on the plains. The Indians had adapted to owning them, even used them for trade and commerce, but they hadn't always been there. It provided a lot of food for thought as the simple farmer kept quiet and worked, providing for her family.

The rains kept coming and interfered with their gathering of the hay. They'd have to leave an extra day for the hay to dry out and be raked up, assuming it didn't rain again. Wet hay could rot and rotten hay would poison the animals eating it. Worse, rotten hay could turn to compost and heat up, sometimes causing a fire. They didn't need a fire in their new barn.

The rains foreshadowed cold weather, which was why Erin had hunted for elk or deer. She was feeling the need to hunt again and build up reserves against a time when they would need it. Their supplies wouldn't last all winter if she didn't have some extra. She already knew they should go into town once more with the wagon. Instead, she chose to look for a log that was hollowed out but not rotten, so they could make a smoker with it. Taking the children and explaining what they were looking for, they collected a lot of wood. They learned the woods nearest them on a hillside and nearly lost Timmy over the bluff as he ran headlong through the woods. Catching him by his shirt, Erin managed to keep him from falling over the edge, but it had been a near thing. She looked for the log alone after that, Molly fearing for the children if they went too far into the woods. The children gathered wood and filled the box of the wagon daily from the edge of the woods as Erin searched deeper.

She didn't find the tree she was looking for in the woods nearest their home. Instead, she went to search out other groves of wood that were strangely growing on sides of hills in unexpected places. Periodically, a lone tree would be growing where two hills converged, which provided it with water as the hills drained. Oddly, it would be alone with no other brush or trees growing around it. She finally found the tree she wanted near the far end of the farm, or ranch as Molly insisted on calling it. She laughed when she teased Molly about that word. As she cut down the dead tree, she saw no sign of bugs. It was completely hollowed out inside. It had died and time had eroded the wood. The outside bands had lived on for a long time. As she cut it, she examined it repeatedly, not wanting bugs in their meat. Taking down the sides of the wagon, she managed to get the tree tied on the bed and the oxen brought it back to the ranch. She didn't want to drag it as it wasn't solid and might get damaged. She realized the oxen's phenomenal strength and appreciated them all over again. She would be using them to plow next spring.

Using the weight of the tree against itself, she toppled it upright into a hole she had dug in the yard and held it in place with rocks and sand and a few posts in case of wind. Next, she carefully cut a door in it as low as she could. She lined the bottom of the log with clay that she hardened slowly, using small fires to create a base that wouldn't burn through the tree. Next, she angled nails in the tree all the way up its trunk and put in another door, again using thin leather for hinges. Finally, she topped it off with a removable roof.

On her next hunting trip, Erin was also able to bag a deer. It was not as much meat as the elk, but she brought it home to butcher it. Pulling it up as she had the elk before it, they cut all the meat into useable portions. They weren't bothered by flies this time as it had frozen that week just after she finished building the smoker. Placing strings through tiny holes in the pieces of meat meant they could hang the meat in the smoker. Erin and Molly both reached up inside the smoker to find the nails to hang the meat on. Then, Erin used a ladder to go in through the upper door and down through the top after temporarily removing the roof. She started a fire in the smoker with good, clean wood, nothing with pitch such as pine, then she closed the doors and watched to see if smoke leaked out around the doors and the roof. She was pleased that most of the smoke was trapped inside with the meat. After three days, they took that meat out and started another

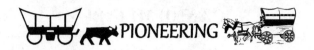

batch, putting the dried and smoked meat in bags and storing it in the loft of the cabin.

While Erin had been hunting, Molly took the children and taught them to look for greens. Wild onions were a popular one to harvest. After the freeze the other night, they'd be especially tasty. She found clover but it wasn't fresh; however, she gathered some of the seeds and folded them carefully into paper, labeling it for spring. Having fresh clover grown in their own fields or garden would come in handy.

They gathered yucca roots, chopping down the ugly, spikey plants that Erin wanted gone from their fields but leaving them on the hillsides where they would prevent the dirt from eroding. Yucca roots were something like a potato, but tougher, fibrous, and a good source of carbohydrates.

"What is that?" Theodore asked after they dug up their first yucca root.

Molly explained. "We will cut this up and boil it in water, which should soften it up. It's great in soups and stews," she also explained. He became more enthused when cutting down the plants, using the axe most willingly, but he was not so enthused about digging it up with a shovel. Molly, sensing his behavior, insisted that he do both. "If you start a job, you have to do all parts of the job whether you like it or not."

They also walked to the nearest pine forest on their land, hiking up some steep hills. Molly explained they would be collecting pine nuts. Pine cones hid the seed within them, what they call the husk. Smashing the husk against a rock allowed them to remove and harvest the pine nuts. They could be eaten raw or they could be toasted, which Molly promised to do. Each of the children tried them. The flavor was distinct but very pleasant. Like many nuts, they were an excellent source of fats, and looking at how lean they were all becoming from their diet recently, she felt they could do with this little treat. They collected many bags of the pine cones intending to smash them up and remove the seeds later.

There were also a few oaks on their land near where Molly herded the sheep. They could gather the acorns beneath their spreading branches. This was another nut they could roast and dry and then grind up to make flour. Molly knew she could make a variety of tasty breads using things other than wheat or corn, and she intended to make acorn flour bread. Having the sheep nearby provided a mowing machine they could use to get through the tall grasses. Having the dogs nearby watching the sheep also provided protection in case of wild animals.

"What is that I smell?" Erin asked as she came in from checking on the latest batch of smoking meat.

Molly smiled at her surprise. Having made do with pan bread for so long on the wagon train, she was pleased to be able to bake bread in the oven that Erin had constructed using the sheets of iron they transported across the country. She'd put it in the fireplace next to the fire and Molly learned to turn whatever was baking in the oven midway. She had big plans for all the things she would make on baking days.

Since they had plenty of butter, it was a nice change to eat it with baked bread instead of the usual pan-fried bread. Their dinner that evening was fresh venison with baked bread and some beans Molly had soaked for hours. This made a delicious meal for them all.

"Do you have your sourdough starter going again?" Erin asked as she enjoyed her slice of bread. Molly had given her two slices, and she was relishing the taste.

"Yes, I got it going again on the back of the sink. This isn't sourdough though," she explained with a mystery grin. She explained about the acorns, and Erin bit into the bread again, realizing she was tasting nut and it wasn't sour at all.

"What's sourdough starter?" Tabitha asked, curious.

"Remember the biscuits everyone made in the pan when we were in the wagon train?" Molly asked her, then continued at her nod. "Well, they would let a little of their bread mix go bad or sour since they didn't have yeast to make good bread. That would start the sourdough. You remember, you ate the bread on the trail."

The girl nodded, filing away that little fact as Molly taught not only her, but Theo, Tommy, and Theresa how to cook. When Theo, who had been influenced by the mountain men and other men on the train protested that it was *girls'* work, she put him in his place. She reminded him what his pa had said back in Ohio. There wasn't women's work, there wasn't men's work, there was just work, and they were all going to do it at one time or another.

"But boys work in the fields and woods with their pas," he had protested.

"I did that too," Tabitha pointed out. She'd cut a lot of wood, just as much as her brother. She'd hauled and chopped it too. "Guess you just don't want to know how to cook and feed yourself," she taunted.

"Girls are supposed to do the gardening, cooking, spinning, weaving, and mending. They are supposed to do the sewing," he glanced at the sewing machine in the corner of the cabin, unused yet. He was curious to find out how it worked. Molly hadn't had time to do

any sewing yet but intended to do some when they were stuck in the cabin over winter. "They make soap and candles too," he finished, evidently having a litany of chores that girls were *supposed* to do.

"I can do all that too," Tabitha added and taunted him by sticking out her tongue. "And I can feed the cows, milk them, and gather hay like Ma does."

"*Now*, are you *both* listening?" Molly raised her voice slightly. "I can do all that and more, and so can your pa!" She wondered how shocked the two of them would be to learn their pa was a woman? "And next year, we are going to pound our own corn to make cornmeal and maybe we'll grind our own wheat too. What if you don't have a husband or wife to do all this for you or with you?" She directed that comment towards the oldest two, knowing the younger children were listening except for Timmy, who was playing with a cat. "You think on that!"

The children were shocked: first, at her raised voice and second, that she could and would do all that. They had known that, of course, but they'd been arguing as they teased each other and were unaware that Molly was not only listening but would put a stop to it by topping them both.

"I think Theo would like to make the next batch," Molly told Erin, much to her surprise.

"You think you can bake bread as good as your ma?" she asked him, enjoying the taste once again.

Theo nodded, remembering the conversation. He was intrigued to learn how to bake his own food and realized that his pa had told him long ago…anything a man can do a woman can do and vice versa. He was eager to learn because he didn't want Tabitha showing him up.

CHAPTER SIX

Molly had knitted the yarns Erin purchased so long ago in Missouri. That purchase had also led them to purchase their sheep as well as the spinning wheel, which was now in their bedroom. Its sharp needle was covered but only so the children wouldn't touch it. Because of Molly's knitting around the fires at night as they crossed the country, they all had plenty of socks, mittens, scarves, and hats. She hadn't enough yarn to make sweaters, but she planned them out with the wool from the sheep they would harvest next spring. When the first snows came down, and even in the cold that came before the snow, everyone would have warm clothes to wear. They'd all grown a little, but by going through their old clothes and adjusting for sizes, they managed to piece out complete winter outfits for all the children.

"Can you find a string for my mittens, so when I take them off to shoot my gun I don't lose them?" Erin asked Molly. Between them, they ran the string through the sleeves of her jacket and down the arms, putting the ends of the strings through the wrists of her mittens, weaving it so it looked natural and wouldn't break too easily.

Erin was out almost every day now that it was cold and had snowed. She was hunting for meat they could store, procrastinating on butchering their own pigs. The wild animals were getting harder to find, but she tried to bring something back every day, even if it was just a squirrel. She knew shooting a squirrel was difficult. It was so small it could be destroyed by a bullet and there wouldn't be any usable meat if she hit it. So, instead, she would bark it—shoot into the bark of the tree the animal was on—hitting just beneath the animal ideally. This would stun the squirrel and it would fall unconscious, allowing her time to kill it and save the meat for their consumption. She had started taking Tabitha out with her and was teaching her how to hunt. Tabitha had cried over her first squirrel and had been devasted when she got a rabbit, but the first time she hit a deer, she was euphoric because she knew the supply of meat in these bigger animals would be a big benefit to her family.

"Do you think I can get an elk?" she asked eagerly. She was no longer afraid of the gun, firing and quickly learning to recharge the gun.

"I don't know. I think my getting one was a fluke," Erin admitted ruefully. Still, they tried, walking miles around the ranch and looking for any opportunity to bring food back for the family.

"It's not fair that I can't go hunting too," Theo asserted. "Someday, I'll be a man, and I need to know how to hunt." It was obvious he was envious of Tabitha going out with their pa.

"Tabitha is older and obviously more mature. When I see you are old enough to go, you'll go," Erin told him sternly. Her voice held a warning, and the boy stopped himself from saying anything more. He knew better than to point out that Tabitha should do girly things and he, a boy, should be doing the hunting with their pa.

Molly had started taking out the wagon and bringing back as much wood as the oxen could pull for their winter needs. They'd already laid in a good supply, but she was worried they would run out. They were all kept busy as they prepared for winter.

On the day that Erin got the second elk, someone came to their yard to buy the Conestoga wagon. Molly had filled the box with wood and was emptying it with the help of Theo and Tommy. Theresa and Timmy were playing with the new batch of kittens, and it was spitting snow in the cold. They looked up in surprise when they heard a wagon coming over their hill, and they were surprised to see strangers riding down into their little valley. Molly told the children to continue emptying the box while she went to see what they wanted. She figured they were there to see the smith, but she had no idea when Erin and Tabitha would return.

"Hello, there. Can I help you folks?" she called as they came to a stop in front of the barn, King and Queenie both barking to intimidate the horses. "King, Queenie, quiet!" she called, and at her command they both silenced, but their body language told the horses not to come another foot closer or they'd be torn to pieces.

"Those are some fine dogs you have there," the man said admiringly as he set the brake even though his horses wouldn't even consider taking a step forward. "I'm Bret Collins, this is my wife Rebecca, and these are our children. I understand you have a Conestoga wagon you are willing to trade or sell?" he asked.

"Ah, you'd have to talk to my husband about that. We're still using it, as you can see," she swept her arm towards where the children were throwing wood onto the growing pile that needed cutting and straightening as it looked all askew. The children, suddenly the center of the adults' attention, quickly got back to work.

"Looks like you have quite a crew there," he laughed. "May I get down?"

Molly nearly laughed. People were always a little *politer* when King and Queenie were about. "Yes, please do," she said welcomingly. "Stay," she said to the two intent Tervurens. She knew if the man bore any ill will towards her or made a lunge, both dogs would be on him in two bounds.

"We're traveling north into Canada. I have a chance of a job up there, and I'm told our wagon isn't up to the rigors of the trip." He patted the wagon he had arrived in almost affectionately.

"Ours brought us all the way from Ohio," she admitted, glancing back to make sure the children were finishing their work. They were going at it with a will.

"Is your husband around? I talked to a man in Sweetwater who said you folks might be willing to trade or sell?"

"He's out hunting for our winter meat. I'm not sure..." she began but King suddenly made a noise. He was on a stay but wanted to bring attention to himself. She looked to where King was staring intently. Queenie looked too but then quickly looked back at the people in the wagon and the man on the ground. She knew her job. "Well, there he is now," she said, seeing the travois behind the mare, Erin and Tabitha both riding.

"Looks like he got something," the man commented, wondering at the young girl with the tall, lanky man.

Molly tried to see beyond the mare. She wasn't sure what was on the travois, but she knew Erin wouldn't go to the trouble of building that large, temporary contraption to bring in meat unless it was much too heavy for her. They all waited until Erin got closer.

"Hello, there," Erin called, seeing the waiting wagon and wondering if they wanted smithy work. She hoped so. They could use the additional money this late in the season.

"Looks like you got an elk there," the man greeted her as she got down from the mare and helped Tabitha down.

"Yep, we shot this one back in the hills early this morning," she admitted. "I'm Erin Herriot," she held out her hand for the man to shake.

"Bret Collins," the man said, shaking her hand. "This is my wife, Rebecca and our children," he gestured to them as he introduced them.

"Ah," she answered. "You've met my wife, Molly," saying that still brought pride to her voice even after a year, "and our children. This is our oldest, Tabitha." The young girl nodded in acknowledgement but shyly looked at the ground.

"I understand you're selling that Conestoga wagon?" he inquired, getting right to the point. It was getting cold fast, and he didn't want to be out here too long.

"Yes. Yes, we are," she said and glanced at Molly, who made a gesture that it was all up to her.

"Let's get the travois under the bar," Molly murmured to Tabitha, so they could lead the mare away and get out of the men folks' way. "It was nice meeting you," she said to Bret Collins in a louder voice, glancing at his wife to include her, then leading the mare away with Tabitha.

"Nice to meet you too," he answered but was more interested in what Erin had to say about the wagon. They began to walk towards the wagon, the children industriously throwing wood on the pile, nearly finished cleaning it out.

They discussed it for a while, and when all was said and done, the man traded his wagon. Erin inspected it carefully and found a few things she felt could be improved on, so Collins gave her some hard cash to complete the trade. They unhitched Collins' horses, brushed out the Conestoga, and hooked his horses up to it. Erin showed him how to attach the bows that she had stored in the barn, and together they put the canvas over them, tying it securely on the wagon box. She waved as the family left with the larger wagon.

Erin looked to see that Molly had put the travois under the block and tackle she had set up for raising their kills and reassured herself the mare was in the barn being brushed down. The new farm wagon was sitting forlornly in front of the barn. She led her team towards it but didn't start hitching it up.

"You sold our wagon, huh, Pa?" Tommy asked unnecessarily.

"Yes, son, I did. We didn't need that big wagon anymore. This smaller wagon is more what we need now," she answered as she tied the team off.

"A fine trade?" Molly asked as she finished brushing the mare.

"I think so," Erin answered, and together they tied off the elk and prepared to lift it in the air. Tabitha quickly pulled the travois out of the way. It was worse for wear and she took it over to where the loads of wood were piling up.

Theo ran to the cabin to get the aprons and knives they used for butchering. Tommy and Theresa brought out the large tubs they used to hold the meat and innards.

"I want to get a meat grinder," Molly confessed as they sliced off the roasts and put them in the tub. They would make one roast tonight, but the rest would be sliced thinly and cured in the smoker. She'd cleaned out the ashes, all fine wood ash, and it was ready and waiting in bags. She saved the ashes to make soap.

"That would be great if we could make sausages and not let all this go to waste," Erin agreed as she sliced off more of the meat. The dogs were watching avidly. They knew they would get their share of the leftovers since their humans made dog food out of the bits of meat they didn't use. If they had a meat grinder they would be able to use even more of the meat they cut up.

Butchering took a long time that day, and Erin had to stop to remove the harnesses from the team, setting Theo and Tabitha to brushing them down before releasing them in hobbles on the nearby hillside. She looked forward to getting a paddock enclosure but hadn't found the time yet. The split-rail fencing had only been big enough to enclose the pigs, and even they kept getting out, which also meant something could get in.

"Did you hear the wolves last night?" Molly asked as they worked. She was trying to cut along a rib to get the meat, but the tendons were strong. Erin took the other side and between them they yanked it apart, aided by a sharp knife cutting at the meat and tendons.

"I think those were coyotes, but they were far off," she commented in return. She was worried this meat would attract other meat eaters. She had left a clear trail by using the travois, but it wasn't like she hadn't done it before. And she would do it again, even though the amount of blood and parts she left behind might have the animals following in hopes of getting an easy meal.

The smoker was going, and the tubs of meat were in the cabin by the time Molly put a roast in the oven. They were still pulling apart the elk, and Erin cut off the head and placed it on a post out back. The birds, the bugs, and she didn't know what else had been at the other head she placed there. By spring, it would be a nice skeleton, but she knew it was the horns that were most valuable because people made things with the horns. She'd heard that knife makers used them for handles, Indians traded for them, and one mountain man had told her that some folks from Asia ground up the horns for medicines. She'd didn't care what people used them for, so long as she could get money for them. She made sure the new head wouldn't fall to the ground as she left it exposed to the elements.

Molly had spread out the pelt for Erin, and together, they tacked it to the side of the barn intending to scrape off the last of the fat and meat still attached, so they could work it and it could be sold.

Finishing up and taking off her apron, Molly saw Theresa crying. "What's the matter?" she crooned to the little girl. She wanted to hold her but was still bloody and dirty.

"I'm sad that he had to die," she said, pointing to where Erin was finishing up on the edges of the pelt. It would take days, and she'd work the rest of it in the cabin as she pulled the tacks to take it down.

"Well, honey, God provides for us to live, and we need food. You love elk meat," she pointed out.

"I know, but it's sad that he had to die," she sobbed.

"I know, honey. Try not to think about it. Could you make sure that the kittens are in the barn and check on the puppies? I see a storm coming, and we better make sure everything is battened down."

The kittens and the puppies were enough to distract the five-year-old, if only for a moment.

"That is a tender heart," Erin commented, the pelt in her arms.

"They all have tender hearts, but they have to learn. We need the meat...."

"I know. I don't like shooting them either. Tabitha was angry she didn't get the shot," she added with a laugh.

CHAPTER SEVEN

Molly's prediction proved true. A storm did blow in. Erin brought the sheep in closer, so they could keep an eye on them. The snow that came down didn't last, but it made it hard to gather their small flock. The cattle could still be seen on the hillside, but Erin could tell they were drifting farther and farther from the ranch yard. Billy wandered looking for food and trying to escape the winds. All the cattle would seek shelter from those harsh, cold winds.

They cut up the meat over the next few days and began to smoke it. Erin then went outside and got the children enthused about cutting up the pile of wood into smaller, stove-sized lengths and building up the stacked woodpile. That lasted a few hours.

"Shouldn't we be splitting this?" Theodore asked. "Why do they split wood?" he asked in the same breath.

"They split it to help it dry out faster," Erin explained as she sawed off another length. She stopped for a moment, so Theresa could pick it up and proudly carry it to the neat stack alongside the cabin. Erin started another length, eyeballing how long she wanted it before setting her handsaw. "Some even build a roof over their pile to keep it dry."

"Wet wood doesn't burn and there's a lot of smoke," Theo contributed authoritatively. He was wrestling with a bigger piece, and it was taking him three times as long as Erin to cut it to length.

"Ma says we should turn the meat," Tabitha announced, coming out bundled up in her winter clothes.

They'd had to start a fire in the pit because the smoker was taking too long for the strings of meat to dry over the smoky coals, and Erin seriously considered looking for a second tree to build another smoker. Still, it wasn't often you got an elk, and they'd gotten two this season. She figured that was only because they hadn't been hunted in this area before. They'd be harder to get each year from now on.

Erin made sure the children were busy indoors when she decided to butcher one of their pigs. They needed the bacon and ham, and while she silenced the indignant squeals with a knife, she felt it straight to her heart. She had known this piglet. She had raised it from birth. It had survived the trip out here, running behind the wagon with its siblings and mother. And before that, it had hung in the sling as the wagon carried it west. She knew getting attached to the animals was a mistake but she couldn't help herself. In that way, she was a bad farmer. She dipped the carcass in boiling hot water and then shaved off the hairs. As she cleaned the insides, Molly came out with the large tubs and silently, together, they filled them.

"Look at this bacon. It's a perfect marble," Molly complimented as she pointed out the fat and meat in the side she was cutting into usable portions.

Distastefully, Erin nodded and then took her tub to place the meat in the smoker. The hams would go into the tree whole if they fit along with the ribs and other choice pieces of meat. Erin was a long time hanging the pieces and helped Molly take the remainder in the tubs into the cabin.

"Are you okay?" Molly asked, concerned over how quiet Erin was.

"Of course," she assured her, pulling herself out of the funk she had allowed herself to fall into.

"More?" the children cried, not realizing it was ham and bacon that would be put up. The fresh bacon served with their biscuits in the morning didn't even faze them. It took half the day before any of them realized one of their pigs was missing and cried about it. Erin ignored their tears as she continued to cut wood, stockpiling it for winter.

"Are you going into town once more?" Molly asked, a day or so later.

"I suppose we better, just to be sure," she agreed, although the cold and the snow they had gotten didn't make her too enthused. She'd gone over the new wagon, tightened a few things, and replaced one piece of iron to ensure the box was good and tight. The horses pulled

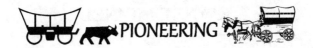

this wagon effortlessly, and they seemed proud that she only needed the one team. The children were in good spirits as they headed into town.

Erin was pleased to get rid of the two elk heads, even if they weren't perfectly clean. She'd scraped more off them, but the birds and the elements had made it easier in some places than others.

"Have you ever heard of a bone graveyard?" Mr. Laydin asked, pulling Erin aside from her wife and children, so his wife couldn't hear either.

"Is that where animals go to die?" she asked, horrified just thinking about it.

The man nodded and added, "I could give you a bit more if you brought me others." He indicated the two sets of heads with the antlers still attached that she had already agreed to trade him.

"You know where it's at?"

He shook his head. "I just heard someone tell of it."

"Well, I haven't seen anything like that, but I'll bring you anything I find," she promised, repulsed by the idea of a bone graveyard. Those were myths, weren't they?

Stocking up, Erin was disappointed by the choices in this small store. Still, it was a lot better than traveling all the way up to Pendletown, which would take a couple days there and back.

It started to snow on their return trip as Molly quietly mentioned to Erin how little cash money they had left. "I know," she fretted, having known how much they used up to get here. Still, despite their frugal ways, the children ate a lot, and they hadn't really been prepared to feed all those mouths. She explained about the check that had come in, the credit they had at the store, and vowed to herself that she would show Molly the money that was left, so she wouldn't worry as much. Erin hurried the horses as the snow started to thicken. She didn't like being off the ranch too long and leaving the dogs alone to guard it.

That snowfall was the first of many as it continued to come down. They were snug in the cabin, and Erin used that time to fit together the pieces of colored glass they had taken from the church window so long ago. Fitting the colored pieces took time, was aggravating, and the window wasn't exactly the right shape or size. Still, she persevered and soon, they had that pretty window to look at every day. She'd cut a second window at the back of the cabin as she had planned. She used greased paper in that window to provide them with additional light and keep out the cold.

"I'd love a window upstairs too. It would allow the children to look out and would give more light up there. When we go into the storage, I don't like using a lantern up there," she confided with Molly.

Erin went out twice a day to do the chores while the snow continued to come down and build up. The winds built up huge drifts, and she shoveled her way to the barn to milk the cows. She turned the cattle out behind the barn, but the cows wouldn't go far because of the drifts. Also, they knew there was food here in the barn. Erin just hoped the hay would last. She'd chosen a good hill to weather the sheep on. It blocked the winds from drifting the snow too deep. Billy had led his cattle, including the oxen, over the hill. Erin had hiked to look for them, but the snow made it dangerous and finding the herd took a long time.

Stripping some saplings, she constructed snowshoes, which she'd heard the mountain men talk about. The first set were horrible and caused her to trip and hurt herself. Then, they fell apart. Molly helped her with the second set and they managed to bend and shape the wood properly using a combination of bark strips and smaller twigs to reinforce the webbing of leather and keep her boots from plunging through. When she tied them on, Molly and the children laughed at how they caused her to walk funny. But the snowshoes did make it easier to search for and find their flocks of sheep and cattle. Taking King, her rifles, and her pistol along, she felt a lot safer out in the blinding snow. She used her tracks to find her way back, but they were nearly drifted over and if not for King, she might have become completely lost. She wasn't the only lost creature. She came across and killed a deer caught in the deep snow. This fresh meat wouldn't be smoked like the others but hung up and frozen. They would cut meat off the carcass for their meals for quite a while. Keeping other animals away from the frozen meat involved the dogs.

"I need to build a bigger barn. Maybe a meat house or something," Erin complained. There simply hadn't been enough time last fall, and the snow had come early. They were close enough to the mountains that this was understandable, but she worried about providing enough food for her family. Buying vegetables and staples had been expensive, and they still had months to go before they could grow their own, much less harvest some of them.

Something, maybe a weasel, had gotten into the barn and killed one of their big geese. The killer hadn't eaten their prey, which puzzled Erin, but she hung the bird up and they had it for Thanksgiving.

Erin spent a lot of her time shaving shingles in the corner of the cabin. It was pleasant listening as Molly worked with the children on their letters, read from the few books they had brought, and told stories. Erin would have preferred to be out hunting every day, but it simply wasn't practical.

For Christmas, they had another goose. This one looked like it had been killed by a wolf. King and Queenie had run it off, but Erin had called them back. This made her decide to keep their flock inside and not let the ducks and geese head for the open stream, which was slowly icing over.

Erin managed to kill another deer between Christmas and New Year's, taking it away from a pack of wolves as she searched for Billy and the herd. She hadn't been successful in finding Billy on her snowshoes, and the wolves had surrounded the lone deer that was caught in deeper snows. She saw by the tracks the wolves had deliberately herded the deer to the deep snow to make it easier to attack. Unlimbering both her rifles as well as her pistol, she hit two of the wolves with careful shots. The first shot had scared the other wolves, and their momentary shock had enabled her to get the second wolf, but she got off no more shots as the remaining wolves took off. Erin used her knife to kill the frantic deer but getting all the meat back to the ranch was a nightmare. Erin skinned both wolves, pulling their longest canine teeth for trophies that perhaps Laydin, the storekeeper, would want. She knew their pelts would also be worth money. Using a rope, she dragged the deer across the snow, slowly and surely. It took hours, and she worried the wolves would come back and follow their trail. Having King and Queenie around was a bonus but not an absolute guarantee to keep such animals away from their stock. Their growing pups ate a lot and were slowly being weaned off Queenie. It had been a poor time to have pups, but the dozen cats they now had, most of them grown kittens, were an equally poor choice. Erin fretted about feeding everyone.

"Are you okay?" Molly worried, seeing how gaunt and haunted Erin looked after pulling that deer God only knew how far.

"Just tired," she admitted, trying not to share her worry with her wife. The children watched them closely. They were trapped in the cabin most of the time. Only Tabitha and Theo got out with any regularity, and then, only to help with chores. Very rarely, on a bright and sunny day, Molly allowed the other three children outside the cabin to play.

Erin could see Molly was restless too. She was trapped in the cabin with very little to do but cook, clean, and teach. Everyone was getting on each other's nerves. Tempers were short, and by February, Erin was spending most of her days in the barn or the sheds. Molly found her there one day as she fired up her forge to melt all the scraps and pieces of iron she had laying around.

"You're using a lot of wood to make that fire," Molly complained, knowing how hard they had all worked to bring that wood in.

"It's got to be done. I can reuse these," Erin indicated the old horseshoes she was melting.

"But why now? Can't it wait until spring?" She wondered if Erin was avoiding her. They weren't intimate these days. Neither of them had the desire for intimacy, and she was worried.

"I thought with the press of other work this spring, we'd have no time," she hedged, telling a half-truth. She'd just wanted to escape the claustrophobia of the cabin, all their children, and the relentless pile of shingles she was making using a knife with two handles. She was certain her father had used this knife. She would tap the knife into the wood and use the hand maul to tap the blade farther into the stump. Slicing off thin shingles of wood, she'd stack them with the others. When she had a stack about a foot or so high, she'd add them to the stacks she was storing in the barn. Sometime next year, they'd replace the sod roof that was currently covering the cabin. The sod wasn't very successful at keeping out the rain and moisture, and they'd had to use buckets to catch the many drips.

"Is something bothering you?" she asked, astutely.

"I'm just waiting for spring," she tried to say cheerfully, glancing to where the sod plow was waiting to bust up the land and create fields for her to plant. The plow had been a beast to reassemble, but she didn't regret purchasing it or bringing it across the country. They had their seed, ready and waiting, but if spring didn't come early, they might be forced to eat it.

Molly had the same worries and wished Erin would talk to her about them. She too worried about feeding all these children and keeping them entertained with songs and reading and educating them all. Her own education had ended after the eighth grade. No one saw any need for girls to go further since they would soon be married. What was the point of educating girls? She wanted more for her children but didn't know if she would be able to find the books. And because of her own limited education, she worried she wouldn't be able to teach them even if she found books. There were no schools in this relatively

unpopulated area. Mrs. Laydin had said they were considering one in Sweetwater, but that was too far away for the children to attend.

Slowly, the seasons changed, and when she was up to her waist in snow and trying to make sure the sheep didn't freeze to death as they gave birth, Erin realized she had made a big mistake letting the ram in with her little flock too early. She realized she shouldn't have bred them until at least December, so they would give birth when there was grass on the hills. Having to bring the pregnant sheep into the barn with those that had given birth under the overhang stretched their already meager supply of hay. The milk cows and pigs had also gone through their fair share of the hay. Feeding this lot while keeping away the wolves, who were drawn to the smell of placentas and lambs, would drive Erin mad. She spent several nights in the barn, her guns loaded and ready to shoot, further alienating Molly in her desire to keep their stock safe.

"You're killing yourself," Molly told her, seeing how tired and thin Erin was looking. They'd gone from three meals a day to two, and still, she didn't eat a full meal, preferring to leave more food for the children.

"We just have to wait for the snow to melt," Erin lied to her convincingly. She was worried there simply wasn't enough food, and they needed their seed to survive until harvest.

"Kill one of the sheep. Find the cattle or even the pigs," Molly told her practically. They'd already butchered two of the pigs: one last fall and another in January. She knew how hard it was for Erin to butcher these animals, but it had been necessary.

Erin wouldn't kill the sheep, and she didn't need to after she lost one mother. Thankfully, she'd been able to convince another ewe to foster the lamb. They'd also lost three lambs, and she worried how many more they would lose before spring officially arrived. The cows were drying up with limited hay rations. They needed fresh grass, so their own calves would be healthy. She eyed the pigs and knew she had no choice. Their own food was running out, and they had no way to get more. They had to feed not only their family, but also the dogs and cats that hunted for them, kept their barn and home safe, and provided companionship. Some would say companionship wasn't necessary, but more than once Erin had found herself petting a pup, a cat, a dog, or a kitten in contemplation, and she'd seen Molly do the same. That companionship saved all their sanity.

CHAPTER EIGHT

Spring slowly crept forward, although a few snow storms tried to negate that fact. Erin had sharpened and re-sharpened the blades on her plow in anticipation of getting her fields ready. She couldn't start until the ground warmed up, and she was getting anxious. The receding snows meant that animals could forage in the previous year's growth of dead grasses, and Erin anxiously sent the sheep, the milk cows, their horses, and the pigs out onto the surrounding hills. Unfortunately, this attracted the meat eaters, who were hunting. They too were hungry from the hard winter. Teaching their growing pups how to protect the animals kept both dogs very busy.

The Herriots ran out of flour, even acorn flour, and Erin seriously considered using the mare and stallion to go into town alone. She didn't dare take the entire family since getting caught out in a blizzard would be the death of them all.

"I don't want you to go," Molly pleaded with her as she outlined her plan.

"We need food, and I can pack it in on the backs of these horses," she said. "I'll go faster without the wagon, and you all can stay safe here at the ranch."

"It's a ranch now instead of a farm?" Molly teased, trying to lighten the mood between them. It had been tense for too long, and she worried about Erin.

Erin smiled slightly, but they both knew a lot could happen on the way into town. They had no idea how deep the snows would be between here and town, but they both finally agreed that she needed to get to town to help with their supplies. She carried what little money they had left on her person, along with the wolf pelts and the deer to trade. They'd used up much of their credit at the store with the high prices for supplies.

"I wish you'd take King with you for protection," she suggested.

"You need King and Queenie here, but I am taking two of their pups to see what I can get for them."

"I won't tell the children until after you are gone," she agreed.

"I'd take more, but if people thought we had too many, we might not be able to get our price."

"Two bits?" she asked, wondering if she would even get that much. Even though there was a scarcity of such fine animals out here, people were as poor as their family, and that twenty-five cents was a steep price.

"I'll try, but honestly, two less mouths to feed will be a blessing," she confessed, then was immediately sorry at the look on Molly's face. She knew she was thinking of the five children they had taken on, not realizing how it would beggar them. "I'm sorry," she immediately apologized.

"No, I understand," she answered and watched when Erin mounted up, the two pups on either side of the stallion's saddle. She led the mare with a pack saddle she had fashioned, the pelts on her back.

"Does Pa have to take the pups?" Theresa fretted, seeing her getting ready despite Molly's attempt to distract them.

"Yes, Theresa, he does. We need to try and find a trade for them. We need the money," she admitted, not willing to hide their dire straits from the child even if she was only five. She glanced and saw that Tabitha looked worried. Tommy and Theodore went to play with the remaining pups, one of which would die for no apparent reason in the day while they waited for their pa to return. Timmy was already playing with the kittens. Some had caught a sort of cold and had mucky eyes and noses. Molly insisted they all wash up as soon as they came back in the cabin to ward off the animals' germs. She didn't know if that would work, so she also didn't allow any of the animals in the cabin anymore.

Erin was extra cautious on her trip towards Sweetwater. She knew it had been a hard winter, and her family weren't the only ones starving. She'd been lucky to get that last deer to supplement their food. And they'd been able to butcher the pig and use the sheep, but they needed beans, flour, and other staples. She smiled as she remembered they still had plenty of salt from that salt lick they had found so long ago. Breaking up those rocks had entertained them many nights as they traveled west to join the wagon train. That wagon train seemed so very long ago. She wondered what had happened to many of those people. Pat Wallace, the leader of the train, had been a competent man. He'd been suspicious about Erin, not because she was a woman, who looked like a man, but because of the reputation that preceded her. She smiled remembering the men who had tried to steal their cattle and the way she had handled it. She had put a gun upside the head of one of the thieves. She'd been scared and bluffing. She'd also been so angry the man had profited from her animals, and she struck without warning, giving the man no chance. She couldn't give them a fair chance. If it were discovered she wasn't a man, it would have gone far worse for her, and maybe for the family she had created. Molly and the children meant everything to her.

Sweetwater didn't have much. They too had suffered through the winter, but Erin managed to get a bushel of beans, a quarter bushel of flour, and a few other canned goods that would tide them over.

"How'd you and your family fare?" Laydin asked her as he tallied up her total, less the pelts she had brought in. The canines from the wolves were of particular interest to the man, and he'd traded for those as well when Erin brought them out.

"Fair to middling. I tell you this, I'll put in a lot more supplies next winter," Erin replied as she checked the figures of the storekeeper before nodding her acceptance.

"So, you're staying? You won't go on to the Willamette Valley?"

Erin immediately shook her head, her hair not moving since Molly had given her a haircut that made her look more like a man. It had gotten shaggy over the winter, and while Erin didn't mind its length, they both agreed she needed it short to keep up her male persona. "No, we staked out the prettiest land I could find, and we'll farm it."

Laydin, a gossip, would have liked to talk more, but Erin was anxious to get home. She had worried the entire way about a storm coming up but the skies remained clear. The little she had been able to trade had netted them maybe enough to last a month or so. Laydin hadn't wanted the pups. She hoped spring would come, warm the ground, and she could eke out a living until harvest.

"Them your pups?" another man asked as she put the supplies in the pack saddle on the mare.

"Yep," she answered warily. The man was big and beefy. He was looking avidly at the pups hanging in bags on either side of her horse.

"Them's shepherds?" he asked.

She nodded, not willing to explain about Tervurens. She wondered if the man was interested in buying them but she wouldn't suggest it.

"You sellin' 'em?"

"Yep."

"How much?"

"Wallll," she said, adopting his way of speaking and stretching the word out, "I got two bits on the others."

"You had more?" he asked, incredulous at the price and the fact there had been others.

Erin didn't tell him that it was previous litters, just nodded. She saw him considering the high price and then come to some agreement in his head. "I'll take one if you'll show me 'em."

Erin unfastened the bag the squirming pup was in. He hadn't been happy to be kept that way, but he had no choice.

"That a male?" the man asked and then leaned down to pick the pup up by the scruff and look himself. The pup went limp as he held him up and scrutinized him closely. "You got a female?" The way he said *female* grated on Erin's nerves, but maybe she was being touchy.

Erin did and unfastened the flap for the other pup, bringing her down. Both pups were thrilled to be out of their undignified holders and immediately set about running in a circle, drawing laughs from both Erin and the man. Their legs were long, and they were uncoordinated as they played in the mud of the street.

"Two bits, eh?" he confirmed, looking at Erin as though to talk her down.

She nodded. "Their sire and dam are the best dogs you could ever want," she added, hoping to convince him.

"Would you take two bits for the two of 'em?" he asked hopefully.

She shook her head, and avoiding looking at the man, captured the male effortlessly. He wiggled and squirmed, not wanting to go back in the saddle bag and trying to lick her face in his eagerness.

"Alright, alrigh'. I want 'em both," he muttered, digging into his vest pocket for the two quarters.

Surprised, thinking he was only interested in the one, she took the money and handed him the squirming pup. Trying to catch the little girl pup was very difficult as she didn't want to be caught. Thinking she would be put back in that uncomfortable saddle bag, she played hard to get. Only Erin, pretending to walk away, had the girl pup curious enough to follow and be caught by the man.

"Thank ye," he said as he walked determinedly away. Erin watched as he went toward one of the other stores in town. He placed the pups inside a wagon hitched in front of the store, which Erin hadn't noticed before. She took her fifty cents and returned to the store to buy more supplies. Unable to get freight wagons in over the winter, the choice was limited, but Laydin did manage to sell her what little she could afford.

Erin was in a much better mood as she made her way home. They didn't have a lot, but if spring finally came and the fields warmed, she'd be able to plow, and they could plant both a garden and their fields. They'd be able to piece out with spring greens and maybe some early vegetables from the garden. She was very hopeful.

"I'm so relieved you're home. Wolves attacked the sheep while you were gone, and King and Queenie are both hurt," Molly greeted her, the shotgun in the crook of her arm. The children crowded around behind her, both excited and frightened by the incident.

"Did they kill any?" she asked, her heart sinking.

"Three ewes and four lambs," she confessed, "but they didn't get the meat. I shot at them with this and even got one wolf," she said, patting the shotgun.

Erin's heart sank at the news. Three ewes meant fewer breeding adults. Four lambs meant four less future animals for their small flock. But at least they hadn't gotten the ram. She kept him separate, so he wouldn't breed with them again until she'd determined the time was right for that chore. "How are Queenie and King?" she asked, her next concern. They were valuable animals to have on the farm.

"I've treated both their wounds. They got into fights with the wolves, protecting the sheep until I could get there with the shotgun."

Erin left the horses to look in on their dogs. She could see where Molly had patched up their wounds. They didn't look too bad but one never knew when infection might set in. *Wolves might have all sorts of diseases too*, she thought. She petted both dogs, their tails thumping on the ground of the barn in gratitude. The remaining pups were playing behind their wounded parents.

That reminded Molly, "You sold the pups?"

"Pa, why'd you take the pups?"

"Did you have to take the pups?"

"What'd you get for them?"

That last comment was from Tabitha, who was realizing how little money they had and how worried her parents were. She knew feeding all the children was stretching their budget.

"I got enough," she answered, addressing each question and the person who had asked it. "And yes, I did have to sell the pups." She went back outside to hand the parcels to the children to take inside the cabin, handling them almost as though they were presents. Once each of them had a bag to carry inside, she whispered to Molly, "They didn't have much in town either."

Molly nodded. She had wondered about that herself. "What are we going to do?"

"Pray and hope that spring is really here," she indicated the melting snow on the hillsides that had already flooded their stream. She'd been right to build the cabin high above the flood plain of the small stream, which was already well out of its banks as the melting snows drained from all the nearby hills.

After skinning the sheep and lambs and hanging their carcasses for proper butchering later, she thoughtfully petted the pelts of the full-grown sheep. The thickness of the coats reminded her it was nearing time to shear them. After the pelts dried, she and Molly would sew them to create a softer mattress for Tabitha's bed. A blanket on top of the two kept the scratchy wool from touching her skin, but she said it was warmer, softer, and more comfortable to sleep on than the straw tick they had left below it. The others protested but promises of future soft mattresses for them to lay on appeased them…for now.

Erin took the mare out again later that week to see what she could hunt. King had wanted to go, but his injuries were worse than Queenie's, so Erin just took her. She knew the bitch wanted to get away from her growing pups. She had come into heat that spring already, but Erin had kept King away from her, so she wouldn't have more pups yet. Right now, it was not a good time for more animals than they could feed, and she didn't know if they could sell them. She wished she could catch their tom cat and castrate him. He had once again impregnated both females in the barn. Whatever had gotten at the kittens had taken off the carcasses, and the children's cries over the loss had been alarming, but Erin was secretly glad to lose a few of the kittens.

Erin, using Queenie to help her search, finally found their herd. Billy's head came up as she whistled her familiar tunes as she got down from the horse and tied it off. He jogged closer, eyeing her suspiciously, but the whistling was too ingrained. He'd known her all his life and associated her with love, affection, and scratching. The enormous bull came to her in greeting. "Whoa, boy," she said at his enthusiasm as he tried to rub up against her in welcome. His massive horns were beautiful but dangerous. She petted and scratched the enormous animal and sent him back to his cows with a smack on his massive hide. She saw they had lost one cow, but the others all looked healthy and happy, and she was pleased to see several calves among them already. "You did a good job, boy," she complimented the bull. He looked pleased, even if he didn't understand her words.

Erin rode to their lake on the ranch. It was very full and there was still ice stretching out across most of the lake. The streams fed this lake. She hadn't had time to investigate where the lake drained, but she would in time. Time...the bane of her existence. Heading back to the ranch, she contemplated the work ahead of her and hoped spring had truly arrived. But Mother Nature wasn't ready to cooperate, and she dumped another snowfall on them. But she was getting tired, so it wasn't as intense. The weather was getting warmer and melting the snow faster. The chickens were already on nests, but Molly hesitated to take any eggs. She checked the eggs to see if they were fertilized, candling them, and returning the fertilized eggs to the nests of any broody hens. Erin allowed the ducks and geese to once again go to the stream but used the dogs to herd them back nightly. The pups learned the difference between chasing the squawking, protesting birds and moving them back to the barn to be locked in their stalls.

"You know, this seems thicker," Erin commented on the bread Molly baked using the flour she had brought from town.

"All I know is, between that and the bacon, it fills you all up," Molly answered. They didn't know in those days the breads they made were heavier and heartier, much less healthy than what would be made in future times. Store-bought or manufactured bread lost a certain something. Their breads filled them up, and the nourishment of the flavorful bacon and ham they ate stuck with them longer, providing more nutrition and calories they all desperately needed.

Neither of them thought about their nutritional needs, of course. They just knew they were hungry almost all the time. Erin was glad when spring finally arrived, so Molly could find the greens they were so desperately craving. While eating fresh clover, she wished they had oils to dip them in. Using bacon grease wasn't the same, but at least these and other greens provided them all with necessary vitamins.

Erin's first foray into shearing sheep was a disaster. She didn't know what she was doing and didn't want to hurt the sheep, and they ended up looking scraggly. Slowly, she learned to hold the sheep down firmly and sheer back their thick, wool coats in neat swaths. The shears were sharp and nicked them periodically. This caused them both to jump—the sheep from the pain of the cut and Erin from having caused their pain. Molly helped her hold the sheep down as they bleated and cried out. Returning them to their upset lambs, they looked naked without their winter coats. Still, they had a good-sized bag of wool that Molly insisted on washing again and again. She washed the wool a third time to get out the smell of the sheep, their dung, and any bugs that might be trapped in the thick coats.

"Can you spin that?" Erin asked, knowing Molly was just as unfamiliar with the sheep as she was. She was just grateful there were so few as she had learned a lot. Next year, she would wash the sheep before shearing them.

"I will learn," she promised, looking forward to it as the children helped enthusiastically.

"What are you doing, Pa?!" Theo asked when he caught Erin mulesing and docking the lambs. They were crying out and bleating loudly, which had alerted the boy to their plight.

"You have to remove this extra skin around their anus to keep the wool from becoming clotted with sh–" she started to say a rude word and caught herself. Realizing the boy's age, she finished with, "fecal matter."

"What's fecal matter?" he asked innocently.

"Poop," she answered, looking down intently at what she was doing, so she wouldn't harm the small lamb. She also cut off their tails, docking them short and dabbing on goose grease to stop the bleeding and keep the flies off, although it was early enough that flies weren't a big concern. She wished she had tar to daub on them, but goose grease would have to do.

"Why are you cutting off their tails?" he asked, concerned at their cries. Erin had chosen to do the mulesing and docking behind the rails of the pig pen, and the mother sheep were calling to their lambs.

"Have you ever seen a lamb with a tail?" she asked instead of explaining. The tails were unnecessary, and they would also grow wool and hold clots of poop. The sheep rancher, who had sold them this small herd back in Missouri had explained, rather graphically since he thought he was talking to a man, what she had to do. She was grateful they had such a small flock and there weren't too many to do. She'd been pleased when the ewes had mostly given birth to twins, one even had triplets, and none had rejected their lambs. The one ewe that had died was carrying a lamb that she'd been unable to save. Again, she realized the many mistakes she had made in breeding the sheep too early in the year.

The books that Erin and Molly provided the children had drawings of sheep, so he could shake his head in response to her question about lambs with tails. Still, he watched avidly as, one by one, she took care of the lambs. She debated a moment before removing the testicles from the male lambs and notching their ears.

"Why do you do that?" he asked, unconsciously covering his own privates with his hands.

"We don't want too many rams among our sheep, and these will provide food for us when they grow up." She left one, the best one of the lot, with its testicles intact in case anything happened to their ram. "The notches in their ears will make them easy to spot, so we know which ones are wethers."

"Wethers?" he asked, not having heard the word before.

"Sheep that can't have babies," she answered, not wishing to explain about castration. She'd already said they would be raised for food.

Once Erin was done and had given the lambs back to their concerned mothers, sending them to the hill behind the barn with King to guard them, Theo drifted away to impart his newfound knowledge to his siblings. Erin scooped up the rather disgusting small testicles and other parts and put them in the pig trough knowing the pigs would eat anything.

CHAPTER NINE

Finally, spring was officially here. Well, it had arrived a while ago, but the ground had now warmed enough that Erin could take a plow to it. She went out and herded the oxen back to the barn. Billy was not thrilled when she took *his* females away, but she could see he had done his job well and two of them were with calf. Any day now, the milk cows would give birth too, and the milk they were giving off was incredible. Since the two pregnant oxen were too far along to use, Erin only had one yoke of oxen to use for plowing. First, she left the sheep on the area they wished to use, keeping them tightly bunched as they ate the grasses. She made them stay even after the grasses were eaten down, using the dogs to keep them on the area, so they would eat every blade of grass. Her only alternative was to burn off the grass, and she didn't want to take a chance the fire would get away from her and spark a fire elsewhere.

She started with the garden. Molly had marked off the area where she felt it should go. Erin had never enjoyed plowing more. The sod plow was incredible to work with, cutting effortlessly into the thick roots. The strong oxen plodded along, and Erin took pride in the fact that she could plow a straight furrow. She plowed the garden both ways, making sure the ground was well tilled.

Erin sent Theo out to the field she wanted to tackle next with King and the sheep. He could leave them for a time to help with the planting. Erin insisted everyone, including Timmy, help them plant their carefully hoarded seeds.

"Should we save any for next year?" Molly fretted after their first day. They'd brought out all the packages they had packed so long ago from their garden back in Ohio. They had saved the seeds and transported them all the way across the country.

"I don't know. Unless we have too much of something," Erin admitted, "I tend to want it all." Still, they erred on the side of caution and left a little of everything aside for next year's planting. The garden was much bigger than the one back in Ohio and would use most of the seeds they had brought with them.

"We'll have to set something up to keep out the rabbits and other animals. The dogs can't be in all places at once," Molly mentioned. Out here, the wild animals had very little fear of humans as there were so few of them. The dogs were enough like wolves to scare any sensible creature, but still, the animals couldn't help but try for this veritable feast the humans were planting for them as it came up.

"You'll have to teach the children how to set traps for some of them," Erin responded. She was already tired from the first field she was plowing. She'd send Theo, and sometimes Tabitha, to watch the sheep since those fields were farther from the house. With King or Queenie and the pups along, they felt the children were safe. Still, Erin hoped to buy another rifle eventually. She had a rifle across her back even when she was plowing. Molly kept her shotgun handy and loaned the second rifle to the two oldest children, admonishing them about its critical use and what a heavy responsibility they had.

Erin, with her family's help, planted corn in that first field. She would later intermix the corn with beans. The corn would grow up and its leaves would crowd out any weeds. The beans could grow and climb the stalks of corn, but as beans grew so much faster than corn, she didn't plant the beans right away. She'd done this repeatedly in her field back in Ohio. The next field was given over to wheat. The third, a smaller field was given over to oats, and another even smaller field was used for barley. Erin was determined to plow up as much land as she could, but when the ground dried out and became too hard to plow, she knew she would have to wait for the following year. Weeding and taking care of her fields became a full-time job. She was also cutting down trees, using the wagon to bring in the trees and splitting them to

make fences, so she wouldn't have to hobble the horses anymore and could have paddocks.

Seeing her come into the cabin at night, sweaty, filthy, and exhausted, Molly worried about her. "You're doing too much," she admonished.

"There is so much for me to do," she answered back, washing up, changing into the only other clean shirt she had, and putting her dirty clothes where Molly could wash them for her. She felt bad she couldn't help with that, but Molly knew how hard she was working to plow up as much land as she could while conditions allowed. She knew Molly was just as busy taking care of the children, working on the garden, and trying to learn how to turn the wool they had harvested into yarns and thread she could knit or weave into clothes for them. The pieces drifted all over her work area in her attempts.

"I think weaving is a bit beyond me," she admitted as they sat companionably one night. She looked over and saw Erin had already fallen asleep, upright in her chair. She was killing herself, trying to get as much done as possible on the farm. Molly smiled to herself. Erin was calling it a farm again. Still, the hard work was sculpting her body. It was harder work than the established farm back in Ohio, and the constant plowing had made her muscles hard and prominent, barely hidden by the shirts that also hid her wrappings. The bindings were wearing out at a rapid rate too since Molly washed them daily. She promised herself she would buy good cloth to make Erin shirts that would hold up under all the work she did. She'd use that sewing machine they had in the corner. It had been barely used since they got here, but she intended to use it a lot when she had the material.

That first meal using produce from the garden, was a delight to the senses. The thinned carrots, fresh radishes and lettuce, even the first beans were consumed with relish as they all ate as much as they could hold. Accompanied by yucca plant roots and the meat they were still eating, everything was wonderful.

"Did you plant dandelions?" Erin asked, alarmed, when she spotted the greens coming up in a corner of the garden.

"I'll be careful with them. I promise I won't let the seeds go anywhere but into a seed packet, and I'll pull up any plants that aren't used."

"Keep an eye on those pests," she teased, looking forward to eating the greens. Many things made her smile that late spring as she plowed their land, working every hour of daylight and bringing the oxen or the teams of horses back well after sundown. She'd plow with the oxen to break up the sods and then go over it again with the horses. It saved her arms, but she was still pleased with how much Molly liked touching her muscular arms, massaging them and helping her relax.

Molly was thrilled that the milk cows were fresh again. Two had already given birth. Growing children needed fresh milk. She knew Erin was waiting until the third one dropped its calf to butcher one of the calves for the rennet they needed. In the meantime, she was making butter again, salting it, packing it in a tub, and keeping it cool in the cellar they discovered they needed. For now, it was a just rough hole beside the cabin; Erin was too busy to do more right now.

"No, you can't drink all the buttermilk," Molly said, rapping Theo's knuckles as he reached for more. "Leave some for your brothers and sisters."

Erin shot her son a fierce look for his gluttony, but they had all been hungry this winter and spring, and now, all this bounty compelled them to eat as much as they could.

Erin was annoyed when someone came to the farm to have her shoe their horses or fix their pots and other metal utensils or wagons. Firing up the forge took a lot of wood, and she didn't have time to stop everything for these sporadic customers. Still, the extra money was welcome, and they now had a surplus of chickens that people had traded. Erin had Tabitha and Theo collecting thin saplings, so they could build another coop for the ducks and geese. They didn't like the barn as they were kicked at by both horses and cows, and they made a mess in the stalls they were locked in.

"This is rich land, Molly. Look at those fields," she enthused, excited at the thought of harvesting them at the end of summer. They were taking a walk, hand in hand, the children running ahead of them and playing.

"Look at that," Molly gasped, looking beyond the field to the hills that hid the lake. Standing on one of the hills was a herd of horses that could only be wild.

"Oooh," the children breathed when they saw them too.

"There's some fine stock in that herd," Erin mused, wondering if she could catch some. They only had the one stallion and one mare, and while her farm horses were due to give birth this summer, she couldn't rely on their offspring to bring them much money very quickly. The farm horses had been crossbred with her stallion, which was not as big boned as their breed. She was certain their offspring would be smaller. Free horses for the taking suddenly aroused a new passion in Erin.

"You can't go after those horses. There is too much work to do to get this farm on its feet. You have to shingle the cabin, you want to expand the cabin too, and what about the paddocks?" Molly asked, almost jealous that Erin could go after the horses. She felt stuck in the cabin with the children even though she spent every moment she could outside in the garden.

Erin knew her wife was right. She didn't have the paddocks needed to hold, much less train horses. But that didn't stop her from dreaming about those wild horses. If she could get a couple good ones, she could sell them, breed them, and start a herd of her own. It would pay to have horses, cattle, sheep, and the farm. This way, they wouldn't be dependent on any one thing. Diversification they called it, and it would ensure they always had enough food to eat.

"Howdy! I'm your neighbor north of here," a man by the name of Roberts introduced himself. "I want to make sure where your property line is, so I don't trespass."

"I'm Erin Herriot. This is my wife, Molly, and our children," she answered, studying the man on his horse.

"My wife and son are with our wagon about a mile over there," he said, indicating the way north with his chin. "I'm hoping you don't mind if I file on the land next to you?"

"Not at all. We need good neighbors," Erin answered with a smile.

"You should bring your wife and son over. Maybe we could have a picnic," Molly put in, speaking up and looking forward to the possibility of socializing with another woman and child, seeing someone other than just family.

"Sounds good," Roberts smiled his appreciation of her friendly offer.

"I'll saddle up and show you my northern boundary," Erin offered. She'd measured, but she had also found where speculators had been through here using sophisticated measuring tools to get reasonably accurate maps made and had left their stakes in the ground. Riding north on her stallion, she kept him in check. She knew he was aware of the band of horses they had now seen on their land a couple times.

"Nice stallion," Roberts commented as they rode along. He noted that Herriot's saddle contained two scabbards with rifles in each of them and Herriot had a pistol poking out the back of his belt.

"Yeah, he's a bit of a young one, but he's game, and he has three of my mares in foal," she answered.

"Where are you out of?"

"Ohio. And you?"

"Southern Illinois. We came out last year and went to the Willamette. I didn't like it, or rather, my missus didn't like it," he amended, flushing as he admitted that. "We heard about land near the Blue Mountains and came looking. I like the looks of this area."

"It's a pretty area. We weathered our first winter this year, and it was hard," she admitted, pulling the stallion back slightly as he was wanting to run in his exuberance.

"I see you got a garden in," he mentioned, admiring the amount of work she had already accomplished on her place.

"And a couple of fields," she added, feeling the need to brag a little.

"Yeah? What did you plant? Is it up yet?"

"I planted the biggest one in wheat, but I also have corn, oats, and barley. It's all up. We'll see if it lasts or if the growing season is long enough." That was her main worry. She didn't know anything about this part of the country.

"If it's as fine as the Willamette Valley, we should do well. You say you got horses?"

They discussed stock, and Roberts said he'd be interested in one of her calves, a good milk cow. "Won't be ready for a year," she pointed out. She told him they'd also had a young bull born just that week and had decided to wait until a third calf was born to butcher it for rennet and make cheese.

"I haven't had good cheese in a coon's age," Roberts admitted as they approached the property line and Erin pointed it out. Then, they headed east along the boundary.

"I had heard of the Organic Laws of Oregon they drafted in Willamette, but I didn't know they extended up here," Roberts commented as Erin explained how much land he could file on. "I thought the Harrison act would apply out here." He gestured to the rolling hills before them.

"Doesn't the Harrison Land Act sell you the land?" Erin asked, having heard of it from other settlers on the trek out here.

"Yeah, they ratified it in 1800, and you can buy three hundred and twenty acres at two dollars an acre. You get four years to pay. Then I was told they revised the law in 1820 and you could buy eighty-acre tracts of land for a buck and a quarter an acre. I tell you, eighty acres for only one hundred dollars sounded good, but six hundred and forty acres just for working the land sounds incredible," he said in awe as he looked around all that Erin owned and realized he too could own the adjoining claim.

"Yes, they decided to adopt the Organic Laws of Oregon over here too, and that's what I filed on when I was up in Pendletown."

"I'll ride up there tomorrow and file," he assured her as they rode along, so he could see where Erin's land ended.

"Do you want your wife and son to come over to our place while you're gone? You might find yourself delayed or something. It is a two-day ride by wagon, but if you ride your horse hard, you can make it in one."

"That's a good idea. I know Rebecca gets scared by herself, but I heard about you from Laydin, and he suggested I make your acquaintance. You a smith by trade?"

Erin shook her head, laughing. "I'm a farmer. My brother did the smithing, but I brought his small anvil with us when we moved. I'm lucky they needed smithy work around here. I introduced myself to Laydin. He had a few horses that needed shoeing and he sent many others my way."

They rode up as far as Erin's eastern property line and then headed back in an arch across country towards where Roberts had camped with his wife. Erin pointed out where Roberts' northern border might be, and he nodded in acknowledgement.

"How do you do, ma'am?" Erin asked respectfully when she was introduced to Rebecca Roberts. Their son Alex was a strapping boy of twelve, who looked competent as he had guarded their small camp with a rifle. They hitched up Roberts' horses and Erin got a glance into the Conestoga wagon they had used. She saw very little in the way of supplies and household goods left in the box.

"I'm sure you'll like my wife, Molly. She's looking forward to meeting you," Erin told Rebecca.

"It will be nice to know there are neighbors," Rebecca said in return. She was a worn-looking woman, who hadn't fared well on the long trip across the country.

"I have a daughter, Tabitha about a year younger than you," Erin told Alex. "My son, Theodore is nine and Tommy is seven. I hope you will all be good friends."

"I look forward to making their acquaintance, sir," he answered respectfully.

Molly was thrilled to meet Rebecca and her son, Alex. The children were soon chattering and showing Alex around their place. Roberts headed off for Pendletown immediately, and Molly quickly made friends with Rebecca. They compared notes about the trip out from back east.   Rebecca was clearly envious of Molly's cabin and possessions.

"We lost a bit on the way out here, and it was so expensive to live near Portland. We weren't prepared for not getting on our own land right off. I told Dan we needed to get away from those people we came out with on the train and start over.   He heard about land near the Blue Mountains, so we came here."

Listening to the woman complain, Molly could see how she might not be a great friend to have, but she was better than having no friends. Erin was Molly's best friend in the world, but she wouldn't be included in any conversations because of the unspoken rule that men speak only with men and women speak only with women. Only husbands and wives could speak together.

It took three days for Roberts to come back from Pendletown. He carried supplies in a sack on the back of his horse. "Wish I had borrowed one of your horses as a pack animal. They wanted fifty dollars for a pack horse up there!"

"Probably be more in Sweetwater, if you could find one," Erin pointed out.

"Well, I got filed on the adjoining land, neighbor," he smiled as he told them his news.

"That's good news." Molly had asked Erin to help the man and his wife get their place going. Erin had argued that they had plenty to do around their own place, but Molly had countered that they needed help, they didn't have much, and it was the neighborly thing to do, so Erin offered right away. "We'll help you get your cabin started."

"Now, you don't have to…" Roberts began as he put his things in the back of his wagon, not taking down the tailgate, so they didn't see how little they really had.

"I know we don't have to, but what are neighbors for?" Erin said heartily, knowing Molly wanted to help these folks.

They ended up going over daily to help the Richards build their cabin, which created a road where there wasn't one before. They left early after chores and returned late to finish their chores, milk the cows, and check on their own animals. Using the same techniques they had used to build their own cabin, they notched the logs to form the cabin walls. Roberts understood more about ridgepoles and forming the peak on the cabin. He'd be using the canvas from his wagon until he could either get more poles cut or use sod like Erin had. He offered to help her re-roof her cabin since she already had the shingles cut.

"Must have been a long winter," he commented when he saw the piles of shingles in the barn.

Rebecca refused to do any chopping, but she would pull the logs along or pile up the branches they cut from the logs. As they worked, they talked about anything and everything.

"I'd love to go for those horses too," Roberts admitted when Erin told him of the herd they had seen. "I think between us we'd be able to tame them, sell them, and make a profit."

Erin liked that she had found a soul who understood her dreams.

"Back east, we'd have gotten a few of the men together to hunt for those wolves and foxes too. Do they have squirrels around here?"

Erin told him of the hunts that she and Tabitha had gone on and about barking the squirrels.

"You took your girl to hunt?"

"I believe both the boys and the girls need to know how to defend themselves and use guns."

Roberts was surprised at her attitude but accepted it since she was helping with the cabin.

Keeping up their regular chores and helping the Roberts family took up most of their early summer. As things got even busier with collecting items from their garden, they finished the roof on their own cabin. Peeling back the sod caused dirt to rain down in the cabin between the poles that Erin and Molly had placed. A lot of sweeping and dusting were in order, but that could wait until they finished shingling the entire roof. Rebecca also wouldn't help with the shingling, but between the three adults they managed to quickly shingle the roof. The children were a big help, handing up bundles that Erin had tied with string.

"May I borrow your plow and oxen? I don't think my horses can handle the tough plowing, and I had to sell my plow," Roberts confessed after his cabin was built.

"You won't get through this," Erin kicked at the dirt with her boot, "this time of year. I'd say you better wait for the fall rains or in the spring. Maybe you can dig up enough for a garden, although it's late." Erin found out later Molly had given Rebecca some of their carefully hoarded seeds. "That was for us to fall back on," she said, annoyed that her wife hadn't consulted her.

"They have nothing. They lost everything on the trail or in trying to survive the winter near Portland."

"That ain't our lookout," she contended hotly. They had helped their neighbors, but they weren't responsible for them. They'd worked hard for what they had.

"Isn't," Molly corrected automatically, knowing exactly what Erin was saying and agreeing with her. Still, she wanted to help them, and they had helped with their roofing. She liked the new roof, and Erin had taken the sods that had started to grow on the roof and built a wall along the stream, creating a catch basin to pool some of the water and making it easier when she wanted to do the wash outside. Pumping the water inside and heating it in the fireplace was for winter cleaning. That pump was something else Rebecca had liked about their cabin but couldn't afford.

"My, look at this colored window," Rebecca had said admiringly, looking at the pieces Erin had carefully soldered together. They'd had to be creative since it didn't fit exactly the way it had back where they found it, but it sure was pretty when the sun shone through it and created colors on the floor of the cabin. The oiled paper window at the back of the cabin wasn't nearly as nice. "Maybe someday we can have glass windows in our cabin," she said, but it was her tone that bothered Molly. It sounded like envy and something else she couldn't quite recognize.

Molly enjoyed her colored picture window. She couldn't see through it well since the colors distorted her view, but it sure was pretty. Erin had promised they would take a trip up to Pendletown someday to get glass for the back window, and she wanted to cut a window upstairs, so the children had more light in their loft. Molly had asked her to wait until they had the glass before cutting the new window since having only shutters would allow too much cold air into the snug cabin. She hadn't thought of the hot summer and being upstairs was stifling. She'd been glad when Erin and Roberts cut it despite her initial objection. Now, the children could breathe that fresh, clean, prairie air.

"Maybe we should get screens too," Erin proposed, knowing the warmer weather would bring bugs, including mosquitos.

"That list is getting mighty long," Molly pointed out.

"If these crops come in, we should be good," Erin said cautiously, but she wouldn't borrow against it. She'd heard that Laydin and other merchants in town would lend out supplies against future crops. A bank had set up in Sweetwater, and it was also lending money against future crops. Erin wouldn't go into debt against the crop, despite how

good it looked. She was too afraid of someone taking their land like what happened to Molly back in Ohio.

"They don't know we ain't a couple," Molly argued, worrying about supplies as the summer continued. "They wouldn't lend us the money if they knew."

"Aren't," Erin corrected her for once, grinning at the irony. "I won't go into debt, and we won't speak of *it* again," she answered meaningfully. They both knew the *it* she referred to wasn't money but the fact they were two women and not a husband and wife as everyone assumed. They were legally married since they had stood before a preacher back in Ohio and had the legal paper that declared they were married, but no one would understand or care if they discovered the truth.

Molly understood, and with the children getting older and listening in to adult conversations, they had to be careful what they said around them, even unintentionally.

CHAPTER TEN

It was a good thing Erin was very frugal and careful. Her barley crop was destroyed by the herd of wild horses traveling through one night. What they didn't eat, they flattened with their hooves, and she was nearly in tears when she discovered it. The field was too far from the cabin for the dogs to have heard the herd, but Erin wished she could go after them and recoup some of her losses.

At least they could harvest the wheat and oats, bagging them up and filling the wagon with the results of their hard work. The Roberts came over and helped with the harvest to earn a share for their hard work. Molly, annoyed with 'Becky' Roberts, who snobbishly insisted on being called Rebecca, let her watch the children who weren't helping to thresh the wheat and oats.

Erin and Molly had cleaned a large area in the farmyard. Using brooms fashioned from their own straw, they brushed away the dust and dirt until they reached the hard-packed surface below. Then they sprinkled water on it, the hot sun baking it, before they used the flat side of shovels to pack down the earth, creating a smooth surface. Bringing in the sheaves of wheat, they cut off the tops and stacked the straw in the barn for winter. Erin, Molly, Roberts, Alex, Tabitha, and Theo all used flails that Erin had carved over the winter. Theo was in tears when he broke his flail, sure he'd get a whipping for breaking it.

But Erin pointed out a crack she hadn't seen when carving it and gave him another to use. They also used the horses with their feet wrapped in rags to keep dirt out of the seed as they threshed the grain. Finally, using pitchforks, they tossed the threshed grain into the wind and watched it blow away the chaff.

"Good thing it isn't raining," was Rebecca's contribution as she watched the younger children, keeping them amused.

Erin wondered that Molly didn't get upset with the morose woman. She treated their children as though they were helpless, and they were puzzled by this behavior. Erin and Molly treated the children as if they were capable of any work that was assigned to them. Even little Timmy sensed this woman was a little too coddling and acted up accordingly.

Slowly, they shoveled the wheat into their limited supply of bags. They managed to fill the wagon and Erin took that first load to Sweetwater. She would trade for supplies, including material to make more bags, and she would also get some ready-made bags and other supplies to hold them over.

"I hear the prices are higher up in Pendletown. The rest of our crop is going there," she said after she returned from the trip.

"Yeah, Sweetwater isn't big enough to handle our crops yet," Roberts agreed with her, having gone along to get his 'share' of the wheat he had helped with. Rebecca had insisted they have supplies too, like the Herriot family. Her obvious envy was a little embarrassing. Still, she wasn't petty about it, just insisting they be treated as though they had all the things the Herriots did. Roberts knew he was no way near as well set up as Erin's hard-working family.

They harvested the oats next. Erin was grateful the horses hadn't gotten into that field. Lastly, she was able to salvage some of the barley, but it was back-breaking work since the horses had trampled so much of the grain. She lost a lot on the barley field but enough was saved that she had seed for next year and could sell a bit.

"Now, don't forget the lists," Molly admonished Erin as she went off to Pendletown to sell the wheat, oats, and barley using both their and Roberts' wagon.

"You have my lists?" Rebecca asked Roberts, showing off in front of Molly as though they were going to have as much as them. She was staying with the Herriots while Roberts accompanied Erin on the trip to Pendletown. They were going to Pendeltown for the possibly better pricing on the harvest and to order things they couldn't get in Laydin's store in Sweetwater.

"I want to apologize for Rebecca," Roberts said around the campfire that night. Erin had Jack, one of King and Queenie's older pups with them. He was gangly, but she had high hopes for him. She didn't know if she would sell him or not, but right now, it was nice to have a dog along. She didn't want to leave the farm without the protection of both King and Queenie.

"Oh?" Erin asked, as though she hadn't noticed the woman's envy over what they had, which was little enough.

"We lost so much on this trip out here, and I don't know if I can make as big a field as yours next year," he shook his head sadly, feeling he had failed his wife and son. Rebecca had pointed out their losses many times.

"You're starting over. There's a lot to be done," she told him, feeling uncomfortable about the conversation. She didn't feel it was right to talk about their spouses like this, at least she didn't discuss Molly.

Roberts acknowledged they were starting out new, but Herriot seemed to have a handle on it. The fields they had harvested spoke of the hard work that he had done all on his own, although Molly was willing to help if necessary. He too wished he had the farm horses Herriot had and hoped someday to buy some. Those oxen were also a plus, and he'd have to borrow them when the time came. He'd looked at Rebecca's ridiculous list and knew he'd have an argument on his hands when he returned from this trip. Over half of what she wanted was impractical until they were better established.

The prices they ended up getting for their grain more than made up for the long haul from the farm. Erin was able to get most things on their practical list first. She filled the back of her wagon with things they could get right then and there, but some things weren't available and would have to be ordered. Supplies came in from Oregon City and Portland, ships coming in from all over the world to bring things that weren't made here in Oregon. She found a beautiful bedroom set she would have liked to buy for Molly but resisted. Instead, she bought practical things like material to make clothes. She saw Molly wanted denim as well as muslin, poplin, and cotton. She bought exactly what Molly put on the list, not deviating despite wanting to give her gifts. The money was burning a hole in her pocket, but she resisted. She did notice that some of the wools weren't very good quality, and she inquired about a loom.

"There's a farmer that said he was selling his wife's loom," the storekeeper mused, trying to remember. "His wife didn't last the winter, and he was selling her things."

"I'd be interested in it, and I'll be back in about a week with another load if you could recall who was selling."

They bought more material to make bags and thread to go in the sewing machine. Even if they didn't use all the bag material or thread, it would come in handy in the coming years. That sewing machine had caused a bit of a stir when Rebecca made it known that she wanted one too. Erin thought if she wanted one, she should help her husband more on the farm he was trying to establish.

"This is quite a load," Roberts commented on their way back. His own purchases had been more modest and sat at the back of his wagon. He had generously offered up the extra space for Molly's list items.

"Well, the prices certainly are more reasonable than in Sweetwater," Erin commented.

"Do you think you will really be back next week and get that loom?"

"I'm hoping Molly and the children will have more of that wheat threshed. Maybe Rebecca—" she started but Roberts put up his hand to stop her.

"She won't do anything but woman's work. She was infuriated when I pointed out that Molly does enough for a woman or a man, and you don't seem to mind. She said it was unnatural for a woman to flail and harvest because that was man's work."

Erin felt sorry for the man, she really did. Without Molly being her equal partner, she didn't know what she would do. "We are just evenly yoked," she said to cover the embarrassment.

"Yoked?" he asked, confused.

"Well, when you have two oxen that aren't of similar size, they don't work well together. I saw a few like that on the wagon train, and they were always disrupting the smooth flow of the train. They caused the most delays, slowing us down. Molly and I help each other. I'd do the dishes if she asked, and I don't even have to ask her to help me with the harvest. The sooner we get it in, the better for us all."

"There is a lot of work to be done, and I don't feel I'm providing enough for her," Roberts confessed ruefully.

"There aren't enough neighbors around here to make it easier on all of us. She doesn't have the women folk around who could use her help, so it is more noticeable that she isn't helping with the harvest."

A bit of silence ensued between them as Roberts thought over what Herriot was saying and agreed with it. Rebecca had been the prettiest gal in his hometown, and he hadn't thought about the fact that she expected certain levels of maintenance. When his farm began to fail back east, he heard about the 'free' land in the west and convinced her to move. He hadn't thought about how the long trip would wear on a woman of her sensibilities or expectations. Leaving behind everything and everyone she had known had turned her into a bit of a shrew. All her pretty things had either been sold or left behind. She simply didn't understand how hard he would have to work to get them re-established.

"Oh, Erin, you shouldn't have," Molly said when she saw the bit of ribbon included in the purchase of the fabrics they needed to make clothes.

"What's a little ribbon for my girls?" she answered, blushing at how happy she had made her wife, and she could see both Tabitha and Theresa looked pleased with the pretty ribbons and had been especially pleased when she said, 'my girls.'

"Oh, Pa, this is fine, really fine," Tabitha said when she fingered the material, her dried and cut fingers catching on the fabrics.

"Plenty of it to make new clothes for everyone," Erin promised. "I'll help," she promised Molly, who laughingly shook her head.

"Now, after we get in the rest of the harvest and winter comes, I'll have plenty to do without you underfoot," she teased. They both knew that Erin could sew just as well as Molly, even without the sewing machine.

The pathetically small amount of supplies in the Roberts' wagon set Rebecca on edge. She was angry and berated him all the way back to their cabin. "All that work, and this is all you got?"

"There is still more threshing to do, and I don't suppose you helped Molly and her children do it?" he felt brave enough to point out.

"I watched the younger children and minded them while Molly did *that*," she answered, disparaging of the work Molly did. It was so...so common. She didn't see the contempt her own son held her in as he exchanged a meaningful look with his father. He'd been helping over at the Herriot's and saw that even Tabitha and Theo, younger than himself, pitched in. They knew if they didn't, they wouldn't eat. They'd told him stories of how slim it had become last winter, and he didn't want to have that worry in their own home. He told his father about it the first time they were alone, and they agreed to hunt for meat that fall.

When they had another load to take to Pendletown and were using both wagons, Rebecca declared she wanted to go along. Feeling awkward at her insistence, Erin didn't think it was her place to say no, and it was obvious Roberts was too cowed to say no.

"Oh, I'll miss your *help*," Molly tried, feeling sorry for Erin, who obviously didn't want the woman along as they would be gone for several days. She hadn't really been of much help, but Molly didn't want to subject Erin, who was exhausted from flailing the wheat and other seeds from their stalks, to the woman's company. All their shoulders ached from the work, the animals only so effective when stomping on the grains.

"Well, we can't expect our men folk to understand a woman's needs," she said. "I'll help with the campfire duties," she promised gaily.

Erin exchanged a look with Molly and another look with Roberts before mounting her own wagon, this time with another pup along. She hoped she could sell this one too. Molly had reported that Queenie had come into heat again, which was why she had kept both dogs tied up and Queenie in the cabin with them at night. Rebecca had complained about having a dog in the cabin, but the children had been delighted.

That week while Erin was gone with Roberts, they finished the wheat, the oats, and the barley. Bagging up the last of it, she was careful to keep out the dirt that inevitably came up from their jury-rigged flailing grounds. Erin had stated they needed a proper floor in the barn and hoped to build one this fall in the time they had before winter. She'd ask Roberts to help, but he was talking about plowing and building his own barn, so she wasn't sure he would have the time.

"Let's pull as much wood as we can from the woods while your pa is gone," Molly said enthusiastically after they put the last bags in the barn. She'd gathered a mess of garden stuff for lunch and intended to can that evening. The beans were drying on planks Erin had brought from Pendletown. The smooth boards cut from a mill were fine, and she hoped to use them to frame in the upstairs window and put in glass. She had told Molly she intended to bring glass home this trip. She was looking forward to enjoying this luxury, but she was not looking forward to Rebecca's reaction when she would see it. She'd already commented on the screens that Erin put on the windows for use when the windows were open and the shutters aside. The screens kept out the night bugs and afforded them a lot of light during the day now that the waxed paper was gone.

"Won't we need the wagon, Ma?" Theo asked, concerned.

"Well, we'll use the horses or oxen on the big logs. You and Tabitha can handle that, I'm sure, and you can show Alex how we do it, so he can help too," she smiled at the youth. She knew Alex wasn't happy that his parents had left him back while they went into the larger town. Still, he was willing and able to help, and they did have to gather wood for winter. "We'll pile up the rest of it and fill the wagon when your pa returns."

Mornings, Molly gathered from the garden, spreading out the beans to dry under the screens Erin had built exactly like the ones they had used back in Ohio. Then, they took the horses to the woods further afield than the ones on the bluff to gather wood for the oncoming winter, stacking it up for the wagon. As planned, they dragged back the bigger downed trees with the aid of the horses or oxen.

"We'll need the oxen for that one," Theo stated, pointing to a tree that was about three feet thick.

"I don't know that we should even try. You just remember to mention that tree to your pa when he gets back," Molly said, not liking how huge that tree was but knowing the boy would enjoy having something to tell his pa.

Erin was miserable on the trip. Rebecca never stopped talking and she was mostly complaining. She wondered why more people hadn't settled in this part of the country and then complained when their trail had to skirt around one farmer's land.

The prices on the grain were still high enough that Erin felt the trip was worthwhile. She gave Roberts his money in full, then later regretted allowing Rebecca to see how much she gave him. She went on to spend every dime. Ordering her own supplies to last over the winter, Erin was glad when the shopkeeper had a couple of sturdy lads roll the heavy casks into her wagon and stack them.

"You wanted that loom?" the man asked, remembering Erin.

"Yep. He still got it?"

"That he does, and I sent for him when I saw you at the granary."

"I appreciate that. I truly do. I'd like some of those yarns over there in the meantime," she said, indicating the brightly-colored wools. She knew Molly would appreciate them but vowed she wouldn't mention how urine was used to set the many colors, which the merchant had confided to her in a conspiratorial whisper. Still, the colors were vivid and beautiful even if the process was distasteful.

Because of the many supplies already in Erin's wagon, she had to impose on the Roberts to put the large loom in theirs. While he was stacking his supplies around it, Erin could hear Rebecca's complaints begin. The last thing Erin put in her own wagon was the carefully wrapped glass squares, well cushioned to prevent breakage.

The trip back seemed to take twice as long because there wasn't a moment of silence. Erin had bought the plowshares to make a regular plow, knowing at some point she would no longer need the sod-busting plow. She was planning on sharpening them up that winter and shaping the handles and other wood parts herself. Rebecca didn't understand why they didn't have the money to buy their own plow and why everything was so expensive. Erin's back was turned while handling her own team and wagon, but she was certain she heard Roberts explode and demand his wife to *shut up* and *be quiet*. The silence didn't last long, but Erin had a smile over what she thought she overheard, even if she had imagined it.

They stopped off at the Roberts' place. Erin would have gone on alone, but she had Molly's loom and some of their supplies in the back of the Roberts' wagon, and she wouldn't put it past Rebecca to try and convince him to keep some of them or just take them herself. Erin helped them unload, noticing that their beds had no straw ticks and were simply blankets on wood slats. That had to be hard to sleep on. Still, it wasn't her lookout. Roberts had cooking utensils and a nice fireplace to cook over. "We'll have to help you put in some wood when we build your barn," Erin commented, looking about the place they had chosen for their farm. She wouldn't have chosen this spot, but Rebecca liked the location, and Roberts tried to please her.

Arriving back at her own farm, with Roberts following close behind in his wagon, Erin was thrilled to see how much more settled it appeared than the Roberts' raw place. She saw that her family had hauled logs of various sizes, and she anticipated the work of sawing them up. She saw everyone in the garden gathering stuff as she came over the hill. Waving madly, the dogs barking their own welcome, she was pleased to jump off her wagon into Molly's welcoming arms.

"Oh, Erin," she said with a little cry in her voice when she saw the loom.

"He had these strings his wife wove too, and he threw them in," she told her, showing her what she had gotten for her—hangs of string as well as rolls that she could weave into cloth of their own.

"There's no room in the cabin," she pointed out, feeling so proud of her Erin right now.

"We'll build it," she promised. Between her and Roberts, they managed to manhandle the loom into the barn and cover it up. They took all the supplies into the cabin and left them everywhere: on the table, beneath the table, by the hearth, even in the bedroom. Molly and Erin would spend days putting it away, storing it for winter, so they wouldn't run out. They put some in the loft and some elsewhere about the cabin. Molly smiled when she saw Erin had even purchased store-bought treats for the children. She whispered to put some away for Christmas or St. Nicholas. They gave the children some of the candy as a treat now for all the hard work they contributed to the harvest, even including Alex in the *celebration.*

"Now, onto the haying," Erin stated. It was long overdue, and she thought that next year she would do one cutting in the spring and one in the fall, so it wouldn't take so long or slow down as it matured. While Roberts would have helped more, he felt he better work on his own place for a while. Taking his son and wife, he left for home.

"That is a sad, sad woman," Molly mentioned, making sure the children weren't close enough to overhear as they scythed the long, tall grasses of the field they wanted to plow the coming year. They were working in the field next to the wheat field, which they wanted to enlarge. The stubble in the field had attracted all kinds of animals and birds to the field to glean the seeds that had fallen in the harvest. Erin wished she had a lighter gun to shoot the pheasants they saw, but instead of lamenting the fact, she released the ducks, geese, and even the chickens into the field. Using the dogs to herd the flocks was difficult as the birds did not want to cooperate, especially the chickens. But they all benefitted as the birds cleaned up the field and fattened up, teaching their ducklings, goslings, and chicks to find food in the large field. Erin didn't hesitate to shoot the hawks that tried to get an easy meal. King and Queenie were both watchful and would alert her to the hawks' presence, teaching their young pups at the same time.

"I'd like to give Jack or Jenny to the Roberts," she said, referring to the remaining pups, "but I don't want to give them one more mouth to feed," Erin told Molly as they worked, raking the sun-dried hay into long windrows.

"I know. There is much I'd like to help them with too, but where do you draw the line? It's not like he isn't grateful, but Rebecca..." she shook her head at the sadness of the woman.

This year, they didn't have the high bed of the Conestoga wagon to deal with. Erin made some slats with thin pieces of wood and nailed them together to form an open box, so they could get more hay in the lower farm wagon. After attaching it to the box, they began to pitch the hay into it, having the children take turns running back and forth in it to stomp down the hay. Even Timmy got a turn, but only when they first started because no one wanted him high up on the load and slipping off.

"This has been a fine harvest," Erin marveled as they brought in another load of hay, filling the barn.

"We still are getting things from the bean and corn field and the garden," Molly reminded her. She'd had to stop cutting to collect the many things in their garden, gathering them in bowls and bags. They would can and put away what they could in the evenings, working quite late. Slicing, dicing, peeling, and washing, the children were put to work as they gathered as much as they could. They had used every bucket, extra bag, and wash pan they had. It was all building up.

"If you don't do a good job, we might run out this winter. Remember how lean our meals were last winter?" Erin reminded the children when they would balk at all the hard work.

"No, Timmy. You aren't old enough to use a knife, not yet," Molly admonished the helpful three-year-old, pulling his reaching hands back. His birthday was coming, and she planned to bake him a cake. Each child would deserve one after all they had helped with this year.

"Am I old enough to use a knife?" Theresa asked, hopefully.

"No, not yet," Molly answered with a smile. She set Theresa to washing the collected vegetables. Her birthday was in a month, and she'd have to make her something special too.

They gathered more hay this year than last year before the rains came and slowed their harvest. In the days when they were waiting for the hay to dry out, Erin would cut wood and split logs to make a floor for the barn. She had been about to install it in the current barn but decided to do another out back, adding to the current barn space. With the help of Molly and the children, they dug down to put the half logs flat, like they had in the house. They would be building this part of the barn behind the other one and cutting a hole in the wall of logs to connect them both, more than doubling the barn space they now had. This would also give them a floor to thresh on next year. She was careful to line up the logs, so there was no space between them. The children had fun again, playing with the sandstone and smoothing out the tops of the logs as Erin hauled more to build up the sides when they were ready. They'd learned a lot building their cabin last year, and she was pleased with the children for their enthusiasm and help.

When they had enough wood collected, Erin rode the mare into town to invite everyone to a barn raising. On the way in, she made a point of riding over to the Roberts' to invite them first, to Timmy's fourth birthday party and second, to the barn raising. They felt having

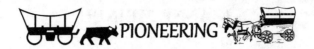

the birthday party separate would make it special for the boy, and the baked cake was his present. He was having a grand time and didn't notice the absence of presents. Molly had managed to whip up a new shirt for him, so he was strutting about in that.

The barn raising brought people from all over. One man had a squeezebox, an accordion, and was willing to play for them in exchange for food and drink. People brought a dish to pass and were willing to work to raise the barn, celebrate the harvest, and get to know their neighbors. Many hadn't met before, but some Erin remembered from smithy work and greeted them by name. They'd set up tables all over the yard, using log stumps and boards as seats.

"Gosh, I wish I knew you were here. We'd have invited you to our own barn raising earlier this summer," one of the women apologized upon meeting Molly.

"No problem. We were all pretty busy planting and gathering," Molly left her at ease as she got to know the many people who had come from far and near.

With a dozen or more men and boys chopping, cutting, and measuring, the sides to the barn went up in no time. Erin panicked at one point, wondering if she had cut enough logs for the project, but they were doing fine, and they even got the lodge poles on the top, laying them and nailing them down tight.

"You have a fine floor there," one man clapped Erin on the shoulder, nearly sending her flying in his enthusiasm. "Perfect for dancing."

The music rang out and dancing started immediately after sundown as people partnered up. Erin was able to hold Molly for the first time in public. She danced with her, enthusiastically stomping her boots to the music and laughing as Molly blushed becomingly in a new dress. They really enjoyed themselves as they all burned off the feast the women had prepared while the walls of the barn were being raised. The open sky above them was waiting for the cross poles that Erin had prepared, but there hadn't been time to lay them that day. She'd cut shingles over the winter, but in the meantime, she intended to use the sod plow to cut up enough to cover the new section of barn.

It was at the celebration of Tabitha's twelfth birthday a few weeks later that the Roberts and Harriots met again. "Didn't you promise my husband that he could use your sod plow?" Rebecca asked shrilly upon hearing Erin wanted to cut up some ground and sod her barn roof.

"Of course, and he's welcome to use it after I break up enough for my roof," Erin answered, being diplomatic and trying not to show how shocked she was at the woman's almost accusatory tone.

Roberts had told her how dismally their small garden had done, wasting many of the seeds Molly had generously given them. Molly was even now preparing to collect seeds from their plants for next year, allowing some plants to grow until they flowered and went to seed.

Despite the unpleasantness with Rebecca Roberts, Tabitha had a nice birthday party and Alex even gave her a chaste kiss on the cheek, causing both to blush.

Erin hadn't mentioned to Rebecca that the sod was already cut. Since the barn raising, she had taken the time to enlarge her fields and the sod was ready and waiting. Roberts rode over with Alex, leaving Rebecca home with a *headache* as they helped to gather the sod and place it on the poles on the barn roof. It was a heavy and dirty job, just as bad as last year when they did the house, but Roberts and his boy had never done it before and they learned, so they could do it on their own place. Roberts had gathered more logs to build himself a barn for his three horses. He wouldn't host the barn raising that Herriot had, but Erin and Molly insisted on helping, and they managed to raise the sides in two days. He was appreciative of their help, even if Rebecca, who had become more waspish and unhappy since they got here, wasn't.

Back at their own place, Erin enlarged the cooling *cellar* she had been digging. She had enough logs to enclose it and built a sturdy floor over the large cave she had dug. It now abutted the house but was not as high. Erin built it with a trap door, so she could get down in the cellar and place sandstone in the corner on the flat of the logs. Onto this sandstone, she put a large barrel, which was waterproofed and cut down the middle on the long side, so they could have a bathing room. She made a drain leading out and running downhill to the stream. After filling the tub halfway with cold water from the pump, they could heat up water over the fire, walk a few steps to this new room, and pour it in the tub. The first time Molly used it, Erin was taken back to their home in Ohio and aroused by the sight of her in her towel. Erin quickly changed into her nightshirt, but the memory of that would remain with her forever.

"Why do we have to take baths?" Theo, nearly ten, complained.

"Because you stink after a hard day's work, and while that is to be expected, we don't want to smell you if we don't have to. It's nice to have this in the cabin, and we needed the cellar," Erin explained. She loved the fact that after a hard day fighting the fields she was plowing

without the benefit of the sod buster, she could sink into the tub with her bindings off and soak in the hot water. She'd put a latch on the door, too high for most of the children to reach, so she had complete privacy. She would have loved to take a bath *with* Molly but could only have her memories of that…for now.

She managed to fit the loom in another corner, closing off the area from the rest of the room once it was in place. It gave Molly a clean spot that was out of the way, allowing her to work with the wool she wanted to learn to weave. Eventually, the spinning loom also ended up in this room.

Molly watched as Erin plowed up the stubble in the grain fields while she chopped down the corn stalks that had dried fully. The beans were also done for this year, and they'd had an abundant crop of both. Molly tied the stalks together, creating teepees that dotted the field. Once the Roberts were done with the sod-busting plow, having plowed a very small part of their farm, Erin used it to widen all their fields while the weather held. Not all the fields could be enlarged due to the hills. She didn't want them to erode too much when the fall rains came. They'd already had a few rainfalls and a couple of gully washers.

CHAPTER ELEVEN

"**W**as this year successful?" Erin asked as they piled hay into the newer section of the barn, making room elsewhere.

"Oh, yes, and I'm looking forward to what we can do next year," Molly answered cheerfully. They hoped the raspberries would produce better as they grew. Erin had seen wild raspberry bushes but none as profuse as the patches on Picket Road back in Ohio where she had dug theirs up. They'd found by fertilizing their plants with horse manure, they were growing very well. Next year, when they were more firmly established, they'd see if they were able to harvest enough to make jams and jellies as well as make more dried fruit for their stores.

"Well, some things will take a few years," she admitted as they discussed what had worked and what hadn't. The garden had been under constant siege by rabbits, and Erin planned to hunt them and set traps. Chipmunks, moles, and other rodents were a problem too. The cats had grown fat on their hunting.

"We could give the Roberts a couple kittens," Erin said. "Maybe the next time we see them?"

"You just want all those kittens gone," Molly teased but she understood. Both cats had had litters, and they had too many kittens around the farm to support if they ran out of food. She looked up in time to see two cats vanishing into the loft.

One or two kittens had already disappeared on their own. There were a million things that could have taken them: weasels, foxes, and birds of prey. The smart ones survived, but even then, there might be a smarter animal waiting for them.

Erin and Molly rode out alone one day to check on the herd and see how well Billy had done. They were pleased to see the number of calves, and they drove a young bull back to the yard with them for butchering this year. He was well over a year old, and Billy was still strong and able to care for the herd by himself without competition. There had obviously been a fight or two already as the young bull bore scratches that only horns could inflict. Butchering him would solve the problem, and they brought him in to fatten him up.

"I should let the oxen out with the herd too," Erin mentioned. They both knew it would save on feed. "I still want to try and double the size of the fields," she mused aloud as she weighed the work waiting for her around the farm.

"There simply isn't enough time in the year to do everything we want," Molly answered. They were gathering more wood for the fireplace, and the children were running about in the woods having fun as Erin and she chopped some of the blowdowns to bring along with the seasoned wood. Erin had a million projects she wanted to do with the wood over the winter, not the least was making more shingles for the new section of the barn. "You think Roberts will want to break more of his fields now that the ground is softening with the rains?"

"Probably," Erin shrugged, willing to lend him the yoke of oxen and her plow but wanting to do her own fields to provide for the large family growing up before them. She wouldn't suggest it to Roberts, not wanting to make it seem she knew better than he did about his farm.

It was as though they had conjured Roberts with their thoughts. One day, he rode over when they were hauling wood to the large, haphazard piles next to the cabin. The children were throwing wood out of the wagon and looked up at the barking dogs.

"Hello, there," he called, holding his horse in check as it shied at the Tervurens, never having really gotten used to the large dogs.

"Hello, yourself," Erin called in reply, stopping the ox that was pulling the large tree she had hitched up back in the grove. "Want to gather wood with us?" she teased.

"I've been pulling trees from my own woods," he told her proudly. "I have Alex cutting and sawing." He saw Tabitha look up at the name from where she was sawing a limb. "I was wondering if you wanted to help me catch some horses?" he turned back to address Erin.

Erin looked up from where she had leaned down to take the chains from around the tree. "You going after the herd?"

"I think there is a second one out there, and yes, I think I will. I could use more horses and selling the extra stock will give us some ready and much needed cash."

"If we could find some buyers?" she answered, rubbing her nose with the back of her glove. It was getting a bit nippy outside and her nose was not only cold but running.

"True, but I was talking to Laydin, and he said he knew some buyers that could use some rough stock, even some that's half broke."

Erin released the tree and stood up, holding her back from all the hard work she had been doing. She glanced at Molly to see her reaction to the proposal. The brunette knew her wife's heart and dreams. She nodded slightly. Smiling, Erin turned back to Roberts and said, "Sure. When would you like to go?"

"Can I go, Pa?" both Tabitha and Theo asked together, looked at each other, grinned, then turned hopefully to Erin.

"No, I don't think that would be a good idea, and I need you here," Molly said before Erin could refuse. Erin turned her back to the children slightly and gave Molly a grateful smile.

"I think I could be ready by the end of the week?" Roberts answered.

"Sounds good. I'll be ready."

After he left, Erin resumed work, releasing the chains from around the tree Molly had dragged in and helping the children finish emptying the wagon of the deadfall they had picked up. "Wow, that one is vile." Erin threw the totally desiccated piece of wood into the wood pit. "You children know not to bring anything like that back. It wastes space. We won't burn it in the fireplace, and it would do better rotting in the woods. The trees and plants get nourishment from such things." She turned away but saw a guilty-looking Tommy blushing. She didn't say anything further as they washed up and ate a quick lunch and returned to hauling more wood. A couple days later, Molly finally said they had enough wood to last them and asked the children to chop and saw while Erin was gone.

"I'm not leaving you to all this work," she replied as she sawed another limb into easy pieces for the woodpile.

"You promised Roberts you would go for those horses. Don't you think you should get ready? We'll be fine cutting all this up," she indicated everything they had hauled in.

"Let me just help with…" Erin replied, sounding doubtful.

"You know you want to go. You might find some good stock." She wanted Erin to have some fun. Dealing with those horses didn't sound like fun to her, but she knew Erin always got a dreamy look whenever she thought about them.

Erin was well prepared with ropes, hobbles, and camping supplies when Roberts showed up.

"I see you've been busy," he said, admiring the woodpiles of almost uniform shape and size that they had been cutting up. "I thought I was prepared, but you all have me beat."

"It's my crew. They are enormously helpful," she answered, smiling and giving the children the credit they deserved. They each took pride in being a help to their pa and ma. That pride often spurred them to work with renewed vigor on projects such as this. Despite the cold, the occasional drizzly rain, and the cuts and nicks, they were a good group, who worked hard.

"How far out are we going?" Erin asked as they left her yard and headed east.

"Beyond your lake, I think," he answered. "I saw them back in my hills when I was scouting to see what I could hunt this winter. We need fresh meat," he almost said it apologetically.

"I'll be butchering a bull and a couple of pigs," Erin mentioned. "I could use some help in exchange for some of the meat."

"I'll gladly say yes to that. I've been craving some good beef and bacon for a while. I'm sick of rabbit," he admitted to the only meat he had been able to provide his family.

"We need to work on getting rid of more rabbits at our place too. They almost wiped out some of our garden. If not for the dogs…" she began.

"I wish we had a dog," he confessed. "Can't afford one of yours though."

"Maybe we can work out a trade of some sort," she said as though she had just thought of it. She'd really wanted to give them one but wasn't sure they could feed it, much less themselves. It wasn't like giving them a setting of chickens as Molly was going to do as a Thanksgiving present, so they would have chickens to lay eggs for them over winter or birds they could eat.

"That sounds like a plan. I want to give the boy a rifle, but Rebecca is deathly afraid of him hurting himself. It doesn't matter how many times I point out that he is a responsible boy, almost a man."

Erin smiled. No fourteen-year-old boy was a man but many of them thought so. He would be a boy for many more years, but yes, he should

have a gun and a dog. She didn't care if they got the bad end of the deal. Alex should have one of the dogs.

They rode out to where Erin had seen and hunted elk last year but didn't see elk, deer, or horses. They searched for two days before finding some tracks that were quite fresh and following them. They found a creek the horses used on a regular basis judging from the repeated sets of tracks they found. "How are we going to do this?" Erin asked.

"I was hoping you might have ideas," he half joked.

"Well, we have to find them first," she indicated the fresh tracks and began to ride in wider circles to get the lay of the land. "If we can find a little canyon where we could drive them, so they can't get out...we could capture them like that."

"That's a wily stallion I saw with the second herd. He's a big son of a—" he left off as he caught sight of the herd. "There," he pointed.

Erin had looked when Roberts stopped talking and caught sight of perhaps a dozen horses. There were paints, like some of the tribes on the prairies favored. She also saw plenty of browns in various shades, and there was a big, black brute with spots on his rump like the Nez Peirce raised. Her eyes focused on him. "Let's back off and find something we can use to trap them," she suggested, not wanting to scare them off. Horses could smell things that humans couldn't and wouldn't be fooled twice unless they were scared.

It took them another day to find something even close to what she'd suggested. The sides were steep enough that only a mountain goat or a determined horse could get up. They circled around to get downwind of the horses when they went to get water. Erin was right. As soon as they smelled the humans they went to a different spot, but unknowingly, they were closer to where Erin and Roberts wanted them.

"How in the world are we going to herd them into that?" Roberts asked, afraid of coming home without something to show for his hard work. Rebecca would never let him hear the end of it. There were a couple of fine-looking horses in the bunch, but some had seen better days, and some were downright ugly. There were no old horses. Those would have been culled from the herd by wolves or other predators. Erin had told him about seeing the mountain lion spore and bears last year. The story the children told of the grizzly they had encountered on the trip out here had been exciting, but Erin downplayed it.

"Let's use their sense of smell against them," she suggested, taking out her fire-making supplies and starting a little fire. The wind took the odor of smoke right to the horses and the stallion's head immediately came up. Erin quickly put the fire out, but the horses were now on alert. "You go around that way and try to keep them going there," she indicated the notch in the hills that would take the horses to the canyon-like area they had marked out. "I'll go this way and keep them from running south."

It wasn't as easy as she made it sound. The horses, used to being pursued by predators, were fast, fleet of foot, and determined to remain free. They lost some as they pushed them towards the notch. Erin could tell Roberts felt the stallion was a sad loss, but he was a beautiful specimen, and Erin wasn't too disappointed. She already had a stallion on her place and didn't need the work of keeping the two separated to avoid fighting. They nudged the rest of the herd into the notch and slowly but surely towards the cul-de-sac. One of the horses managed to climb the almost vertical walls in her desire not to be trapped.

"Let her go. She deserves her freedom," Erin said regretfully. She didn't want anything that wild. They would have their hands full with the six they caught. They quickly used ropes to close off the opening. The whites of the horses' eyes showed as they charged around the area trying to find a way out.

"Do you know how to throw a lasso?" Roberts asked.

"Nope. Do you?"

"No idea. Wish I had a whip."

"Molly's good with a whip," she mentioned.

"She is?" he sounded amazed as he grinned at the incongruity of that statement. She was so…delicate, and yet, she could do anything. He really admired Molly and her grit.

First, they let the horses settle down. Anytime the horses came near the rope strung across the opening, they chased them back. This scare tactic was not in their favor though, and they rethought it until Erin had the idea to tie little bits of cloth to the rope. This would cause the bits of cloth to flutter in the breeze, and that would scare the horses, at least until they became familiar with it. Next, they had no source of water for the beasts, and it was obvious they needed water after their run. They cropped the grasses as they settled down, but they had no water.

"Wish we had a trough or something to entice them with water," Erin mentioned.

"I could fill our canteens…."

"Not enough," she admitted as they made a cold camp, eating jerky and drinking from those canteens.

The horses didn't need water badly yet, but enough that they were pacing and wanting to get out of this little area. They were used to the

wide-open plains. The humans that had captured them still had no idea what to do with them. Erin started whistling to them as she came up to the rope, bringing brush with her as she made a fence on this side of the rope. Their ears twitched at the unfamiliar sounds. Roberts, catching on to what Erin was doing, started copying her, bringing other deadfall and wood to form a barrier. He couldn't whistle as well as she, but his different whistle attracted the horses' attention too.

Using food and water as motivation, they slowly earned the horses' trust. It was a slow process. The horses had plenty to eat in the uncut grasses, but they were becoming desperate without water. Finding a type of wooden basin that still leaked, Erin used the water from her canteen to entice the horses. By the time the horses got past the human smells on the rope, the water in the wooden depression appealed to them, and they lapped it up quickly. This allowed the humans to get closer to them. Erin and Roberts took turns going back to the creek to fill their canteens. The wall of debris had gotten higher and now, there was only a space wide enough for one horse to get through at a time. Erin took down the rope and placed a shorter piece across the entrance. It rained one day, and the horses managed to get water from that. The humans had to start over in their efforts to entice the horses to allow them near them.

Cutting the long rope she had brought into equal size pieces, she and Roberts made loops in the ends. When the horses began to wait for them to come into the area with water, they started trying to pet them. They naturally shied away, but their desperate need for water soon had them coming back. They progressed from giving them water in the depression, to using their plates to feed them, and soon, the horses were allowing themselves to be petted. One of the horses, a big appaloosa, was the hardest to convince. Next, Erin began carrying her rope with her, and Roberts copied her. They let the horses sniff the ropes. The horses didn't realize that once the rope was around their necks, they practically belonged to the humans.

This process was taking a tremendous amount of time, and Erin worried that Molly would be upset. So much could have happened back here in the hills, and Erin knew Molly would think the worst. She also desperately wanted a good wash, dreaming of the room with the half cask to bathe in. She'd told Roberts about that and described how difficult it had been cutting the cask in half the long ways and having it come out even. Not very fastidious himself, he wondered why Herriot would go to the trouble.

Eventually, they got ropes on all six horses. The horses weren't happy about it, but one by one Erin and Roberts led them from the enclosure to drink at the creek. They wouldn't let them drink their fill, but they took their time and got them used to being led by the rope. The appaloosa was the last and the most difficult; she struggled with the rope. Erin had thought she was a he at first, a younger stallion than the one that had gotten away, but it turned out she was just a big mare and feisty as all get out.

"Well, can we take them back and work on them at home?" Roberts asked. He knew Rebecca would be furious, but if he returned with horses he could sell, she might calm herself down. He'd chosen three that looked nearly identical and were almost completely brown except for small, white splotches.

They dismantled the barricade and loaded up the horses with their camping gear. Leading three horses each, they nearly had their arms jerked out of their sockets when the horses resisted. Erin was pleased with the fact that Roberts thought the appaloosa was ugly. The other two were black and dun respectively. They were all a little feisty, especially as they passed the creek where they had been led to drink repeatedly. Once beyond that, it was a struggle to lead them towards the ranches.

"I'm going to head for home," Roberts told her at one point.

"You don't want help?" she asked, knowing her place was more likely able to hold these wild creatures.

"I'm going to take these to town right after I let Rebecca know I'm alive," he told her, sounding guilty for being away from home so long and enjoying it.

"I'd like to sell these two myself," Erin indicated the black and the dun. The appaloosa was pulling back on the rope again, not liking that the rope was leading her. Erin slowed to let the horse have her head and saw this calmed her enough to allow her to continue without fighting them.

"You won't sell that big appaloosa?" he asked, having learned what kind it was from her.

"No, I think I'll keep her and breed her to my stallion."

"I should give you one of these horses in trade for the dog and to build some credit with you," he answered too quickly and then immediately regretted his impulse. "We need the money or I'd...."

"Don't worry. I understand completely. After you check in at home, come by my place and we'll go to Sweetwater together and see if we can get a decent price on the five horses."

"I'll do that," he answered as he turned off in a direction that would put him on his land in no time. Erin watched him for a while as she went along towards her place, now in familiar territory.

"Pa, you got some," Theo nearly shouted upon seeing her.

"Shhh, you'll spook them," she warned as she felt some yanks on the ropes. She called to the boy, "Take my mare, and I'll tie these off." Theo cautiously came forward to take the mare's reins as Erin dismounted.

"Well, what did you get there?" Molly said from the barn, coming out to look at the horses. Tabitha came out to look over her shoulder, and Erin could see the other three children behind her.

"I think we will need to build those corrals," Erin said with a grin.

"My, isn't she pretty?" she said, admiring the appaloosa.

Erin was pleased she liked it too. "I'm going to try to sell these two."

"You're keeping that one?"

"I think she'll breed up strong horses with our stallion."

Molly nodded as she looked the wild horses over. Three horses weren't much for the time Erin was away, but she could see she had enjoyed herself. "Where's Roberts?"

"He went to his place to show Rebecca that he was alive. She come over here?"

"Twice. She wanted to send the sheriff out looking for you two."

"What sheriff?"

"That's what I said. I told her you'd be back when you got back."

"Well, I don't know how much these will fetch, but I hope to make it worth the time away." She looked at Molly almost hungrily, wanting to convey how much she had missed her.

"What are you going to do?" she indicated the three horses which were rolling the whites of their eyes, showing their distress as the four dogs approached. The dogs looked like wolves to the wild horses.

Erin signaled them to stay and they obeyed instantly. She started to whistle to calm the horses, and their ears flickered forward at the sound. "I'd like to put them in a corral, but we are going to have to tie these off and maybe hobble them," she indicated the horses with a slight motion of her hand, trying not to gesture and spook the horses. If they realized they could drag her with their combined efforts, they would. Right now, the strange sights and sounds on the farm were spooking them. "Easy there," she crooned. She ended up hobbling all three and leaving the ropes on them as she put them out back of the barn, so they could crop the grass and settle down. There had been too much for them to adjust to today. She was surprised when Roberts came over first thing the next morning, ready to go to Sweetwater.

"I was planning on working on–" she began but Roberts cut her off.

"I've got to sell these or Rebecca is likely to take to my head off. We need supplies for the winter of course," he added lamely.

Erin could imagine how bad it had been and nodded. Turning to Molly, who had come out with her, she started to ask her something and Molly held up her hand. She was glancing at the three horses Roberts was selling, wondering if Erin had generously given him the better of the deal.

"I'll pack for you. You get your mare ready and then go get the other two."

Erin smiled gratefully at her wife's thoughtfulness, adjusting her hat as she went to get her mare saddled. In no time at all, they were leading the five horses towards Sweetwater.

"I'll give you five dollars a horse," Laydin offered.

"*Walllll*," Erin began, drawing it out, "I think we'll take them up to Pendletown. We can probably get as much as twenty dollars each for them."

"They aren't broke, and I don't think–"

"I'll give you fifteen," a voice in back offered. They turned to see Daniel Baxter approaching.

"Hello, there," Erin said, recognizing him from the shoe work she had done last year.

"You sell that Conestoga wagon?" he asked with a smile, recognizing her too.

"Shore did," she told him. "We've been out capturing these," she indicated the horses.

"Rough stuff," he said, examining them closer now. Five dollars a horse was pure stealing. "I'll still give you fifteen a head."

"Naw, we want twenty. Once they're broke, they will be worth twice that. They are healthy stock too. We let loose the ones that weren't healthy."

Roberts was dumbfounded. They hadn't *let* any go. Those others had escaped and…then he realized what she was doing. Horse trading had an age-old custom of lying. He kept his mouth shut since she apparently knew the man. He certainly wouldn't be selling these three to Laydin for five dollars a head if someone else was offering fifteen. He was already spending the money in his head.

"True, but they are fresh from the range."

"True that," she repeated back to him. "I'm sure there will be someone up in Pendletown that wants to break 'em in." She turned to Roberts and nodded towards his horse. "Let's go."

"Now, hang on there," Laydin began. This had been his idea. "Maybe I can go as much as ten dollars a head?"

"No, thank you, Mr. Laydin," Erin said kindly as she mounted the mare, glad the horses weren't pulling her arm off and making her look bad.

"I'll go to twenty then," Baxter agreed.

"A head?" she confirmed.

He nodded. "I could use some more if you got any."

"Maybe in the spring," Erin told him as he handed over twenty-dollar gold pieces. Erin gave Roberts his three and handed Baxter the two ropes for her horses. Roberts leaned over to hand Baxter his three ropes and nearly got pulled off his horse when they backed away suddenly.

"Easy, there," Baxter said gently. He quickly tied three of the horses to the hitch rail in front of Laydin's store. "I'll be back for these," he told the shopkeeper whose mouth was wide open and would catch flies if he didn't close it soon.

"I'd like to get a few supplies," Roberts told him as he got down off his horse, clutching the sixty-dollars in his hands as though it were a fortune.

"I'll see you back in the hills," Erin said, giving him a little salute as she touched the edge of her hat.

"Thanks, Erin. See you," he acknowledged, watching as she rode off on her mare.

Erin's heart was beating hard. Forty dollars for two horses! That was incredible! She knew that horses were pricey out here, but these weren't even broke! She couldn't wait to tell Molly.

CHAPTER TWELVE

As the winter progressed, they both had to admit they were far better off this year than they had been the last. They had plenty of house-bound projects for the winter. Even with the cold and snowy weather Erin managed to get out and work with the horses, especially the appaloosa. She desperately wished she had a fenced-in field or paddocks she could put her in but suspected the sturdy horse would simply go over or through the fences she had. The split-rail fences had been easy to build with the logs they brought in, but they weren't strong enough to hold a determined horse. Erin had her work cut out for her trying to gentle the wild beast. She broke her hobbles twice, and only her fear of King and the other dogs kept her from bolting back to the wild. She liked the brushings Erin did on her coat to clean it of dust and debris, and she also liked the pats on her sensitive skin.

"Pa, she's real pretty, ain't she?" Tabitha admired.

"*Isn't*," she corrected automatically. "And yes, she is pretty."

"Can I have one like her someday? Can I, Pa?"

"Well, she's a strong-willed horse, Tabitha, and we have to see if we can gentle her. She's going to have wonderful foals," she added, hearing the note of longing in the young girl's voice. She hadn't gone into it with the children present, but she wanted to put the appaloosa with the stallion soon, so they would get her pregnant. She didn't want a foal in the winter here though, so she was going to wait until spring. She'd learned her lesson with the sheep.

Erin worked on some of her wood projects in the barn when she had the horses in munching on some of the hay. The appaloosa learned to like her whistling and talking and seemed to look forward to seeing her as she worked.

"You sweet talking to your new girlfriend?" Molly teased as she came to the barn to milk the cows.

"Shore am. She's a looker too," she smiled up at her wife as she stood to steal a kiss.

"She is," Molly agreed, admiring the big horse. "Wonder how she ended up in a wild herd?"

"I don't think she always was, but she sure is shy of us."

"What makes you think she hasn't always been wild?"

Erin shrugged. "Nothing specific. Just something I sense. I bet some fine Indian brave had her and is upset over her loss."

"She's had someone on her back?"

"Not me...not yet."

"Are you going to try that?" she worried, looking wide-eyed at her wife in alarm.

"Not until spring, maybe summer. She's a strong one, and I can't afford any broken bones."

Molly laughed as she was intended to. She had worried about this part of capturing wild horses. She just hoped it would cure Erin, but with the money it had brought in, she didn't think so.

"I don't think it fits," Erin said as she showed Molly her mistake. They shared a laugh. One of the arms was much shorter than the other. She went back into the bedroom and closed the curtain to change, nearly starting in alarm as it opened to admit Timmy.

"Timmy, that curtain was closed. You aren't to come in here when it's closed," she told him sternly, holding the shirt up to cover the wrappings that hid her breasts.

"Sorry, Pa," he said, turning around and walking out.

"Close the curtain," she called angrily. He turned to close it, glancing at her curiously before pulling it shut. Erin quickly changed into a shirt that fit and returned the other one to Molly, who showed Tabitha what she had done wrong. Erin was still angry at Timmy's invasion of her privacy and discussed it with Molly later.

"I better put up walls for our bedroom," she stated, sounding aggrieved.

"Didn't we agree it would make the room feel too small?"

"I can't have the children walking in on me!"

"Yeah, you were upset that time we were making love and..." she started to laugh but knew it wasn't really that funny. They would be in a heap of trouble if the children ever realized that Erin was a she and not a he.

Erin let the ram in among the sheep in December this year. That meant they had almost five months before they had to worry about lambs. The wethers had turned into good mutton chops, and Erin was glad they hadn't sold them. She hadn't been able to get an elk this year but had managed to get a deer. In the new section of the barn she had left a longer log sticking out about eight feet up. She'd attached a pulley to the end of it and attached the windlass to make it easier to lift animals they needed to butcher. They had pork, beef, mutton, and venison that winter. The large variety of meats with the vegetables they had dried and canned made for tasty meals every day. Both Erin and Molly taught the willing children how to cook.

In February, there was a knock on their door that surprised them. Roberts showed up and asked for some supplies, shamefaced. "We ran out of your chickens last week. I've been trying to get a deer or something, but even the rabbits are hiding." The children sat at the table, their lessons forgotten as they stared.

Erin had him sit and warm up by the fire as Molly and she packed him a sack of food. When he left, he had flour, dried fruit and vegetables, pork, beef, and mutton in the large bag he put behind his horse.

"I can't thank you enough for this," he told them sadly as he headed out. He had been about to go to town and beg for credit, so he was grateful the Herriots were so generous. "I'll pay you back when–" he began before Erin waved him off.

"What are neighbors for?" She knew this neighbor would probably never be able to pay them back.

"How bad do you think Rebecca has gotten with them all alone in that cabin?" Molly asked her later when the children had gone to bed. She was disappointed that all the chickens she had given them to start their own flock had been eaten.

Erin shrugged. She hadn't thought about the Roberts too much as their own family kept busy through the long, winter months. "I worry more about that boy and what he is seeing."

"You know he's sweet on Tabitha?"

"That's a matter of proximity. He doesn't have a lot of choices."

"Still, it wouldn't be a bad match," she whispered in case the children were still awake and could hear them.

"No, but I wouldn't want our blood tainted with hers."

"Our blood?" she asked, laughter in her voice.

"I do think of them that way after all this time."

"Me too," she admitted, snuggling in to go to sleep.

Something got into their chicken coop and slaughtered almost all their birds. Molly was in tears over this loss. "I kept them alive all the way from Ohio," she lamented. They'd also added to their flock in trade for the smithy work Erin had done.

"I know, I know," Erin comforted as they cleaned up the slaughter. Erin saw their dogs and noticed Jack slinking off guiltily. She looked closer at the pen, and when she saw no signs of varmints in the snow, she realized there was a possibility Jack was the culprit. And if that was the case, she was going to have to shoot the dog. They couldn't have a dog on their farm that would kill their stock. They cleaned up the mess and the few chickens that were left. The birds were clucking in despair, obviously upset, some looking bedraggled after their feather loss, and Erin couldn't help but draw the conclusion she had. She shared her thoughts with Molly.

"Jack? No, he couldn't possibly…" she began, but he was nowhere about as they cleaned up the mess. King, Queenie, and Jenny were looking on as though they understood how upset Molly was. "How can we find out for sure?"

"Well, he will know if I sit out here with a gun and will avoid coming here. I don't know what to do. Most farmers would shoot a dog that kills chickens."

"But King and Queenie don't kill chickens and neither does Jenny."

"We don't know for sure it's Jack."

"But you think it is, don't you?"

"There is a paw print," she pointed in the dirt of the pen.

"It could have been there before?" she offered lamely. Her heart was sinking as she came to the realization that Erin was probably right. "What are we going to do?"

"I don't know," she admitted, feeling devastated at the thought of shooting one of her own dogs. "We'll just have to watch."

It was the death of their mean old gander, the pride of the flock they had bought back in Ohio, that finally convinced them. The gander had gone up against Jack, and Molly had witnessed it. The gander had been a fierce fighter, but Jack had lain in wait for it. The fight lasted long enough that she pulled her shotgun out and shot the dog herself, crying as she pulled the trigger. As he lay there twitching, she worried that he was in pain and pulled the other trigger, firing the second barrel into the dog. He'd already killed the gander, who lay there with a broken neck.

"Oh, Erin," she sobbed into her wife's arms when the gunfire had brought her running with her own rifle from where she was shucking corn in the barn. They both continued carrying guns but never thought about it; it had just become automatic. The thought of needing a rifle and not having it near had been their fear for a long time. "I didn't think twice. I just shot him," she cried. The children were all coming running from the cabin.

"You go back," Erin ordered them. "Get back inside now!" She saw them reluctantly head back to the warm cabin, looking over their shoulders as Erin once again took the sobbing Molly in her arms to comfort her. "You did what you had to," she told her, rubbing her back as she cried. "Get away from there," she ordered King, who lowered his tail and ears as he realized Jack was dead. He did as he was commanded and looked on from a distance. Queenie and Jenny joined him. They all looked sad.

Erin had Molly hold the dogs in the barn as she took Jack far out onto their land and dumped his body over a crevice near one of the clumps of trees. It was snowed over, and she nearly missed it as she rode the mare. She finally managed to place it by nearly walking into it herself in the deep snows. Putting the dead dog's body in the crevice, she piled snow on it, knowing wild animals would smell the fresh blood and dig it up. She didn't want to think about it, but there was no way she could bury the carcass in February. She headed back to the farmyard.

That night, as Molly wrote in her journal, Erin could see her crying again. When she was done and came to bed, Erin just held her, knowing she was playing that shot over and over in her head.

After Erin plucked and dressed the old goose, she cut it up and fed it to the dogs, cats, and pigs rather than have it for dinner. She knew Molly couldn't have eaten the mean, old gander. They had other up-and-coming ganders to service the geese, but none with the personality or meanness of that old bird. He had lived a full life, tormenting animals and people alike with his orneriness.

Erin saw Molly make something special for the children with his feathers—quills for them to write with. Each of them also had a feather pillow from the various birds, and she was hoping to gather enough feathers to make a feather bed from those they would butcher.

"With the wool we get this year, we should be able to make another wool mattress," Erin commented, seeing her sew the edges of the large swath of material that would become a mattress.

"That will be sold," Molly pointed out. She was looking forward to the increase in their herd of sheep. Erin had kept them close to the barn in their pen to feed them frequently, but they still heard wolves howling some nights. King and Queenie probably had their work cut out for them. She hoped that Jenny learned their good ways, and as she thought about Jack again, she couldn't help the tears that came to her eyes.

The children had asked about Jack, of course, but Erin hadn't let them see the corpse she took off. She'd explained that Jack had gone bad. He had killed the chickens and the old gander, and their ma had to shoot him. She explained their ma felt bad about it and they shouldn't talk about it with her.

"I'm sorry you feel bad, Ma," Timmy said wisely as he comforted her during one of these crying jags.

Molly was appreciative of her young son's compassion, but it made her want to cry more. She also knew her period was due as Erin's had just started and her emotions were up and down.

"Pa, are you going to let King and Queenie breed this year?" Theo asked, out of Molly's hearing.

"Yep, she had a year off and is stronger for it," she answered.

"My ma didn't," he answered, and Erin turned to him in surprise. At first, she was not sure he meant to say what he had. They rarely talked about their natural parents anymore.

"Well, sometimes that is how it goes," she tried to be comforting but failed. She saw the boy had something to say.

"I think having too many children killed my ma."

"That could well be," she agreed, watching him carefully.

"I miss her sometimes, you know?" he asked, trying not to cry. Ten-year-olds didn't cry.

"I miss my mother too. She's been gone many years now. You always miss your ma," she answered since they were sharing feelings.

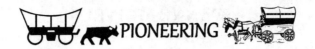

She knew men didn't normally do that, but she hoped to raise her sons to be compassionate young men.

The boy looked up with big tears in his eyes, sniffing and trying not to let them fall. "It's not that I don't love you and Ma..." he began awkwardly.

"We know that, son."

"I appreciate all you've done for us..." he continued, still sounding uncomfortable.

"Sometimes it's just hard to say," she admitted, hoping to help him.

"Yeah, it is," he agreed, relieved that she wasn't mad at him. It felt like some sort of betrayal to these people who had loved them unconditionally from the first day. As he got older, he realized how hard it had been to saddle them with so many children. Last year, they had nearly starved. Thankfully, this year, there was an abundance.

They both stood there awkwardly until Erin pulled him in for a hug and a squeeze. Sometimes, saying nothing at all was the best message. She felt the boy wipe his eyes on her jacket but didn't mind.

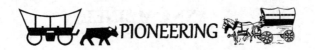

CHAPTER THIRTEEN

Spring came early that year in comparison to the previous year. They'd weathered the winter well and still had enough food to last them a while. Erin had plenty of shingles to put on the barn when they had time to replace the sods. She sharpened the plow shares in preparation for plowing the fields. The deep snows caused a heap of mud to tumble into the stream, leaching it off from the surrounding hills. Erin was anxious to get at her plowing and get her seed into the ground, so it had the maximum amount of growing time.

Roberts came over, talking to Erin about plowing his own small field and garden. "I'm thinking of throwing it in," he admitted after the winter they had had.

"You have several years to prove up on that land," Erin pointed out. She had one year up on him but still knew it would take time to produce enough to support her family indefinitely, but if last year was any indication, she was on the right track. "Do you have enough to start over somewhere else?"

"I was thinking if I went for more horses..." he began.

"You don't think others are coming out here with horses? We got a good price because Baxter wanted them right then and there. You might not get that good a price on a horse again," she pointed out. "Plow your field and enlarge it. Don't give up too soon." Thinking for a moment, watching him contemplate his decision, she asked, "How's Rebecca?"

"She didn't fare too well. The isolation is getting to her. I think I may have to leave because she needs neighbors…near neighbors."

Erin nodded, understanding. The isolation could get to a person out here. She was grateful they had a large family, but she would have been fine with just Molly. Molly was her world.

Erin ended up lending him the two yoke of oxen and her sod plow, so he could expand his field. First, they had to go out and find the herd where she had sent the oxen to live off the land over the winter. It took some searching as they had drifted far and wide on the land, even moving onto Roberts' lands. Billy objected when she tried to take the oxen, but once Erin sweet-talked the bull and whistled him down from his anger at their invasion, he finally allowed them to cut the oxen out of the herd. Erin got them heading back towards the farm.

"That bull's dangerous," Roberts stated as he looked over his shoulder at the snorting bull they had left behind them. He'd been amazed when Erin wasn't even scared of the big animal. Whistling and going near him with the utmost confidence had told the bull this was *his* human, and it was that confidence that reminded him of the pats, caresses, and scratches of the past, which calmed him down. She didn't touch him this time, but he did allow her to cut the oxen out and for that she was grateful as she eyed the sharp horns.

"He's an old sweetheart," she understated. She knew he was dangerous. He was perfect for a life on the range, protecting his growing herd from all invaders. She was sure he had fought off wolves and other predators. He'd be very effective against them with those impressive horns. She saw last year's calves and knew there were going to be some good offspring from her bull. She'd have to consider letting some of the younger bulls grow up instead of harvesting them all, just in case something happened to the older, mature bull.

She had her teams of horses and the other light plow to go over her own fields. "You have a week, maybe more before I'll need them back," she told Roberts, indicating the two yoke of oxen and the plow. She knew he'd have some trouble with the oxen, who had become accustomed to their freedom all winter. He'd have them broken in by the time she got them back. He'd also have a lot more plowed if he used them wisely. Two yokes of oxen hooked up to that plow could cut up an amazing amount of turf. She'd brought in the oxen's offspring too, wanting to get them used to being around people again, and if she found the time, she would also work with them.

Erin started with the garden using her regular plow. She had widened it last fall with the sod plow and now overturned those rotted grasses, breaking them down further into dirt as she readied the ground for Molly's carefully-gathered seeds. Then, she moved on to her other fields, deciding that one of the fields they had used for hay last year could be turned over this year and others farther out could be made into hay fields. She was determined to win her bet with Uncle Sam that she could farm this wild and distant land. They had four years to prove they had worked this land and lived on it. She gladly started their second spring with vigor.

Before Roberts could return with the plow and oxen, it started to rain. The spring rains were coming to wash away any pockets of snow that remained closer to the mountains. The resulting runoff filled the creeks, marshes, ponds, and lakes. It also made the fields soggy, and the runoff was ruinous to the work they had already put in. Molly had been about to put her seeds in the garden and was glad they hadn't or they'd have been washed away.

Erin chose to look on this as a bountiful thing and took advantage of the downpour to wash the sheep, one at a time, using soap Molly had made last fall. She'd dip her hand into the soft soap and lather it deeply into the wool of the sheep, allowing the rain to rinse out the suds. Later, she would come back and pull the deep wool back and forth to ensure the soap was truly rinsed out, taking the dirt, grass, and anything else she could find with it. It didn't remove all the bugs and twigs, but the cleaner wool would be nice when Erin began to shear her sheep. Shearing was a few days off since the rain showed no signs of stopping, and the sheep were miserable in the rain. Erin could see she needed to build a sheep fold with an overhanging roof where they could get out of the rain. The pen was fine to keep them enclosed, but it didn't keep out the weather. That meant more winter evenings slicing shingles from wood blocks.

The sun fought to shine through and dried the beleaguered sheep. Erin was grateful it hadn't turned cold or they would have frozen in their wooly coats. This year, she was better at the shearing, but there were more sheep to do, and her arms and shoulders ached from the unfamiliar activity. She got them all shorn on her clean barn floor, the children and Molly stuffing the wool in bags and the bags of wool stacked up along the walls waiting on her to take them to town when Roberts returned with the oxen and plow.

"Sorry I kept it so long, but with the rain, I'm sure you understood what happened to my fields. I had to go over them again, and I got even more done despite the rain. It was miserable walking behind them," he indicated the placid oxen chewing their cuds and waiting to be unyoked. "I was sinking in the mud," he exclaimed, but it was obvious he was happy about the amount of work he had gotten done despite the rain.

"Yep, I figured," she answered, happy for him. "I got my sheep washed and sheared."

He looked beyond her to the naked sheep dotting the hillside beyond the barn. They looked so odd, and he wondered how much sheep's wool would bring in. He was envious of his friend's foresight in bringing flocks out here despite not knowing what the land would sustain. Still, Herriot had treated him well, and he owed them a lot. He wouldn't let his envy color their friendship. "I'm going to town to get some seed to plant my fields," he told her proudly.

Erin waved him off, sad that he had to go into debt to get his seed. She planted her own the following week, choosing the early morning to spread the seed. The winds usually came up about ten in the morning, so she chose to do it as soon as the sun was high enough to see over the fields. She used a bag she wore around her to dip into and spread the seed by hand. She'd heard there were steel harrows being made nowadays, but she didn't have enough iron to make such a thing, so she had taken a log and drilled spikes through it for Molly to drive behind the horses. Molly came out about an hour after Erin started spreading the seed and used the tines or spikes to cover the seeds with the dirt. This way, the seed wasn't left exposed for birds and other animals to simply eat them off the fields. Erin stopped when the winds came up. Her practiced throw caused it to be too thick in some places and too thin in others, and the winds would make that worse. Molly finished off as she returned to the farmyard to hitch up the oxen and plow until the next day when she was out early to continue seeding their fields.

"Whew, glad that is finished," she said as they finished the enlarged barley field, which was always last. "Now, it can rain again."

"Now, the real work begins," Molly teased as they planted the corn and much later, the beans. Erin had plowed the field into hills two ways, so it was squared off. They planted the corn, four kernels to a hill, on the four corners. Much later, she planted the beans, four inside the outer four corn, so they would grow up and wind around the stronger stalks of growing corn. Since the corn grew slower than the beans, she waited until she saw the corn stalks up about four to six inches before planting the beans. Molly had planted a few things in the garden, but with the other fields needing work, she and the children had helped with planting the corn first. Then, they went back to working the garden until it was time to plant the beans.

"It's a good thing some of these crops need different weather," Erin complained good-naturedly as she helped plant in the garden. She couldn't work in the garden for too long as the sheep had begun to give birth. Normally quiet and forgotten on the hillside, now their needs were paramount. She spent many hours helping them. The younger ones were the worst, and she determined she would never breed yearlings again. She lost more young sheep to their stupidity, unlike the older, more sedate sheep, who simply accepted their lot. The loss of even one lamb was sad, and Molly ended up making a bottle board for three they managed to save. She would raise them by hand, and the children were delighted to help until they realized how much work it was.

"Not as if we don't have enough to do around here without hand-feeding lambs," Erin grouched. Still, they would be valuable someday.

"You're procrastinating on our spring trip to town," Molly reminded her. The wool needed to be taken in, and she'd already started spinning the small lot she was keeping.

"We can't both go, can we?" Erin wondered aloud.

"I need to get off this ranch, or I'm going to go as crazy as–" she began jokingly, then realizing where her comment was going, she stopped short and decided not to finish that sentence. The children were listening. "I think we could leave Tabitha and Theodore in charge and take Timmy with us," she said instead.

"I don't know. That's a huge responsibility," Erin said, but she knew Molly was forcing them to grow up a little quicker than they would have otherwise. Taking responsibility for their brother and sister would weigh heavily on them, but their responses told her they were up for it.

"We can do it!"

"Can we, Pa?"

"I don't want to stay with Tabitha and Theo," chimed in Theresa, who wanted to go to town with her parents. Sweetwater, as small as it was, was exciting to the little girl.

Surprisingly, Timmy didn't say anything, but he was sucking his thumb and Erin swiped at it. "Don't make me put pepper on that," she warned him. "You'll end up with buck teeth."

Molly and Erin ended up heading out early after the cows had been milked. Tabitha promised to make sure everyone ate, no one would touch the fire or oven, and she'd start the milk in the rocker, so there would be butter to pack by the time they got home.

The day was turning into a fine day as Timmy rode comfortably ensconced on top of the bags of wool and looked at the passing scenery. "Look at the little beggar," Erin murmured to Molly, and they shared a laugh at the little boy's expense; he looked entirely too happy.

Sweetwater was busy for once. Other farmers and ranchers were taking the opportunity to come into town. Their bags of wool generated some interest because few in the area had sheep.

"Can't raise 'em out here with the wolves," one of the men contended.

"Funny, we are," Erin returned, not liking his attitude.

"Real ranchers raise cattle," another put in his two cents.

"You should see my bull. His horn spread has got to be at least six feet now," she answered dryly, her arms spread to show the width of the horns. She wanted to ignore these know-it-alls and wondered if people like this existed all over.

"Yeah? Six feet? And I bet he's as gentle as a kitten," the man answered, laughing at her expense. Others joined in on the laughter.

"Here's your receipt for the wool," Laydin showed her the amount they had agreed on. He could sense it was getting ugly in his store, and he didn't want that.

"As a matter of fact, he *is* as gentle as a kitten. I'd bet you five bucks I could walk up to him and pet him. You, he'd try to gore," she returned, looking at the receipt, adding it up, and nodding at the merchant to show she found it fair.

"*Erin*," Molly tried pulling her away from the group of men who were trying to egg her on.

"Oh, yeah?" the man took up the challenge. "Five bucks? You're on!"

"I'll take some of that," another man put in, and before Erin knew it, there were four men betting on her boast.

"Look at that. Now that we've put our money where our mouth is, he looks all yeller," one of them joked, causing them all to laugh uproariously.

"Let me get this straight. If I can walk up to my bull and pet him, I win all this," she indicated the four men who had put up five bucks and were now pulling out coins and dollars. "But if I don't, all I lose is five bucks?" she clarified.

"No, you lose *twenty bucks*," one of them said ominously. The way he said it, he sounded like he would back it up with his fists too.

"Who will hold this money?" she asked, trying to avoid getting angry at their continued badgering. She knew that one or two of them hoped she would start with her fists, but she knew her odds.

"*Erin*," Molly tried again. Twenty dollars was a *lot* of money, more than a man could hope to make in a month, but the men were crowding around, edging her away, ignoring her because she was female.

"Laydin. He'll hold the money," the first man said, turning to the storekeeper who had no choice but to take the money since many of these men were important customers.

"How will we determine if he wins?"

"He ain't gonna win."

"A bull that size isn't going to be *gentle as a kitten*," the man said in a derisive voice. They all laughed.

"Laydin will have to come out to see this bull." Laydin looked like he didn't want to leave the comfort of his store, but they had pulled him into it.

"*Erin*," Molly tried a third time, trying to convey her alarm with her eyes.

"Deal," Erin said, holding the receipt up to Laydin, "Take my twenty dollars from this and my credit here at the store."

The men all chuckled evilly as the storekeeper counted out twenty dollars and put it in with theirs. He wasn't happy with this bet either.

"When do you want to do this?" Erin asked, her heart beating hard. If these men figured out who she really was…this would be about more than a bull with horns. This was cattlemen versus sheepmen, and this was men against women, even if they didn't know it. Their bullying tactics were used against men they considered less masculine than they or easy to abuse. She was angry, but at the same time she was confident.

"No time like the present," one of the men assured her.

"I couldn't possibly…" Laydin began, trying to point out how much business he would lose if he wasn't there.

"Your wife can run the store while you're gone," someone put in. They were laughing, and the way they were speaking and egging each other on, Erin had to wonder if they were intoxicated. The man clapped his hand on Laydin's shoulder, propelling him forward and *encouraging* him to go along with them.

It was obvious Laydin didn't wish to go so suddenly. A voice rang out, "Let's make it worth Laydin's while. Everyone put up another dollar!"

"*Erin*," Molly said warningly again. That was a lot of money, and though she knew Erin had a good relationship with Billy, he was out on the range and protective of his herd. He hadn't liked when she took from *his* harem when she fetched the oxen. He might not be as willing to let her come near him again as he had growing up on her farm. Out on the range, he fought wolves, big cats, and who knew what else. He was becoming wild.

Erin knew they were deliberately costing her money, but they didn't know she had raised that bull from a calf. Five dollars to win twenty wasn't too bad, and an extra dollar for the sake of goodwill with Laydin, the only storekeeper in Sweetwater, also wasn't a bad idea. "Yes, let's give Laydin five dollars for his time."

Presented with five dollars for his time, Laydin was suddenly willing and able to go along. His wife and son could get along without him for a time. He took off his apron and grabbed his hat.

"Pa?" Timmy called to Erin, getting her attention immediately. She looked down at the worried face.

"It's all right, Timmy," she assured him as she picked him up and carried him out of the store, the other men buoying them along as they went. She put him over the side of the wagon and helped Molly up onto the seat.

"I thought we were going shopping?" Timmy asked, confused, watching as those men got on their horses. They waited for Laydin to get his ride. It was obvious he wasn't used to riding horseback when he joined them. Fortunately, because of Herriot's wagon and because none of these men knew where the ranch lay, they had to ride slow.

"What is this foolishness?" Molly asked under her breath, furious that their shopping trip had turned into a circus.

"I don't know, Molly," she admitted, shaking her head and keeping her voice equally low, so the men wouldn't overhear. They probably couldn't hear anyway since they were riding along with Laydin behind them, talking loudly and teasing him about riding a horse…finding someone else to pick on for a while. "Something about the way they were ready to tie into me about the sheep angered me, and I let them make this ridiculous bet."

"You know better than to give into bullies. Ignore them!" she hissed.

"Yes, it's been a while since I had to deal with the likes of these." She thought back to Ohio when she had been teased because she looked more like a man than a woman and no one would marry her. They had been wrong but didn't know it. Someone had married her…her best

friend. She glanced at Molly, likening her anger to a wet hen. She was one of the prettiest gals around, and she had been so grateful to Erin for offering her a place to live with no strings attached. Falling in love hadn't been part of their bargain, but they had. Taking the initiative to move beyond friendship had shocked them both, but when they realized they both felt the same, they were determined to make it permanent. The move across the country had been a way to escape everyone who had known them back in Ohio. Now, no one would know that Erin was born a woman who looked like a man, and she had become that man. Molly didn't care. Man or woman, she loved Erin.

"What are you talking about? You dealt with bullies like that on the wagon train all the time," she stated, still sounding furious. What a wasted day. All this way into Sweetwater and for what? Entertainment for bullies? Well, she hoped Billy was in a good mood and would show them. She intended to be there when Erin won the bet. The ride back to the ranch was deathly quiet. Timmy was the only one who spoke, and his parents answered in monosyllables.

Arriving back at the farm, Erin leapt off the wagon to go saddle her stallion. He wasn't happy about it. He had been agitated all day by the scent of the appaloosa coming into heat. Erin's interruption of his pursuit of this female really irritated him. Erin came out of the barn leading this uppity stallion and saw the men looking around curiously at the barnyard and the raw outfit and making comments between them. Laydin looked very uncomfortable in this group. Molly had gotten off the wagon with Timmy and taken him inside. Erin tied off the stallion to go saddle the mare for Molly. The mare wasn't too pleased either when Erin locked her newly delivered foal in the barn and forced the mother to go with them. The foal cried plaintively.

The men stared as Molly came out of the cabin wearing men's pants. The five children trailed behind her, looking on curiously. They'd seen their ma come in and asked questions immediately, but she just instructed Tabitha to please watch Timmy and the others. She explained she and their pa would be back in a few hours…probably. She wouldn't tell them what was going on, wouldn't explain where the supplies were, and then they looked out the windows to see five strange men in their yard.

Erin mounted the stallion and handed Molly her reins when she mounted the agitated mare and took her firmly in hand. Erin shoved her rifle into the boot on her saddle, adjusted her hat, and said, "Shall we go?" The men laughed raucously, sure they were going to win their bet and making to follow her. "Unhitch the team," Erin said to Tabitha and Theo, who nodded in awe as they watched them ride away.

It took a couple hours to find the herd but Erin, who checked on them regularly, knew some of their favorite valleys. Following some fresh tracks, they eventually found them spread out against a bluff.

"So, where's this bull you all are braggin' on?" They looked around, seeing no sign of the herd bull. There were a couple young ones, but nothing like she had described.

"Wowee, that is *some* bull," one of the men breathed, seeing Billy for the first time. His head had come up over the backs of several other cows. He'd been calmly grazing with some of his favorite cows. He snorted slightly, scenting the wind to see who these invaders were.

"Well, you're right about them horns," another admitted, earning him a glare from his companions for giving away some of the bet.

"He ain't petted that bull none," one of them pointed out.

The last man was staying strangely quiet. Yes, he had put cash money on this bet, but something about this was off. Something about this whole situation was familiar and yet...not. That rancher was entirely too confident about his bull. He'd only seen that once and that was...it was at that moment he realized who Erin was, but by then, she was already getting down from her horse, handing the reins off to her pretty wife, and walking down the hill towards the herd and the bluff...whistling.

Molly watched as Erin got down from her horse and began to walk down the hill towards Billy. Erin adjusted the gun she had in the back of her pants under her jacket, drawing attention to it. She'd bet none of the men knew she had been carrying the pistol. They'd only be focusing on the two rifles she carried on her saddle.

A couple of the cows ambled away as though they had planned to move anyway. As she got closer, she smiled at the bull, still whistling. She was so proud of him. He'd exceeded any expectations she had for him. He'd been such a little bull. Her father had wanted to butcher him, but she'd pleaded for him and had been allowed to keep him as a pet. She had taken full responsibility for him. Now, look at him. He was one of the largest bulls she had ever seen and had survived crossing the country with his herd. As she glanced around at the various calves in different stages of growth, she knew he was responsible for this. He was the father of this herd and his genes continued.

Molly wondered how Erin could be that confident in the bull. He was a wild thing after living out here on the range. He'd survived two

winters out here. He could be very dangerous; he certainly looked it. She looked around at the other men, seeing the varying looks of incredulity on their faces, but one of them looked...furious. None of them had been introduced, so she didn't know their names.

Billy snorted ominously to show he wasn't going to let anyone near his herd. It carried across to her watchers. Molly was alarmed. Maybe Billy didn't recognize Erin anymore. Those horns looked alarmingly sharp.

"Hey, there, Billy boy," she crooned, putting up her hand to show she didn't mean him any harm and keeping it at just the right height to pet the large beast. He snorted harder as the cows parted between them. Erin smacked one cow on the rump to hurry it along, not in the least afraid of them or him. She whistled a tune she had used since he was a calf, a tune she had made up and put to words a few times, "Hey, Billy boy," she sang a little, stopping when she realized it could carry to her watchers. She continued to whistle, watching him as he dug at the turf, letting her know he was getting angry.

"That bull isn't buying his act," one of the men crowed, thrilled to be seeing him lose the bet.

"I'll bet you he flattens 'im in no time flat!"

"How much you bet?" the man countered, and in a moment, they had exchanged another bet for more money.

Molly shook her head. She didn't understand these men. Money was hard-earned and not to be treated so frivolously, although she was tempted to bet them since she knew Billy and Erin. She glanced at the man who was frowning again. He looked more than furious, but she could no longer read what was on his face. She glanced back at Erin, who was now about five feet away from the bull.

"Billy, don't you know me anymore?" Erin asked him sadly, wondering if she could get out of his way if he tried to trample her. His horns looked like they had grown since the last time she had seen him. In that short time, they seemed sharper, more ominous, and deadlier. She remembered how enraged he had been at the grizzly and how effective those needle-sharp horns had been. "Hey, big boy," she crooned, reaching up and forward to touch the horn nearest her. He shook his head, not wanting it to be touched. She dodged the sharp end, ducking, and saying, "Billy, that's *enough*. You come over here right now." She snapped her fingers and pointed at her feet as she had always done with the dogs and had taught the bull as he grew up. Billy answered with a resounding bellow, sounding enraged. Several cows trotted away from the encounter. Whatever he had said, they wanted no part of this. It was meant to intimidate, and Erin wondered if she were crazy to be attempting this.

"He's going to attack," one of the men said, assured.

"I'd love to own him. Look at the spread on his head. It would make a great ornament."

"He's eyeing Herriot like he isn't sure what he is."

"He's closer than I thought he'd get."

"Look at that! He's still walking towards him."

"He's crazy! Loco!"

"What's the matter, Billy boy?" Erin asked him gently, putting out her hand to calm him. She took two steps closer. He only had to turn his head to hurt her. She waited. He waited. Billy was eyeing her as though to make certain who she was. He was breathing hard and scenting her. The onlookers waited, some holding their breath. One was breathing hard, but he was not excited, he was angry. "You okay, my Billy boy?" she sang to him under her breath, so no one else could hear.

He turned his head slightly, looking at her more fully as though to say, "Why aren't you petting me?"

That was the look Erin had been waiting for. Smiling, she lifted her hand, took a step forward, and began to pet the big behemoth. Using her fingertips, she dug into his neck and shoulders, scratching his pelt. He arched, so she could get at the itchier places under his neck, turning his head and looking ridiculous. No longer the fierce bull, he had a silly, contented look on his bovine face.

"I would *never* have believed it!"

"That's amazing!"

Molly smiled. She hadn't wanted to believe Billy had turned mean, but a lot of bulls were, and he'd be deadly if he did. She nearly laughed as Erin hugged the big bull and scratched him harder, pushing him a step over. He didn't have to move but he did because it was his Erin doing the pushing, and he was going to accommodate her.

"You, big boy," she told him fondly as she released him and scratched some more. Patting him, she let him know her goodbye, and he watched her walk away, turning her back confidently on the dangerous bull. It was as she started up the hill again that he let out a bellow. He let everyone know he was the king of this herd and this was *his* kingdom. It really was quite impressive.

"I wouldn't have believed it," one of the men repeated, smiling, delighted that he had lost the bet, "if I hadn't seen it with my own eyes."

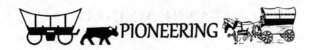

"Will you sell that bull?" another asked eagerly.

"Mr. Herriot, here are your winnings," Laydin offered the money, which she gladly accepted, putting it carefully in her pocket.

"No, I won't sell Billy. He's the founder of my herd," she nodded her head towards the cows spread out in the field, chewing unconcernedly as they pulled tufts of grass.

"Amazing bull. I'd be interested in buying one of his offspring," one of the men mentioned as they watched her mount up.

"I'd be glad to accommodate you there," Erin said with a self-deprecating smile. "I can't guarantee they will all be as friendly or amiable as Billy though. He's a special case." She was about to start the horse and return to the ranch but pulled up at the last voice.

"You're Erin Herriot, aren't you?" the angry man suddenly spat.

"Yes, I am," she admitted, frowning at the man. He looked...familiar.

"You're the bloke who wouldn't sell any of his animals to help out other settlers. I barely made it to Oregon because you wouldn't sell to me!"

Erin fixed him with a look. It took a moment. It had been well over a year since she had last seen the man. He'd let his hair grow much longer and much, much greasier. It was probably why she hadn't recognized him. "It wasn't *my* lookout to see you were outfitted. I raised those animals on my farm back in Ohio. Why would I sell them when I needed them to get my *own* family to Oregon?"

"You might have helped out a fellow traveler."

"I did help out my fellow travelers, time and time again, if you recall. I used my animals to help people get out of the mud or up steep inclines. I used my dogs to keep the herds going. I worked with those herds, fed people, and if you recall, I shot at Indians attacking our wagon train!" She was getting heated over the hard words, and Molly put her hand on Erin's arm to calm her. Nodding slightly, acknowledging that she was there, Erin didn't take her eyes from the man, staring him down.

"You might have sold me one of your teams," he muttered defensively as he broke eye contact and looked down.

"I needed my teams," she repeated.

"What is wrong with you? You are holding him responsible because you lost all your stock and family when you got to Willamette?" one of the men asked him, wondering what this resentment was about.

"We might have been in better shape if he had sold to me..." he began in a complaining voice.

"Wasn't my lookout to make sure you were outfitted," she repeated, watching the man, wondering if he was still holding a grudge about the bloody nose. "I have work to do, and if you all will excuse me, we needed supplies before you started your fun and games. I won the bet," she reminded them. "You got your fun and saw the bull. I don't need to tell you that you are trespassing," she addressed the man, still unable to remember his name. She remembered him now, recalled seeing him on the train, but she had never learned his name, which she found odd. She'd learned a lot of names on that train. He had been sullen, unwilling to help, and rude to many of their fellow travelers. It was obvious by the company he kept that he was a born troublemaker.

"Let's go. He's right. We've had our fun and learned our lesson," the man stated, smiling in Erin's direction to show he held no ill will. "I still want one of those young bulls."

"Then, we should talk. I don't think Billy wants his sons around too long." That was the nature of a good herd bull, they would chase off any potential competition for their harem.

Molly started her mare walking, and Erin let the stallion have his head, so they could start. The man who wanted a bull hurried to catch up with them and discuss the terms of buying a young bull. The other four men started following.

"That was something to see."

"I wish he'd sell that bull. Imagine those horns on a wall. Maybe I should bring my cows over and have him service them. Imagine the calves he would throw." He considered the viability of that. He only had a scrub bull on his place now and offspring from that enormous bull would be far superior.

"That was truly spectacular," Laydin put in, urging his horse to go a little faster to catch up with the group in front and immediately regretting it. He had no business being on the back of a horse and knew it.

The two interested in the bull both hurried to catch up to Erin and hear the terms she set for one of her bulls. The other man held back behind all of them, glaring at the back of the man who had refused to sell to him so long ago in Missouri.

CHAPTER FOURTEEN

Their day wasn't over. Returning to the ranch, Erin and Molly waved off their visitors and hitched their team to the wagon again. This time, the children went to town with them. Leaving the dogs on guard, Erin chirruped to the horses and they were on their way back to Sweetwater. The children had a million questions about what those men had wanted.

"You made a bet?"

"Isn't betting a sin?"

"You won!"

Erin explained about Billy. They already knew most of the story About how she'd raised him, and he followed her around like a puppy. She'd trained him and loved him as much as King or Queenie. She glossed over the betting part or how much she had won, but she stressed that she didn't approve of betting.

As they approached Sweetwater, they saw another wagon parked in front of Laydin's store. It was the Roberts. Pleased to see their neighbors and friends, they gladly went in to greet them. Roberts was friendly, amiable, and delighted to see them. Alex equally so. But Rebecca was strangely quiet, nodding coldly when she was greeted and ignoring them and their questions about how they were doing.

"I'm so grateful for you lending that plow. If I can make a decent crop this year, I think we'll get on our feet," Roberts enthused.

"There you go," Erin encouraged him, looking at the odd expression on Rebecca's face. It was almost…vacant, as if she wasn't totally there with them. As they waited for Laydin and his sons to fill their order, Erin told Roberts about Billy and the bet. Laydin heard and contributed his own viewpoint, thrilled with the unexpected bonus of five dollars he had gotten for his participation. To him, Herriot's bet was a godsend and a bonus. He had gossip he could share for a long time. "All for holding the money," he exclaimed. "You find that boneyard yet?" he asked, feeling as though he and Herriot were the best of friends now. At Erin's quick shake of her head, he returned to finish filling customers' orders, a genuine smile on his face from his windfall that day.

Molly quickly ordered what they needed, wanting to complete their day as they had intended. Two trips to Sweetwater were one too many in her opinion. It was late, and those many miles had made her tired. Rebecca was unnerving her and the children, and she distracted the children with questions about merchandise they might be interested in. Laydin had laid in a little more in his remote store as customers requested things he hadn't carried before.

"Whew, glad to have that done," she said as they all got in the wagon.

"Yes, it's been a full day," Erin agreed, looking back at Rebecca and feeling as though the prairie was maddening the woman…maybe it already had. She felt sorry for Roberts. He was a nice man and had raised a fine boy.

Two of the men from the bet had talked to Erin on the way back to the ranch. One wanted to buy one of Billy's offspring outright. The other wanted to have his few cows serviced by the bull. They discussed the details, and Erin agreed to bring in the young bulls and allow the first man to choose one in the next few days. She wanted to bring the young bulls in anyway. She needed to know what she had out there and just inspecting her herd from time to time wasn't enough. Billy had scared her a little this time. It was only her confidence in the fact that he would know her that had enabled her to approach him.

"I'm going to need both King and Queenie, but I'm going to take Jenny too, so she learns more," Erin told Molly a couple days later at the breakfast table.

"Want me to saddle up and help you?"

"I'd love that, but what about the children? Will it be okay if we leave them with Tabitha?"

Timmy had a cold and was fretful. Molly followed him around with a handkerchief to clean his runny nose, so he wouldn't wipe it on anything. It also looked like Theresa and Tommy were coming down with something.

"No, I suppose I should stay and keep an eye on them," she sighed, really hating being a mother right now but understanding. Erin was going to get those bulls to sell. They would need the money.

"Can I go with you, Pa?"

"*May* I go with you, Pa?" That came from Tabitha, who was working extra hard on speaking properly. Molly had been teaching her certain manners beyond what she taught all the children, including articulation and proper speech.

Erin smiled. "I think you can go, Tabitha. That is, if you can get the horses saddled in time before I get done with my breakfast..." she left off as the young girl ran out of the cabin, banging the door behind her. Theo raced out after her, banging the door too.

"No, you don't, you two," Molly told Tommy and Theresa, who would have raced after their siblings. "You stay indoors today."

"Awww, Maaa," they said in unison, both clearly whining.

"You heard your ma," Erin said sternly, trying to hide her smile as she bit into her toast. Both Tabitha and Theodore had left their breakfast half eaten.

"You be careful," Molly admonished her, hiding her own grin from the children as she prepared a lunch for her husband and daughter to take with them in the saddlebags. There was no telling how long it would take for them to bring in those cattle. She also scooped Tabitha's eggs onto a piece of bread that she had toasted, topping that with another piece of toast and wrapping a cloth around it for the girl who had been so enthused she had forgotten to eat her breakfast.

Erin and Tabitha rode out. The foal was once again locked in the barn, much to the mare's distress. "Keep a firm hold on her or you are going to get tossed," Erin warned the girl as she attempted to eat the egg sandwich and ride at the same time.

She nodded, taking a firmer hold on the horse with her legs, wishing she were wearing a pair of britches like her brothers or Pa. She'd seen her ma wearing pants the other day, and they looked a lot more comfortable than her skirts, which were hiked up too high for comfort. "Pa, could I wear pants like you and Ma sometimes?" she asked in between bites while attempting to control the mare, who wanted to go back to the barn. They both heard the appaloosa call longingly to the stallion. She thought she was in love with him now.

"Well, out here on the range I wouldn't mind but not in town where folks could see you," she answered, hiding her grin at the question. She felt a little bit of a hypocrite telling her daughter something like that when her own *pa* was wearing pants, just like the man they thought she was. Still, she knew Molly wanted the children to be proper, as evidenced by the manners she was imparting to them.

They looked for the herd where Erin had last seen them near one of the bluffs, but they were long gone. King, Queenie, and Jenny all put their noses to the ground when Erin told them to 'search.' "Find Billy," she ordered them. She knew both Queenie and King recognized the name as they headed off. Following the dogs, she noticed Tabitha was having a little trouble with the mare. "Firmer on your grip," she advised, wondering if she should take the horse and give the stallion to the girl. No, that was a bad idea. The stallion had grown a lot on the trip out and was now full-grown and cocky. There was no way she would let the children ride him.

Billy seemed surprised to see the dogs and looked up at Erin on her horse, scenting her and looking fierce. When Erin began separating some of his offspring from the herd, he didn't like it at all. The dogs obeyed Erin, even the younger one, Jenny. Jenny looked back frequently at Erin, who ignored her after the initial command. Whistling to catch their attention, a hand gesture soon had them circling around, another way to cut bulls from the now restless herd. Slowly, but surely, they got five young bulls of various ages cut from the herd, and Erin started heading them back to the ranch. It was dry and dusty work. Billy, snorting through his nose, began leading his herd away from the scene, and one by one, the cows and other cattle followed him until they were out of sight.

"Pa, you think animals have feelings?" Tabitha asked as she rode on one side of their small herd while Erin rode on the other. The dogs kept at the young bulls' heels to keep them moving in the direction they wanted, being careful not to get kicked. They were ready to growl or snap at the young bulls to maintain their fear of the dogs, so they could do their job.

"I sure do," she said without hesitation, wondering where this conversation was going.

"I do too," she admitted thoughtfully. "I just wonder if we've hurt their feelings from time to time?" she explained. "Like when Ma had to kill Jack. Do you think Queenie and King felt bad?"

"They did, Tabitha," she admitted, remembering that terrible day. Their tails and ears had drooped. They may not have known Jack as their *son* anymore, or the pup they had raised, but he had been a part of their pack. He was a companion, and they had acknowledged his loss with their sorrow.

Erin was so proud of this thoughtful and intelligent young girl they were raising. She enjoyed their conversations. They brought the cattle into the yard, putting them in the split-rail fenced area behind the barn. She hoped it would hold them. Although they *thought* it would hold them, if they wanted to get out, they could. The pigs proved that all the time.

"Think that man will want one of these?" Tabitha asked as they unsaddled their horses, the mare anxious to get back to her foal. She was very agitated, and they could all hear the plaintive calls of the foal for her mother. The pups greeted King and Queenie, who resigned and let them begin to feed on her.

"I hope so. I don't want to upset Billy any more than we have," she admitted. Seeing him twice in the past week had been more than she had planned.

"Erin? Oh, thank God you are back. Do I have a story for you!" Molly came running out of the cabin carrying Timmy. She was followed by Theo, who had bandages on his arms, and the other two children, who looked wide-eyed around them.

"What happened?" her eyes took in Theo and looked around. She adjusted the rifle she had just slung to her back and held tighter to the one she had just taken from the second boot on her saddle.

"You are not going to believe what happened after you left," Molly admitted.

"Tell me!" she demanded, worried.

"Everything is okay now, but after you left..." she began.

Molly watched for a moment as Erin and Tabitha rode off, the dogs trailing the horses and looking happy to be going, especially Queenie, who was escaping her always demanding pups. She'd only had four this time but they were a handful. There was a big male that Erin wanted to keep and three smaller females. The male was a glutton too, always feeding on Queenie and tiring her out.

Molly returned to the house, listening to Timmy's whining and finally putting him to bed in her and Erin's bed, so she could watch him. Both Tommy and Theresa were fretful and cranky, but neither had fevers yet. They were, however, flushed and looked like they were coming down with something.

Molly did her normal chores, setting Tommy and Theresa to making butter by using the converted chug-a-lug, now on rockers that Erin had cleverly made, so they could rock the milk back and forth inside the barrel instead of the dash up and down motion like most butter churns.

"Easy there, not so hard," she warned them from time to time as she knitted. Erin had brought her some beautiful yarns in vivid colors, and she was excited to make them all scarves, mittens, and maybe even sweaters for next winter. They grew out of their clothes so quickly and occasionally lost scarves and mittens, even wore them out sometimes, and she wanted them all well-supplied. She was hoping to eventually weave her own wool. Erin had sent away for special threads that she could learn to weave with. She was excited about doing that this winter. It was just one of her many projects. She wrote of that and other happenings in the past few days in her journals, smiling as she remembered the bet on Billy. Although she didn't approve of gambling, this time she was so proud of Erin.

As she went to check on the barn at noon, her shotgun slung along her back, she looked off to the east where Erin and Tabitha had disappeared to look for the herd. She didn't expect to see them back so soon, but she looked anyway. It seemed quiet without the dogs as she approached the barn. She heard the young filly neighing for her mother, the needy little thing. Most foals were very quiet but not this one.

"Ma! Come quick!" Theo called, and Molly picked up her skirts to run the last few feet to the barn. What she found inside was astonishing.

No longer quiet, the barn seemed full of growling and hissing cats. Only a couple of the cats were theirs. They had never seen the others before. The cats' ears were back, their spines were arched, and they were all hissing at each other. There seemed to be four she didn't know. Her cats, including the kittens, were upset at this trespass and making as much noise as possible. Then, she saw what they were

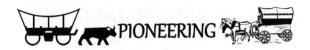

fighting over…the pups, who looked terrified not only of their own cats but also the invaders.

"Go on! Shoo!" Theo said, waving his arms at the strange cats.

"Careful, Theo," she told him, wondering where they had come from. They looked feral, unkempt, and wiry.

The waving of his arms seemed to set them off, and they attacked. They didn't go after the terrified pups, who yelped anyway, and they didn't attack the hissing cats all in a line and ready to defend their barn. No, they attacked the human who had instigated their premature attack. They ran right for Theo, who screamed as they jumped on him and scratched his arms when he automatically raised them to protect his face. "Maaaaa!"

Molly had never seen the likes of it. She had seen cat fights before but nothing like this, and she had never seen them attack a person. "Hey!" she yelled, trying to distract them. Two of them leapt off the boy to head aggressively towards her. She unlimbered her shotgun, intending to use it, but then she saw the angle was wrong and she would hit Theo or one of the pups if she fired. Instead, she used it like a club, batting one of the attacking cats aside. That only knocked it away for a moment, and now, their own cats were attacking. She could see Theo was getting the bad end of the deal, the cats scratching at his arms. She fended off the other cat, who turned fast to come at her again. Dropping the shotgun into its sling on her back again, she picked up a shovel. Every time the cat came at her, it was met with the iron face of the shovel. It finally backed off when the other cats distracted it by hissing and spitting at it. The whole thing reminded Molly of schoolyard children egging each other on to fight. She held the shovel up in front of Theo, annoying the cats, who didn't like to be faced with metal they couldn't scratch or bite. She shoved at them with it, trying to get them to scatter and retreat. She saw a bucket half full of water, picked it up with one hand while still fending off a cat with the shovel, then dropped the shovel long enough to throw the water on the fighting cats. Before she knew it, the four strange cats took off with several of their own cats chasing after them. They were soon lost in the long grasses surrounding the farm.

"Are you okay?" she asked the boy, who was trying manfully not to cry despite the pain in his arms

"Come on," she said, glancing back in the barn. She could see the pups were calming down, almost as though nothing had ever happened. One of the female cats was climbing in with them and licking them, almost like a surrogate mother, which was soothing them further.

Theo had deep scratches that bled a lot. Molly washed them thoroughly. She knew cat claws had lots of dirt in them and frequently the scratches got infected. In the cabin, he hissed when she pumped water in the pan and had him put his arms underneath it. After putting rags on the scratches to absorb the bleeding, she worried she'd have to stitch up some of the wounds. Instead, she used a poultice to slow the bleeding and wrapped his arms in bandages. He wore his wounds as a badge of honor, relating the fight to his siblings proudly. "Ma, do you think they were rabid?" he asked, having heard of the disease from Erin.

Molly hoped not. She hadn't thought of that. She thought perhaps the cats were looking for new territory and chose the wrong barn to make a stand. She'd heard of something like that before, but the memory was vague. It was probably a story someone on the wagon train told, and she'd dismissed it at the time. She worried after he asked that question but shook her head in answer. "Tonight, you are going to have a hot bath and soak those arms again," she warned him, and he groaned at the idea. It was bad enough he had a weekly bath every Saturday night but now, he would be taking an extra one? Well, maybe he wouldn't have to take one on Saturday too.

"Wow, did you see where they went?" Erin asked as Molly finished telling her the story.

"No, not really. Our cats chased after them and they were back by the time I finished bandaging Theo. I went to check the barn, and the cats were back and behaving as though nothing had happened."

Erin was concerned, and when Molly repeated Theo's question later, she too worried. They would watch the boy closely over the coming days. He didn't get out of his Saturday bath. Even though he'd had one just two days prior, they insisted he take another. As the scratches healed, they itched, and they admonished him for picking at the healing scabs. "Leave them alone or they'll scar," Erin told him.

"Don't make me wrap them again, so you can't reach those scabs until they are healed," Molly warned him. They were healing nicely, and she was pleased how the cool, clean air of the ranch was helping them along.

They never saw those cats again.

CHAPTER FIFTEEN

As summer progressed, Erin sweated over her fields, pulling weeds as she found them, and picking beans to supplement their winter stores. She was concerned as the weather got hotter and hotter that year. It was much hotter and drier than the previous year. The prairie grasses turned from green to brown to dust in some places. Roberts rode over to talk about going for horses, but Erin was concerned about fires. Despite the dry conditions and rock-hard ground, she tried to plow around the farmyard and fields in one huge circle, but her attempt failed. She had no idea how to protect her place in case of fire, but Roberts had a suggestion…fire.

"If you keep it under control in a large swath around your place, the fire would have to jump the burnt grass if it came along. It's not much different from the idea you had about plowing up the ground around your place."

Erin nodded, envisioning what he had suggested. It was very hot. She wondered if the fires of hell could be much hotter. "Could you help me? I'd like Molly to watch the children while I do this in case it spreads faster than we can control."

He nodded musingly as he considered what they would need. "Let's do it in small swaths, so it doesn't get out of control. If a prairie fire does come through, you can back fire from the ring."

Molly came running when she smelled the smoke. She had spoken with Erin on the subject many times. In this heat, their biggest concern was running out of water, and the stream was way down right now with no sign of rain on the horizon. Still, their pump worked, and it didn't look like the well was going down from what they could see when they checked under the sink. "What are you doing?" she asked when she saw them battling the fire they had started, one on each side of flames that quickly whipped up.

"Stay back, Molly," Erin called as she smacked at the flames, beating them down. They did about a ten-foot swath and would have continued, but Erin got a little too zealous when putting it down and it was completely extinguished. Roberts used a shovel to bat out the still smoking spots in the section.

"Want this coal to start it again?" he asked, lifting a shovel full.

Erin nodded, not willing to pull out her fire-starting materials again. As he walked over with the live coals towards the dry grasses, Erin explained to her wife what they were doing. "If we do it in sections in a swath around the homestead, we can stop small fires that might get out of control or a prairie fire."

Molly realized this made sense. "Why don't I help?"

"I really want you to keep the children in the cabin and out of the way, so I don't have to worry about them." Already, from behind Molly, she could see the children climbing the hill where they were doing the burning. The children were naturally curious about what they were doing and were being drawn by the fire. "Get back in the cabin," she called to them, and Molly turned, shooing them away as she walked back down the hill. She didn't make them go back in the heat of the cabin. Instead, they all kept watch from the farmyard, doing chores that required them to be out of doors, so they could watch the men work.

All day long, they could smell the smoke as Erin and Roberts burned a swath along one side of the homestead nearest to the farm and its buildings. Over the next two days, they would burn around each side of the farm and up to the stream as well as around the fields.

"Looking mighty parched," Roberts commented, wiping his forehead with his handkerchief, looking at Erin's fields and worrying about his own. It was midmorning and already quite hot. He desperately needed a good crop to hold him over in the next year. Rebecca had taken to sitting in a chair in the cabin, doing absolutely nothing but fanning herself and drinking water in an uninterested fashion. Nothing motivated her. She just sat, and he finally had to do something, which was why he had come to find Erin and asked her to go with him for more horses. He'd brought Alex along, so he could also escape his mother's odd behavior and left Rebecca sitting in the cabin alone, staring off into space. He looked up as Alex and Tabitha arrived carrying a bucket of water. Both were fascinated by the fire, as were all the children. They brought the bucket of water, each saying it was for the men to drink and for the fire, then staying long enough to watch them burn away the grasses, put out the fire, and then burn some more. They created about a ten-foot swath, sometimes more, sometimes less, around the entire farm, and Roberts wondered if he should do the same. He didn't want Erin to see how bad Rebecca was though, so he didn't suggest she come help at his place. He wondered if he should send his wife somewhere for help but didn't know where.

"Yeah, we definitely need a good rain," she said, wiping her brow as she smiled at the children, putting out a patch before they got there and gladly taking a drink from the bucket. "That hits the spot," she thanked Tabitha with a smile. She knew the cool water was from their well instead of the stream as it tasted different.

There had been a couple of times when the flames did get a little out of control, but they had worked hard to beat it back. A fire now, would be tragic to anyone in its path.

"You know, this might not work," Erin had pointed out, but she realized they needed to do something...anything. She'd seen rabbits, chipmunks, and other wild animals race off from the smoke and flames, panicked by it.

"Still, we're trying," he answered. "What would you do if one of those prairie fires came through here?"

"I'd let all the animals out to fend for themselves and head for the lake with Molly and the children," she answered right away, proving she had given this some thought already. "You?"

"We've got a large set of creeks on our place. They probably empty out into your lake. I'd head for those, but if that wasn't enough I'd come to your lake." They both laughed at that, but it was a weary laugh.

"Pa? Ma wants to know if we could all go for a swim in the lake?" Tabitha piped up.

"We'll be done with this today, and that sounds like a goal for after the work is done," she replied with a smile, liking the sound of that. "The stream not enough to play in anymore?"

"No, it's really shallow now and not very cool. Tommy fell on the rocks and skinned his knee."

"He okay?"

She nodded. "Ma patched him up. She asked me to bring you this," she indicated the pail of water, "and ask about the lake."

"Sounds good," she admitted, wishing she could go in the water too. But the water would reveal her shape, and she couldn't do that. Even the bindings would be clearly visible through her wet clothing. Maybe some night by the light of the moon she and Molly could– She dismissed the thought as soon as it came to her, knowing the children would be frightened if they woke in the night and their parents weren't there. And a ride out to the lake and back would take hours.

They both watched as the children left, leaving the bucket of water as they resumed burning the swath. "You know, Rebecca thought those two would..." Roberts began, suddenly feeling awkward for bringing up the subject and for mentioning his wife.

"Yeah, Molly has said the same," she answered, not even realizing he was uncomfortable. "Maybe someday. We will see.

After finishing their section and ending up back at the big, black mark where they had begun, they made sure the fire was completely out, pouring the last of the water in the bucket on anything that was still smoking, then turning it over with a shovel, pounding it out in the dirt, and waiting to see if it smoked anymore. That old adage, 'where there is smoke, there is fire,' wasn't always true, but they couldn't afford any mistakes, not when the prairie was this dry.

"Seems to be out," Erin said, feeling around carefully with her bare hand for good measure. She'd only been wrong once as they fired the perimeter around the farm, but that burn had taught her to be mighty careful. Although very small, it still hurt.

"Let's go for a swim," Roberts said, gathering up the tools they had used. Erin grabbed the bucket. They walked down to the barn to put them away and hitch up the team. Molly heard Erin whistling and came out with the children. Alex and Tabitha were carrying a picnic basket.

"Can the dogs come?" Theo asked, looking at their hopeful faces.

"Well, someone's got to stay home," Erin began and then, seeing the disappointment on her children's faces she decided the best person to stay home would be her since she couldn't swim. If she left one of the dog's home, they could at least picnic together; however, she knew there would be questions about why she didn't go swimming with them. She knew Molly was teaching them to swim, something she knew how to do very well because of her brothers. She sighed as she smiled. "Why don't you all go, and I'll keep watch here."

"No, Erin, we can leave the dogs."

"Bosh," she answered, still smiling as she waved at them, gesturing for them to go. "Take the dogs, they need a cooling off and they need to teach those pups to swim."

"But, Pa, I wanted to show you...."

"Pa, it won't be fun without you...."

"I'll stay with you, Pa."

"Nonsense. I insist you all go."

"*Erin*," that was Molly.

"No," she answered with a smile and a stern look. "Go!"

All too soon, and with a lot of lifting and pushing, the children had the pups in the back of the wagon. King, Queenie, and Jenny jumped up with encouragement, their tails gaily wagging. They looked like they were laughing in delight, looking forward to wherever their family was going. The children each grabbed a pup, trying to keep it in their lap, but their efforts were unsuccessful since they were all too excited. Molly glared at Erin for a moment, Roberts on the seat next to her and Alex in with the other children fending off the enthusiastic pups, and then, they were off.

"Bye!"

"Bye!"

"See ya, Pa!"

"Later!"

They all called back and forth as Erin waved at them, pleased to see them going off to enjoy themselves and happy that Alex and Roberts were going along as well. They deserved it, and she only wished she had thought of sending them on their own earlier. She turned to the eerily quiet barn, the chickens clucking almost as though in whispers. With no puppies yapping and no children shouting or talking incessantly, the silence was almost ominous. Erin sighed. It was too damn quiet without the children and dogs. A cat meowed at her inquiringly and she pet it, noting it had a snotty nose and wondering if it were sick.

Remembering she was all alone, she decided to take a cool bath. With the children gone, she could relax. No one would be banging on the door, and no one would be calling through the door asking her incessant questions. She was completely and utterly alone. She looked around once more, closing the barn doors and hoping it would be cool inside in the shade for any animals that chose to be indoors. She looked over the pigpen fence towards the horses to check if they had their hobbles on and determined that a corral was her next project. *A strong one,* she thought as she looked at the appaloosa. *I'm going to ride you this year,* she thought to herself, wondering how that would come about without causing her broken limbs or too much pain. As she walked towards the cabin, she thought about the lake and wondered if she rode the horse into the lake how hard it would try to buck her off?

Sitting in the cool water she had freshly pumped from their kitchen, she locked the door as she always did. The lock protected against children or anyone who might come upon her. She didn't want to be *accidentally* discovered in the buff. It was a good thing she did too. She had just finished her bath and was standing in clean trousers and draining the tub when she heard, "Hello the house!" Startled, she finished wrapping herself and grabbed a shirt, finger-combing her hair quickly and then buttoning up to cover the fresh, clean bindings.

"Hello?" she opened the cabin door to see who was there, grabbing up one of the rifles she had put beside the door when she came in. She glanced at the pistol she had laid on the table. She was surprised to see one of the men who had bet against her months ago sitting on his horse in front of the cabin. He smiled upon seeing her, looking at her curiously where she stood bare-footed and with wet hair. "Can I help you?"

"Herriot, right?" he asked.

She nodded, squinting at him in the strong sunlight. She'd been enjoying herself in her bath and that room had no windows, so he had caught her by surprise.

"I'm Graebel. Do you remember me?"

She nodded again and then asked, "What can I do for you, Mr. Graebel? You interested in some of my bulls?"

He laughed as though she had made a joke and asked, "May I get down?" He looked pointedly at the rifle she was holding, her hand right by the trigger, so all she had to do was lift, point, and cock it. She nodded again and watched as he got off the sweating horse. "You can water your horse at the creek while I put on some socks and boots," she offered.

"That's very kind of you. I'll do that," he agreed and started to walk his horse down to the small stream that was even smaller due to the drought. Erin quickly shut the door to race and get clean socks and stamp into her boots. She shook them out as a matter of course, surprised when soot drifted out of them. She'd have to sweep that up before Molly saw the mess.

"What can I do for you?" she repeated as she came up behind Graebel. She still had her rifle in her hand and now, the pistol was firmly tucked into her belt.

"I was wondering if you know about the Organic Laws of Oregon?"

Surprised, Erin nodded, peering at the man and wondering what he wanted. "I'm familiar with them, yes."

"If you're married you can claim six hundred and forty acres?" He took off his hat to wipe his sweaty brow, using the back of a sleeve to sop up the moisture. He gazed intently at Erin.

"I'm aware of that. I filed on this homestead that way," she admitted.

"Then you know of it. That's good. That's real good!" he said enthusiastically.

"Can you tell me what this has to do with me?" She was puzzled about his visit.

He put his hat down, gripping it with both hands and looking very uncomfortable. "Well, I want to file on a claim. I was thinking I'd like to file on a claim adjoining your'n. If I were married, I'd have as much as you do."

Erin nodded, still not getting the man's point. She felt a slight breeze come up. It was hot but it felt good in her wet hair. She waited for him to continue.

"Well, women are at a premium out here..." he hesitated and then went on. "There ain't...*isn't* no age limit, and we could be married in name only."

"Who are you thinking of marrying, Mr. Graebel?" she asked, thoroughly confused as to why he was involving her.

The man sighed. He'd hoped Herriot would understand and he wouldn't have to spell it out. "Why, your daughter," he answered, as though that were obvious.

Erin was struck dumb for a moment. Her first thought was to point the rifle at the man and order him off her place. Instead of making the man her enemy though, she stared at him, a hard look coming into her eyes. "My daughter is only twelve years old."

"That's good. That's rightly good. I thought she was only ten!" he said as though he meant it. Erin was appalled.

"She's too young to get married."

"Well, we wouldn't be like *really* married. We'd have to get a justice of the peace or a preacher to sign the paperwork saying we were hitched, but I'd wait for her. She could even live here with you while I work the land."

"So, you are proposing that you marry my twelve-year-old daughter and take on a claim next to mine in your and her name," she slowly stated the facts as he started nodding eagerly, "in order to cheat the government out of an extra three hundred and twenty acres?" At the word *cheat* she saw the anger rising in his eyes.

"I ain't no cheat," he protested. "I didn't squelch on my bet, did I?"

"And that's another thing, *Mister* Graebel," she stressed the one word. "You gamble. What father would let his daughter marry a gambler?"

"I ain't no gambler. My friends and I were having some fun, and that was a harmless little bet. You won it, and you kept our money," he pointed out.

"That's because for me it was a sure thing. How many times have you lost such impetuous bets...lost your money to foolish gambling? You are proposing to take my daughter as your wife but you mention nothing of love or of providing for her. Instead, you talk of working the claim while she lives here with her ma and me."

"It weren't exactly like that," he protested. "I'd want her to have my children when she was ready."

"And how old would she have to be to have your children?"

"Fourteen or..." he hesitated, seeing the look on Erin's face, "maybe sixteen?"

"Do you even know my daughter's name?" she asked, feeling the itch to use the rifle again and gripping it tightly instead.

"Umm...Betty?" he asked, and at Erin's shake of the head he tried again, "Sue?" Again, he tried to think of a name and this time, Erin waved him off using the rifle.

"Don't even try again, *Mister* Graebel. I suggest you leave. I won't be giving my daughter away to the first man who asks to marry her, especially when he's not asking for her out of love but to get more land from the government. You wouldn't make her happy and–"

"But I would," he protested, leaning forward to plead his case. "I'd treat her real fine. We could get hitched, and then I could court her while I get our place in shape like you've got here. You could give us some cattle and maybe some sheep, and we'd have a real good start."

"So, now you want me to give you a dowry for my daughter, who you don't know, so you can court her?" At the man's eager nod, she said, "Get off my land, *Mister* Graebel. I'll give you to the count of ten before I start shooting."

"But you ain't listened to a word–"

"One...two...three..." she brought the rifle up, lining it up dead center on his chest, "four...five...six..." she watched his eyes widen as he looked at the hole in the barrel of the rifle pointed directly at him. He quickly mounted his horse and kicked it savagely. "Seven..." she raised her voice, so he would be sure to hear her, "eight...nine...ten," she said and pulled the trigger, making sure she shot behind the hooves of the horse. She was thrilled when she heard the bullet hitting rock. She was certain he heard it too because he looked back, contemplating returning in the amount of time it would take her to reload. She pulled her pistol from her belt, and he turned his horse again and rode off.

"Of all the nerve," she muttered as she put the pistol back in her belt and began to methodically reload her rifle. She was still fuming as she prepared her lunch and thought again of that odd conversation.

CHAPTER SIXTEEN

Molly returned with the children, all of them looking refreshed and tired from their exertions. Erin greeted them happily. She had just finished the chores and was carrying the milk to the cabin when she saw the wagon.

"Have fun?" she called, putting the milk pails down. The cows were giving less and less milk as it got hotter and hotter, and she worried they would dry up. The family depended on the milk they gave for drinking, to make butter, and a host of other uses.

She heard a cacophony of answers as the children all tried to answer at once. The dogs joined in on the noise everyone was making as they jumped from the wagon, Erin helping the pups down one by one.

"It was wonderful," Roberts said, his shirt still looking slightly damp. The children all looked wrinkled but very clean, their hair in disarray. "We'd better be going."

"Don't you want to stay for dinner?"

"We would, but I'm sure Rebecca is waiting for us, and it's late. We do need to get home."

Erin understood and didn't try to convince the man. From the little she had gleaned, Rebecca was a bit touched in the head, and she didn't envy him. She wished him well as he saddled his horse and Alex got up behind him. They rode away with everyone waving them off as Molly started to unhitch the horses.

"Would you two take these in the house?" Erin asked Tabitha and Theodore. "We'll be in in a minute." She waved off the younger ones, who were still telling her what a great day it had been.

"They are going to sleep well," Molly said as they ran off. "So much enthusiasm. I bet they wore their feet down an inch or more with all the running."

"We had a visitor while you were gone," Erin began. She looked around to be sure none of the children were nearby to listen, then began to tell Molly about Graebel and his proposal. She told her exactly what they had both said while it was still fresh in her mind.

"Of all the nerve!" she stated, enraged at the idea.

"That's what I said," she snorted, finding it funny that she had said those *exact* same words. She could laugh now. She'd had the afternoon to think it over.

They discussed it a little more, realizing that it maybe wasn't so far-fetched and that others might make a similar offer or Tabitha would start getting courted. Women *were* scarce out here, and she wasn't that young to some.

"I won't consider allowing her to get married to anyone until she's at least eighteen!" Erin asserted.

"What if it's Theodore and he wants to marry at sixteen?" Molly asked, giving her a look.

"He will have to wait until he's eighteen too!" She had been about to shrug it off but realized Molly was making sure she wasn't being sexist about the situation. Boys tended to be allowed to do things before girls, and it was hard not to follow the norm of what others believed sometimes. She liked to think she was above that. That was a good reminder Molly had given her.

"We'll see about that," she contended, no longer outraged at that Graebel. Erin swatted her buttocks, surprised the dress was still damp.

They put away the horses, quickly brushing down their sweaty traces, feeding and watering them, before releasing them with hobbles behind the barn. Erin looked over at Molly and smiled. They were both clean, right down to their fingernails, and she could tell by the look on her wife's face that she was thinking about sex.

They closed the barn, shutting the animals inside. The dogs were able to get out by leaping through one of the windows into the pigpen and then jumping the split-rail fence if they wanted out, but the pups weren't big enough yet. Erin wanted to start letting people know they

had pups for sale including a bitch old enough to breed. Jenny had already come into her first heat and keeping King away from his own offspring had been difficult.

"Is that lightning?" Molly asked as they walked hand in hand towards the cabin, already able to hear the children squealing and calling loudly to each other.

"I hope it isn't *just* lightning. I don't want to worry about fire," Erin squinted above the hill to the west to make out what she hoped were storm clouds. They so desperately needed rain. She wasn't convinced the burn ring around the place would work, and the crops were going to be a total loss soon. Even the garden was suffering despite them watering it by hand.

Erin's prayers were answered during their cold dinner as they suddenly heard raindrops on the shingled roof.

"It's *raining*," a couple of the children called in wonderment, looking thrilled.

Erin got up to look out the back window, the glass getting splattered by the wet. The window was dusty and mud-streaked at first, but the mud was soon washed away as the rain came down in earnest.

"Oh, this is wonderful," she smiled as she looked at her sleepy children, knowing they would sleep well tonight from all their activity that day.

Molly sent them all up the ladder early that evening, instructing Tabitha to open the window upstairs slightly to let in the breeze from the rain and air out the hot loft. "Don't open it so wide that the rain comes inside. I don't want anything getting wet or mildewed up there."

Within fifteen minutes, Molly checked on the window as well as the children, who were sleeping soundly under sheets, their blankets neatly folded at the end of their beds. It was simply too hot to sleep with a blanket and the sheet would be enough. She looked at Tabitha for a while, worrying that some man would try to marry her daughter too young. She had been shocked by Graebel's offer, but she understood there were few women out here. She just wanted her daughter to have a chance to be a young girl for a while longer before she had the responsibilities of an adult.

"The children are so worn out, I don't think they could hear a herd of stampeding buffalo," she murmured as she came back down from the loft, smiling at Erin.

"Oh, really?" her wife responded, pleased with that news. Molly came right into her arms, wrapping herself around the taller woman.

"Did you want something?" she teased as she leaned down for a kiss, enjoying the fact she had her wife to herself. She felt good in her arms.

"Yes, I want...something," she murmured as she reached up for a kiss. It wasn't often they could be so impulsive, so affectionate, but tonight, the children were completely exhausted. She was tired too, but not so tired that she wasn't going to take advantage of this time together. The kiss captured her wife's warm lips and she immediately deepened it, her tongue licking to entice them to open, immediately fencing with Erin's slick tongue.

Erin smiled into the kiss, pleased to see this side of Molly. They were usually too tired from working hard or interrupted by children before they could indulge in the lovemaking they had taken for granted so long ago in Ohio. Being alone those first two years, they had learned a lot about each other as they experimented in their new love. Now, more established and parents to boot, they liked to think they knew what turned the other on. Their time was valuable, and they didn't have many opportunities for lovemaking, so they had to be happy with hasty couplings or interrupted lovemaking. Tonight, both sensed they wouldn't be interrupted and could indulge a little more.

Slowly, Molly maneuvered Erin into their bedroom area, bringing the lamp along and placing it on the bedside table. She would have blown it out except she liked the idea of seeing her wife as they made love. She liked the idea that they could take their time and wouldn't be interrupted by children. She'd thought about that out at the lake as she'd let the children get a wee bit too exuberant in their water play, indulging them as they wore themselves out. Roberts had been surprised that she didn't curb their enthusiasm, but Alex had enjoyed it too. Molly had a secret agenda, and now that it was coming into play, she was going to play too.

They undressed unhurriedly, helping each other out of their clothes and touching lightly, almost accidentally as they disrobed. The light of the lamp cast delicious little shadows on the planes of each other's bodies. Erin's body looked muscular despite her lanky frame and Molly's was curvy. Erin couldn't help herself as she reached out to touch, her hands cupping the roundness, smoothing her work-roughened fingers over her wife's body. Molly enjoyed feeling the sinewy muscles, remembering how Erin looked lifting a sack of grain, her body slightly sweaty from the hard work necessary on the farm. It was incredibly erotic to indulge slowly and without interruption in their explorations.

Molly reached around, feeling the muscles rippling under her fingers and hands as she caressed down to Erin's buttocks, her hands squeezing the taller woman closer to her.

"Mmmfh," Erin groaned into the kiss, her own fingers finding the roundness of Molly's body, wrapping a leg around her, so her slightly spread legs could grind at the apex against her wife.

"Oh, gawd. You're so wet," Molly breathed as she ground against that wetness.

"I've been thinking of you," Erin breathed in return, her breath quickening as she felt her wife's warmth against her naked body.

"I desire you so."

Erin stepped back slightly, looking down at the smaller woman. With a gleam of delight at the puzzled separation of their warm bodies, she picked Molly up in her arms and gently laid her on the bed, placing herself on top as she joined her, grinding down slightly as she indulged herself in the pleasures of the flesh.

"Oh, Erin," Molly breathed, thrilled with the sensations as their skin came into contact again. Momentarily confused until Erin picked her up, she enjoyed the helpless feeling for that moment, suddenly coming back into her own power as Erin couldn't seem to stay away and immediately covered her body with her own, the warmth between their bodies inflaming them both as they kissed, nibbled, and licked at each other.

Erin slowly kissed her way along her wife's neck, tasting the clean skin, scenting Molly's own unique essence, all the sweat and dirt washed away by her afternoon at the lake. She smelled wonderful and there was the distinct odor of her arousal tantalizing Erin's nostrils. She couldn't wait to taste it as she kissed her way down her wife's torso, stopping to tease each of the erect nipples before she caressed and kissed her way over the rounded stomach. Slowly, inexorably she made her way between her wife's outstretched legs, feeling the heat radiating from her center. She parted the folds, pulled back the hair, and took her first taste, kissing her wife lovingly.

Molly's breath began to come in gasps as she arched into Erin's hot mouth, feeling moisture pour from her body as she responded to her wife's ministrations. Her hands crept down to encourage her wife to go *there….*

Erin smiled into the kiss between her wife's legs, the wetness pouring down her wife's body. Her exploring fingers found the gush as she placed first one and then another finger within Molly's welcoming portal. She pressed in and up at the same time, able to tell by her wife's now clasping fingertips that she enjoyed the pressure she was exerting.

"Oh, God," she blasphemed as she arched into the sensations, her body slightly convulsing as she ground down into Erin's face.

"You like this?" Erin asked, teasingly, to be sure.

The muscles of the legs wrapped around her head locked as she held her in place and gave her the answer to her silly question. She couldn't hear for the thighs against her ears, but she smiled against her wife's wetness as she tasted, lovingly lapping at it. She was having a hard time breathing and indulging her wife by giving her the attention she deserved. She took a deep breath before going in again, holding it, so she could delve in, her fingers pistoning inside the woman beneath her. The muscles around her ears began to quiver as the feet against her back began shaking, the heels pounding tattoos against her back almost painfully as Molly began to lose control. Erin tried pulling back slightly to take another breath, but the muscles convulsed, not letting go and not allowing her a full breath before they pulled her in again. She was smothering…but what a way to go!

Molly pulled her hand back from where it was fisting painfully into Erin's hair. She suddenly realized what she was doing and let go to shove the back of her hand against her lips and smother the cries of pleasure. Despite their exhaustion, the children would have heard her if she wasn't aware on some level. She noticed her lips were freezing as the blood drained from them and centered around her middle where Erin's lips were working their magic. Her toes began to tingle as they too lost blood to the cause, curling painfully as the powerful feelings caused her to convulse. She shoved the back of her hand against her mouth, flattening her nose and making it hard to breathe as she fought against her need for the sensations Erin was triggering versus the need for oxygen. Somehow, she compromised and got both.

Erin was relieved when Molly's legs relaxed. Her back would be bruised from her wife's heels pounding on it. Her hair had been pulled painfully by one hand, and the other hand had dug its nails into her shoulder. She was pleased with all of it as she kissed her way up her wife's voluptuous body, covering its cooling skin with her own overheated body. Molly's legs fell to her sides as her limp body relaxed…but only for a moment. Molly suddenly wrapped her legs around her spouse again, rolling to put Erin beneath her and climbing onto her, grinding down to feel the residual orgasms as she worked to make Erin feel as good as Erin had made her feel. Erin smiled as Molly enthusiastically touched, caressed, and kissed her, leaning down

to give her intimate kisses between her legs as she had done to her wife. Suddenly, impulsively, as Molly leaned down, Erin turned her wife's body, so she was once again between her legs in a sixty-nine position, something they had never done before. She still wanted her wife's passions on her tongue, and she wanted Molly to kiss her *there* at the same time...

At first, Molly was surprised. She had never imagined they could both indulge at the same time. Molly suddenly liked how it made her feel. She was in control, and yet, the residual convulsions to her body meant she could continue to enjoy her own body's feelings. She indulged fully as she clasped Erin's body to her, her fingers digging into Erin's buttocks, pulling her mons closer to her face as she lapped at her center, feeling the surge of wetness against her nose. She let go of one buttock to plunge her own fingers within, hearing a slurping sound as Erin realized her own excitement. The splashing against her face was a surprise as her wife bore down and the wetness gushed out of her.

"Oh, my love," Erin moaned as she began to come, her body convulsing beneath Molly's, clasping the warm body against her, shaking and sweating and enjoying the sensations that only her wife's body and ministrations could give her.

"I could use another bath," she said a while later as they both lay replete from their lovemaking.

Giggling madly at the naughtiness they had indulged in, Molly went to get some water and clothes to clean them up.

Seeing her wife's curves wrapped in a towel to hide her nakedness, Erin wanted to start all over, but fatigue and an early morning won out.

CHAPTER SEVENTEEN

The rain saved their crops. It was the first of many regular rains that came late that summer, and they were able to look forward to gathering their crops. First, they cut hay and stacked it in the barn as well as around the barnyard. Everyone helped with the stacking, and Erin went with them to the lake once or twice but only when she could take the appaloosa. The children didn't focus on her bindings, but she pulled her shirt self-consciously away from her wet body as she came out of the water with the spotted horse, who couldn't buck that well in its depths. She didn't like it; she worried they would notice. She knew Roberts and his son would have noticed if they were there, but Molly told her she was worrying for nothing.

They now had one paddock. Erin cut poles and posts and dug post holes to place them in. The children helped put the rocks in the holes around them and make them firm.

"Come on, we don't want our horses or cows to get away!" Erin egged them on as they built it. It was not large, but it was strong. It was a very good beginning. It allowed them to finally remove the hobbles and let the horses roam freely behind the barn. Erin had even started a fence in a large area behind the barn, so the cows and horses could graze out there, but the rush of harvest halted that project.

"I was wondering if you wanted to trade work again this year?" Roberts asked.

"Sure, bring Rebecca and Alex over, and we'll have a fine time," Erin said gregariously.

"Um, I'm not so sure we should have Rebecca come, but Alex will be a help."

"Do you think leaving her there is a good idea? Maybe seeing Molly and the children would cheer her up."

"I don't know if anything would cheer her up," he admitted, looking extremely uncomfortable. He simply didn't know what to do for her. He'd tried talking to her reasonably, and he'd tried yelling, but nothing worked.

"Well, I'm going to begin cutting my wheat next week if the weather holds. I think it will be dry enough by then. Bring her that first day, and if that doesn't work out, you can do what you think best." It was the least she could offer. She didn't know what to say to the poor man. He was a good man, and he didn't deserve the lot life had given him.

"Will do," he agreed and rode home thinking about what she had said. He wondered if it would make any difference to Rebecca or if she was too far gone. She was a shell of the woman she had been when he had married her. Alex had asked him a couple of times why she was this way. "I don't know, son. I think these prairies turn some people mad because they can't handle the endless spaces and the rolling hills. Some people expand and grow out here. Others shrivel and..." he couldn't finish that sentence, but Alex was a bright boy and picked up on the inference. His mother was the kind that shriveled and would probably die. He didn't like the thought of losing his mother at all, but eventually, he would become resigned to it. For him, she had already been gone for a while. She was here physically, but the mother he had loved as a boy was long gone. The shrew she had become was the most memorable, but the shell of the woman she was now was nothing to him.

They started at the field nearest to the cabin and worked their way around the edges, cutting the wheat as close to the earth as possible to get as much of the stalk as they could. This wheat was valuable not only for its rich heads of grain but for the endless straw it provided. Tabitha had begun learning to weave. Her initial results were disastrous, but now, after repeated attempts, they had a couple of useful

baskets including some that were waterproof with a little bit of coating. They were planning to use several of her baskets to help with the threshing.

The bundles of wheat were made into teepees all over the field, shocks of grain put across the top to shed rain if it came up. Erin hoped to gather it as quickly as possible and avoid the rain completely. They had that fine floor in the newer part of the barn for threshing. She'd kept the animals out of there for a couple of weeks as she and the children swept and shoveled and cleaned it all. Molly had taken buckets of water and scrubbed it even cleaner. It practically shone and was ready and waiting for their grain to be threshed on its surface. Working in the hot, fall sun, she was now thrilled with the heat as it dried out the grain. By starting at the outside and working their way inward, anything that hadn't already dried out would be dry by time they got to it. The field, larger than last year, took more time.

King and his pack of pups were chasing birds, especially pheasants that were attracted to the ripening grain. They'd been unable to sell any pups in Sweetwater this year. Even after lowering the price, no one was interested. Erin, ready for the birds this year, had the shotgun filled with birdshot—smaller grained balls of lead. Alerted by the dogs' stance, she had it off her shoulder in an instant, the sling spinning it into her hands and ready as the dogs pounced at the birds. As the birds took off, she shot first with one barrel, sometimes both, and a couple times she was lucky enough to get pheasant for dinner. Calmly, she reloaded the gun, ignoring the shocked or stunned stares of her family, who hadn't been watching the dogs as closely as Erin.

"Fetch," she told the large dog and was pleased as the pups learned the word by watching their father. If they could learn not to slobber all over the birds, she'd be even happier with their progress.

Erin had decided to thresh *all* the grain this year before taking it up to Pendletown. It was too long a trip and she wanted to make as few trips as possible. Roberts had already volunteered his wagon. He needed smithy work done on it too, and they'd worked a deal for it against the work he was trading with Erin. They were going to help him harvest his much smaller field, and Erin would help him transport that grain with her wagon.

"Maybe Alex could drive my wagon this year, and I can start gathering my grain?" Roberts proposed, anxious to get it in, to get started. They'd stopped to grab a quick lunch in the hot sunshine.

"We can visit you then. Won't that be fun, Rebecca?" Molly tried to include the woman, who stared dully off into nothingness and didn't answer. Now, she'd do only what she was told: eat, sleep, use the outhouse. Embarrassingly, she'd had several accidents, and Roberts had been humiliated when he noticed Molly changed her clothes for her. She hadn't said a word to him about it, and Rebecca no longer spoke.

"If that's what you want to do, that would be fine," Erin agreed, wondering how they lived with the woman in that condition. She'd watch out for Alex, and if he could drive the wagon, that would help Roberts, who was anxious to start his own harvest. Molly and the children would certainly help Roberts with their harvest.

Roberts anxiously agreed as they went back to work and later headed home.

"Pa, may I come with you to Pendletown too?" Tabitha asked that evening, trying not to sound too eager.

Erin smiled, not fooled in the least. It wasn't Pendletown that interested the girl, it was the fifteen-year-old young man that enticed her on the trip. "Yes, you can go," she answered and got a hearty hug from the young woman.

"You are going to have to watch those two like a hawk. Don't let them sleep near each other, and..." Molly went on and on, instructing Erin what not to do.

"Molly, I've been a parent as long as you have. I know how to keep young lovers apart."

"Don't call them that," she objected, frowning at the word.

Erin laughed at her, and Molly realized she sounded like an overbearing wife and mother. She laughed. She realized Erin would do the best she could.

"You'll have to walk over to Roberts' place since we'll be taking both wagons."

"You're leaving the mare. I'll put the children on her back and ride the stallion," Molly informed her a bit spiritedly.

"Of course," Erin backed down, realizing her mistake.

It had been a good year despite the heat. Some of the kernels in the center of the field were a bit small, but that could be due to a variety of things besides just the drought. Erin hoped when the granary saw the quality of her wheat they wouldn't notice the smaller kernels since they were mixed in with the others.

The trip took a long time, even with both the oxen and horses pulling the very heavy and very full wagons. The trail was as undefined as the previous year, and it began to rain, making it even more difficult. Erin was grateful for the tarps across the beds of both

wagons keeping the bushel bags of wheat dry. She also had cages on her wagon that she had altered to hold a couple of the gangling pups. They weren't happy to be confined, but she didn't know how else to keep them without tying them up, and she had no other room in the wagon. The wheat was more important than these pups' comfort. She also brought Jenny, who sat with her on the wagon seat. Tabitha sat with Alex in the other wagon, and the other two pups were in the cages, one on each side. She'd combined the cages she had made for the geese so long ago, glad she had saved them and could use them again with only minor adjustments and repairs.

Erin was astonished at the prices she got for her wheat. Apparently, the drought had been widespread and not everyone had gotten the rains that saved her crops. She asked around to see if anyone was interested in the pups and surprisingly, she sold them both for the two-bit asking price she had started with, although she had been willing to be talked down. As they filled both wagons with her supplies, she tapped her foot, impatient to get back home from the three-day journey. The rain had made the hills dangerous, and they rode their brakes as the horses tried not to slip on the grassy tracks.

"Can I go see my pa and tell him we're back?" Alex asked as they pulled into the homestead yard, parking as close to the cabin as possible. Erin had known he was homesick for his own place, looking repeatedly to where they would have turned off as they passed the turnoff. She saw the mare, the stallion, and the appaloosa looking at them curiously from the paddock, which meant Molly and the children were around somewhere.

"Of course, just saddle my mare and go. If your pa needs you, let me know. Maybe he wants to go this next trip?" She laughed as the boy ran off and Tabitha looked disgruntled by his eagerness to leave. "Come on. Help me get these unloaded and into the house." She started to unload the supplies from the wagon, pleased when Molly and the other children came out to help.

"I'll bet we got forty bushels to the acre," she told Molly as they worked. "That's sixty bushels to the wagonload. We'll be transporting this for a long time," she said, anticipating an outburst.

"I thought I saw someone on our land," Molly admitted quietly as they put the supplies in the cabin. She intended to put them away neatly later. Right now, it was important to get everything under their roof and fill the wagons with the bushels of wheat to take on the next long trek north. She went on to explain she had thought the dogs were barking for no reason, but later, she thought she saw two men on horses riding east across their land.

"You had your shotgun nearby?" Erin asked unnecessarily. They both still carried a gun everywhere. It was not always convenient, but it was better to be safe than sorry.

"I did, of course," she answered, almost sounding indignant and then laughing at herself.

Erin couldn't worry about two travelers using her land to cross, but she did worry about her wife being alone with the children. They were all alone in this remote valley, miles from town. She wished Theo were a little older, so she could give him a gun too, but she simply wasn't ready to do that. That night, they hid the money that was left after buying supplies and selling the dogs, placing it under the pump in a box Erin had constructed. There were no banks out here, and Erin didn't trust banks anyway, not after what they had pulled on Molly so long ago. She remembered that a new bank had gone up in Sweetwater. Maybe they would put a little of the money in an account there.

"We're rich, if we can get all this to market," she whispered as they snuggled that night. She was excited and knew of one sure way to express that excitement. Despite her fatigue, she began to caress her willing wife, smiling as she heard the telltale sounds of arousal coming from her wife. Slowly, their bodies began to dance against each other. Molly lifting her nightgown as Erin began to unbutton her nightshirt, feeling the bare skin they revealed rubbing against each other. They had been kissing avidly, enjoying the feeling engendered in each, when they were rudely interrupted.

"Pa?" a voice asked from the darkened area beside the fireplace.

"We have *got* to get a wall and a door that *locks*," she whispered to a giggling Molly. "Yes, what is it?"

"Can I go with you to Pendletown this time?" It was Theo, and he sounded hopeful.

"I'll think about it. Now, you get back up to bed," she ordered and heard him on the ladder. Why she hadn't heard him coming down, she didn't know but then, she had been a little busy. "Now, where were we?" she asked a still giggling Molly.

"Oh, you think that is funny, do you?" she asked, delighted to hear her wife laughing.

"Why, yes, I do," Molly responded. "What are you going to do about it?"

"Make you laugh some more. You need laughter in your life," she answered with a corresponding chuckle of her own. Molly didn't laugh

long as the feel of Erin's skin against hers made her suddenly serious in her intent to gain pleasure from her wife and give it to her as well. Her teeth in Erin's shoulder told their own tale as Erin found spots that seemed to pulsate from her touch.

"Oh, my love," she breathed softly, not wishing to raise her voice as they indulged in an age-old display of passion. She knew the children had overheard them a few times over the years, but she didn't wish to draw attention to it unnecessarily if she could help it and muffled her groans of pleasure against her wife's pliant body.

"How do you know to do that?" Erin asked as Molly seemed to learn things instinctively, giving her so much joy and pleasure as they explored, indulged, and loved each other under their covers.

Molly smiled. If her wife could read her mind, she would know she wasn't always thinking of the tasks before her on the farm. She frequently thought of things they could do when they found time to be together like this. Frequently, these thoughts got her wet, and she'd had to put a rag between her legs on more than one occasion as she indulged in her salacious thoughts and ideas. Now, she could put them into action, and the wetness only enhanced both their enjoyment as she attempted to recreate her daydreams and bring to life those thoughts that had merely been ideas before.

"Oh, oh, ohhhh," she pushed her mouth against her wife's breast to keep from crying out at the enjoyment she was experiencing from her wife's incredible capacity for lovemaking. She barely managed to keep from biting the luscious flesh that was before her, indulging herself just ever so slightly. Her fingers dug into her wife's body, pulling her close against her as she convulsed.

Feeling the pleasure-pain against her own body as her wife came, she increased her efforts, her body looking for its own release as she ground against her, and together, they achieved nirvana.

CHAPTER EIGHTEEN

Roberts came back with Alex, who returned the mare the next day. "I've got to bring my wheat over here. There is nowhere on my place where I won't get dirt in the mix."

"Well, why don't you then," Erin told him as she continued to load sacks of grain in her wagon.

"But I'll need my wagon to do that," he answered, sounding worried. He'd heard the price that Erin had gotten for her grain and wondered if he would get his done in time to get it to market. So much depended on his crop.

"You got *all* your grain cut?" she asked, stopping for a second to look at him. She wasn't about to give up his wagon if she could prevent it.

"Nope, not yet." He was doing as much as he could as fast as he could, and Molly and the children had come over to help. As he had warned them, Rachel did nothing but sit all day in the cabin; she didn't even look at the children.

"Maybe by the time I get back from this trip we can bring your grain over here to thresh and bag?"

"That sounds like a plan," he said, enthused. "I'll help you load up."

"It'd be appreciated," Erin answered as they all worked to load the heavy bushels of grain. The younger children were of no use and were playing with the kittens. Tabitha and Theodore could, between them, pull a bag over to the wagon, but they could not lift it. Alex showed off for Tabitha by lifting the bags for them and fetching another himself. Erin grinned at his *enthusiasm*, knowing he'd be worn out that night despite his youth and strength.

"I better get going," Roberts said when both wagons were as full as they dared. The oxen and the teams of horses were each in use to pull the heavy loads. "Alex, did you say goodbye to your ma?"

"She wouldn't know…" he began, then realized how that sounded. "Sorry, Pa. Yes, I did say goodbye."

"I'll see you in a couple days," he told the youth as he left him to hurry home. Before he left, he looked at Molly, envious of Herriot. That woman was a keeper. He'd gotten to know her as they all harvested the grain. He was attracted to her but would never act on it. He was faithful to Rebecca, even if he couldn't reach her. It was his lot in life, and he would cling to his vows, if only to show his son how a man behaved. But it didn't keep him from envying Erin for having such a woman. Erin was a very unattractive man, and he didn't see what Molly saw in him. He was a good man, and he supposed that must be enough. He would try to be a good man too. "See you all later?" he asked Molly hopefully, unaware that he lit up a little just looking at the woman.

Erin saw the look. Molly, who was bringing out food for them to take on their trip, didn't see it as she looked at her husband and smiled. "Yes, we'll be over later to help," she called absentmindedly and handed Erin the foodstuffs. "Now, you two behave," she cautioned her and then smiled over at Alex. Theodore was going this time, so Tabitha could help with the harvest. Erin had them catch the other two pups, so they could try and sell them too. She waved as Alex chirruped to the horses, who were slowed by the lumbering oxen. He was keeping them to a pace as they headed out of the yard with their harvest of their precious seed. It was enough to make them all rich. She worried as she watched them slowly make their way up and over the hill and out of sight. Would they be able to keep up this pace of coming and going with the grain they all depended on? Already, Erin and she had enough to get them through the next year, but they hadn't even threshed Roberts' grain yet. They still had the oats to harvest and thresh as well as the barley and corn. She shook her head at the worry.

Erin was worrying too. She'd lain awake long after she made love to Molly last night, wondering what she was going to do about her harvest. They were very far away from the grain elevator in Pendletown and Sweetwater didn't have one. It was taking far too long to travel this distance, and they had barely made a dent in their harvest on this second trip. She wondered how long it would take to get it all in.

Erin decided to hire freighters for the third trip—men with wagons that could come to her farm and haul away the grain. For safety's sake, they would travel in a caravan or a wagon train together with the precious load. Apparently, Erin wasn't the only one in this part of the state with this problem. There were other farmers, who had gotten rain and prospered, and they were desperately trying to get their grain to market. There were many other farmers equally desperate to earn some money to tide them over until next year's harvest, and they were willing to hire out their teams and wagons to take farmers with grain to market. Erin hired several of them, having them follow her as she returned to her farm and they all pulled up in her yard to begin hauling the grain away.

"Erin, thank goodness you are finally back. I wondered if we would get my grain over here with the rains," Roberts greeted her when she returned. She was unpacking her supplies into the cabin and some into the barn. She'd also bought boards for building various things around the farm.

"Why don't we use my freighters and bring it all over here at once instead of using just our two wagons," she suggested. "Men," she got their attention as they unloaded the wagons she had her supplies in. "My neighbor here wants to use my threshing floor for his grain and needs to hire you to bring it over. It will delay us maybe a day, if that's okay with you? I'll pay you for your time," she offered generously, seeing Roberts becoming upset over the added expense. The men agreed and three of the empty wagons hitched up and followed the man back towards the Roberts' place. Already, there was a deeply rutted path between the two farms. In no time at all, the remaining three wagons, along with Erin's and Roberts', were heading over to load up the bundles of grain from the field into the wagons. They were careful not to shake the grain out of its husk as they placed the shocks in the wagons and then transferred them into her barn. Then, they loaded the wagons with the bushels of grain from the Herriots' harvest. There was still a little left as Erin once again left to make a trip to Pendletown. This time, Tabitha and Alex were both allowed to come.

Erin was pleased to pay off the freighters. Their language had been choice, and she was surprised that many of them were farmers. She'd protested their conversations, pointing out she had two young children and one of them a girl, who didn't need to be hearing that sort of language. The return trip hadn't been pleasant. She still frowned as she recalled what had happened:

"Careful, that's Herriot. Remember what Wallace said about him," one of the men cautioned another who was ready to fight Erin when she objected to his language.

"You know of me?" she asked, knowing the name Wallace well. He was the man who captained their wagon train from Missouri.

"Yeah, I've heard of you and that bear fight you had. He also broke some man's nose," he laughed as he told the tale to the others, who may or may not have heard it but would love to hear it again in any event. No matter how many times such tales were told, they enjoyed hearing someone else tell it. They could hear it a dozen different ways. Erin was embarrassed as she heard, yet again, the tale of her hitting a man upside the head with her rifle and retrieving her stolen cattle. Alex was all ears, impressed with the tale that he had heard at one time or another from Theo and Tabitha.

"Think you're tough, eh?" one of the men asked after the second day had ended and they were around the campfire. Someone had pulled out a bottle and they shared it around. Erin had refused to drink.

"Nope, not at all," Erin replied cordially. She couldn't afford to be in a fight, and they didn't know the other times had been accidents of fate. If they found out she was a woman, there was no telling what these men would do. They were coarse and rude people she wouldn't normally have chosen to associate with. It didn't matter that she had hired them to do a job. They hadn't been paid yet.

"Careful there, Carl. Remember his reputation," another of the men taunted. They kept it up until Carl was caught up in the teasing and attacked to save his dignity. Unfortunately, as he walked toward Erin to take out his perceived grievance, he stepped in a hole in the ground that his fuzzy mind didn't see. He lurched forward, and Erin tried to catch him, but her knee was coming up as she walked forward, and it caught him squarely in the face. She heard the crunch of his nose breaking. The other men hadn't seen the hole either and hadn't seen that he was falling or that she tried to catch him. Instead, they saw him lurch forward and it looked like Erin came toward him, her fists cocked, and she clocked him with a knee to the face. He was knocked

out and Erin had a terrible feeling of deja vu from the fight back in Missouri.

"Why don't you take your buddy over there and clean him up," she indicated the river they were camped alongside. The fire was a little too big as they held their fears at bay with the waste of good firewood. "You might want to set his nose before he wakes up." She turned away, disgusted.

"Why, that's my friend, and I won't have you–" began one of the burlier men. He stopped his charge and whatever he had been about to say when Erin turned and pulled her pistol from her belt. They had all seen the pistol and the ever-present rifle. A lot of men carried either or both. Erin also took the added precaution of pulling her knife.

"C'mon, you want some of this too?" she asked. She wasn't being polite. She was angry and sick of this bullying. "You know what you'll get now," she nodded towards where someone was cleaning up Carl.

The man saw the hole of the gun's barrel pointed at him, and he couldn't miss the shine of the blade in the firelight. He gulped and backed down immediately.

"That's it. I don't want to hear any more about it. The next man that comes at me is going to die," Erin promised. "I don't want you talking like that around my children anymore!" She went to sit down by her astonished children. Alex looked impressed. Erin didn't sleep well that night. She worried that someone would take her up on her threat and she'd have to kill them. She alone heard the moans of the hurt and drunken Carl. Fortunately, it didn't keep him from tending to his horses and driving his wagon the next day. He kept his eyes down or averted whenever Erin was around.

Erin was never so relieved to get all her grain weighed and paid for. She paid off the men, including their time for hauling the bundles of grain over to her place from Roberts'. It wasn't much, but this added money would help many of them make it through the winter.

"Let's get home," Erin told Alex when they were done.

"Don't you need supplies?" he asked, surprised. He had thought they'd go to the store here in town once again. Pendletown wasn't that big yet, but someday, it would be big as it grew from the agriculture around this area. Its stores were a lot bigger than the one in Sweetwater, and it offered many things that Laydin would have had to order special.

"No, we got enough for winter," Erin admitted. She just wanted to be gone and far away from the freighters she had hired. She knew they would talk, and she didn't want anyone else challenging her to show what a big man they were. Bullies like that were all over, and she already had a reputation, which was apparent from what happened. She didn't want any more violence. One of these times, she wasn't going to be so lucky.

Roberts' wheat took longer to thresh than they anticipated, but Erin made one more trip with Roberts and Theo. Tabitha didn't want to go anymore, especially since Alex wouldn't be going. He would be staying home to take care of Rebecca.

Erin thought about what Molly had told her. "She's pathetic. She does nothing but stare all day long. Sometimes she hums, rocking herself in a chair, but she does nothing all day."

"There is nothing we can do, and it's Roberts' decision what to do with her." She felt bad. She'd thought over their situation many times, but there was absolutely nothing more they could do besides helping him with his crops.

Erin was surprised at the supplies Roberts bought with the money from the sale of his crop. For the first time in two years, the man had an excess of money, and he spent it. It wasn't frivolous, but it also wasn't very judicious of him. There were things that he simply didn't need and was buying just to please Rebecca. She would never even realize they were there as she stared sightlessly off into nothingness, but Erin didn't interfere. There was very little that held appeal to her in the town, and she was pleased when they left. Helping Roberts unload the two wagons of supplies into his cabin, she was unnerved watching the woman sit and not reacting to anything. Erin returned home, the extra oxen and team behind her wagon. She was glad to be home and not have to worry about getting the rest of her wheat to market. It had been a lucky year. She still had the oats and the barley, but she wondered if she could talk Laydin into taking those. Maybe she would see what they could work out. It was a long way to Pendletown, and surely, she wasn't the only farmer in the area with crops.

She began to get in her oats and barley, the family stacking it in the barn to thresh it as they gathered the last of the field crops. As always, they'd leave the corn and beans for last.

CHAPTER NINETEEN

In the rush of getting the grain to market, Erin had forgotten the men Molly mentioned seeing on their land. One day, she took a break from threshing to ride out on the range. She took the big appaloosa, pleased with how she was coming along. Erin hadn't been sure about using the water trick that was explained to her, but it was working well. She now rode the appaloosa a little faster than the mare but not as intense as the stallion. Still, the horse's strong limbs were evident, and Erin could feel the muscles beneath her as she rode. She really enjoyed the ride, looking for Billy but not finding him that first day. Taking King the next day, she was determined to find the herd, wondering at the new births and if there were any missing after this hot summer and harvest. She had a couple of carrots in her pocket to give Billy as a treat.

She didn't find Billy that day either. She did find where the herd must have been not too long ago. She also found two horses, their backs riddled with saddle sores from wearing saddles for too long. Their reins were trailing and tangled in brush, which prevented them from getting away, and the bits prohibited them from eating, so they were gaunt. Looking for the owners in an ever-widening circle, the appaloosa shied away from what she eventually found.

It was the remains of two men. As Erin looked around trying to figure out how they had died, her first thought was wolf or mountain lion. It took a while to work it out, but the only tracks she found belonged to cattle. She wasn't certain, but it was possible that a big bull had done in these two men. What was left of them made it hard to tell since the crows had picked them nearly clean. Erin threw up her breakfast as she turned them over. Worms were already attempting to get their share of the corpses. Both men wore pistols that had been fired.

Erin took blankets from the backs of the two horses as well as ground sheets. She wrapped the men up in them and attempted to put them on the saddles of the horses. The horses balked at the putrid smell of the corpses, and Erin gagged again as she nearly lost parts of one of the badly decomposed men. Finally, she had them tied to the saddles and led the poor horses toward her appaloosa, who also shied at the smell that was now on Erin. She got back on the bigger horse and led them away. She wouldn't go to the ranch. Her children and wife didn't need to see this. No one needed to see this, and yet, someone would miss these men. She took them to Sweetwater and called to Laydin when she arrived in front of his store.

"We got an undertaker in town?" she asked. She could see people had noticed the two bodies on the horses when she rode in, and they came to see what was going on. Several of them could smell the decomposition emanating from the men's bodies. It was a hot, fall day, and the flies were following. The horses' tails were swishing madly to brush the flies away, but it wasn't working well. The horses shook their manes repeatedly, trying to brush the flies away that way as well. Flies could drive a horse mad.

"What do you got there?" he asked as he came out of his store.

"I found two men out on my range. I don't know what they were doing there. I don't even know who they are. They'd been dead at least a week or more. I think a bull gored them or something…maybe they were trampled." She'd had a lot of time to think during the miles from her ranch into Sweetwater.

"Yeah, yeah, the barber also has undertaker duties," he said, holding a rag to his nose as the scent of the bodies wafted up.

"We got a sheriff around here yet?"

"There's one up in–" he began, and others chimed in.

"Well, if someone could fetch him, I'd be grateful. He can come out to my place, and I'll show him where I found the bodies." She didn't want to stop too long. The smell was making her nauseous

again, and she didn't want to embarrass herself by throwing up in front of spectators. She led the horses over to the barber shop and helped the man unload the bodies. The poor horses were miserable.

"Who is going to pay to bury them?" the man asked. His name was Peyton.

"I have no idea," Erin admitted. "Doesn't the town have a fund for things like this?"

"Well, I gotta get paid, and then, there's the cost of the coffin."

"I didn't go through their pockets. You're welcome to any money you find on them. I'm going to put in for the horses and their gear, and anyone who wants to talk to me about that can come out to my place." Erin could use a couple more horses on her place. One of these was a gelding, the other a mare. The saddles had been fine once but would need a thorough cleaning after the corpses leaked on them and also from the horses' saddle sores. Erin was just glad to get away from the stink and back on her appaloosa, who could still smell the rot on her and shied away, making it hard to get in the saddle. Erin could smell it on herself all the way through the little town. People stopped and stared and pointed as they discussed things. Erin had been sweating the entire way, worrying and wondering what would happen. She was glad to get back to her farm.

First thing, she got the saddles off the poor horses. The saddle blankets were almost bonded to the damaged skin of both horses, the sores oozing and leaking into the material. Erin didn't want to hurt either of them. The children came out to see what she was doing, and she ordered Tommy, Theresa, and Timmy back in the house. Gently, she eased the blankets off the horses, one by one, using water to loosen the soaked material until she could pull it away.

"What is going on?" Molly asked when she came into the barn to see what Erin was doing and saw the sores.

Erin explained what she had seen and done as she worked. She used goose grease on their backs but knew that fresh air would be the best healer as she treated both horses. Molly helped her brush them down, their behavior suggesting it was probably the first for both. Erin and Molly were careful to avoid the sores as they rubbed them down.

"Hey, there. Hey, there," Erin crooned as she worked with the poor animals. She whistled, and both twitched their ears, the whistling probably another first for them.

"Who do you think the men were? Do you think it was the two men I thought I saw?"

"That was weeks ago...but maybe," she mused.

Letting the horses off their bridles, the bits gone from their mouths for the first time in who knew how long, they fell to voraciously eating the hay Erin put out. The other horses started to come over, smelling the new horses and checking them out from curiosity. A pecking order would eventually ensue.

"Do you think you can claim them?" Molly asked as she watched them eat.

"I don't know. I do know they are getting better treatment than they are used to. Look at those ribs."

When Roberts came over to ask about going after more horses, he was surprised to see her two new additions. "What's this I hear? In town, they're saying you killed two men trespassing on your range?" He smiled to show he was teasing, watching as Erin lifted split rails to add to the fences she was building.

Erin didn't find it amusing, even coming from someone she considered a friend. "I didn't kill anyone," she said tightly. "Are they saying I did?"

"Well, some are. I set them straight," he admitted. "You wouldn't kill unless you had no choice. I heard how they looked. Are you okay? What do you think happened to them?"

"I think they were killed by my bull," she admitted as she worked, not looking at her friend.

"Billy?" he confirmed. There wasn't another bull on her range, he just asked to make conversation.

She nodded, putzing to keep her hands busy. "I'm going to wait until they send for the sheriff, so I can answer questions, but yes, I want to go for horses. I think I'll eventually need more mares and a stallion. If not this year, next."

"Why another stallion?"

"Well, I won't be able to breed all of them with my black, and I don't believe in breeding back to the father like some do. Eventually, all the faults come out in the offspring," they continued talking about horses, breeding, and how much they might get for the horses. They even talked about taking them to Pendletown or even farther to get their asking price.

"Molly won't be happy with me for suggesting it," Roberts grinned unrepentedly.

"Molly won't be happy to have me underfoot mooning about going either," Erin added, laughing.

"Molly would like to go," she put in, having listened to the end of their conversation when she came into the barn as they were discussing

it. "Would you like to stay to dinner?" she turned to a blushing Roberts.

"No, no. I should get back to Rebecca. Alex is watching her now, but I like to be there."

"How is Alex going to cope when we go for horses?" Erin asked, looking at the man.

Roberts looked uncomfortable at the question. "Alex will watch his mother," he said, but he sounded sad at the thought.

"She's no better?" Molly asked softly, feeling sorry for their situation.

Dan shook his head. "Well, I better get going. I'll send Alex over in a few days to see if the sheriff was here and when you want to go."

"Tabitha would like that. She's been mooning after him," Molly told him, the three adults grinning at young love.

"Maybe I'll send her over to tell you," Erin countered his offer.

"Either way, those two will be happy for the chance to see each other," he answered as he went to get back on his horse. "Hey, you see any strange cats?" he asked after he mounted.

"Yeah, we did, last year. Why?" Molly answered for them both.

He told how three cats had attacked them in his barn. They'd evidently been living in there for a day or so, but he had shot one and the other two took off.

"Black and white cats? Obviously of the same litter?" Molly asked, to identify them.

"Yeah, that was them. I'm glad you told me to always have a gun near. The one I shot was a big son of a–" he left off, realizing his female company. "Anyway, she's dead, but the other two took off."

"There were four of them when they attacked here. Between Molly, Theo, and our cats, they were chased off, but Theo got some scratches." Erin shook her head, having thought that was the last of them.

"Think they were rabid? I've heard of skunks being rabid, and racoons maybe, but not cats."

"Anything that gets bit can get it, but no, I think these are just territorial cats looking for a place. Wherever they came from, they want something a little more domesticated but don't know how to be sociable."

They said their goodbyes and watched as Roberts made his way down their driveway. "I was just thinking…" Molly said quietly.

Erin put an arm around her wife. "What about?"

"We have a regular road to our farm now," she indicated the path Roberts was on with his horse, riding west so he could make his way to his own farm.

"It's a farm today?" Erin teased.

"Well, if you get some more horses and start breeding them, then it's a ranch."

"If I plow some more land and plant crops, it's a farm," she countered, both grinning at their joke.

"You raise cattle, it's a ranch." They shared a laugh.

"You, Herriot?" the big, burly man asked from his sway-backed gelding's back. He had a badge pinned on his shirt and his gut hung over his belt.

"You the sheriff?" Erin countered, not sure she was going to like this fellow.

"I understand you brought two bodies in to Sweetwater the other day."

Erin nodded, her hat bobbling on her head, and adjusting it angrily. "Yep, that I did. They were badly decomposed. I probably should have buried them where I found them, but I was hoping someone could identify them. I want to make a claim against their horses and gear since I found them out on my property."

"You said they were gored by your bull?"

"Who said that?" she asked, trying to remember who she had told.

"I'm not at liberty to say," he said, sounding pompous.

"Well, I never said *my* bull gored 'em. I said *a* bull gored them."

"You got a scary bull, I hear?"

"He ain't scary," she countered, angry at the implication that her bull had killed the men. She was sure it had, as it was the only bull on that section of range, but she was sure he had good reason.

"I heard of the bet you had. One of the men was—," he gave the name, but it rang no bell for Erin, who looked at him blankly. "The other man's name was Graebel." At this name, Erin realized who he was.

"Yes, I know that man. He was interested in my bulls and lost the bet. He came back to the ranch and wanted to make an offer for my daughter."

"He did, eh?"

"That's right. I told him no."

"Why'd you tell him no?"

"Because she is only twelve years old."

"Yeah...so? He wasn't good enough for her?" he sounded like that was a perfectly reasonable question.

"She's too young."

"Girls that age get married all the time."

"I heard that," she admitted but wasn't about to debate it with the man.

"I see we have a visitor," Molly said as she came up. She had seen the man arrive in the yard and she suspected who he was.

"This is my wife, Molly," Erin said proudly.

"Mrs. Herriot, ma'am," he said, making a gesture of saluting her with his hat but not removing it.

"Would you like some coffee, Sheriff?" she saw the badge.

"No, no. I'm here on *official* business."

"Oh, yes, those two men Erin found. Terrible wasn't it?"

"Yes, ma'am," he agreed, a little flustered by this woman. With the dark good looks and the long lashes, she was a very pretty woman. He looked back at Herriot, wondering what she saw in this tall, lanky man.

"You want me to saddle up and take you where I found them?" Erin asked, not liking the way the man stood admiring Molly. Molly was hers and....

"Yup, if you would," his tone changed from respectful back to slightly intimidating.

Erin saddled up the appaloosa and calling King along, she put double boots on the saddle.

"You won't be needing those," the sheriff told her, sounding resentful.

"You might not, but I don't go out where I might need them and not have them. It takes too long to reload when you need them."

The sheriff had to admit that Herriot was right, but he didn't have to like it. He made a grunt of dissatisfaction.

Erin led the way, but she was sure the sheriff held back because he wanted to keep an eye on her. She was also certain his poor horse couldn't carry his fat body too quickly. The appaloosa ate up the ground under her long legs with King keeping up effortlessly. When they got to the area, Erin started to cast about.

"What are you doing? Didn't you say you knew where you had found them?"

"Yeah, it's around here but it's been a while," she returned, looking about at the long grasses and watching King to see if he smelled anything. She made a gesture as though he were to round up the sheep and he began to circle around.

"What's that for?" he asked, seeing the dog head off.

"I'm hoping he'll herd any cattle in the area, so I know where they are and don't get myself gored."

"I thought you said your bull ain't scary."

"He isn't. However, there are other cattle out here, and maybe they will mind us being here," she added as she looked for the bushes the horses had been tangled in. She found them and then got off her horse to show the sheriff where the bodies had been strewn on the ground.

"You sure you didn't have a problem with Stewart?"

"Who?"

"The man you brought in?" he asked, his tone sounding angry at what he perceived as Erin's games.

"Oh, yeah, you mentioned his name. I don't know anyone named Stewart."

"The others say you do."

"What others?"

"The ones you had the bet with."

"Someone thinks I killed these men over the bet?"

"Or because he was angry over you not selling him stock at some point."

Something began to click for Erin. "This Stewart fella, he come out on a wagon train a couple of years ago?"

"That's him," the sheriff confirmed.

"Now, I know who you mean."

"Apparently, you broke his nose at one point?"

"That was an accident," she told him honestly, "and yes, I wouldn't sell him stock that I needed to get out here with my family. Apparently, he held a grudge."

"Well, I don't see no sign of them," he pointed where Erin had shown him.

Erin saw King returning, looking for instruction, and she signaled him to come in. He hadn't found any cows or sheep or anything to herd in the vicinity. "Well, of course you don't. Enough time's gone by that anything left behind would be picked over by the birds and other creatures." Not everything was gone though. The Sheriff found a button off one of the men's shirts.

"This yours?" he asked, picking it up from the grasses.

"Nope," she shook her head. "I haven't seen it before."

"Looks like it could be off one of those men's shirts."

"Could be. Makes sense. They were pretty torn up."

"Hmmph," he said, snorting through his nose.

Erin stood there, watching as the sheriff made a thorough search, looking for anything else he could find. It took a long time and she spent her time looking around, liking the rolling hills, the beautiful sunshine, and…what was that noise?

King heard it too and cocked his head. "Um, Sheriff? I think you better get back on your horse," Erin called, backing away from the site and heading for the appaloosa. "King, come," she ordered the dog.

"Why? You see something?" he said, looking up. It was then he saw the cattle. They were moving quickly, almost as though something were chasing them. He began to run towards the horses, his stomach flapping with each stride, his legs getting tangled in the long grasses as he loped over them.

Erin got up on the appaloosa and just stayed there behind the brush, hoping if the cattle ran this way they would be split up. King sat watching at the feet of the horses, his tongue hanging out as though he were laughing. The sheriff sat his horse on the other side of Erin, his chest heaving from the exertion of running and getting back on his horse. He was wondering why Herriot didn't move. It was then, he saw the huge bull that everyone had been talking about. He really was impressive. He could see why one of the men he talked to wanted to mount the head. As the cattle got closer, Erin started to whistle loudly.

"What's that in aid of?" the sheriff asked her, but she shook her head, still whistling.

The cattle had gotten closer and whatever had started them running, was no long scaring them, so they slowed down. Only a few cattle passed them by before they stopped running, began walking, and then started to graze. Erin watched the herd as several others slowed and started grazing. Her whistling didn't stop, and Billy looked towards the sound. After a while, several others joined him, and he began to amble his way towards the brush. It was obvious he remembered the spot as his head went down like a dog and he sniffed around the area, still watching the people on the horses.

"Billy boy, you smell something?" Erin crooned to the bull. He lifted his head from the ground, filing away details that only he or King could fathom. She whistled again, a monotonous tune that brought the bull towards them again. The sheriff's horse side-stepped, and the appaloosa followed suit. "Hold my horse?" Erin asked the sheriff, getting off and handing him the reins.

"Wha–" he began, but the farmer had walked away. He headed towards the enormous bull and started whistling again. He only stopped when he was within arm's reach of the dumb animal.

"Billy boy, what have you been up to?" she asked as she reached to pet him. He looked fine, but she could see some healing marks on him. He'd been scratched up somehow. He was missing hair along his side, and she petted and scratched him as she examined him. He didn't move, chewing his cud as he half closed his eyes, enjoying the scratches. A couple of cows had followed him, also drawn by the whistling human. They'd stopped to watch and fell to cropping the grass, their tails flicking away flies in the afternoon sunshine.

The sheriff couldn't believe his eyes. That was the largest bull he had ever seen, but Erin didn't seem concerned, and the bull was enjoying her attention. He looked at the horses, noticing they were both unfamiliar with the beast and agitated. He looked down at the dog, who didn't seem concerned in the least. He looked like he was enjoying himself. The sheriff looked up in time to see Erin finish her examination and petting of the bull and signal to the dog, who got up and made his way up to the bull, wagging his tail. They extended their noses, both snuffling a greeting.

"Billy boy, you behave yourself," she told him as he exhaled, blowing snot all over the dog, who was sniffing just as avidly. King pulled back slightly, his tail still wagging. Erin finished scratching Billy, patted him a final time, and then ducked as he turned his head and his long horn came around. "Easy, boy," she told him as she turned her back to him and walked away towards her horse.

"That is some bull," the sheriff admired as she took the reins and mounted up.

"Yep, he's a sweetie," she said nostalgically, remembering how small he had been when he was born. He was one of the few links to her father when he had been alive. They hadn't been sure he was worth saving and look at him now. She watched as he rejoined the cows who had been brought out from Ohio. They all eyed the humans before falling back to the grasses.

"I can see why people want bulls out of him or to breed their cows with him."

"Yep, I can too. Although that man I spoke to about breeding his cows to Billy never came back."

"Oh, Billings. He went under and had to leave," he told her.

"Leave? What about his cattle?" she asked as they started away, the bull staring after them. Erin whistled, and King began to run after the horses.

"I have no idea what he did with them, but I know he just couldn't afford to stay."

Erin looked back at the herd, now chewing placidly. She wondered what had set them running in this direction and towards this exact point. "Hey, do you mind if we take a little more of a ride?" she asked suddenly.

"Um, no, but this is taking a lot longer than I had thought it would."

"You thought I killed those men, didn't you?"

"Not from what the barber and Laydin told me, but I had to meet you. I had to be sure." He realized this tall, lanky man wasn't as dumb as he first thought upon meeting him. He had to be smart to bring all these animals west with him, and even he could see that the cattle were prospering. There were yearlings and even younger cows in the herd, and he'd seen the fields the man had plowed. He was a hard-working man and that raised his respect for him. As they turned around and headed well around the grazing herd, he asked, "Where are we going?"

"Well, cattle don't run unless they have a need to, like they been spooked," Erin said as they headed back on the path the cattle had taken, which wasn't hard to determine since the grasses hadn't yet sprung back after being trampled by their hooves.

The sheriff realized the truth of that, and he settled himself into his saddle, feeling the ache of his years and riding on, wondering what they would find.

Erin could tell where the cows had been grazing. It was obvious: the grass was eaten, there were cow pies, and there were even some spots where the cows had lain down to chew their cud and relax. But something had startled them into running towards where Erin and the sheriff had been investigating.

"Do you even know what you are looking for?" the sheriff asked as Erin rode back and forth in ever-widening circles.

"Tracks. If a wolf scared them or–" she didn't voice her suspicions aloud, but when she saw the shod hooves, she knew she was on to something. "Did you have a deputy out here?" she asked, looking up at the overweight sheriff. "Maybe someone who came out here to investigate first?"

The man shook his head, puzzled. There were very few out here who would take this low-paying job, but he had thought it would be a cushy job and he could sit in his office most days and read the few newspapers that came in from the coast. Only occasionally, he had to arrest a lawbreaker and take him up to the jail because his own office didn't have a jail.

It was getting late in the day and Erin would have just settled in for the night, but she could see the sheriff was getting uncomfortable. And he still had the ride from her ranch to Sweetwater and on to wherever he resided.

"I think someone scared those cattle deliberately. There may have been a third man and he saw what happened to his partners."

"What makes you think that?" the sheriff asked suspiciously, wondering if Erin was just trying to deflect from her own participation in the crime.

Erin showed him the shod hoofprints that looked vaguely familiar to her. After shoeing horses around this area, she recognized some shoe marks, but she wasn't positive yet. They followed the tracks to an outcropping where rocks had been pried away and thrown at the herd. They found the rocks among the shorn grasses.

"See, this one fits," Erin showed the sheriff because he had scoffed at her theory. The rock fit right back in where it had been pried out. The sheriff was beginning to believe her.

"You see where the horse goes off that way…" Erin said, her heart beating as she realized where it headed…not farther into the mountains, but west towards the two farms and Sweetwater. "Well, I think there was someone else out here," she said, dusting off her hands and mounting the appaloosa.

"I'll have to find this person and see what they know."

"I'm going to head back to my place. You know where to find me if you have any further questions."

"Yep," he said, nodding and resigned to spending the night out. He had hoped to find a bed back in Sweetwater, but this had turned out to be more of an investigation than he anticipated. He watched as Herriot rode off, sitting almost ramrod straight on the appaloosa until she kicked it to go faster, the dog easily keeping up. It was getting dark. He should probably go back to the ranch with Erin and sleep in his barn, then start the investigation again in the morning, but he was curious now that Erin had made him aware someone else was involved. He followed the tracks while he could still see them. They stopped for a time at a rise. He got off his weary horse and ground hitched it. Following what were obviously boot tracks, he walked to the top and looked over. He wasn't surprised to see the herd down below, settling in for the evening. He recognized the brush Erin had shown him where

the horses had been found, and he could see the cows were avoiding the spot where the two men had met their demise, probably put off by flies, residual smells, or maybe even worms.

That night, the sheriff made camp just north of the ridge, out of line of the tracks he was following, hoping they would still be visible in the morning.

"Well, does he believe you now?" Molly asked as Erin unsaddled the appaloosa and picked up a brush to clean her with. She'd seen Erin ride in, and of course, the dogs barked to welcome both their master and King home.

"I think so," she said hesitantly. "We found the place, and I showed him where I found the bodies." There was something in her voice though that had Molly asking further questions.

"But...?"

Erin should have known her wife would detect what she wasn't saying. She smiled slightly as she applied the brush to the horse's flank. "Someone set the herd on us. Unfortunately, they miscalculated, and the herd settled down before they got to us." She chuckled as she said, "I showed the sheriff how friendly Billy can be."

Molly smiled, shaking her head. As a bull, Billy was incredible. As a puppy, he failed. She would think twice before approaching him now. Back on the farm in Ohio it had been different.

"We followed the path of the running herd, and we saw where they had been grazing and found some tracks nearby. Someone threw rocks at the herd to startle them and get them running. Then, they rode off."

"Where?" she asked, her dark brows beetling in perplexity.

"Back this way but on towards Roberts' land. They must know that area because they sure seemed to know where they were going."

"We should warn the Roberts."

"I think the sheriff will."

"What'd he say about those horses?" she indicated the two in the corral they hadn't had too long.

"He said if no one came forward, they are mine."

"Did you go through their saddlebags?"

"Yeah, I was hoping to find out who they were. There wasn't much there, so they hadn't planned to be out too long. There was nothing to identify who they were. The sheriff told me they were Graebel and Stewart." She stopped to look at Molly and see if she recognized the names.

"Wasn't Graebel the one that wanted to marry Tabitha?" she frowned as she remembered. It had been distasteful to her.

"Who wanted to marry me?" Tabitha asked, coming into the barn and hearing her parents talking.

"How long have you been standing there?" Erin demanded angrily. She didn't like it when the children eavesdropped.

"Long enough. Who wanted to marry me?" she asked again, looking from one parent to the other.

Erin exchanged a look with Molly, who nodded slightly and said, "One of those men who bet with your pa over the bull."

"One of those old men?"

"Not so old," Erin put in, wanting to laugh.

"But...but, they were so grown up," she put in, proving Erin's point that she was still a child.

"Apparently, that didn't matter," Erin added, not wanting to hurt her daughter's feelings, but wanting to be truthful all the same.

"And you said no?!" she confronted her father. She sounded outraged.

"You wanted me to say yes?" she asked her daughter. "As your pa, I felt I should say no since you didn't even know him."

"But couldn't I have at least met him?" She was flattered that someone wanted to marry her.

Erin glanced at Molly again. She looked ready to jump into this conversation. "He didn't even know your name."

"But we could have gotten acquainted at least." She sounded like a little girl not getting her way.

Erin was sick of it already. She'd made her decision, and the man was dead. She really didn't want to hurt her daughter's feelings; however, she needed to be taught her place. "He wanted to marry you to claim six hundred and forty acres adjoining our ranch. He didn't want to live with you. He suggested you would continue to live here with your ma and me. Is that the kind of man you would have wanted me to give you to?"

She only thought about it for a moment, then shook her head. As she thought more about her pa's words, she was suddenly angry. She was glad that man was dead. If her pa had given him to her, she'd be a widow now. What would have happened to that land the man wanted? She'd have nothing to show for the marriage. Suddenly, she was grateful her pa hadn't given her to that man. Impulsively, she hugged Erin, who looked at Molly, startled. "Thank you, Pa. I'm glad you

didn't give me to that man. He wouldn't have made a very good husband."

Erin hugged her back, noticing how tall she was getting. At thirteen, she was filling out too. Molly had confided she'd had her first period. "I only want what's best for you young'uns. You know I'd never let you get into a bad situation I could prevent."

She nodded, giving her a squeeze before she let go. "I know, Pa," she admitted, and smiling at them both, she left them alone in the barn.

Molly looked to see that the girl had headed back to the cabin. Standing up again, she asked, "That other name, what was it?"

"Stewart?"

"Why does that name sound familiar?"

"It didn't sound familiar to me until the sheriff told me he had been on the wagon train and he'd also been in on the bet."

"Now, I know who he was!"

"Well, I don't know what their plans were, but Billy took care of it for us."

"But there was a third man involved?"

"That's the sheriff's lookout, not mine," she answered, but still, something about it made her uneasy.

CHAPTER TWENTY

Erin rode over to the Roberts'. It wasn't as fine as her homestead, but she could see where they were trying. He was using the sod-breaking plow and both yokes of oxen again to enlarge his field. He wanted to keep it going for as long as possible. He hadn't had oats or barley to harvest and was using his remaining time this fall to expand his field.

"Do you need your plow back already?" he asked. He'd only had it a week, but in that time those two sets of oxen had plowed up an incredible amount of land. Their strength was phenomenal. He wished he could buy the offspring the two of them had last spring.

"No, not at all. Have you taught Alex to use them?" she asked from where she sat on the appaloosa.

He looked almost guilty at that question. Stopping the teams, he stood chatting with her, worried that she wanted them back. "No, to be honest, I wanted to do this myself."

"I hear you," she understood. He'd know it was done right if he did it himself, and what a sense of accomplishment that would be. "I was wondering if you wanted to work with me? I know of some abandoned cattle and thought I'd round them up and push them out on my range. I could use some help, and I thought you could use the money for the work."

"Why don't I go in on shares?" he asked, suddenly eager for the idea. He needed stock on his range too.

"Because I know where they are, and I'd rather pay you wages. If you don't want to do that, I understand."

With wages, he would at least make sure they had plenty of supplies for the coming winter. They'd been lucky that they were having a nice, Indian summer. The thought of snow was long off and nothing in the air indicated snow was coming any time soon. He'd taken advantage of that to plow as much as he could get in. He did owe Erin for borrowing her oxen teams and the plow, and he felt guilty thinking about refusing, but he did have a fourteen-, nearly fifteen-year-old son that could do the work while he went. Thinking it over, he nodded. "When were you thinking of going?"

"As soon as you can get ready. Molly knows where we'll be and is okay with it."

"You aren't going to plow your fields?"

"Actually, I don't think I will until spring. I noticed they are eroding into the creek, and I don't want that. Leaving them unplowed over the winter, the roots of whatever I planted will hold the dirt in the fields where I want 'em."

That made sense, and he nodded, realizing Herriot was a better farmer than he would ever be. He sighed. "I'll go get Alex."

"Why don't I tell Alex you've decided to go with me, and you can continue plowing while he gets your horse ready and packed up for you?"

"That's a good idea. Maybe I can get this small section done before you both get back."

"How'd you find out about the abandoned cows?" he asked as they rode along on the other side of Sweetwater.

"Sheriff told me. If I lay claim to the cows that he wanted to breed to my bull, there isn't going to be anyone to stop me."

"What if I had insisted on a share?" he asked, visibly uncomfortable and Erin could see it.

"Since you agreed to come with me, I thought you were working for wages. If not, tell me now. I don't want to lose your friendship over this," she told him firmly, stopping her horse to stare him down.

"I'll work for wages," he confirmed, stopping his own horse but feeling some resentment building.

"Maybe we will have time to hunt for horses when we get back?. We made some good money that way last year."

"That we did," he agreed. "That we did."

It took some riding to find the spread that Billings had abandoned. He hadn't been a farmer, and Erin was surprised that no one else had come for the cows. There was a scruffy-looking bull among the few cows, and they searched quite a ways looking for them. The cattle that had stayed close by plus the few King found only amounted to about a dozen in total, and they herded them back towards Sweetwater.

"H'up, h'up, cows," Erin said as she slapped her leg and herded them to the road that would take them to the ranch. She mentally laughed at herself for thinking of it as a ranch instead of a farm. She didn't think paying Roberts for the small round-up was worth it, so she suggested he help her with the branding. She'd heard that more and more ranchers were branding to identify their cows. Her own cows were notched, something she had done back in Ohio to identify them as their cows, but branding seemed to make sense now. Alex could continue to plow, and they could herd these cows with hers and release them together, so Billy could keep an eye on the herd. There were offspring she hadn't notched, and the branding would at least identify all of them as Herriot cows.

"I'll meet you in a few days. I have to fire up my forge and make a brand."

"Don't you have to register that brand too?"

"I'll do that next time I'm in Sweetwater. They can send it on to the county seat."

Erin paid him two whole dollars for his time, and he nodded as he headed back to his place. She put the few new cows on the hill behind the barn with King to keep them in line.

"That's all there was?" Molly asked as she came outside to see Erin firing up the forge.

"Yep, wasn't really worth it to pay Roberts."

"Still, it's a start, and if they were truly abandoned...."

"I don't think Roberts liked working for wages. He wanted a share of them."

"There isn't enough to parcel them out, is there?"

"Still, he could have sold them or butchered them out. I just want to get them out on the range."

"Why are you firing up the forge then? Why aren't you pushing them out by Billy?"

"I want to make a brand for our place, something that will identify our stock as Herriot cows."

"How will we be able to tell?"

Erin hunkered down and drew an H in the dirt. "What do you think of that for a brand?"

Molly looked at it a moment and then put a line across the top and another line across the bottom. "Isn't that how they make an eight?"

Erin had to admit she was right. There were people that would make a brand and then alter it. There were things called a running iron that would make it easy. So much for quickly making a brand. "How about this?" she asked, making the H again with an E next to it.

"I think you should make something with a curl to the letter, so it makes it harder for them to alter it." She showed Erin what she meant, making the H and E in cursive and interconnected.

"My, that's fancy," Erin said, pleased with the idea.

"Can you make that with your iron?" Molly asked, pleased that her *husband* had consulted her; most would not have.

"I think I can make anything with enough time and practice. I'm going to make two, so Roberts and I can get those cows branded first." She nodded to the few cows on the hill. "Later, I'll bring in Billy and his herd. Those calves are large enough to brand, and there are a few yearlings."

"Won't you have to pay Roberts for his time?"

"Of course, but I'll be able to trade some of it for the use of the oxen and the plow."

"Wish we could just let him have some of that to be neighborly."

"We do. He helps us, and we help him. That *is* being neighborly."

"Still, not expecting anything in return is more neighborly. I wish we could help him with Rebecca somehow."

"She just wasn't strong enough for this life," she admitted sadly, getting up and looking at the brand Molly had come up with. The script writing made a difference.

Molly watched for a while as Erin prepped the forge, using a homemade bellows to get the coals hot and ready for the iron she slipped into them. It took a while and the children made an appearance to watch too. It was fascinating to watch, but when the hammer began striking the iron, the noise caused a couple of the children to go off and play elsewhere.

Slowly, Erin bent the hot iron to the shape she wanted, glancing frequently at the dust where Molly had written the letters. She cursed when the children unknowingly walked in it and scattered the dust, but her memory was good enough that she shaped the letters from the red iron and then plunged it all into water to cool it. She did this repeatedly until she got the shape she wanted. It took her many hours to make two that looked identical. She tested them both by burning the iron into large wood chips.

"My, doesn't that look fine?" Molly said when she returned to see how Erin was doing. It was getting quite late. She'd hung one of the wood chips on the wall.

"Your idea," Erin gave her all the credit and smiled. It did look good, and she was proud of her work. "We need to register it too."

"How do you do that?"

"Well, I think you are supposed to go to the county courthouse, so no one else can register the same brand."

"Do we have a county courthouse?"

"I don't think so. I'd like to find out how to register it as soon as possible though, so if anyone steals more of our cows, we can at least set the sheriff on him."

"More of our cows?"

"Remember Jacob Marlow?" she asked, and that name had Molly remembering back to Missouri. She'd been very scared when Erin had gone to retrieve the missing cows. Then, the town sheriff had come out to accuse Erin of not only stealing her cows back but striking the man, which she had.

"What if they already have brands on them?"

"Well, if I bought any with brands on 'em, I'd put my brand below them. If you put it over them you are trying to hide the original brand and people can tell. Depends on how old they are."

"How do you tell?"

"Skin the animal. From the back side, you can see when someone burns over the old brand."

"Doesn't it hurt the animal?"

"Yep, but only for a while."

"You think someone was trying to steal our cattle when Graebel and Stewart got trampled?"

"I think they were trying to steal Billy, and he wasn't having any of it. That's what I think."

Molly had to admit that was plausible. Billy could be quite disagreeable. Even she, who had known the bull for years and used to feed him from her own hands, was now scared of him. She didn't know how Erin got past those huge, deadly horns.

Roberts rode into the yard early in the morning a day later. It was getting a little cold and a little rainy, signifying that fall and winter weren't far off and the Indian summer they were enjoying was coming to an end. Roberts was annoyed. He had wanted to go for horses, and now, he was helping Erin with her cattle. He'd spent all day yesterday pulling wood from his own groves of trees for winter while Alex continued plowing with the oxen. He'd instructed the boy to keep at it, so they could have the maximum amount of their field plowed for next year's planting. The boy was tired but game.

"We'll practice on these," Erin said, nodding towards the hillside where the cattle and sheep were intermixed.

"Practice?" he asked.

She showed him the two irons she had made and the burn marks in the chips. Even he had to admit it looked nice.

They brought one cow down to test out the brand. They used the hot fire that Erin made in the forge to get the end of the brand red hot. They tried to wrestle the cow to the ground, finally realizing the futility of wrestling with a full-grown animal. They finally decided one of them would hold the cow while the other quickly applied the hot tip to the cow's hide on the left shoulder. The smell of singed hair and skin was horrible, and the bellows of the cow were sad. It was also dangerous to whoever was holding the cow as she lunged away. However, it looked fine when they were finished with her, so they released her and went to get two more. All that morning, they branded the few cows, and when they were done, they had only the scrub bull to brand.

"I don't want this bull to breed with my cows," Erin admitted as she applied the last brand. "I'm going to sell him."

"Why not give him to me?" Roberts asked, feeling resentment that Herriot wouldn't share the cattle with him.

Erin looked at him in surprise. "You don't have any cows to breed him to, and I thought we agreed I would pay you a daily wage?" She felt uncomfortable now.

"I did agree to that," he admitted in a defeated voice.

"Let's go get the other herd. We'll tie this fellow up here," she told Molly, who had come out to bring them both something to eat. Roberts ate as though he didn't get regular meals.

"I could take him into town and look into registering the brand," Molly told her. "I need to get a few things at Laydin's Mercantile anyway."

"If you don't mind doing that, it would be a great help." She smiled at her wife, pleased with how self-sufficient she was. She caught the look Roberts was giving Molly and frowned. She could see he was comparing her to Rebecca and coming up short on his end. She turned away and saddled up the appaloosa. It was stronger than the other mare, and she didn't want to ride the stallion because his gait wasn't that smooth. She enjoyed the power of the muscles in the larger appaloosa.

"Ready to go?" she asked Roberts, who was helping Molly hook up on the wagon. It annoyed her. She should have helped her wife. She tied off the appaloosa and went to tie the bull behind the wagon for her. She saw the children coming out and swung Timmy into the bed of the wagon followed by Theresa. But when she was about to lift Tommy, she shook her head. "You're getting too big for this and too heavy for your pa. You better climb up." The boy puffed up with pride and climbed right up. Molly exchanged a smile with Erin, knowing what she was doing.

"Pa, can I go with you?" Theo asked.

Before answering the boy, Erin asked, "How about you, Tabitha. You want to go and gather cows with us?"

"No, thank you, Pa. Ma and I are going to look at fabrics. I want to learn how to make a dress I saw in the catalog in Laydin's store the last time I was there."

Erin was surprised. Their daughter was becoming a young lady and obviously wanted the attention of the opposite sex. She glanced at Molly, who nodded.

"Well then, Theo, I guess it's you and me. Go saddle the mare, and we'll leave King to guard the place."

"What about the pups?"

"We'll take Queenie, but I think the pups would scatter the herd. Better teach them on the sheep first." She looked over at her wife. "Ask Laydin if he knows anyone who might want a pup. Maybe we can get rid of one or two before the snow flies."

The wagon went one way, the riders the other, and King looked after both, unhappy to be left home alone with his pups. Still, he knew his people depended on him to guard the place. To escape the pups, he made a circuit, his longer legs soon outdistancing the determined pups.

It took them a good hour or more to find the herd, who were spread out over the hillside. Billy's head came up immediately, seeing the riders and hearing Erin whistling. He relaxed a little at the whistle but didn't like it when they started riding towards his wives, the dog nipping at their heels to get them moving.

"That is a dangerous bull," Roberts said as he avoided him and started gathering cows.

"Not at all," Erin contended, directing Theo away from Billy anyway.

"Why do you whistle, Pa?" the boy had asked.

"It gets them used to me, and some of them associate it with the food I used to give them when they came into the barn back in Ohio. It also prevents them being startled and thinking I just appeared out of nowhere."

"But you use the same whistle around the dogs and sheep?"

"I use the same whistle for you children too," she teased, smiling to show the boy she was kidding. "The ducks, the geese, even the chickens and cats know me by my whistle."

"Easy there, Billy," she called to the bull when they started herding him with his cows. He would have gone anyway, but she wanted it to be his idea. He was snorting, thinking about charging Roberts whose horse let him know that it was afraid, but he calmed when Erin started crooning to him. "Billy boy, where do you think you're going?" whistling along before repeating the verse in a sing-song.

It took time, but slowly, they gathered the cows, their calves, and the yearlings and got them heading towards the home ranch.

"Why don't we make them run?" Theo asked as they paced behind or beside them at times.

"We don't want them all heated up, excited, or out of control. Running does that, and it also burns off fat. They are going to need that fat to survive the winter. Sometimes, they can't get at the grass under the snow, and that is when their stored fat will come in very handy."

It was already getting late when they stopped the animals just out of sight of the home yard. They fell to eating the grasses, and Erin got off her horse to give Billy a carrot she had brought along for a treat. "Atta, boy. Just keep them here tonight, and we'll start in on them tomorrow," she told him.

"What did you do before you branded them?" Roberts asked as they rode back into the ranch yard.

"I notched their ears. Back in Ohio, that was enough to prove ownership, but I heard from someone that down Texas way they do it with branding, and it made sense to me."

"I'll see you two tomorrow," Roberts promised, waving as he rode away. He stopped on top of the hill to talk to Molly, who was returning with the wagon half loaded with supplies and eager children full of questions for him. He was anxious to see how much Alex had gotten plowed in his absence, and he wanted to see if Rebecca was okay. They waved him off, not wanting to keep him from his home as Molly started the wagon down the hill. By the time she got there, Erin and Theo had unsaddled their horses, put food down, and were brushing them. They stopped to help her with the horses and packages.

"Mr. Laydin knew how to register the brand," she said excitedly to Erin as she showed him the paper that Laydin had made a copy of. "It cost me a whole dollar," she confided, horrified at the expense.

"Whew," Erin replied, wondering if they had paid too much. Laydin would go out of business if he pulled stunts like that on others who might know better. It was fortunate they had gotten a lot for their crops. They were going to thresh the oats, barley, and corn over the winter and hoped to get a good price on any that was left in the spring.

"How'd the gather go?" she asked.

"Billy and his herd are over there," she pointed beyond the fields to a hill that jutted out slightly. "We left him to bring them into the yard tomorrow."

They unpacked the wagon, the children chattering excitedly. They soon had it emptied. Molly waited until the children were in the cabin and Erin was leading the team away to put them up in the barn for the night before she spoke to her. "Do you notice something different about Dan?"

"Dan?" she asked, wondering who Molly was talking about.

"Roberts," she frowned.

Erin nearly laughed. She'd always referred to him as Roberts and just assumed it was his full name. How foolish. "Yes, I know he wanted a share of the cattle, but it wasn't like I cheated him or anything. I gave him a fair day's wage for a fair day's work."

"He just seems *different*," she muttered, wondering what it was but not able to put a finger on it.

Erin thought it was because he wasn't getting ahead. They had moved here with stock, and he was starting from nothing. Still, he had the farm and was making his fields bigger. In a couple years' time, he would be able to prove up on the land and own it outright. They just had a year up on him. All they could do was be good neighbors, which is why Erin had lent him not only her sod-breaking plow, which she'd had to sharpen the blades on time and again for him to use, but also her oxen. There was no cause for any resentment.

Molly intuitively knew part of it was Dan's attraction to her. She had known he admired her, finding her much more adaptable to this environment than his wife. With Rebecca in the shape she was in, she knew he couldn't help but compare.

They were both right. Rebecca's envy was about so many things: what they had, that they were a full year ahead of them in plowing, that they had brought stock on the hoof, and all their beautiful things. Rebecca's envy and resentment had transferred to Dan Roberts. At first, it was her snide comments and her harping that wore on him, but now, with her silence, he felt guilty that he hadn't been able to give her the things that made a woman happy in her home. He felt if he had been able to give her those things before she fell ill, she wouldn't be in the shape she was in. They didn't dare leave her alone anymore for more than a few hours at a time. Alex had to stop at noon to check on her and eat. Instead of taking food and water to the field and stopping for a few minutes to eat, he had to waste a full half hour to an hour making sure his mother ate, cleaning her up, and taking her to the outhouse. They couldn't afford to hire help for Rebecca, and they couldn't afford to hire anyone to plow either. Roberts was deluding himself that with more money and stock they might get Rebecca back to where she was. His resentment and his own envy over what Molly and Erin had, or what he perceived they had, was rising.

CHAPTER TWENTY-ONE

The branding went well the next day. Both Theo and Tabitha rode to bring in the cattle, cutting them out one by one, but sometimes they brought in a cow with her calf at her side. Molly would use the whip if she needed to, but she and the dogs would get the cow to Erin and Roberts to brand. After branding, they'd let the cow go out the far side of the barn and up onto the back hill. This was how their cattle began getting to know the new cows too. Branding was physically demanding work. It was hot and dusty, and the bawling of the cows was loud and unnerving. Their pain couldn't be helped; the branding was necessary. When they were done, they herded their cattle and the new cows back to where they had spent the night and let them spread out. Billy calmed down after Erin had gone to get him herself. He too had been branded, but Roberts refused to do it. When Erin leaned in with the hot iron, she thought this time for sure he'd gore her. He hadn't been happy about the branding, bellowing in rage, but he had been happy to be reunited with his cows and find there were new ones for him to sniff and become acquainted with. There were a couple coming into estrus too. He had his work cut out for him.

"Well, that's one chore finished and just in time, I think," Erin said as she looked at the clouds building on the western horizon. She'd paid Roberts for his time and he was hanging about chatting Molly up.

"Yes, it smells like snow. I better get home and see if Alex has finished the patch he laid out for himself. I'm also going to see about laying in some more wood for winter." Roberts mounted up, gave them a wave, and headed off down the driveway.

"Shouldn't we be getting our oxen and plow back?" Molly asked, concerned.

"I would think so," Erin answered, frowning. That was the bad thing about lending to neighbors…sometimes, they didn't bring things back. "Maybe you should go visit Rebecca if it doesn't snow tomorrow and see how she is doing?" Erin asked meaningfully. Molly took the hint and nodded.

It wasn't to be though. It started to spit snow that night, and they were kept busy readying their own animals for winter, harvesting the last of the garden and corn, and putting things away. Even with the children to help it required a lot of time and effort. The next day, it was snowing, not much but enough to make them miserable. Molly had hauled a lot of wood in from their woods and that still needed to be cut and stacked for winter. There would always be something to do, so they simply didn't have time to go after a neighbor.

Roberts was counting on that as Alex and he switched jobs. He wanted to get as much plowed as possible. He didn't care too much when he damaged or dulled the blades. He justified it with thoughts that Erin was a smithy and could sharpen them. He fed the oxen very little and staked them out on the grass, so they could eat it instead of his valuable hay, which he put aside for his team of working horses and his riding horse.

When it became apparent he wasn't going to return the yokes of oxen in a timely fashion, Erin was forced to go over with her wagon and ask. She didn't like it, but the oxen were hers. She'd agreed to only two weeks and it had been more, much more. She wasn't surprised to see the size of the fields that Alex and Roberts had plowed. She knew what her teams could do. She was just glad he was out hauling wood when she and Alex put the plow in her wagon bed and tied the oxen to the back, so she could head home. Not seeing Roberts was probably the best and least awkward way to handle things. As it was, Alex had been ashamed and worried that Erin would want to see his ma. He was glad when Erin drove away with her plow in the wagon and the two yokes of oxen plodding along behind it.

"I'm sorry you didn't get a chance to go for horses this year," Molly said as they started their winter chores, things that would keep them busy indoors in the cold months.

"Yeah, me too. Maybe next year," she admitted as she tapped the knife with a mallet that would cut some of the shingles she was trying to shave off the log.

Molly had brought the spinning wheel into the family area near the fire, so she could spin their own wool into string that she could weave. She'd carded their wool too and was proud of this achievement. She'd determined to make them all warmer clothes this winter and had gotten Tabitha and Theresa enthused about it. Tommy was enthused too, but he thought it wrong to knit because that was a *girl's* job. Erin was angry at that and showed him that she too could knit if she wanted, and he was surprised when she showed him how.

"I don't want to learn to knit," Theo confessed.

"But if you don't have a wife to take care of you, you can take care of those things yourself," Erin repeated something she had told the boy before.

Theo was intrigued by the sewing machine, and Molly had no trouble showing him how to work that and how to measure patterns using paper from bags first to figure out the size. He was pleased by the first shirt he made even if it was off slightly, but Timmy didn't care that he had to roll up the sleeves, so he wore it. "My brother made this," he told everyone proudly. They knew that of course; they had all watched it in progress.

That winter wasn't as hard as the previous one. The snow was lighter, and their hay and straw seemed to go further, or maybe it just seemed that way because there was more of it. Roberts was surprised to see her feeding her horses corn when he finally found a clear day to come over and talk to Erin about the spring plowing. Erin was surprised when Roberts acted as though nothing had happened last fall.

"Corn is good for them and gives them staying power. They will run farther, work harder, and last longer than with just hay," she explained. Roberts felt a bit guilty because he had sold every bit of grain he had raised to buy supplies and had nothing left to give his horses.

As a present, Molly presented Roberts with a goose for their Christmas dinner. He expressed his appreciation as he tied down its wings to transport it back to his place. Both Erin and Molly wondered why he had come over. He could have come in the spring to discuss the plowing and seeding he had brought up. Erin had shown him the harrow she made. They both decided it was so that Alex could see Tabitha, and both could escape Rebecca for a few hours. But they were surprised they had just left her alone in that cabin.

They had two rams now, and Erin let them in with the sheep in December hoping they would do their jobs well and they'd be lambing sometime in May. Feeding the sheep that year was no hardship. There was no deep snow to fight, and the stream didn't quite freeze over, the running water keeping it open.

"Someday, I'd like a sleigh," Erin teased.

"With silver bells?" Molly teased in return as they decorated a small tree Erin had insisted on bringing into the cabin to decorate. That year, the children had learned to make popcorn balls and sew popcorn into long strands to hang on the tree. The cabin smelled wonderful with the piney tree and all the things Molly baked for them.

That night, as they filled the stockings with store-bought candy and a toy each for the children, Erin whispered, "I'd like to build you a house next year."

"We'll see how our crops come in. We had a good year this year, and I don't want to be house rich and crop poor. What if a drought comes again and it lasts longer?"

Erin had to concede that her wife was wise. As Molly wrote in her journal that night in bed, Erin asked, "Will I be able to read those? You have several now."

Molly looked up, surprised. "I never thought about it. You never asked before, so I didn't know you were interested." She had thought of the journals as solely hers. She wouldn't let the children read them because she had talked about the fact that Erin was a woman and not a man. Now, she felt the need to explain she had shared that information and her feelings, so whoever would read it after she and Erin were long gone would understand. They hadn't wanted to deceive anyone, but not everyone would understand their relationship. Everyone out here in Oregon accepted Erin as a man; no one questioned it. That also changed some of how she wrote in her diary, not just the daily happenings.

"Of course, I'm interested. Maybe I should write in it too and tell my side of things?"

Molly thought about it and nodded. "You should write your own feelings too, tell your side of things and maybe reference what I write."

"My handwriting ain't as–" she started but Molly interrupted before she could continue, "Isn't as neat as yours," she amended.

They both laughed at the automatic correction. They both did it with the children and each other. They always tried to speak properly, but old habits die hard and laziness caused them to make the odd mistake. Molly had warned the children never to correct each other and especially not to correct their parents in public.

Each evening after the children were in bed, Molly would write in her journal. If she had something to say, she'd write a lot, but if she didn't, she just wrote a few lines. Occasionally, she would skip writing. She watched as Erin read what she had written in her journals since Ohio, occasionally stopping to write in her own journal, which she had started. She would reference the story, the date Molly had written it, and give her own version of events. Sometimes, she even argued with Molly in writing, which was amusing to them both. She might not have fine handwriting, but she did have a dry wit about her and wanted their offspring to understand they were loved. She wanted the children to know they were wanted and they hadn't resented working hard for their family. She also told of her love for Molly, that she didn't consider it unnatural or a sin, and that she believed God wouldn't have put them into each other's path for no reason. They were all together in this thing called life and working towards a common goal...a home. And from what she could see, they were all happy despite the hard work.

That winter, Erin started a lifetime habit. Molly was months, even years ahead of Erin's own writing, but they both enjoyed their writing time when the children didn't interrupt. Naturally, the children were curious about what their parents were writing. They told them the journals would tell their story after they were long gone. Maybe their grandchildren or great-grandchildren would read them, and they didn't feel their children needed to read them now.

CHAPTER TWENTY-TWO

A bear got into Roberts' barn that winter. It hadn't gone into hibernation and was starving. It killed both his horses. All that remained was his riding horse and one other horse in poor shape. He'd heard their screams, but his gun hadn't been loaded. With Rebecca in the shape she was in, he hadn't dared keep a loaded weapon in the house. They ate horse and bear that winter because he hadn't gotten an elk or a deer, and the rabbits were getting scarce around his place. He noticed Erin and Molly hadn't invited them over for butchering that year, and he missed the bacon and hams and beef they had previously always generously shared. What he didn't know was they had invited him and Alex to bring Rebecca over for their butchering in late November, but he hadn't seen the note pinned to their door. Rebecca had picked off the note and eventually shredded it while he and Alex were out hunting for a few hours and left her alone.

Roberts would have walked over to tell his neighbors about the bear but didn't dare in case a storm came up. His riding horse was in no shape to make the journey, so he stayed near his place. By the time the winter storms were gone, the horse was healed, and he finally made it over to their farm, he found Erin already plowing up her fields in preparation for spring planting. Knowing that she'd come when he was away to take back the oxen and the plow, he didn't know if he dared ask to use the plow or her horses for his own fields. Instead, he stayed around, telling her about the bear.

"I sure hope I get something for the pelt," he said, sounding defeated.

"I'm sure you will. We should have gone for horses. Maybe after we finish planting?" she offered, knowing that wouldn't work because then she'd be busy with the sheep.

"It's going to be hard as I'll have to bring all our supplies in on this," he indicated his riding horse and hoped that Erin would offer the use of her extra pair of farm horses. She was switching off which ones plowed the field, and he could now see that Theo and Tabitha were working with the oxen in a far field. "You breaking more ground?" he asked, flushing because of not having returned the oxen last fall.

Erin noticed the blush and chose to ignore it. "Yeah, they wanted to learn, and this way, they won't hurt anything. I think the oxen know more about plowing than they do," she joked. They chatted a while, talking about going for horses, so Roberts could possibly find a couple to keep and sell the extras for money to buy better stock. At no time did Erin offer to lend him oxen or horses and finally, he asked, "May I borrow your plow when you are done, so I can get my fields ready?" He felt humiliated for having to ask.

"Of course. I'll bring 'em over when I'm done and ready to seed," she indicated the pair hitched up to her regular plow.

"Thank you. I'd appreciate it," he said.

She noted there was no mention of trading work or paying her back, so she asked, "Why don't I send Theo or Tabitha over on a horse when I'm done here, and you can help me seed. It'll go faster, and Molly can harrow for us?"

Feeling he had to pay his neighbor back for the use of his horses and plow, he nodded tightly and turned to go. All the way home, feelings of resentment built in him. Realistically, he knew it wasn't Erin's fault he lost his horses and couldn't afford the things they had and he felt aggrieved at having to ask for help. They had been generous and helpful, but he still didn't like that he felt he had to pay them back.

"Molly, would you go to town for me?" Erin asked that night after dinner when she had washed up.

"Can I go?"

"Can I go?"

"Me too?"

Three of the children chimed in at once, and Erin looked at them steadily until they looked down, ashamed for having interrupted an adult.

"What do you need?" Molly asked, ignoring the rude children. She could see Erin's look had chastised them as effectively as if she had spoken aloud. Theo and Tabitha looked on, surprised. No one went to town during planting season, and Molly had been getting the plowed garden ready, staking out plants and stretching strings to make rows, digging in some spots and smoothing others.

"I'd like another plow. We have two teams of farm horses, and we could use another plow. The fields are getting big enough that we could work them both at the same time."

"I thought you liked giving the horses a day of rest as you switched back and forth?"

"They can rest when we've finished planting," she asserted, knowing that every other farmer worked their horses like that and she'd just been indulging hers. "Can we afford it?" she asked.

"I'll check our funds, but I'll go in," she promised. Erin knew they could afford it. Last year's crop had really given them a large profit. Even after hiring the freighters, they had come out way ahead. Neither of them had seen that much money before, and they hadn't spent as much on supplies either. They knew Laydin didn't like that they had bought winter supplies in Pendletown, but they had to get rid of their crops and even with the time wasted traveling that far, they got better prices in the larger town.

Molly came back with the new plow and some news. Laydin and merchants from other small towns were getting together to put up a grain elevator. It was much closer than Pendletown, and they hoped the farmers would bring their grain to them for the top prices they intended to give.

"Well, we shall see," Erin said, not sure if she was more pleased by the news or the shiny, new plow. Molly had gotten other supplies too, and Erin helped carry them into the cabin.

Molly had bought material to make Tabitha the dress she so badly wanted. She'd practiced over the winter and had done a fine job of making a nice dress for herself and a smaller one for Theresa, though not of such fine material.

"I also found out they are building a church!" she told Erin, who looked up when she brought in a box from the wagon filled with supplies.

"I take it we will be going into Sweetwater a lot more often?" she asked, dryly.

"The minister is going to try to be there at least twice a month. He goes from town to town, so everyone contributes a little to his expenses."

"Who is paying for this church?" Erin wondered.

"Well…the town," she answered.

Erin noticed the hesitation. "How much did we contribute, Molly?"

"Ten dollars," she said, looking shamefaced.

"Ten *whole* dollars?" Erin nearly shouted. That was a third of a month's wages for most men. It was a lot of money.

Molly nodded, looking at the floor. "I know I shouldn't have done it, but you should have heard how enthusiastic they were about the church and listened to them brag about how much free labor they were all contributing. When they said they had to buy the boards and the glass, I almost told them about our colored glass window," she gestured to the front of the cabin where the light shone through the pretty glass.

"I'm not giving up our window for a church in town," Erin spat angrily. *Ten dollars! Ten whole dollars she had given them!* Erin got up and walked out of the house to finish emptying the wagon and put the horses up. Molly caught up with her and helped her lift the new plow down.

"I'm sorry, Erin. I just got carried away. I'll go ask for it back."

"You can't do that now, and you know it."

They both knew it. It would make Molly look bad and Erin even worse for making her do it.

"I'll work harder this year to make up for it," she promised.

Erin looked at her wife and shook her head. "You are the hardest-working woman I know. You do more than your fair share."

"But what *you* do earns us money," she countered, near to tears for her impulsive action.

"What *we* do, honey. What *we* do," she assured her, taking her in her arms and comforting her. "We are in this together, remember?" She looked up and saw a couple of faces smashed against the window watching their parents fight. They hadn't missed the angry undertones. She waved them away and they disappeared.

The anger didn't last, it never did, and Erin took out what little anger remained by working harder in the fields to prepare them for seeding. She gave Tabitha and Theo turns using the old plow. The horses did most of the hard work but plowing a straight furrow required skill and there was a learning curve. They learned fast and were soon

helping her prepare the fields. Tabitha rode over to the Roberts' under the guise of inviting them to help seed but she really wanted to see Alex, and he was delighted to see her too. She didn't stop to visit. She'd brought two of the farm horses to hitch up to their wagon, so they could bring Rebecca with them and take home one of the plows for their own fields. Erin lent them both plows and both teams of horses. Roberts was astounded at the new plow and felt some kernels of resentment building again over their ability to buy it. He and Alex would be able to prepare their own fields in record time once they finished seeding over at the Herriots'.

"Won't this look fine when all the carrots and radishes and lettuce are up?" Molly spoke to Rebecca as they worked in the garden, the younger children helping to plant the seeds half an inch apart. Rebecca sat in a chair, a cat on her lap, but she didn't pet it. Apparently, the cat didn't expect it either and they both just sat in the early morning sunshine. It was a warm spot and that's all that mattered to the cat. Rebecca looked off into the hills where the sheep ponderously walked among the tufts of grass, eating. Their big, wooly coats looked bushy about them. Molly turned to look where Rebecca was staring. The sheep needed to be washed and shorn soon. Erin was hoping to do it during the next rainstorm, having learned that was an effective way to clean the wool. Molly had made soap last fall that was extra soft and just for washing the sheep. It was stored in the barn, waiting for just the right time to use it up.

"Ah, I see you are watching the sheep. It will be nice to have lambs again. I also heard in town that someone had a boar for sale. I'll have to remember to tell Erin," she said as she leaned over to cover up the seeds the children were planting. She'd forgotten about the boar with all the hoopla over the church. "Did Dan tell you about the church they're building in town?"

Rebecca seemed to focus for a moment. "Church?" she repeated as though tasting the word for the first time.

Molly stopped and stared. She'd just been making conversation and didn't really expect a reply. She hadn't heard Rebecca speak in a long time. "Yes, won't that be something to look forward to? They are building a church, and a traveling preacher will be coming around twice a month, so we can have services...proper services. I'm sure others could take turns reading from the good book on those other Sundays."

The word seemed to mean something to Rebecca, but she didn't speak again as they planted the garden. Erin and Molly had discussed it and decided Alex, Dan, Tabitha, and Molly could spread seed this year. Theo could harrow, running the horses behind them and turning the dirt over the seeds they were throwing.

When they stopped for lunch, Erin was pleased to see a nice ham steak on her plate. Roberts looked at his and then glared at Erin for a moment before digging in. The beans Molly had set to soaking last night were a good accompaniment, and the dried raspberries from last year's crop were set in cream for dessert.

"That was fine, real fine," Erin said, standing up after drinking a big glass of water to finish her meal off. She patted her stomach as she reached for her hat. She normally wouldn't keep seeding after ten in the morning, but today the winds hadn't come up and she was taking advantage of that and the extra labor to get as much done as possible. The others finished lunch and one by one, they got up and went back to work. Theo was last, and Molly admonished him for lingering and keeping his pa waiting.

"I gotta give them a head start," he explained as he went to hitch up the horses to the homemade harrow.

When they finished that day, the two plows were loaded in the back of the Roberts' wagon. Then, as they were leading one of the teams to hitch up to the wagon, Erin insisted that one team stay, so they could harrow tomorrow. Molly pulled Roberts aside to tell him about how much the word church had meant to Rebecca. He didn't hear a word she said, just gazed at her, nodded politely, and got up on his wagon seat. Rebecca was already seated in the wagon.

"See you tomorrow," they all called and waved as they headed home in the twilight.

Erin was annoyed when Roberts showed up the next day with Rebecca and no Alex. They walked over since the team was needed back on his farm to plow his fields. "Got to get them prepared for our seeding, don't we?" he asked, heartily.

Since they had walked, they were late. Erin had been at work for nearly an hour with Molly and Tabitha helping to seed. Molly stopped working to get a chair for Rebecca, so she could *watch* the children play near the field with the pups from last year. Erin didn't say a word to Roberts, and he repeated his actions the next day it took to finish seeding their fields. Theo had no trouble finishing up the harrowing. The horses did most of the work, and he just held the reins and followed behind them. Roberts hung around until Theo was done, helping with Erin's chores, and then carefully tied Rebecca sideways to one horse and mounted the other to head home.

"That situation is starting to annoy me," Erin admitted that night as they both relaxed after the hard day, not writing much because of their fatigue.

"I know, but you are a good friend and neighbor to be helping them."

"Well, at least I won't need the horses or the plow to finish planting the corn," she responded, trying to look at the brighter side of things. They'd already plowed the corn field both ways, creating squared-off hills as they always did. They would plant four seeds on every hill again, and later, on every second hill of every second row, she'd plant four beans. There was no harrowing in this field, but all the children would be expected to help, even Timmy who had turned five this year. Erin was planning to plant squash in this field too this year, having heard of the trick from another farmer. The leaves from the squash vines would crowd out the weeds that weren't held back by the beans.

Erin was thrilled when she sheared the sheep. The quality of the wool seemed better this year, maybe because they had washed the sheep in the creek. Molly had suggested they use the retaining wall to rinse them in, one by one. Soaping and washing them in the rain and then making them swim in the trough had turned out well. The sheep dried out over the following sunny days. And it was just in time too as they went into labor the following week, and none of the gunk from birthing their lambs got on their valuable wool. Their flock more than doubled that year and Erin kept them close to the farmyard while they were young and vulnerable.

"Why don't I get a party for *my* birthday?" Theo asked as Tabitha preened in her new dress. Alex and his folks were coming over, and she wanted to look her best.

"Because your birthday is in February, and no one travels in February out here. That's why there are two cakes. This is for your birthday too," Molly told him with a smile. They hadn't been able to afford it last year, but she thought this was a good idea and would make the boy feel special.

He smiled and then had a thought. "I had a cake on my birthday." He worried she'd take the extra cake away when he reminded her.

"Yep, and you get another one since you didn't get a party," she told him, grinning at the chagrin on Tabitha's face. "Help me set the table, you two."

There was no designated men's work or women's work in this home; they both chipped in with no argument.

It was a lovely, little party and Molly insisted on *gifting* the Roberts with a third cake she had made after she found out they had missed Alex's fifteenth birthday. She knew Rebecca certainly wouldn't have baked one.

Roberts returned the two plows in his wagon, and he promised to return the team the following day. "When are we going for more wild horses?" he had asked eagerly, but Herriot was knee-deep in lambing and couldn't commit. Roberts brought it up again a couple weeks later and they agreed to go the following day.

"Let's take King," Erin said as they checked their packs one more time. She was riding one of the horses she had gotten from the dead men and leading the other, which carried their supplies. Both her mares, including the appaloosa, had given birth that spring, and she didn't want to separate them from their foals. She was pleased one had a filly and the other a colt, both out of her stallion.

As they headed out, Roberts wasn't as chatty as he had been in the past. Erin let the silence stretch between them. Their friendship wasn't what it had once been, and she didn't know how to heal it. If she talked about it, it would embarrass them both…men didn't discuss feelings. She was hurt though. She felt used, and Roberts seemed ungrateful. He seemed to resent her for some reason, and while she had her suspicions why, she certainly wouldn't bring them up or air them with the source. Molly and she had talked about it many times.

"I haven't seen a one," Roberts said three days later as they came together at the camp they had made not too far from where they had herded the horses two years before. "I found some tracks, but they are weeks old."

"I thought I had seen some, but it turned out to be deer," she said with a sigh.

"Should have shot one for dinner."

"Naw, wrong time of year, and they have young. That's why I brought enough supplies for us to be out here a while. Molly understands."

At Molly's name, Roberts looked away. He was ashamed for the feelings he had for his neighbor's wife. She was a pretty and caring woman. She was everything that he had hoped Rebecca would be and

had been for a brief time until she changed. He didn't recognize her anymore.

They broke camp and went farther into the hills towards the mountains. On the second day, they found tracks, and King, finally realizing they were searching for horses, was put on the trail. He led them to the wild herd that third day. They scouted the herd, but the horses were skittish, and when they smelled the horses, the men, and the dog, they took off. Roberts and Erin circled wide. It was harder to do as they came closer to the mountains, but they managed to find a place to camp and a place to trap the horses if they could find them again. This location was better for trapping. It not only had the high, steep walls they needed but there was also a small spring in the corner of a large meadow of deep grass. They managed to block off the entrance with brush, leaving space for the horses to enter.

They finally managed to find the horses and get them moving in the direction they wanted. If not for the dog, they wouldn't have found the horses or been able to get them into the trap. It was a different herd and contained none of the horses they had let escape from the first herd. Erin saw the most incredible stallion. It made hers look shabby. The beast was quite a find for a wild stallion, and it looked to be quite young, from what she could see at a distance. The stallion immediately fought the trap, using its body to fling itself time and again against the brush they had woven into the high walls. Erin had remembered to bring Molly's whip, and she used it to frighten the stallion. Even when the whip no longer frightened the horse, the sting kept it back.

"There's some fine stock in there," Roberts commented as he watched Erin keep the stallion at bay. "I've been practicing roping, and I hope I'm better than last time." He seemed in better spirits now that they had a chance to take some of the stock.

"Theo is better than I am at roping things," Erin admitted. She too had practiced from time to time. This outing, they had several ropes ready, so she wouldn't be cutting up any more.

Having learned from the last time, they took more horses. They let go those that were too old, too ugly, and too cut up from living on the range. They kept only the best for their own use—the young and those in their prime. Erin could see the greed in Roberts' eyes and let him have the best pickings out of a sense of guilt, but she insisted on keeping the stallion.

"You can't have two stallions on your place," Roberts objected.

"Tell you what...I'm going to keep that stallion, and you can have breeding rights for five years for either of my stallions on the horses you keep."

"Five years, eh?" he asked, contemplating and then finally, agreeing. He was going to keep at least six of the horses and sell the rest. He saw that the ten Erin was keeping weren't as good as his own, but he felt that the stallion more than made it an even split.

As the weeks went by and they calmed the horses, getting them used to human touch and the ropes, they both agreed it was time to head home. Spring work had turned into summer work. Erin had Molly and her children, but Roberts had only Alex to look out for Rebecca and their crops. That was a lot for a fifteen-year-old boy to handle.

Erin could see Roberts was in a better mood. She wasn't planning to sell any of these horses. They would be the start of her herd, and she hoped to gentle them all and breed them. Cattle and horses would be a good investment, and she intended on fencing in more of her place this year, so they could keep them.

She watched as Roberts turned off for his place, leading his horses. She wished him well. What he did with his horses was his own concern. She'd been more than fair. She was even more pleased to have had an opportunity to explore more of the land east of her place. She had seen a couple places she would like to hunt next fall. She hadn't had time to hunt last fall but fortunately, the beef and pork they raised had been enough.

"Pa, you got horses," Theo said happily when he saw her leading the long string of horses. King was at their heels to make sure they behaved, dodging them if they tried to kick out at him, and punishing them when they did. The stallion was the worst, and Erin worried about him breaking out or hurting the others.

"Easy, there. Open the corral and get the black stallion out of there and into the barn. I've got another stallion here, and I don't want them fighting," she told Theo as she slowed. He ran on ahead to open the gate, and she rode in with all the ropes and her pack horse. Roberts hadn't offered to pay for the supplies they had used or help with bringing the horses in, and she had to let that go too. She untied the horses one by one but left on the rope bridles she had made for hers. She felt getting them used to domestication this way would make it easier in the long run. She was planning on breaking a couple in the lake in the coming weeks.

Molly and the children listened avidly as she told about the hunt and what she had done during the weeks away. They told her about all they

had done at home too. "We've got poison ivy in the woods where we got our wood from," Molly told her, nodding towards Tommy and Theresa, who both had bandaged arms.

"Bad?" she asked, wondering why their arms were bandaged up.

"It's the only way to keep them from scratching," she informed her. "I'll take the bandages off tonight to bathe them, then I'll apply some more ointment and put new bandages on. They must wear socks on their hands in bed too, so it doesn't spread. It also keeps them from scratching."

"We'll have to pull that wood out and burn it," Erin said. "We'll wear gloves that we'll wash, throw out, or burn afterwards." She knew it was the oils in the plant that caused the itch.

"If we burn it, won't the smoke cause us to break out?"

"Yeah, but we must get rid of the plants, and if we bury them, we would just be replanting them. I think goats eat it," she confided.

"I don't know anything about goats. There was a farmer that came out for some smithy work. I told him you'd be back any day now. He was interested in some sheep."

Erin nodded, knowing Molly was more than capable of taking care of things if anything happened to her. She liked that Molly kept up the pretense of being dependent and directing people to her husband, as any woman would. Still, the smithy work would be welcome.

"I saw Billy's herd while we were away. Looks like we have a lot of young ones. I also saw a wicked scar on Billy's side. Looks like he got in another fight, maybe with a bear or some other large animal. He wouldn't let me get close enough to check it out, and with all those horses to look after, I didn't have the time to argue with him."

"Is it healed, or should we go get him?"

"It looks like a scar. He's fine."

Everyone contributed to the dinner conversation as they ate their fine meal. It was a lot different than the meal over at the Roberts' where they had hardtack and the last of the bacon Tabitha had taken to Alex. Rebecca had burned some of their supplies in the fireplace when Alex left her alone while he weeded the fields. Roberts was angry, but there was nothing he could do. He had gotten the horses he went for, more than he had planned on, and he hoped to have time to work on them. Now, he would have to hurry to sell those he planned to get rid of, so he could buy more supplies. He was tired. He was eternally tired of the struggle. It seemed a lot easier over at the Herriots', but they had more people to do the work and Molly was competent.

Erin was thrilled that Molly had had the foresight to haul in wood. She'd known they needed to extend their fencing program, and that was what they all concentrated on between weeding the fields, collecting produce, drying it, and doing their usual summer chores. Erin had the added work of breaking in horses, causing her to be away from the ranch yard. She spent hours taking unbroken horses to the lake and getting them used to the saddle and bridle by riding them into the water and breaking them that way. It didn't get her out of other necessary work on the place though. Erin dug post holes using a new contraption Molly had picked up at Laydin's store, which was easier than a shovel. It made digging easier, and if they didn't hit too many rocks it made for a nice, round hole that the post could be placed in when they got it to the perfect depth. The children helped by kicking in rocks when they had the homemade posts set.

"I'm running out of nails," Tabitha admitted when she was helping Molly set up the fence.

"I bought a keg last time I drove into town," she answered as she held the board in place and allowed the young girl to hammer it. Erin was working with Theodore, who was a lot more nervous about it.

"Ow! Hit the head of the nail, not my finger!" Erin told him, getting angry. She looked away for a moment as she sucked on her thumb. Tommy and Theresa were bringing boards one by one because of the weight, but she was pleased that everyone was chipping in and helping. Even five-year-old Timmy was bringing nails. He would pick up any nails he spilled, spilling even more in his attempt to pick up the others. It was funny to watch, but they had to be careful and pick up the ones he missed because the loose nails could get stuck in the feet of animals or people, and nails were expensive.

By the end of the summer, they had two corrals up, and the horses were split between them.

Erin decided they would go into town for the Fourth of July celebrations. There was a race to watch, and they saw many of their neighbors, who had helped raise the barn. They were invited to two more barn raisings and enjoyed socializing. They were pleased to meet some newcomers and see the area settling even more. It was sad to see Roberts leading Rebecca around. She stared blankly as strangers tried to converse with her.

"May I take Tabitha for a lemonade?" Alex asked respectfully, his Adam's apple bobbing painfully because he was so nervous.

"Of course," Erin agreed, sharing a look of amusement with Molly, who was holding onto her arm.

"Herriot, I'd like to talk to you about any extra bulls you might want to part with," a farmer attempted to engage Erin.

"Sounds good. Come out to the ranch, and we'll round some up for you."

"You got extra horses?" another asked.

Erin noticed the male farmers ignored their women whenever they talked stock. It was nothing she hadn't experienced growing up, but it sure irritated her that Molly didn't mind.

"Why would I mind?" she asked when they discussed it later. "They think a wife has nothing in her head but her garden, knitting, and minding the children. You are one of the few that realize a woman's worth is as valuable as a man's."

Erin blinked at this. "I'm a *woman*. Of course, I would realize that."

"But they don't know that," she pointed out. "They think, since you look like a man and we live as man and wife, that you *are* a man."

"Yes, I realize that, but it still annoys me when they ignore their women like that."

Molly and Erin realized how lucky they were to have the type of relationship they did. They were raising their children to believe that men and women could all do the same jobs. They realized that message had gotten through when Tabitha returned from the Roberts' one day, irritated by something sexist Alex had said unintentionally. The boy was excruciatingly apologetic while trying to get back in her good graces. He even rode over to court her a little, but his time was limited by how much work he had to do on their farm. His father was breaking the horses, and he was badly bruised and beaten from trying to ride them. Erin thought about telling him to use the lake that had worked so well for her but knew he wouldn't appreciate her interference. She had few, if any spills that resulted in bruises. Not all the horses were receptive to being ridden, but it sure beat how Roberts was doing it.

Erin took her horses, one by one, out to the lake to break them. It was more difficult for them to buck in the water, and by the time they tired from trying to buck her off, she was riding them. It was very time-consuming going all the way out to the lake, and the water was ice cold since it came directly out of the mountains, some of which had snow well into summer. The streams from the range that fed it, barely warmed its deep waters.

The children clamored to go with her, but she didn't want them to see her shirt plastered to her body when she exited the water.

"They will see I have breasts. How can I let them go?" Erin asked Molly. She would have liked to take more than one horse at a time because of the distance but didn't have anyone to hold them. Molly couldn't go because of the younger children, although she would have loved to. Tabitha and Theo both would have been tremendous helps.

"I don't think you can, and anyway, they are needed around here," she pointed out.

They finally compromised one day, and all went for a picnic. The children frolicked in the water in old dresses and clothes, screaming and playing in the cold water. Erin wouldn't go near the water, although she longed to join in.

"Pa, you can swim, right?" Theo asked, soaked with water and coming over to sit with Erin, who was watching them play.

"Yep," she admitted.

"Then, why don't you come in the water? You must get wet when you break the horses?"

"I don't like the water," she admitted, lying and not liking that. She'd always tried to tell the children the truth. She'd told them all about her older brothers and her parents, but she had never alluded to her own gender.

"Oh," he answered, disappointed. "Is that why you don't bring us when you break the horses?"

Erin shrugged. "I just feel it's better with me and the horses alone," she lied again. "Someday, you will do this too. Maybe you will like having an audience, but I don't."

It was the excuse she had used many times when they asked to go along. She didn't feel comfortable lying, but Molly backed her up.

"Easy there Timmy," she called, warning him away from going in too deep in the lake and glaring at Molly for not watching him closer. Molly looked up from where she was playing with Theresa and went to bring the five-year-old closer.

They sang on the way back from the lake, the horses' ears twitching along with the tunes. Theo's voice was changing and cracked now and again, and Tommy and Theresa both had no sense of volume. Erin whistled along with their singing and drew smiles. The children all assumed she couldn't sing. She remembered how much she had enjoyed singing in church back in Ohio, her fine voice raised in harmony as she praised the Lord. She missed that.

"Timmy has a fever," Molly admitted later, when they tucked the children into bed.

"We'll have to keep a watch on him."

They watched Timmy carefully, but the fever continued to spike. Molly made a pallet for the boy in their bedroom, so she didn't have to climb the loft ladder to check on him. She also washed all his sheets and blankets in case he was infectious.

"Pa, Theo and Tommy were trying to watch me dress," Tabitha complained.

"Well, I hope to prove up on the claim this year, and next year, maybe we'll build a bigger cabin or a house. Then, maybe we can have a girls' room and a boys' room."

"I'd have to share with Theresa?" she asked, aghast at the idea.

"You share with all your siblings now. What is wrong with sharing with your sister?"

"Can't I have a room of my own?"

"I don't think we could afford to give you a room of your own."

Tabitha stomped off, upset with her father for not understanding her needs.

Erin watched her go, understanding far more than the teenager realized but not willing to give into her little fits of temper. She'd share with her sister so long as she lived under their roof. She'd seen the looks Alex Roberts had given Tabitha. She also saw the looks other farmers and young men had given her when they went to town and everyone realized Tabitha was maturing.

"They are talking about putting in a school next fall," Molly informed Erin as she wiped Timmy's brow with a cooling cloth. He kept throwing off the covers and then shivering as he dealt with whatever bug he had picked up.

"The children could ride horses to town," Erin mused aloud, "but not before harvest and not after the first snow."

"Harvest is late in the season," she pointed out. "They would expect the boys to stay and help with harvest but not the girls."

"Too bad. They are our children, and we need everyone's help."

Molly understood that, but the teacher they had hired might not. She'd already promised they would come in for church, and Erin had grumbled about the disruption to their work. Depending on the season, she often hadn't stopped for a day of rest. There was a lot she wanted to do, and the fencing was only completed around the two corrals. She was slowly working her way up the hill in between trips to the lake to break horses. Her summer was full, as was everyone's.

CHAPTER TWENTY-THREE

Erin was thrilled after harvest that fall when she was finally able to file for ownership of her six hundred and forty acres. She'd proved up on it after the required four years, and they were all happy to know the Herriots owned their farm-ranch. Erin and Molly still teased each other about the wording, the children joining in on their little joke. The only one not happy with them proving up was their neighbor, Roberts. He had another year before he could prove up on his place, and he was jealous.

"Did you want to go for horses again?" he asked, hopefully, after they brought the last of his crop to Sweetwater. Both were relieved that prices were the same as Pendletown and they wouldn't need to spend money for expensive freighting or waste their valuable time. Laydin had expanded his store when his son came on board to help full-time at sixteen years old.

"I don't know. I don't like leaving Molly alone at the ranch. With all the children except Timmy going into town for school, that's a lot of alone time."

"I leave Rebecca, and Alex has his chores."

That was an unfair comparison, and they both knew it. What Erin didn't know was Rebecca had been starting fires in the cabin, and the only thing that prevented the entire place burning down was their dirt floor. Roberts didn't know how to stop her except to hide the fire-making materials from her and leave no fire burning in the fireplace. He was frustrated and hoped the money from the sale of his first big crop would alleviate some of his worries.

They ended up going for horses, but either the herds had moved on, or they were gone from this section of Oregon, because they didn't find any. After a week, they both returned, irritated with each other and the waste of their time.

Erin was surprised to learn Alex wasn't going to school. She supposed at fifteen, he felt himself a man. He sure was a nice-looking, young man. Molly had mentioned this because he was coming over more often to court Tabitha, and they needed more than stumps for them to sit on outside. Tabitha had complained that they didn't have *decent* furniture.

"Well, if they don't like what we have, then they don't have to sit on it," Erin had countered. "It's been good enough up until now."

"Pa, do I have to wait until I'm eighteen to marry?" Tabitha asked one day out of the blue.

"Yep, and I won't allow just any man to marry you either. He has to have a bright future and be able to support you," she answered almost absent-mindedly, assuming she was talking about Alex. Later, she found out from Molly there were also a couple boys at school who were also interested in Tabitha.

"Don't be surprised if someone comes over to talk to you about courting her. Their crops are in, and they are thinking about the long winter ahead," Molly warned her, having heard that a girl of fifteen and another of fourteen had been approached after church.

"That's nonsense! They are still girls at that age."

"Most men figure they are women once they bleed, and we both know Tabitha has her monthly."

They sure did know. She'd synched with both her parents, and her moods were mercurial at best. More than once, Molly had pulled the girl aside to calm her. She was lashing out at her siblings, and Molly explained that a well brought up, young woman didn't behave that way. She learned to control her emotions.

Erin, who still suffered from horrible cramping, found it especially hard to be sympathetic towards the girl. She was grateful Molly knew where to find aspens to make a brew to calm the pains. Erin claimed a headache when the children asked why she took the concoction, and she hoped that allayed their suspicions.

"Why do children ask so many goldarned questions?" Erin asked one day when Timmy pestered her.

Molly laughed, having been the recipient of many such sessions with all the children.

That winter came earlier and was a bit harder, but they weathered it well. The first snowfall had put an end to the children's trips into town for school. They had enjoyed the ride to and from, Tabitha on one horse with Theresa and Theo on the other horse with Tommy. Now, they had to study at home once again, and Tabitha, for one, didn't like it. She'd liked meeting other children her age and enjoyed all the attention she had been receiving from the boys and older men. School and church were her only social interactions.

"That's not how they do it at school," became a familiar refrain from the girl.

"You aren't at school, and this is how we are going to do it," Molly's tone brooked no argument from the young girl, who was missing the social aspects of school.

"Why don't we get a buggy or a sleigh?" the girl asked, imagining the impression they would make going to school in this manner. She thought it would look very impressive.

"When you have your own place, you can spend your money the way you and your husband see fit," Molly told her, and Erin, who had been ready to give the girl a good set down, was pleased. Her own tongue longed to tell off Ms. Smarty Pants. Molly was fair but firm.

Erin was first approached by a settler to the north of town and then by one of the boys Tabitha went to school with. The settler, a man of about twenty-four, was an up-and-coming young man and had potential. The boy was a gawky youth. Both were told Tabitha was too young; however, if they cared to come out and talk to her, Erin wouldn't object. Alex objected...vocally!

"That boy thinks he has an in because they've known each other for years. I think a healthy dose of competition is good for him," Erin told Molly when she objected to the others coming to talk with Tabitha.

"They aren't doing any harm, and the girl can use some of that attention she seems to crave...but only if her chores are done."

It was interesting until Alex got stuck at their place overnight because of the weather. After that, Erin refused to let anyone come again until spring when the danger of snowstorms had passed. Roberts displayed great upset over the treatment of his only son and heir, and that was enough to sever what remained of Roberts' and Erin's friendship.

Roberts had his own plow and horses now. He even asked Erin to repair them once he realized the rocks he hit damaged their effectiveness. She pounded on the metal to work out the aggravation she felt about how he had borrowed her plows and never cared for the blades. He had never once been apologetic about the damage he had caused to her equipment.

Still, there seemed to be competition between the Roberts and Herriots now that Erin had announced she wanted to build a house for her family. The land was proved up on and she would be paying taxes, so it was time they had a home. The cabin was okay, but it was cramped quarters, and she wanted to give Molly a real home.

"We have enough set aside that we can order the boards, glass, and other supplies," Molly pointed out as they discussed what kind of house they wanted.

"Yes, but we don't have the *time*," Erin pointed out, busy with the rush of spring work. Something—she suspected a fox—had attacked the sheep and they'd lost quite a few.

"Could we hire...?" Molly began and realized her mistake immediately. Erin wanted to do it herself. She'd plotted out the dimensions with Molly, decided where they'd put it up and what they would need. The children talked of almost nothing else when they had the opportunity, but school was also a topic of conversation. Their world was limited.

"I'm nearly fifteen years old! I should be able to–" Tabitha began, not for the first time.

"You *are* fifteen years old!" Erin interrupted. "You will behave in the manner your ma and I have raised you, and you will obey us until you live in your own home. We won't discuss this again until you are at least eighteen years old." Erin was sick of hearing the child talk about getting married and having a home of her own that would be better than this place. That upset Erin. She was very proud of what they had accomplished. They were the owners of six hundred and forty acres free and clear, and she was looking to buy more someday. How they eventually came into more land saddened her and hurt Tabitha more than she had ever imagined. It all came about after the next harvest....

"I got my patent for the land," Roberts told her, but he wasn't happy about it. It had been hard-won, and Erin thought he'd be thrilled. "We're selling out and heading back east. Rebecca needs help, and I can't give it to her here."

"I'm sorry to hear that, Dan," Erin told him, using his first name for what was probably the first time in all the years she had known the man. "Do you have someone interested in the land?" She wondered what kind of neighbor they would have now that the Roberts were leaving. No one had settled south of them, that she knew of.

"No, you're the first I told. I thought maybe you'd be interested in my land and some of my stock."

"How much do you want for the land?" She knew he had six hundred and forty acres, the same as they did.

"One and a quarter an acre," he told her, lacking conviction in the price because he knew that most people didn't have that kind of ready money.

But Erin did have that money. Molly hadn't let them spend frivolously, and they'd saved every cent they hadn't needed for supplies. The sale of their horses and bulls and even grown cattle had paid off, and they kept the best for breeding. Eating what they grew along with their own pork and beef, they'd kept expenses low. "I'll discuss it with Molly. Give me a day?"

Molly thought it an excellent idea. It would double the size of the ranch, and while Roberts' place was rockier than their own, it still had some good fields that he had plowed up and there was good grazing land. She was sorry to see their closest neighbor go, but she knew it was for the best. Rebecca would never again be the woman she had been, but maybe Roberts could know some relief from the constant worry. Alex had confided in Tabitha, and she told her ma the things Rebecca had unknowingly done. Poor Tabitha. Her main beau would be gone.

"What about Alex?" Molly asked Erin and saw Erin hadn't thought about that.

"We could offer him a place here. He's nearly a man grown."

"I don't think Roberts will give up his son, and wouldn't the boy resent that we bought his parents' claim and expect to inherit it?"

Erin hadn't thought of that either and agreed it was a possibility. Remembering Rebecca's envy of what they had, she supposed she might have taught that to the boy. It wasn't until they were packing up Roberts' wagon after buying the farm that another incident proved the decision not to offer the boy a place was a good idea. Roberts was carrying out the last of his things and tore his shirt on an exposed hinge on a trunk, exposing a nasty scar across his rib cage. "What is that?" Erin asked automatically, although she wouldn't have wanted anyone to ask her something like that.

"Oh, that's from your old bull, Billy. He got Pa that one time," Alex said innocently as he put some things into the wagon.

Erin looked at Roberts, and in that moment, she realized beyond a shadow of a doubt that he had been the third man, who had tried to steal the bull with Stewart and Graebel. She'd had her suspicions but dismissed them because she'd hoped a friend wouldn't have done that. He must have also been the one who set the animals unsuccessfully stampeding towards Herriot and the sheriff. Roberts looked guiltily at her before turning away, ostensibly to find another shirt to put on.

Erin returned home with the horses she had bought from Roberts and found their household in an uproar over the *defection* of Alex, who had, of course, left with his parents.

"What's going on?" Erin asked Molly, hearing Tabitha sobbing dramatically from her bed up in the loft.

"Apparently, Alex's ties to his parents are more important than the ones to…" she nodded towards the loft.

"Come outside. I have something else to tell you," Erin said. Once outside, she proceeded to tell Molly what she had seen and her suspicions that Roberts had been the third thief.

"You have no proof," she pointed out.

"It was a feeling, but I'm sure I'm right."

"Still, there's nothing you can do about it now. They're gone."

Erin lowered her voice further as she replied, "I'm glad they're gone. He was always damaging my things when he borrowed them. He didn't feed the horses or the oxen properly, and he seemed to resent me more every time he borrowed them. It wasn't my fault."

"No, it wasn't your fault, and you were a good friend and neighbor. Now, there are others moving into the territory, and you should make more of an effort to make friends through church." Molly knew Erin didn't like going to church. She felt like a hypocrite, and yet, she missed the singing she had done as a child. But she couldn't sing now; her voice would give away her gender.

CHAPTER TWENTY-FOUR

They built their house that year. It had two small bedrooms upstairs under the eaves: one for the girls and one for the boys. The girls did indeed have to share a room, much to Tabitha's dismay. However, they were proud of their home, built with sawn lumber and sporting new windows and doors. The cabin became part of their kitchen and work area, the house much too fine for some of the realities of farm work that included butchering, harvest, canning, et cetera. They did all their work in the old cabin and lived in their fine house.

Later, they lost the cabin and the house to a fire that roared across the prairies, burning down Sweetwater and many other homes in its path. They had some warning, so they managed to load their wagons with things they wanted to save, which included the journals. They let their horses out with the cattle, herded their sheep and pigs, brought what cats they could catch, called to the dogs, and they all headed for the relative safety of the lake. The back fires Molly and Erin started helped to keep the wall of fires that were headed their way at bay temporarily. The smoke and sparks sometimes caused more damage than the actual fire as it jumped the back fires and spread. Still, the lake saved them from losing everything, and they could rebuild.

The cabin they rebuilt was a little larger than their original cabin. They also built a barn with boards from the mill, having a barn raising with the neighbors who survived the fires and were themselves rebuilding where they could. It was nice having neighbors who cared and contributed, only expecting them to attend their own barn raisings in return.

Erin admitted that plowing was easier that next year without all the growth slowing them. The fires had come after a rather poor harvest, the heat of the summer having slowed the growth and even killed a lot of their grain. Still, they'd gotten some money for the small seeds, and it was all in before the fires came. It was hard to find feed for their animals that winter, and Erin left the horses out on the range to fend for their own food. A few came back, having become too domesticated and looking to their humans to feed them.

With the ease of plowing that following year, they expanded their fields and used their savings to buy the necessary seed. Fortunately, the rains came in earnest that year. They also had their wool crop and lambs. They weren't helpless, and they replaced things the fire had burned. They replaced their homemade posts with milled posts, enclosing their fields once again to protect them against their own animals. They also enclosed the animals' pens, corrals, and grazing fields.

Slowly, they rebuilt all they had lost. They were lucky. They had savings, which had been tucked away and judiciously guarded by Molly. Even the children didn't know how much money they kept on the farm or where it was hidden.

CHAPTER TWENTY-FIVE

In 1849, the Herriot family received bad news. The land they had so carefully tended, including the land they had bought from Roberts, might not be theirs. The Organic Laws of Oregon, that had so generously granted settlers either three hundred and twenty acres for single adults or six hundred and forty acres for married couples, were written by a provisional government. That meant they had no authority, and the claims were not valid under United States' law. It created an outcry from those who had proved up or bought claims from settlers who had previously proven up. Since Erin and Molly had done both, they were worried that all their hard work had been for naught. They still had their cattle and horse herds, which had grown proportionately through judicious purchasing and breeding, and they'd raised extensive fencing on their lands to protect their crops and herds; however, they would be out all those years of hard work. And where would they go?

"Will we have to get off?" Molly fretted.

"I don't know," Erin admitted.

"We will fight...with guns if necessary," Molly said fiercely, protectively.

"Will we have to go to war?" Theo asked, sounding excited at the prospect.

"No, we will not go to war. The politicians we elected will have to fight for our rights," Erin patiently explained to the boy. She didn't really understand it herself, and there were many settlers up in arms over it.

Already, the vultures were circling, buying land for very little money from those too scared to stick it out. They were speculators, who had the wherewithal to pay cash to those who were frightened. Erin bought cattle and horses from settlers that didn't have the stomach to fight or stick it out anymore, but she paid fair prices. Those settlers had used up their stamina in the fight with the land, surviving and building their homes on what they had thought was free land.

Erin and Molly didn't know if they would have to take the animals they owned outright and move off the land they had worked and fought so hard for. Thoughts of moving again made for a very stressful year.

"There is nothing we can do until they work it out," Erin consoled Molly, who was becoming frantic at the thought they would lose it all. They were doing well, had plenty to survive, but losing the land they had worked so hard for would be a huge blow.

"We will continue as though we are staying," she decided, and they did just that.

As she worked in the fields, Erin worried that far off Washington D.C., where such things were decided, wouldn't realize the impact they would have on so many. While they waited to see what would happen thousands of miles away, work awaited them in a never-ending cycle.

They worked hard to keep up the land. They continued to mold it to their needs, expanding the fields, watching the natural increase to their herds and suffering the losses due to unexpected deaths.

The government of the United States finally honored the settlers' claims in the Donation Act of 1850. The patent or ownership certificate Erin received for their lands "as the free gift of a generous nation" meant more to them than anything. They could breathe a sigh of relief that nothing was wasted; their years of hard work hadn't gone for nothing. President Millard Fillmore's Donation Act would be in effect until 1854.

CHAPTER TWENTY-SIX

A few years later, Tabitha did marry. It was well after her eighteenth birthday and not to Alex, from whom they received only a few letters after his family left the area. She married a hard-working rancher, who moved into the area with his herd of cattle. She loved her husband deeply, and she would have three children with him.

Theo, who had thought he would inherit the ranch by right of being the oldest son, was disabused of that notion and resentful. He started up his own ranch south of them when he was old enough to have his own land. He grew up considerably doing the hard work for himself. Erin helped when she could, so he could make something of the place. He married the town's school teacher when he was thirty, and they had two children.

Tommy grew up and wanted nothing to do with the ranch. Having done so much work on it through the years, he was sick of ranching and wanted to be a merchant in town. He started up a leather shop where he made fine leather goods, eventually moving to a larger town. He never married, but that didn't stop him from enjoying the ladies.

Theresa, always so close to Tommy, grew up with a preference for town living as well. She eventually married Laydin's son. He was about ten years older than she but provided her a nice home, and they had two children.

It was Timmy that surprised everyone. He was totally enraptured by everything on the farm, as he called it. He expanded, buying out his older brother's adjoining land when Theo decided he wanted a bigger ranch and was forced to move to New Mexico when he was unable to buy enough land in the local area. Theo's farm became a ranch that was triple the size Erin and Molly had started with. Eventually, Timmy also bought out his siblings' interest in the original land their parents had been willing to divide between the children. Although his siblings squabbled a little about how much they were paid for their share of the land, they respected the way Tim cared for their parents into their older years.

There were good years, some were *very* good years, and Erin and Molly saved their pennies. Molly was always very practical with their money.

Another prairie fire consumed their barns, the second cabin, and the house that Erin rebuilt for Molly. But once again, they were able to drive their animals and wagons to the lake and save their most precious belongings...including their journals. They had to start over, but they were familiar with this, and they just laughed and carried on, not wasting time crying over their losses.

The cabin they rebuilt with Tim's help was smaller than their original but more practical. The barn was more important, and they used store-bought boards to build that again, making it larger and much more efficient. Later, they would build a fine house where they raised their last son, and he would use it one day to provide a home for his new wife and family. Timmy's wife, a settler's daughter, was a hardy girl, who gave him a fine son they named Benjamin. His son grew up to inherit the Herriot Ranch, which was finally named Falling Pines Ranch. Ben's son, Keith would have eventually inherited the land if he had been interested, but instead, the ranch was left to Ben's granddaughter, Fiona, who became a fourth generation Herriot on the lands, but this wouldn't happen for many years.

Erin watched the passage of years with delight. Finding herself growing old, she contented herself with watching her son Tim slowly take over the farm and build it into something more. Tim took pride in the Herriot name, and he turned the ranch into something they could all be proud of. The cattle, horses, and sheep from Falling Pines Ranch were top quality. He sought and found better bulls, stallions, and rams to breed to their current stock, improving the lineage over the years. Using the land acquired from his brother to expand, their herds became so vast they had to build outlying shanties for the cowboys who were

hired to watch over the stock. Erin and Molly watched Tim with pride, knowing they had raised him right. Tim's wife, Maggie made sure his parents were comfortable and didn't have to do much, especially once arthritis curbed their abilities to help on the ranch. They had worked so hard and for so long, it took years to convince them to finally slow down. Their minds wanted to work, but their bodies couldn't keep up.

Erin was saddened that Tim didn't have the time needed to breed the fine dogs she and Molly had brought out with them. They watched King and Queenie age, and when their beloved dogs died, they buried them in the hills they had loved running in. The few remaining offspring of King and Queenie weren't bred, but each was loyal and faithful to the day they died. Billy disappeared one winter. They liked to think he was still running his harem out in the hills because they never did find his enormous carcass. The horns alone would have given him away. Billy's offspring were prized and even the expensive bulls Tim bought to improve their herds never compared to this original seed stock.

Molly loved sitting on their porch with Erin in a rocking chair beside her as they watched their grandson Benjamin grow up on the farm they had started. It was now a fully operational ranch, and Ben seemed to have a strong sense of purpose about the ranch he would someday inherit. He was a little more serious than Tim had been. When the other grandchildren came to visit with their parents, they seemed so much younger than Ben. Erin and Molly marveled at these offspring of theirs.

Erin passed first, which was a relief since Molly could hide the fact that Erin had been a woman. She was the only one to bathe her "husband's" dead and aged body. She lovingly took off the bindings that held in the sagging breasts, dressing her in a clean shirt, her favorite Sunday go-to-meeting trousers, perfectly fitting, tooled leather boots made by Tommy, and finally, her favorite Stetson covered her hands. No one suspected that Erin Herriot had been a woman, a *two-spirit* human being having the body of a woman but the soul of a man. Erin had looked like a man but had the brains and heart of a woman. Molly made sure Erin's dignity remained intact as she was laid to rest in the church cemetery. Tim made sure his father's grave had a headstone with his name proudly carved on it. Molly smiled her goodbyes, not realizing she would join her spouse a mere month later. The promises they had made to each other long ago on the farm in Ohio had been kept: they had grown old together. They had also kept the promises made that day before the preacher…they remained together until death they did part.

"Grandma and Grandpa were some of the first settlers, weren't they, Papa?" the little boy asked Tim, who stood there proudly. Tim's siblings, Theresa and Tabitha, were the only ones of their generation to watch as Molly was laid to rest next to her beloved Erin. There were a few settlers still alive that managed to make not only Erin's funeral but Molly's. The Herriots were remembered fondly. They had been generous with their help and had gone out of their way in times of need. They hadn't been alone at their lake the times the prairie had burned.

"Yes, Ben, they were. When you grow up and take over the ranch, maybe you'll repeat those same tales they told us coming from Ohio," he answered.

CHAPTER TWENTY-SEVEN

"**W**e should burn these," Tabitha stated with authority upon reading her mother's and father's journals. Erin's were started years after Molly's in response to what she had written, but she had never disputed the fact that she was a woman living as a man. Tabitha was embarrassed and horrified that they had all been duped. It had taken several days to read all the journals. She had been forced to stay on as Tim wouldn't let the journals out of the old farmhouse his parents had built.

"Ma and Pa didn't want us to know until after they both left this world." Tim gestured to the small trunk of journals, all neatly dated and in Molly's beautiful copperplate handwriting indicating which were Molly's and which were Erin's. "When Ma gave me these, she said, 'Don't destroy them after you read them...*all* of them. Think about what I wrote and what your Pa wrote, then leave it for a while as you think it over. You're gonna have questions, and I hope those journals tell you what you want to know. I loved your Pa greatly, and Erin loved me. We loved you kids more than you can understand. You read those journals and think about that. Think about how these journals might help your offspring.'" Little did Tim know that one day his grandson would have need of those very journals for his daughter, who was born a lesbian. The journals would, in a small way, help

Keith to better understand his daughter. They certainly helped him to accept her. He realized this had happened before in their family and would probably happen again.

"It's disgusting! I don't want my children to read these. I think we should burn them," Tabitha repeated, embarrassed to learn that her parents had lied to them all those years. "Think about what people would *say* if they knew of their lies!"

"They didn't lie. They just let everyone assume. They ain't, *aren't*," she smiled at the automatic correction, remembering her parents doing the same, "responsible for what people thought. They simply never corrected their assumptions. You didn't read them all," Theresa put in, more willing to give their parents the benefit of the doubt. "Sure, it's shocking, but how else could they have lived and loved together all those years without Pa pretending to be a man?"

"They shouldn't have done it at all!" Tabitha answered prissily, judging them by *her* morals and standards.

They were all sitting in Tim's living room, their parents' living room in the house they had built after the fires destroyed their cabins, houses, and barns. They'd rebuilt time and again. The will had been read and the ranch was left outright to Tim since he'd paid his siblings a fair price for their share years ago. The spouses and the children were outside. They would not mourn. They were having a picnic to celebrate the Herriots' lives and the loss of two such wonderful pioneers. The siblings had come together for the day to finish reading the journals they had shared, but Tabitha had refused to read the last of them, outraged at what they contained.

"Where would we be if it wasn't for the love of these two?" Tim asked, gesturing to the stack of journals in the trunk. "We were stuck in that orphanage back in Ohio. No one would have taken on *five* children." He had been so young, and the Herriots were the only parents he remembered. They had been firm, loving, and kind. He had a good life and cherished his memories of growing up here on the ranch with them. Never would he besmirch their memory. He didn't care what they had done to achieve the goals they had set out and accomplished. They had been his parents. He had never felt adopted, and he had been their dutiful son. He would honor Molly's request to keep the journals. That woman had been wise in her own way, and now that he thought about it, so had Erin in thoughtful ways.

"They wanted a family so badly, they took us all," Theresa reminded Tabitha mildly, not willing to be intimidated by her older sister, who always tried to get her own way. She had very vague

memories of the orphanage. They were blurred by a lifetime of happy memories with her parents, the Herriots, who had so lovingly raised them as their own.

"We'd still be Harrises instead of Herriots," Tim put in. "I say we don't tell anyone for now, and we certainly won't tell Theo or Tom unless they ask to read these. They have a right to know but only if it's their choice. I say, let the story remain in the trunk."

"I'm going to burn these. I don't want—" she began again, trying to bully her siblings into her way of thinking and reaching to grab more of the volumes.

"No, Tabitha. Pa and Ma left these to me, and I say no," Tim said quietly but forcefully, interrupting her and staying her hand. He was a big man. He'd always had plenty to eat and had grown strong and tall under the love and guidance of Erin and Molly Herriot. He wouldn't let his big sister intimidate him. "I'll keep these in my attic and give them to any of the grandchildren who wish to read them. I am not letting anyone burn them or the story they contain."

Theresa wanted to applaud her little brother. She was proud of him standing up to their daunting and bossy older sister. She could see that Tabitha was furious as she threw one of the journals back in the trunk.

"It's disgusting!"

"Maybe," Tim conceded, nodding to show he acknowledged her opinion. "To you it is. To them, it made sense because that's all they knew how to do. Love is not wrong. They never loved us less for having loved each other." He waited for her to acknowledge his statement, but he saw she was being angrily stubborn. "As Ma says here," he indicated one of the journals he was still holding, "she didn't think about the fact that Pa had been born a woman. She just loved her and was grateful for the love they shared. Pa saved her from the tricks the bank pulled on her. Erin saved Molly and they fell in love. That isn't wrong."

"Two women shouldn't—" she sounded prissy and looked like a mad, wet, angry hen, a victim of the Victorian times they were living in and her own narrow-minded views.

"Then, don't think of them that way. They gave you a good life. You wouldn't have met your husband if they hadn't adopted us and brought us west. They raised us and taught us morals. There was no indication they weren't what they seemed...a loving couple. Heck, I got the nerve to kiss my Maggie because of Pa saying you shouldn't wait for things in life—just grab life by the horns and do your best. At one point, I thought he meant Billy." He chuckled as he remembered how he had misunderstood the horns reference at first.

Tabitha was sick of being lectured by her little brother and huffed out. Theresa looked at Tim and laughed. "She isn't going to let it go. You'd better hide that trunk well and tell Ben to keep it away from her."

"I'm not planning on dying any time soon, but yeah, I know just the place where she won't find the journals and my son won't ask about them. Reading isn't important to him. He'll be a good man to run the ranch, but his interests lie elsewhere."

"Can you imagine the fears they had in those days? What if Pa had been found out?"

"God works in mysterious ways. Wait until Tabitha gets her second wind and starts in about how it's a sin," he said with his sardonic sense of humor. They shared a laugh in anticipation.

"She really should read that last one," Theresa advised, and Tim nodded. Molly had been getting old and a little more nostalgic when Erin died, and she'd written in her old lady, spidery, shaky, but still elegant scrawl as she explained some final thoughts.

Keith was the one who asked his father, Ben about the trunk he found in the attic of their house one day. His father gave it to him, never having read about his grandparents' long drive from Ohio or the early years on the ranch. He never knew that Erin was a woman's name. It never occurred to him to question his parents about his grandparents. He only knew about his grandparents from his father's stories about the wagon train and things he could remember as a young boy.

Most of Tim's memories were on the ranch. The trail out here was a very vague memory as he told his children the stories. Benjamin Herriot couldn't have cared less. He was a simple man, a single-minded man an unassuming rancher, who worked the land and raised cattle and horses. He would eventually get rid of the bothersome sheep and other animals when he began to slow down in his old age and needed money to help his granddaughter through veterinarian school. He would help to raise his granddaughter, Fiona but that was further in the future when he and his wife were given another chance to raise a child whose father couldn't or wouldn't.

When his own pa died, he'd inherited the ranch. Aunt Tabitha was long gone, and no one had known of the journals until the will was read and they were advised they were to be kept in the family. The story lay abandoned for many years until Keith found it. Keith cherished the old journals, understanding the need for secrecy and shocked, yet also

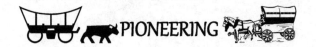

thrilled, at the colored history of his family. He knew he must keep the story alive…

~The End~

❦ About the Author ❧

K'Anne Meinel is the BEST-SELLING author of LAWYERED, REPRESENTED, SAPPHIC SURFER, DOCTORED, VEIL OF SILENCE, and VETTED as well as several other books including her first, SHIPS which was written in 2003 over the course of two weeks. A gypsy at heart, she has lived in many locations and plans to continue roaming. Videos of several of her books are available on YouTube outlining some of the locations of her books and telling a little bit more…giving the readers insight into her mind as she created these wonderful stories. As of this date she has more than **88** published works including shorts, novellas, and novels. She is an American author born in Milwaukee, Wisconsin and raised in Oconomowoc. Upon early graduation from high school she went to a private college in Milwaukee and then moved to California for seventeen years before returning to the state. Many of her stories have Wisconsin in them as settings for her wonderful, realistic, and detailed backgrounds. Named the lesbian Danielle Steel of her time, K'Anne continues to write interesting stories in a variety of genres in both the lesbian and mainstream fiction categories. Her website is www.kannemeinel.com.

If you have enjoyed **PIONEERING**, I hope you will enjoy this
excerpt from

VETTED

Allyssa is a young college student living her life to please her upper-crust family who want her to take business courses, join her father's business, and marry the "right" man. Allyssa loves animals and yearns to take courses that speak to her heart, but her family are deaf to her pleas and she is unable or unwilling to stand up to them.

Fiona is an older, more established woman; a veterinarian working towards the goal of starting her own large animal practice. When a young woman arrives on her doorstep one night carrying a dog she may have fatally injured with her car, Fiona is thrown for a loop.

Vetted—a life that neither woman anticipated, but each learns they want desperately.

Will their families, the fates, and rustlers finally bring these women to their knees? The only way they can survive is to stand strong together, but are they both ready to fight for what they want? Only time will tell....

Chapter One

Allyssa pushed the gas pedal to the floor of the Volvo station wagon, cursing under her breath as the vehicle slowly responded. Driving her mother's old family 'mobile' was humiliating, uncool, and not at all what she wanted to be driving. She had eyed the sports vehicles for years, but felt a nice Jeep should be in her future. Unfortunately, her funds were limited. Being a student at Colorado State meant she had to take what she could get. This vehicle, not even her mother's station wagon, but the maid's occasional use vehicle, was all she could manage. She was saving her pennies though. She wanted something hip, something cool, and something more in line with her style.

Today, she just wanted to feel the wind whip through her dirty blonde hair and had all the windows down. It was the first time snow wasn't paramount in her mind as the cool spring had turned warm. As she sped past the speed limit, dangerously so, she became more alert and watched for any state troopers hiding in the turnouts or on-ramps; their radar guns aimed at the traffic. Fortunately, this far out on the prairie they were easier to spot, lazier actually, and they rarely came

out here unless someone phoned for help from the call boxes on the side of the freeway.

After a while she slowed, took an off-ramp, went up and over the interstate, and onto the on-ramp leading back onto the interstate the other way. She cautiously merged, slowing enough that several faster cars passed her on her left until she was in the slow lane and she began to accelerate. She pushed the gas pedal to the floor again and waited interminably for the old vehicle to respond. She sighed. The speed, the rush of air, and the adrenalin weren't going to do it for her today. She was going to have take what she got, again.

She headed back to the university and her boring dorm room. She had to prepare for her fourth quarter. She'd gotten her midterms from each of the classes. The grades weren't bad, but they weren't stellar and her parents were going to flip. She could already hear her mother, "Allyssa, we expected more of you. Your sister was getting much better grades than this and she managed to be part of a sorority. Why can't you be more like her?" Allyssa knew why she couldn't be more like her sister. She was completely the opposite of her, that's why. Another tactic her mother was sure to throw at her was, "Your father's money isn't really being well-spent, now is it?" The guilt would be heaped on long before her father came home from his day in the office, but his silent condemnation would be worse. He had tried to reason with her mother after the first set of grades came in.

"Now, they said that freshmen frequently falter, and Allyssa is obviously being a typical freshman," but he too would subside under her mother's nervous condemnation of Allyssa's numerous faults.

Allyssa had started to hate going home on weekends. She'd started a job at the cafeteria at school to earn extra pocket change, but as a newbie, she got the less choice hours and weekends, when there were few students to cater to. Those that needed the job more got first choice and she was too new to pick and choose. Her mother had been furious when she found out.

"Are you trying to embarrass us? Your father makes good money and you have an adequate allowance. You don't need to work!"

Allyssa felt compelled to work, to earn her own way. They wouldn't let her do anything she wanted without their opinion, their choices, or their consultation…whether she asked for it or not. Even her choice in career was already mapped out for her.

"Allyssa, you will want to take these business classes if you intend to work for your father when you get out of school. He's made a good living for this family and I'm sure he can get you a job in his office," her mother told her, certain that Allyssa couldn't possibly get a job on her own.

Allyssa didn't want to take business classes. She found them boring and many of her fellow students agreed, some even daring to sleep during the long lectures where some professors preferred to hear themselves speak.

Arriving back at the dorms, she saw it was getting dark and looked for a place to park. She didn't like the way some of the boys were looking at her as she climbed out of the old Volvo. Sure enough, they had to say something to her as she passed by them, looking down at her feet and trying not to be noticed.

"Hey, baby," one of them called.

"You're a tall drink of water, aren't you?" another asked.

Allyssa kept on going, hoping they would stop and leave her alone. She worried that one of them might physically try to stop her. She'd had that experience at a party where they simply wouldn't leave her alone.

"C'mon, baby, a tree like you is meant to be climbed," had been the corny come-on. It had left Allyssa feeling distinctly uncomfortable.

Why anyone would want to be around horny guys all the time she never understood. Still, the silly girls were worse with their giggling and talking about make-up and guys all the time. She shook her head. It was no wonder STDs were so rampant in college-age kids. Half these people were stupid enough to have unprotected sex and then wonder how in the world they contracted something or gotten pregnant. It wasn't just the guys screwing everything in sight, but the girls that were just as bad. The assumption that all girls were like that was what made Allyssa so uncomfortable.

"Whatcha saving it for, baby?" one guy she had dated had the temerity to ask.

It wasn't that she was saving 'it' for anyone. He and his sweaty hands just turned her off.

Even the nice young men at the country club that her mother insisted on introducing her to had some of the same corny come-ons and raging hormones, despite being nicely dressed. Her mother couldn't see it and she tried again and again to introduce Allyssa to her

friends' sons, grandsons, and nephews. Many had no desire to date her either, but obligingly went along with their own mother's, grandmother's, or aunt's hopeful intrigue. After all, Allyssa Webster was a catch despite being as tall, if not taller than most of them.

"You have to date a lot of frogs until you find your prince," her father had laughingly warned her as he danced with her at the country club one Friday night. He was one of the few men taller than her and she smiled up at him, wondering how many women he had dated until he found her mother.

Allyssa frequently wondered what was wrong with her that she wasn't interested. She liked the kissing, the cuddling, and the caressing, but when they tried anything more intimate she didn't like the invasion of space or the heated breathing that followed. It reminded her of a panting dog and made her want to laugh.

"Don't worry about her, Helen, our Allyssa is just a late bloomer," her father assured her mother.

"Yes, Allyssa is just our ugly duckling," her mother agreed smilingly, talking as though Allyssa couldn't hear her, couldn't understand, and certainly couldn't make her own decisions.

Tonight, she was feeling restless and the drive had cleared her head for a while, but not long enough. She soon felt the pressures, even unconscious, that her family had put on her broad shoulders. She put out her clothes for the next day, neatly folding her dirty laundry and putting it into a laundry bag to take home the next day for washing. She laid out her books for her classes on Friday and looked once more at the schedule on Monday to be sure she was prepared. She smiled to herself, her mother hadn't noticed when she had dropped Introduction to Business Mathematics and instead took a biology class, something a little more intense than what she had learned back in high school. She hoped her mother would just assume it was something every freshman had to take.

The next day Allyssa went to her classes, plodding along like the masses, looking up as guys her age and even those a little older roughhoused like they were still in grade school. She had been sure she would find more mature people here, after all it was a university, but she was frequently disappointed. The people she was drawn to were more mature, like her professors, who she enjoyed listening to. Their wisdom and knowledge was something she enjoyed. She even attended extra lectures when she could. Anything to avoid the avid drinking and partying that a lot of the freshmen participated in.

As she began to pack up her Volvo for the weekend, two of the girls from her dorm came over to ask her for a ride to the local mall. She knew it was just a way to cop a ride, not to include her in their plans. Still, she was nice enough to give them the ride and was pleasantly surprised when they offered to buy her something at the food court. Looking at the time, she had to decline. Her mother was expecting her for dinner and wouldn't appreciate her being late.

"Can I get a rain check?" she asked carefully and the two of them blinked, not understanding. Sighing inwardly, she asked again, "Another time?"

"Oh yeah, sure," they answered with a smile and turned to go.

Allyssa was sure that people their age should know what a rain check was. She was also sure they had only asked her out of a sense of obligation for the ride, and while a piece of pizza sounded like more fun than her mother's stuffy dinner, she knew she would have had to call first. She really hated her life.

As she pulled up into Regal Crest Gardens where her parents had their home, she closed her eyes momentarily as she saw her sister's car was already parked in her spot. She pulled up in front of the well-manicured lawn and pulled her laundry bag and suitcase from the back seat. Carefully locking the door, she made her way up to the front door only to have her father open it.

"Hey there, Sweet Pea. How was your week?" he asked with open arms to give her a hug. He took her suitcase from her and ushered her into the house.

"It was fine, Daddy. The final quarter starts on Monday," she informed him with a smile as she looked up at him.

"Wow, your first year already finishing up. You didn't think you'd make it, did you?" he teased, knowing she hadn't been thrilled to go to the university. Still, Helen had insisted, and while he didn't agree that everyone needed a college education, he could see her sister had benefited. After all, she had met and married a fine, young man.

"Yep," she agreed, rather than disagree with him as she carried her laundry bag to the laundry room to deposit. The maid would start a load of laundry for her after she got done cleaning up in the kitchen.

Already, she could smell the delicious aromas coming from there. "What's for dinner?" she asked as she came into the kitchen, her father already there. He had deposited her suitcase at the top of the first landing for her and returned to where everyone was congregated around the family room that opened into the kitchen, creating a homey atmosphere.

"It's Friday," her mother said as though that explained it all.

"Can I help?"

"Let your sister do it, dear. She knows how."

Allyssa was used to that response and didn't take offense. Her sister knew all about how to take care of a house—cook, clean and be the good little housewife. She was four years older than Allyssa and seemed to have life well in hand. She and her husband, Derek had a house already as he was well-established in the business he had inherited from his father.

"Hi, Derek. How's tricks?" she teased him as she greeted her brother-in-law.

"Hey there, Beanpole. Where's your beau?" he teased back, never noticing the fleeting hurt look in her blue eyes.

"I can't find one to measure up," she returned, but it was more than what she was saying and no one ever caught it.

"Set the table, dear," her mother ordered her.

Allyssa turned to the small powder room off the family room to wash her hands. Heaven forbid she got germs on her mother's silverware or one of the men in the family set the table.

"You're doing that wrong," Carmen told her as she brought the mashed potatoes to the table, setting it on a heat-absorbing doily so it wouldn't ruin her parents antique dining room set. She quickly reversed the table setting where Allyssa had put the knife on the outside of the spoon instead of the other way around.

"Who cares?" Allyssa mumbled as she finished setting the table. Her mother's Friday evening dinners were monotonous and were only on Fridays because Derek had to work on Sundays. Allyssa would have preferred pizza with someone from school, but who would she have invited?

"Well, you should. What if it were someone important eating with us? The table should be set just so," she indicated as she straightened out an imaginary crease in the tablecloth and then lined up the silverware, glasses, and plates that Allyssa had already put down.

Allyssa didn't argue, Carmen would have come behind her and fixed it anyway if her mother hadn't. Why they bothered to ask her for help she had no idea. She never did it right anyway, at least not to their specifications.

"Go up and change, Allyssa dear," her mother came in carrying the other vegetables, making sure that a cover was on them to hold in the steam.

Allyssa smiled sweetly and did as her mother bid her, changing from her jeans and sweatshirt to a nice dress. She had been tempted to put on a pantsuit, but her mother wouldn't have thought that proper attire and she didn't want to irk her any more than she normally did. Her father would have backed her up and it would have delayed her mother's dinner, ruining it as far as she was concerned. She shrugged into the dress, knowing it wouldn't be up to her mother's standard even though her mother had purchased it for Allyssa.

"Can't you hold your shoulders back and act proud to be wearing that dress?" her mother asked as soon as she saw her daughter. "Stop slouching," she advised, as she brought the main course into the dining room and passed Allyssa.

Allyssa nodded, trying to throw her shoulders back and towering over her mother in the process. She only slouched because her mother always made a big deal about her height. She advised her never to wear her hair up since it made her appear to be even taller.

As they all took their accustomed seats Allyssa wondered what they would do if she sat in a different one. They would probably have minor heart attacks at her temerity. No one would find it funny, and while it might be worth it to see their looks of astonishment or shock, she knew the uproar wouldn't be appreciated by her mother. She expected perfect obedience to her wishes as it was her home and her rules. The rest of them just lived by them.

The talk was first about her father's week and what had happened that might be interesting there. It was the same monotonous job he had had for years and rarely anything different occurred to make it interesting. Allyssa nodded and smiled when expected, eating carefully, one hand on her carefully spread out napkin on her lap, so her mother couldn't find fault. Her sister was watching her like a hawk, quick to find fault if she dared to put her elbow on the table or something equally socially wrong in her eyes.

Next, they discussed Derek's week. His assertions that he was doing well in his business made it sound like boasting. He had increased his father's business by at least thirty percent since he had taken it over right out of college. "They don't do it like that anymore," he had asserted time and again as he modernized things to what he felt they should be doing. Younger meant fresh ideas and more energy in the established business. Some of the old-timers in his father's business had balked at his ideas and plans. One by one they had either quit or retired, preferring not to fight with the original owner's son.

Next, they talked about her mother's week and plans for the next week, which included social engagements since her mother was not allowed to work. Her father insisted she was needed at home to make a happy house for him to come home to. He liked his comforts and he liked how she kept his home for him. He provided Juanita, the maid they had known and employed for the past twenty years, as a sign of his success. She kept the house just the way Helen wanted it.

Next came the conversation about how Carmen was doing. She too was a stay-at-home wife since Derek was doing so well. Occasionally, when they had a rush of orders, she went into work at his business, but for the most part she wasn't using that fine college education they made such a big deal about.

Fortunately for Allyssa, they managed to finish dinner, including a nice meringue dessert her mother had made, before they could start in on her and her week. Hearing about her studies week after week was boring. Nothing changed, and for Allyssa it was hard to come up with anything new and exciting they would want to hear.

"I noticed the Volvo is due for a checkup," her father informed her as they sat in the family room once again and Juanita cleaned up the kitchen and did the dishes. "I'll inform the garage that you'll bring it in next week?"

Allyssa knew she wasn't really being asked as much as informed that it was her 'duty' to keep the old car in good shape. Juanita had been given the new Volvo they purchased to do errands for the family, shop for groceries, and keep their home in order. "Yes, Daddy. I'll do that," she agreed, not wishing to argue.

Allyssa knew that at nineteen they still considered her a kid and treated her as such. Carmen, so much older in many ways, was included in the 'adult' conversation as they discussed current affairs from the newspaper or what they had seen on the television. Children were to be seen and not heard, and Allyssa was relieved when eight came around and Derek announced they better be going.

"I have a golfing date tomorrow if you wish to join us. We tee off at nine," he informed her father who agreed immediately, pleased to be included.

"We could have mimosas at the country club," Carmen told her mother excitedly, including herself in their little outing.

"It's a bit too early for that," Derek admonished and Carmen quickly agreed, subsiding into silence with his greater wisdom.

Allyssa was ready to pull her hair out as she watched her family interact. Why did no one stand up for themselves? Why were they always so polite? If her sister wanted a mimosa at nine in the morning on a Saturday, why couldn't she have one?

"We'll go shopping while they are golfing. Won't that be fun?" Helen asked her daughters, including Allyssa.

"I'd rather..." Allyssa began only to be cut off by Carmen.

"Oh, that sounds great, Mommy. Where will we go?" she enthused.

Without consulting or even really including her in the discussion they mapped out her Saturday. Allyssa knew she would have a headache by noon with their enthusiasm over shopping. She was grateful when Carmen and Derek finished up their plans with her parents and left. She escaped to her room to change out of the uncomfortable dress and pull on a comfortable nightshirt. Sighing deeply, she longed for an escape from this life. She had thought by escaping to live in the dorms, she would have something different. Her life wasn't horrible, but the monotony and sameness of it got on her nerves.

TO BE CONTINUED...

~End Sample Chapter of VETTED~
For more go to www.Shadoepublishing.com to purchase
the complete book or for many other delightful offerings

~ Because a publisher should stand behind their authors~

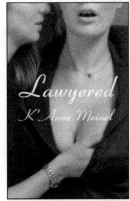
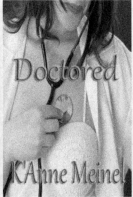

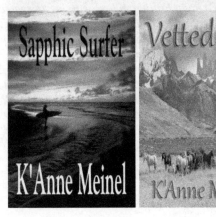

www.shadoepublishing.com

What do you do when you meet someone who changes everything you know about love and passion?

Paige Harlow is a good girl. She's always known where she was going in life: top grades, an ivy league school, a medical degree, regular church attendance, and a happy marriage to a man. Falling in love with her gorgeous roommate and best friend Alyssa Torres is no small crisis. Alyssa is chasing demons of her own, a medical condition that makes her an outcast and a family dysfunctional to the point of disintegration make her a questionable choice for any stable relationship. But Paige's heart is no longer her own. She must now battle the prejudices of her family, friends, and church and come to peace with her new sexuality before she can hope to win the affections of the woman of her dreams. But will love be enough?

www.shadoepublishing.com

~ Because a publisher should stand behind their authors~

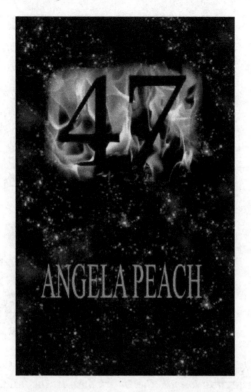

As I watch the wormhole start to close, I make one last desperate plea..."Please? Please don't make me do this?" I whisper.
"You're almost out of time, Lily. Please, just let go?"
I look down at the control panel. I know what I have to do.

Lilith Madison is captain of the Phoenix, a spaceship filled with an elite crew and travelling through the Delta Gamma Quadrant. Their mission is mankind's last hope for survival.

But there is a killer on board. One who kills without leaving a trace and seems intent on making sure their mission fails. With the ship falling apart and her crew being ruthlessly picked off one by one, Lilith must choose who to trust while tracking down the killer before it's too late.

"A suspenseful...exciting...thrilling whodunit adventure in space...discover the shocking truth about what's really happening on the Phoenix" (Clarion)

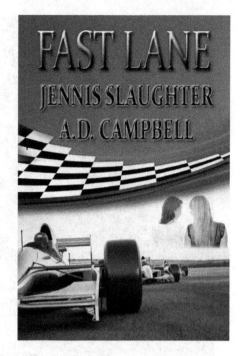

In the male dominated sport of Formula 1 racing, Samantha 'Sam' Dupree is struggling to make her mark against the boys. She hears about a driver who is making a name for herself in NASCAR and goes to check her out. Little does she know that she's in for the race of her heart.

Addison McCloud wants nothing more than to drive. She doesn't care about fame or fortune; she just wants to be fast enough to get herself and her family away from her abusive father. Meeting Sam, changes her world and revs her life into overdrive.

When the two women meet, sparks flies like the race cars that they drive. Will they be able to steer their relationship into something more and win the race, or will their families make them crash and burn. The boys of Formula 1 are going to learn that Southern girls are a force to be reckoned with.

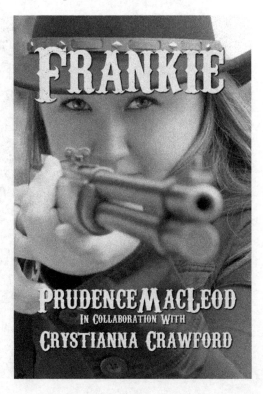

Carrie flees from the demons of her present, trying to protect the ones she loves.

Frankie hides from the demons of her past, and the memory of loved ones she failed to protect.

A modern day princess thrown to the wolves, Carrie's only hope is the rancher who had spent the better part of a decade in self imposed, near total, isolation. Frankie's history of losing those she tries to save haunts her, but this madman threatens her home, her livestock, her sanctuary. She knows she can't do it alone, has she still got enough support from her oldest friends?

Amelia Gittens had the credit of being the first and only woman thus far in the United States military of being a sniper in combat, made possible by being in the Military Police unit of the crack 10th Mountain Infantry Division. After retirement she joins the City of New York Police Department, and suddenly finds herself involved in a suspect shooting incident which soon encroaches upon her entire life. In order to protect her therapist who has been targeted as a revenge killing, Amelia takes on the responsibility as if she was still in the Army, treating it as a tactical maneuver.

www.shadoepublishing.com

~ Because a publisher should stand behind their authors~

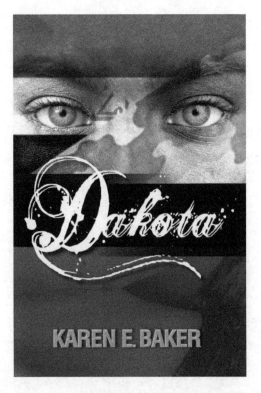

When U.S. Marine Dakota McKnight returned home from her third tour in Operation Iraqi Freedom, she carried more baggage than the gear and dress blues she had deployed with. A vicious rocket-propelled grenade attack on her base left her best friend dead and Dakota physically and emotionally wounded. The marine who once carried herself with purpose and confidence, has returned broken and haunted by the horrors of war. When she returns to the civilian world, life is not easy, but with the help of her therapist, Janie, she is barely managing to hold her life together...then she meets Beth.

Beth Kendrick is an American history college professor. She is as straight-laced as they come, until Dakota enters her life, that is. Will her children understand what she is going through? Will she take a chance on the broken marine or decide to wait for the perfect someone to come along?

Time is on your side, they say, unless there is a dark, sinister evil at work. Is their love strong enough to hold these two people together? Will the love of a good woman help Dakota find the path to recovery? Or is she doomed to a life of inner turmoil and destruction that knows no end?

If you have enjoyed this book and the others listed here
Shadoe Publishing, LLC is always looking for first, second, or
third time authors. Please check out our website @
www.shadoepublishing.com
For information or to contact us @
shadoepublishing@gmail.com.

We may be able to help you bring your dreams of becoming a
published author to life.

CPSIA information can be obtained
at www.ICGtesting.com
Printed in the USA
LVHW081630080421
683869LV00010B/786

8